THE INSIDER

Jeff Nesbit

THE INSIDER

a novel

ZondervanPublishingHouse
Grand Rapids, Michigan

A Division of HarperCollinsPublishers

The Insider
Copyright © 1996 by Jeff Nesbit

Requests for information should be addressed to:

📖 ZondervanPublishingHouse
Grand Rapids, Michigan 49530

Library of Congress Cataloging-in-Publication Data

Nesbit, Jeffrey Asher.
   The insider : a novel / Jeff Nesbit.
      p.   cm.
   ISBN: 0-310-20098-9 (pbk.)
   I. Title.
PS3564.E73157   1996
813'.54—dc 20   96–11932
                                                          CIP

Edited by Dave Lambert
Interior design by Sue Vandenberg Koppenol

Printed in the United States of America

---

96 97 98 99 00 01 02 /❖ DH/ 10 9 8 7 6 5 4 3 2 1

To Casey,
Who put as much into this as I did.

PROLOGUE

The intercom buzzed. The intense young man—sitting behind an immaculate mahogany desk in a spacious corner office on the second floor of the White House's west wing—picked it up immediately.

"The president will see you in half an hour. His secretary just called," an aide said.

"Thank you." The young man set the phone back in its cradle. This was it—the moment of truth he'd been dreading. Did he have the courage for it?

Jon Abelson flipped the little switch on the side of the phone, which automatically forwarded any incoming calls to the front reception area. They'd take his calls there. They always lied so well for him there.

Oh, I'm sorry, Mr. Abelson's in a meeting, they always said so politely. *Can he get back to you?*

Sometimes he did, and sometimes he didn't. Jon could afford not to return phone calls now. In fact, not returning calls was the true test of power in Washington. The ability to ignore calls—even dozens of them in a day—was even more important than getting your own calls returned.

And *everyone* returned Jon's calls. Always. They had no choice, really.

Jon swiveled his black, leather, high-backed chair to face the window that looked out over the south lawn of the White House. The chair squeaked a little, which he hated. He had always meant to get that fixed. Today, though, it didn't seem to matter much.

The line of people waiting for the White House tour stretched all the way along the south gate today, at least three hundred tourists waiting to get inside the most famous house in America. How they could wait for hours just to get a glimpse of his working world boggled his mind. Didn't they understand? There was nothing special here. The people running this place were just like them. A little smarter, meaner, more self-centered, or driven than they were. But still mostly like them.

These walls were like other walls. These doors were just doors. The floors had tile and wood on them, like other floors. The curtains were a little fancier, but still made of textiles from places like South Carolina.

But that didn't seem to matter. The crowds gathered nearly every day for the famous tour of the White House. The president's house. Where decisions that shook the world were made.

If only they knew, Jon thought. *If only they realized how decisions are made and carried out. They wouldn't think so much of the place then.*

But, in fact, they did know. Or, at least, they ought to. There had been enough books and articles written about the place by those who had been here. And yet the people who cast the votes every four years—who were supposed to be in charge of the country—didn't seem to care. They still worshiped the place, despite the all-too-human faults of its occupants.

Jon had worked very, very hard to get where he was. Countless sixteen-hour days and seven-day weeks. Endless discussions to make sure events went as planned. Hundreds of hours of "orchestration" to make sure that meetings and events unfolded as they were supposed to.

There was no questioning his success. The marks of it were everywhere. A fishing picture signed by the Speaker of the House of Representatives. Several intimate photos with the president of the United States, his boss and mentor. Another picture of him making an impassioned point at a national security briefing at Camp David.

He had three secretaries, a staff of thirty or so housed over at the Old Executive Office Building across the way from this office in the cozy west wing of the White House, a government-issue car, and anytime-at-all privileges aboard Marine One.

Everyone in the nation's capitol returned his calls. Immediately. He couldn't remember a time in the past year when he'd had to wait even an hour for someone to return a call.

Because they all knew: Jon Abelson spoke for the president, sometimes even more than the president himself did. Jon was the chief spokesman for the "new politics" movement that the president had forced upon a reluctant Democratic Party—a brand of politics that empowered blacks in the ghetto even as it sent more police into those very same neighborhoods.

Jon gave shape to the president's vision. He gave it form and function. Everyone knew it. Or, if they didn't, they guessed it.

Waiting to see the president, Jon closed his eyes. The events of the past week—the revelations he'd tripped across—tumbled through his mind in random fashion.

8

Against his will, his mind drifted further back to his days at Princeton, working on his doctorate in English and trying to find a niche for himself in the world. Oh, yes, he'd been "on fire" then, a new servant of Christ, driven to bring truth to the deceived of the world. The truth of things—that's what he had wanted to uncover, and then to write about. That had been his mission.

The pain of those memories was searing. It made almost every part of him ache. But this was important, Jon realized; he had to remember where he'd begun, before politics. Especially now.

As painful as it was, remembering seemed to be the only path he could manage at the moment. The present was simply too terrifying.

CHAPTER ONE

The bizarre part was how straight the roads were. And flat. Straight and endless and flat. Right through the heart of small towns, out the other side, and straight on to the next town.

Massachusetts hadn't been like that. The roads there had curves and bends and turns to them. But not here in Ohio, where Jon was headed—for reasons he still had a hard time understanding—for his first job interview since getting his doctorate.

All his life, Jon had really wanted to do only one thing—become a writer. Any kind of writer; he wasn't particular. But no straight line exists from college to a writing career—at least not that Jon had been able to find. After his undergraduate work, he'd tried his hand at a few short stories. He'd even started a couple of novels. But no one had been willing to pay him anything for his efforts.

So, eventually, after several years of trying to write in the evenings while working first as the assistant manager of a record store and then as the district manager for a daily newspaper's circulation department, Jon decided that he needed to hone his craft as a writer. So he plopped himself into a Ph.D. program in English at Princeton and tried to learn how to teach and write at the same time.

Now, at twenty-nine, with a Ph.D. and a few years of experience teaching undergraduate students how to write at least passable prose, Jon wondered why he was no closer to his goal of becoming a writer than before. He'd discovered, somewhat belatedly, that he had no desire to become a tenured professor. He didn't even like teaching. He'd only stuck with it to finance his doctorate—a degree that, as it turns out, is almost worthless since it qualified him to be a professor and not much else.

He'd never finished a novel or anything else of significance while teaching and studying at Princeton. He'd been too busy grading papers or studying or working on his dissertation. And when he'd finally completed all the requirements for his doctorate, he woke up one morning, looked out the window of his one-bedroom studio apartment, and realized that he would never pursue an academic job. He would go stark raving mad if he spent the rest of his life as a professor. He poured himself a cup of coffee and admitted that, for the first time in his life, he had no goals, no ambition, and nothing real to aim for and work toward.

It was like waking up from a very long dream only to discover that now he was in the middle of a nightmare. He'd dreamt about being a writer for so long, he'd somehow convinced himself that it must be God's will and that God would somehow reveal the right path to him and nudge him in the right direction. But nothing of the sort had happened.

Which meant that Jon was now on his own without a career and without a way to pay for the necessities of life. He had to find a job—a real job, and if he was lucky, with some kind of writing as part of the deal.

Jon tried, again, to shift into fifth gear in his ancient, two-door Honda Civic. Most of the paint had long ago peeled off the Civic, with the bare metal showing through all over. The brakes were shot, as that unpleasant grinding sound reminded him every time he stepped on the pedal. The seats sank just about to the floorboards. But at least it got great mileage. If only he could get the dumb thing into fifth.

Despite his despair over ever finding a writing job, he still gritted his teeth about this particular job interview. It was crazy. He had a doctorate, for crying out loud! From an Ivy League school! He wanted to write short stories and hugely successful novels. Maybe a nonfiction book every now and then when he got bored.

So why, oh why, was he driving out into the middle of nowhere, where the roads just ran in straight lines, to interview for a job as a reporter? *Journalism?* Yeah, right. Everybody hated reporters. They were scum—lower than ambulance-chasing lawyers and used-car salesmen.

But journalists got paid—not a great deal, but they did get paid. That was something. And they were writers. Kind of.

He'd heard about the job from the sister of a friend of one of his old frat brothers who'd been visiting the campus toward the end of the school year—his last at Princeton. The sister knew the publisher of the paper, and she said she'd get the guy to call him.

Jon had promptly forgotten about the whole thing. But last week the editor had called, demanding to know when he'd be there for an interview. Jon had stammered out a promise to get there sometime soon. The editor had set a date, and Jon was stuck.

Singleton, Ohio, was like a lot of small, midwestern towns. A couple of big, dying industries, a heavy dose of blue-collar workers desperately trying to change careers, one fairly new shopping center, a few downtown bars and restaurants, a whole bunch of tiny retail stores where everybody seemed to work, and a couple of planned suburban communities with two dozen cul-de-sacs.

Jon had no desire to work here. He wanted to work somewhere exotic or interesting like Palm Beach or Aspen—or maybe Sonoma, Arizona. Or Juneau, Alaska. Not Singleton, Ohio. Not a town where people put bowling trophies over fireplaces they never used. But jobs were tight all over. So far, his job hunt had come up with zip. The degree that was supposed to guarantee him a job was instead making it harder— "overqualified," everyone said. He had to follow every lead that came up. Even in Singleton, Ohio.

As Jon entered Singleton, he began to look for a sign of intelligent life. He figured he'd know it when he saw it. At the first traffic light in town—where the highway became Main Street, naturally—Jon glanced over at a small crowd gathered just outside a shop on the right side of the street. The crowd was agitated about something.

Curious, Jon pulled over to the curb and parked. He didn't bother to lock the car. They could have the thing if they really wanted the trouble. Jon tossed the keys onto the floor mat—he hated it when the keys jangled in his pocket—slammed the door, and sauntered over to the edge of the crowd.

Nearly everyone in the crowd was black, which surprised him. He hadn't expected to see so many blacks here, in a town like this. He wasn't sure why he'd thought that. The thought had just been there.

They were all staring at this white guy who'd jerked his cheap tie down and rolled his shirt sleeves up. He was wearing khakis and scuffed, brown work boots. He looked like a working stiff. Either that, or he was trying to give the impression that he was a working stiff and the clothes were just props.

Either way, it didn't matter much, Jon could see. The crowd loved the guy. They cheered just about every other word, regardless of what he said.

Conspicuous because there were so few white faces in the crowd, Jon worked his way toward the front. People gave him dirty looks.

15

"So do you want your streets back?" the man bellowed with a deep, baritone voice that carried well.

"Yeah, brother, we do!" someone yelled back.

"Do you want your kids safe?" the man yelled, his hands placed squarely on his hips.

"Oh, yeah!" came the answer.

"Schools safe? Drugs off the street?"

"Amen to that, brother."

The man leaned forward. "You have to *take* them back. They belong to you. *Take* them back!" The crowd swayed with him. They were clearly into this.

Never mind that what he was saying made no sense. You couldn't just snap your fingers and get safe schools, crimeless streets, or drug-free neighborhoods. You couldn't just *take* those things and claim them like you'd just discovered them in the community lost and found.

But this guy thought you could. Or at least he was convincing these gullible fools that he thought they could. Was there a difference?

Jon glanced over at the little table off to the side. "Adams for Congress" bumper stickers were spread out across the table. Jon shook his head. Just another two-bit political candidate, pumping the crowd for a two-bit local race. He started to leave.

"Hey, kid!" the man called out. "You walkin' away?"

Jon froze. Did this guy mean him? Jon turned. The guy was looking straight at him. His eyes didn't flinch. They bored straight in, like rifle shots frozen in a time warp.

"Yes, you!" the guy said. He jabbed a menacing finger at Jon, even as he was looking at the rest of the crowd. "He doesn't get it. He doesn't see it." The guy pounded his chest, over his heart. "You have to feel it, in here. A heart for change."

"Amen, brother," a few in the crowd called out.

Jon couldn't believe it. The guy was using him for a prop. Just like that. Without a second thought. Jon almost admired him for it.

Jon wanted to say that he'd just gotten to town, that he'd only stopped because he was just curious and didn't really know anything about local politics. But he didn't bother. He doubted anyone would care a whole lot.

"Nothing to say on your own behalf?" the man called to him. A broad, sunny smile burst across his face, almost as if a computer program had queued its release. "Then take off. You have to be part of the solution. If not, then you're the problem."

16

A chorus of amens went up again. Jon stared at the strange, intense man just a moment longer and then turned to leave. The crowd made it tougher for him on the way back through. An elbow here, a heavy lean there, legs that wouldn't move out of the way.

Only when he'd gotten clear of the crowd did the thought that had been rattling in the back of his mind strike him more forcefully. Why in the world were these black people listening to this white guy? What spell had he cast? It made no sense to Jon. None at all.

CHAPTER TWO

Jon eased his car into a space on the street in front of the newspaper office, turned it off, and sat there for several minutes, staring at the bleak surroundings. He really didn't want to do this. Not now. Not here. Especially not here.

The newspaper building was at the heart of the downtown area, literally at the corner of First and Main streets. But prosperity had fled this area long ago. Even in a city as small as Singleton, anyone with any sense or money had long ago moved about fifteen minutes away, to new streets that led nowhere and houses that would all begin to crumble and decay in about two decades.

A yellow hamburger wrapper fluttered by, swirled once, and then whipped onto Jon's windshield and got stuck against the wiper. It flapped every so often as the wind caught it.

Jon jerked the car door open angrily and slammed it behind him. He didn't lock the car. He left the wrapper on the windshield.

As he crossed the sidewalk, a middle-aged woman missing the better part of her front palate took several halting steps toward him. He tried to avoid her, but she was clearly an expert at this sort of thing.

"Jes' a quarter," Jon heard her mutter.

Jon stuffed both hands into his pockets and pretended to search, trying hard not let the beggar woman hear the change rattling. "Sorry," he mumbled.

The woman's eyes, unfocused, narrowed. "You got sumpin' fo' me? I know you do."

"Really, I don't think—"

"God know ya heart," the woman said breathlessly, the words sounding more like a hiss than part of the English language. "He know ya lyin'."

Jon grimaced. Lying? He hadn't actually *told* the woman he didn't have any money. But he'd been about to. "Look, lady, I gotta get inside for a—"

"God ain't blind," the old beggar woman said, taking a slightly unsteady step toward Jon. "He ain't blind, ya hear? He see alla way through. Yeah, he do."

Jon tried to walk around her and hurry into the building. But he stopped halfway up the low stairway and closed his eyes. He hated beggars. They made his skin crawl. He didn't want to touch them, to get near them, to have anything to do with them. He wished they did not exist. They were misery. They were abject and utter failure.

But the lessons of the Christianity he had adopted in college wouldn't let him leave it at that. Beggars, too, were created in God's image. Like Jon. Like every single human being on the face of the earth, whether Jon liked it or not. And, for that reason alone, they deserved his attention. More than that, he knew they deserved his help. But it wasn't easy for him.

Jon's conversion in college had been dramatic. In his first year at Princeton—his first year of liberation away from a home that had been loving and nurturing—Jon had careened wildly off the path that his parents had helped him carefully set.

He'd had no real reason for what he'd done. He'd just done it. At the first party he'd gone to at Princeton, someone had handed him a thin, black pipe. He had asked, somewhat shyly, what was in it. Hash oil, someone had answered with a wicked grin.

Jon didn't know what hash oil was. It had burned his throat fiercely as he'd taken several long drags. Several minutes later, Jon felt as if an invisible mist had somehow surrounded his brain and locked it into place, as if his eyes were a mile wide. Everything seemed to come at him in slow motion. He felt as though he could understand every word uttered around him, that he could divine some hidden meaning in each and every syllable.

He didn't sleep that first night, the night of the hash oil. Whenever he'd start to come down from the high he was on, someone would offer him more, and he'd go sailing right back up.

He was hooked. The feeling was so overwhelming, so powerful, so extraordinarily unlike anything he'd ever experienced that he wanted to stay that way forever. You could stay high for hours if you wanted. When it started to wear off, you could just take a couple of hits, and the lethargy that came over you would disappear.

They said you couldn't get high the first time you tried. Clearly, they'd never tried hash oil the first time out.

Jon fell hard and fast after that first night. He made friends easily with a small circle of kids who had the money to buy as much as they wanted. Over time, Jon had tried other things—a little cocaine, a little mescaline, some Quaaludes, even strange mixtures of barbiturates and other drugs. But he always returned to the best pot that money could buy. It was safer, not as threatening. He could function in class—barely—and sort of drift through life. The other, harder drugs didn't let you do that.

By the end of his first year at college, Jon was so strung out he couldn't see straight. He'd barely made it through his classes. At the end of the second semester, he'd been forced to pull four all-nighters in a row just to get his final papers done. He'd been lucky to walk away with average grades.

His parents had moved to Charlotte, North Carolina, two years before. He went back there for the summer and landed a job delivering newspapers for the *Charlotte Observer*.

He tried, at first, to find a source of drugs in the city. But it was much, much harder out in the real world, on actual streets in places where people worked and lived.

At some point during that summer—Jon was never sure where or when—he'd made a decision. He had to quit, had to get away from the drugs and the drifting. He had to just quit, cold turkey.

But he found immediately that he could not. He didn't have that ability. That power was not within him. And as his personal supply of Colombian Gold marijuana brought from Princeton began to dwindle, Jon began to panic. He was lost. Very, very lost.

One day he stumbled across a funny little book at a bookstore, tucked in between books about angels and crystals. It was a book about the end of the earth from an author he'd never heard of before.

"Is this the age that Moses and Jesus predicted?" the book jacket had asked in large letters.

Jon knew vaguely who Moses was. In elementary school, they'd taken a religion course in a trailer just off the school grounds every Tuesday morning. The two teachers were Jewish and had taught the kids a little about the Old Testament figures. He knew that Moses had led the Jews out of Egypt to the "Promised Land."

But who was Jesus? Oh, sure, he was the Christmas baby and everything, but when Jon heard his name, it was because someone was using it to curse with.

Jon's parents hadn't gone to church at all. They had made sure that he studied hard in school and stayed out of trouble. But their values had been moral values, not Christian ones. The Abelson family life did not include church. At all. Which meant that Jon knew very little about what millions of others, who went into those churches all over town every Sunday, must have surely known quite a lot about.

Jon turned the book over and over in his hands. The age that Jesus and Moses had predicted. What age? What had they predicted? Who was Jesus? And did it matter at all?

Later that day, Jon scrounged around his parents' house until he found an old, unused Bible. The book's spine nearly snapped from disuse as he opened it. He looked at the front of the Bible to find where it talked about Jesus.

It had plenty of chapters called "books." But none called the "Book of Jesus." Many books existed about all sorts of people named Job or Luke or Peter or Samuel. But none about Jesus.

He leafed through the Bible, finally noticing Jesus' name in the gospel of Luke. Settling into a quiet corner of the house, he started at the beginning of the first Gospel and read straight through. He finished all four Gospels, then read Acts, and was several books past that when he finally stopped reading.

From the first sentence, a profound sense of calm had come over him. For the first time in he couldn't remember how long, Jon did not feel the corners of his mind pulling his senses and his emotions in all directions. He felt a reassuring sense of serenity and saneness in response to what he was reading, as if the world did, in fact, make sense. It was as if someone was helping guide his mind—not bludgeon it.

"Jesus know what you doin'."

Jon opened his eyes. The beggar woman stood on the stairway beside him, her hand held out. Jon reached into his pocket and fished for a quarter. He laid it in her hand. She closed her hand around it greedily, mumbled thanks, and returned to her post, ever vigilant for the next passerby who might help her get enough to buy a bottle of wine before lunch.

Jon glanced up at the top of the building just before he ducked inside. A long mesh net ringed the building five or six feet from the top, extending about three feet out from its brick facade. Very strange, he thought. Very, very strange.

It didn't take long to find the newsroom or the editor's office. It was straight ahead, down the long corridor. The building was small enough that you could probably find anything in it by just wandering around for a few minutes.

Nothing fancy here. Nothing new, either. In fact, the whole place looked as though it would collapse into a big pile of rubble at any moment. He ambled over to the desk just outside the editor's office—the only enclosed office in the open newsroom—and announced himself to the secretary.

"By the way," Jon asked the secretary, an incredibly fat woman who barely managed to fit into the chair behind the desk, "what's with the net around the top of the building?"

The woman didn't smile. "Catch the bricks."

"Bricks? You mean like old bricks that just fall off the outside of the building?"

"You got it."

Jon shook his head. Quite a place he'd stumbled into.

Several minutes later Jon was waved into the editor's office. An elderly man who looked as if he'd smoked about twelve packs of cigarettes every day of his life sat behind an incredibly unkempt desk. He didn't look up as Jon entered and took a seat.

"What's that name again?" the man growled at him finally, not bothering to look up from the copy he was reading as Jon replied.

Jon tried not to get angry. No one ever got his name right, no matter how many times he said it. "Jon Abelson . . . sir," he told him, keeping his voice polite and respectful.

Jon looked out the grimy window. No view except for the side and corner of another building. This place was nasty. The man's office looked as if it hadn't been cleaned in years. At least one hundred shriveled cigarette butts littered five different ashtrays. And at least two of the coffee cups littered throughout the office had what looked like a thick green mold growing over cold coffee.

Man, oh man, why am I here? Jon thought miserably. *I mean, I have a doctorate from Princeton. The Ivy League. What am I doing sitting here in this—*

"You bored, kid?" the man barked at him, his voice sounding as though he had a few bits of gravel stuck in the back of his throat.

Lawrence Sanders—that was his name, Jon recalled. "You wonderin' why you got stuck in this hole?"

"No, of course not," Jon lied. He didn't like lying, but he couldn't just tell the guy what he'd been thinking: that his town was pathetic, that his dinky newspaper meant nothing in the grand scheme of things, and that his office—if not the whole building—deserved to be condemned.

Sanders tossed the copy he'd been looking at off to one side. He leaned forward in his chair, which groaned as if it might collapse, and placed both elbows on top of a pile of papers on his desk. He rested his graying, stubbly chin on both thumbs and held his forefingers over his lips for a moment.

"Look, Abalonian, this is the deal," Sanders said. He cleared his throat. "You don't lie here. Not here. This is the place where the truth is told—or whatever pieces of it you can round up. This is where you go after truth with everything you have. If you don't learn anything else the rest of your life, remember this: There is no higher calling than the search for truth. That's why people hate reporters—'cause we call 'em as we see 'em. So I'll ask you again. You bored? Maybe wonderin' why you're here?"

Jon blinked once, twice. Was this guy for real? "Okay," he answered, with only the slightest hesitation. "Yeah, you're right. I was wondering exactly that."

"Why you're here?"

"Yeah, why I'm here, in a dump like this."

A crooked smile spread across Sanders' face. "There. That wasn't so hard. Now get used to it. I want you fightin' for truth. I want you in people's faces, rippin' the masks off, if you have to. Don't pull any punches, especially not with me."

Jon grunted. "So does that mean you're offering me a job?"

Sanders plucked the resumé Jon had brought with him from the top of one of the many mounds of paper on his desk. He held it out before him with two fingers, as if it carried an infectious disease. "You think this thing qualifies you to be a reporter with the *Singleton Gazette*?"

Jon started to answer—to lie—that certainly it qualified him for the job. His doctorate from Princeton was in English, which newspapers pretended to aspire to. But he stopped short. "Well, actually, no, I guess not."

"And you didn't do anything at Princeton—didn't study journalism or write for the school newspaper—that might have given you a little experience?"

"No, I didn't. But—but I can do the job."

"Yeah? You can?" Sanders eyebrows arched. "How do you know that?"

"I just know," Jon said with some emotion. "I've always been able to get jobs done. Always."

Sanders shrugged. "Maybe. I guess we'll see."

"What's that mean?"

"Look, Ablepan, what are you doin' right now?"

"This very minute?" Jon grinned broadly. "Sitting in your office."

"That's good, kid. A sense of humor. You'll need it in this job, believe me. No, I meant what are you doin' in your life right now? Do you have a week to give me?"

Jon thought about it. Despite all his recent despair about what to do with his life, he didn't really have any immediate plans, other than to find a job eventually. He'd stumbled into this thing by accident. "No, I mean yes, I have a week, I guess."

"Yes or no, Abelman. Do you have a week, if we put you up in a hotel around the corner?"

Jon looked directly at Sanders. "Why just a week?"

Sanders folded his hands. He had Jon hooked, and he knew it. "Simple. Gives me a chance to see what you're made of, before I have to hire you and then go through all the hassle of tossing you out on your ear if you don't work out. And it gives you the chance to see if you're tough enough to last in a place like this."

"Oh, I'm tough enough," Jon said quickly.

"You think so, huh? They teach you about things like that in Princeton?"

"They taught me plenty."

"I'll bet," Sanders snorted. "So do we have a deal? We put you up for a week, and you see if you can cut it?"

Jon tried at least to look thoughtful. "So what do I get out of the deal?"

Sanders leaned back and spread his arms wide. "All this, kid, and more. You get the benefit of my vast years of experience and brilliant insights."

"That's it?"

"You get a byline, which'll get you your next job, whatever it is. And, of course, you get the chance to live in beautiful, picturesque Singleton, Ohio. There's no other place like it on earth."

"I can believe that," Jon said ruefully. "So is there anything else?"

"Well, yeah, one thing. Your first assignment."

"Which is?"

"To cover one of the two congressional races here."

24

Jon remembered the stump speech he'd stumbled across on the way into town and tried to keep from groaning. "Yeah, and what's so special about this race?"

Sanders picked up the copy he'd been reading before and started reading again. "Trust me, kid. If you got even half a brain, you'll see it right off. Go see Samuel Adams. Follow him. You'll see. And if you don't, I'll help you pack your bags."

CHAPTER THREE

The fleabag Sanders put him up in didn't even qualify as a hotel. It was more like a cross between a brothel, a crack house, and a home for destitute alcoholics.

The front "lobby" had a couple of chairs and a sofa in it that reeked of wine and stale cigarettes. At night, the place was a haze of smoke and women in short skirts. Jon didn't have to ask who the women were or where they went when they weren't in the lobby.

That first day on the job Jon was absolutely dead certain he'd be gone by the end of the week. No way was he putting up with this. Not Sanders, not this crummy hotel, and not a newspaper that had nets to catch falling bricks before they bonked people on the head.

He hated everything about it. Every five minutes he asked himself why he was here. The answer, he knew, was simple—because he was a writer, because he had to earn money somehow in a writing profession of some sort. And the newspapers that hired people like him right out of college with no experience as reporters were in places like Singleton, Ohio. That was why.

Intellectually, he understood that answer. But physically and emotionally, he couldn't stand it. The people in the hotel and on the streets and even in the newsroom made him want to gag. There had to be more to life than this. There just had to be.

To make matters worse, Jon discovered from Sanders that he had to pull overtime on his very first day on the job. That evening, there was to be a pig roast at the farm of one of the area's prominent Democrats, who owned about half the land surrounding Singleton. Sanders instructed Jon to go hang out at the event, even though anything he heard there would be "off-the-record."

"Good way to meet folks," Sanders had growled.

"Is it some kind of official event?" Jon had asked.

"Ain't no such thing with the Dems," Sanders had laughed. "They don't have that word in their vocabulary."

"But will Adams be there?"

Sanders had just shaken his head and wandered off.

Jon had never been to a pig roast. Did they kill the pig right there, with all the guests watching? Roast the carcass over an open fire, while everybody licked their chops? How many people did an entire pig feed, anyway?

Jon didn't get the answers to those questions that night because it took him nearly forty-five minutes just to find the farm. No street signs were posted anywhere near the place—just road numbers, and those were few and far between. He had to ask half a dozen people either sitting on tractors or working in their gardens before he finally found the place.

More than one hundred cars—ranging from brand-new BMWs to beat-up Chevy station wagons—were pulled off to the side of the road. Jon parked his wreck at the end of the line and walked up the dusty road to the farm.

Because the guy owned so much land, Jon was expecting some huge mansion. He was disappointed. The house itself was just a regular old white structure, with an addition on the back. But the barn was huge and new. In fact, the barn dwarfed the house.

A few dozen black cows hung out near the fence that bordered the backyard. Kids were pitching apples in their direction, which explained why all the cows were strolling up and down the fence near the party.

Jon spied the pig-roast area right off. Thin streams of smoke rose into the air over an absolutely huge grill, five times the size of the usual backyard barbecue. Slabs of meat roasted on top of the grill—no whole pig and no pig head anywhere in sight. Jon was vaguely disappointed.

Dozens of people, most of them men, were gathered in knots all around the spacious backyard. One rather large group of women were gathered near the back door that led to the kitchen. Jon, of course, knew none of these people. He felt completely ill at ease.

He jammed his reporter's notebook deep into his back pocket and wandered over to the back fence, toward the pack of kids tossing apples at the cows. As he drew near, he could see a few of the cows munching happily on the small, green apples.

He stood off to the side for a few moments, just watching. Three older kids sat up in the apple tree that bordered the fence, shaking apples loose. The younger kids gathered up the apples and tossed them over the fence. A couple of brave kids stuck their hands through the fence to let the cows pluck apples from their open, extended hands. Jon winced as he watched.

"Want one, mister?" a blonde-haired little girl in red, white, and blue bows asked him, holding an apple out.

"Ah, that's okay," Jon said, smiling down at the little girl.

"C'mon, it's okay. Don't be 'fraid," she insisted. "They won't hurt you."

Jon glanced over at the cows. "I didn't know they liked apples. I thought they, you know, just kind of munched on grass."

The little girl cocked her head to one side. "Where you from, anyway? You don't know about cows?"

Jon almost laughed out loud. *I'm from Princeton, New Jersey*, he thought. *I've never even seen a cow up close in my life, never been to a pig roast. And I never knew cows ate apples.* "No, I don't know about cows," Jon answered. "Why don't you tell me about them. Off the record."

The little girl picked up an apple and thrust her hand through the fence. One of the large creatures ambled over, lowered its massive head to meet the little girl's extended hand, and plucked the apple from her palm with a quick smack of its lips.

"See?" she said. "You try it."

"Oh, no," Jon said quickly. "I couldn't."

"You afraid?"

"Of a cow? Of course not," Jon lied. In fact, he was terrified. Those teeth looked huge. His fingers would fit nicely between them and undoubtedly mix well in one of the cow's many stomachs.

"Try it," she insisted, holding out an apple. Jon hesitated. She stepped toward him and thrust the apple into his hand. "Go on. They won't hurt you. You'll see."

Jon looked down at the apple, then at the little girl, then at the big, black cow waiting patiently just on the other side of the fence. Jon could have sworn there was a gleam of curiosity in the creature's large, somber eyes.

"Oh, all right," he sighed. "Might as well."

He took a couple of tentative steps toward the fence. Slowly, careful not to startle the cow, Jon eased his hand through the fence. The cow took a step toward him. For a second, Jon panicked. The cow was going to rush him, grab his hand, and start chomping hungrily on his entire arm!

But no, it lowered its head and started probing Jon's hand for the apple. He realized that he was clutching the apple tightly, rather than letting it lie flat on his palm. The cow's massive tongue licked at Jon's enclosed fingers, trying to pry the apple loose. Jon shuddered and opened his hand. *Click*—the cow's teeth snapped up the apple. Jon pulled his hand back so quickly it scraped against the fence.

"See, silly," the little girl said gleefully. "That wasn't so hard." She turned and raced off, joining her friends. Jon stood there, trembling slightly, his view of cows now altered more than a little. He would think twice the next time he ordered a hamburger from McDonald's.

"That was quite impressive, young man," a deep-throated voice said from behind him.

Jon turned, startled. Facing him was a man in his late fifties, maybe early sixties, judging from his fine, grayish hair. He wore black leather cowboy boots, creased jeans, a huge leather belt with a massive buckle, and a light cotton shirt open at the collar. "I, uh—I've never exactly been around cows much," Jon stammered.

"Somehow I figured that," the man said, smiling. Before Jon could react, the man reached a hand around Jon and plucked his reporter's notebook from his back pocket.

"Hey!" Jon said, startled. "That's mine."

"I know," the man said softly. "But I want you to put it away. This is a private dinner. Off the record. You can watch and listen. But I don't want you taking notes."

Jon felt himself getting angry. "Who in the—"

The man extended a hand. "Name's Jim Jenkins. Pleased to meet you."

Jon took the man's hand and shook it once. "Yeah, well, I'm Jon Abelson."

"I know," Jenkins said. "You're a reporter for the *Gazette.*"

"How did you know that?"

"I make it a point to know all my reporters. Even those who haven't been officially hired yet," Jenkins said casually.

Jon blinked furiously for a few seconds. James Jenkins. *Oh, man,* Jon thought miserably. *This guy's the publisher of the newspaper. I'm dead. Why didn't Sanders tell me he'd be here?* "Mr. Jenkins, I didn't know you'd be at this," Jon said, trying to keep his voice even.

"I go to all sorts of functions. Important to get around, you know." Jenkins handed the notebook back to Jon. "Now, do us both a favor. Put this away, out of sight. You won't need it this evening."

Jon tucked it inside his sport jacket. "I didn't know," he offered lamely.

"Understandable." Jenkins turned and looked out over the sea of faces at the party. He pointed toward a knot of people gathered around a younger man who was speaking and gesturing. "See that man?" he asked. Jon nodded. "Well, that's my son, James number two. He's at First Merchant Bank. He's coming up fast in the world. Very fast. I want you to keep an eye on him."

"Now, at this party?" Jon asked, slightly confused.

"No, in general!" Jenkins snapped.

"Okay, well, sure. But . . . if I can ask. Why?"

Jenkins turned back to Jon. There was more than a hint of anger, perhaps impatience, smoldering in his eyes. "Because that's the way the world works, young man. I told you to do so, and your answer is nothing more than 'Yes, sir.' Got it?"

"Yes, sir," Jon said, doing his level best not to grit his teeth.

"Glad we understand each other," Jenkins said brusquely. "Now, enjoy yourself. But don't drink. You'll make the paper look bad."

"I never drink, sir," Jon said quickly. "Haven't for years."

Jenkins eyed him curiously. "Not one of those born-again, fundamentalist Christian types, are you?"

Jon swallowed hard. No one had ever quite put a question like that to him so directly, especially not a potential employer. "Well—to be honest, sir, yes, I am a Christian. And, yes, I would say that I am born again. I know people hate that phrase these days—"

Jenkins held up a hand. "No need to apologize for your convictions, boy. Better to have some than none, I say. I'm a church-goin' Christian myself. No need to worry on my account."

Suddenly feeling quite uncomfortable, Jon decided to change the subject. Quickly. "By the way, will Sam Adams be here tonight, do you know?"

Jenkins' jaw clenched. There was no mistaking it. "No, I can say with some assurance that Sam Adams will not be here this evening."

"Really? At a Democratic Party shindig like this? So if he's not going to be here, you wouldn't know how I can track him down, would you?"

Jenkins smiled wickedly. "Why don't you try calling him, boy, like any decent reporter would?"

"I will, sir!" Jon answered quickly. "I just thought that maybe—"

"That maybe I'd have a couple of connections?"

"Well, yeah, something like that."

Jenkins nodded. "Tell you what. I might have one or two of those. But you try to track down Adams yourself. If you come up short, let my secretary know. I'll arrange for you to sit down with Linda Hunt. She can help, no doubt."

Jon had no idea who Linda Hunt was. He should have done his homework, at least read through the newspaper's clips on the Adams race. But everything had happened so fast that day that he hadn't gotten to it. And he was most certainly not going to ask Jenkins who Linda Hunt was. Not now. "Great," he said quickly. "I'll do that."

"But tonight, you keep an eye on my boy, you hear? You ask folks here—discreetly, of course—what they think of him." It was a direct order. There was no mistaking that.

"Yes, sir, I will," Jon answered.

For the rest of the evening, Jon did exactly that. He never actually met Jenkins junior directly, but he ran across plenty of folks who knew all about him—and who, apparently, admired him and his talents immensely. Either that, or they admired Jenkins Senior and the wealth that he and his son brought to the local party.

By the time the party had ended, Jon had acquired a number of possible future sources for stories but not a whole lot of help in tracking down Sam Adams. Most people he talked to didn't think much of Adams, which made Jon wonder where Adams's support in the party was coming from.

Jon had the feeling that he was missing some piece of a puzzle, but for the life of him, he couldn't figure it. Everyone at the party seemed to know who he was—or, at least, that he was a reporter. And for that reason, they were all quite guarded with him, even if the whole thing was off-the-record. But so what? He'd done his duty. He'd attended. Now he could get on with his work. Tomorrow he'd track down Adams.

CHAPTER FOUR

Sam Adams, it turned out, was a hard guy to find. Jon struggled all morning to get through. Adams's campaign organization didn't return Jon's first two phone calls. On the third try, he refused to get off the phone until he talked to someone who could give him Adams's schedule.

The Adams aide who finally got on the line still wouldn't give out the candidate's schedule. Jon blew his stack.

"But I'm a reporter with the *Singleton Gazette!*" he yelled into the phone.

"Yeah? So?" asked the kid on the other end of the line, who clearly wasn't impressed.

"You *have* to tell me," Jon said through gritted teeth.

"Says who?"

"Says the First Amendment! You know, freedom of the press."

"So be free. Write whatever you like," the aide shot back. "The *Gazette* always does anyway."

"What's that mean?"

"How long you worked there, anyway?" the aide asked.

"At the *Gazette?*"

"Yeah, the *Gazette*, you moron," the aide said sarcastically. "How long?"

"That's none of your—"

"You just started, didn't you?" the aide interrupted him.

"Well, yeah, I guess I started a little while ago," Jon stammered.

"Thought so," the aide said smugly. "Well, you'll see. You'll get with the program."

"What's that supposed to mean?"

"Look. I gotta go," the aide said. "Call anytime."

And he hung up. Just like that.

Jon slammed the phone down. Something weird was going on, and he knew he'd better figure it out in a hurry. He angrily pushed back his chair from the desk Sanders had given him in a corner of the crowded newsroom. The chair made a hideous scratching noise as it scraped across the crummy tile floor underneath. No one even looked up. Nearly every head at every desk had a telephone jammed in one ear.

Jon stormed down the hall, turned left, and headed to the "morgue" of the newspaper, the place where they filed old clips from past issues. He asked the clerk in the office to pull everything from the past six months on Samuel Adams, and then camped out in a chair to wait for the clips to arrive, mentally kicking himself for not having done this first thing when Sanders assigned him to Adams.

They were in his hands five minutes later, jammed every which way into a brown folder titled "Samuel Adams/Congress." Jon took the clips back to his empty desk and spread them out. Except for one coffee break an hour later, he read them straight through.

The clips seemed to split right down the middle. Half were just straight news stories, basically reporting on what Adams had said or done to attack constituencies, go after certain interest groups, lambaste the other party, whatever. Those stories had no real "slant." They were just basic, grind-em-out political stories. There were also a couple of quite lengthy profiles of him, done by feature writers, that gave Jon almost everything he wanted to know about who Adams was and where he'd come from.

But the rest of the clips, the other half, were anything but neutral. In fact, they sounded almost as if the newspaper had gone to war with Adams. Whenever Adams did something controversial—or, at least, big and public—the *Gazette* always managed to find people, usually several of them, to criticize what Adams was doing and no one—at least no one reputable—to support him.

By the time Jon had finished the clips, he felt that he had a pretty decent idea who Adams was. At least who the public Adams was. Clearly, Adams was good copy. He was controversial and nearly always sideways with *Gazette* reporters. Jon couldn't believe the amount of coverage Adams was getting and how hyped so much of it seemed.

What made it especially strange was that Adams did not have an announced opponent in the Democratic primary, scheduled for the end of the summer. The fireworks right now were all aimed at the race in November, six months away.

Jon also discovered from the clips who Linda Hunt was. Although she was rarely mentioned in the news coverage on Adams and his initiatives, she was his Republican opponent for the open congressional seat. Jon was glad he hadn't opened his mouth and revealed his ignorance last night. Boy, would he have sounded stupid to Jenkins! And what about Jenkins: On the one hand, he had seemed so at ease at an informal Democratic Party pig roast—on the other, he spoke of the Republican congressional candidate as if she were a close personal friend who'd be more than happy to help out. Small-town politics could be curious, Jon figured.

From the clips, Jon could tell that Adams was big on going after groups of people. He'd singled out rich folks, developers, "country clubbers," banker-types, corporate officials, and just about every stereotype attached to the Republican Party.

But it also sounded as if he had attacked a central constituency of the Democratic Party and gotten away with it. He denounced the "liberal welfare system" with a vengeance. That was where his "take it back" message came from. He wanted groups of people in poor communities to organize and "take" their neighborhoods back, block by block—using force if necessary, or so it sounded.

Adams also sounded like a fierce protector of the Second Amendment to the Constitution, the right to bear arms. An easy way, Jon figured, to pick up more than a few votes from the disaffected crowd who hated the government or who joined the National Rifle Association to fight to keep their guns. Adams described it as the right to protect your home—or your neighborhood—from thugs and rapists.

Adams had coined a new label for himself: "Lincoln Democrat." He painted himself as a "man of the people" who looked after the interests of the downtrodden and who challenged the authorities who stood in the way of progress for entire classes of people.

Adams had somehow managed to get a significant portion of the poor, black communities in his congressional district to rally to his cause as their "defender" against the authorities who were denying them their rights. He also railed against corporate chieftains who threatened to roll back some of the hard-fought victories of the unions in the two largest plants in the congressional district—a farm equipment plant and a huge auto-parts warehouse that supplied parts to three separate car makers in neighboring states.

But even as he was locking up two critical parts of the usual Democratic Party coalition—disenfranchised blacks and union workers—Adams had also pulled off a neat triple by going after conservative and evangelical Christians who usually voted Republican. At first, he had focused just on blue-collar Catholics. He was a pro-life kind of guy, he had told them, and he liked the idea of a little prayer in the schools. But as he had warmed up to this constituency, Adams had also begun to reach out to Protestant denominations as well with traditional, family-oriented messages.

And the curious thing, Jon noticed, was that it seemed to be working. Adams was building an unusual left-right coalition that mixed healthy doses of anger, compassion, and good old-fashioned religion, depending on the audience at hand.

Only the newspaper, the *Gazette*, seemed to stand in the way of Adams's march to victory. But, as Jon knew, people no longer read newspapers. Word of mouth meant everything in these races, and the word of mouth on Adams right now had to be very, very good. Jon guessed that, short of a really nasty, corrupt picture of Adams on the pages of the *Gazette*, he was a shoo-in.

Which explained why Adams's campaign staff were treating him as they were. They had no need for Jon. He was their enemy, and it made no sense to consort with the enemy.

Which also meant, of course, that Jon would have to find other ways to get to Adams. If the candidate would not cooperate, then Jon would have to find someone who would.

So he decided to take Jenkins up on his offer. He called Jenkins' secretary and explained who he was and what he needed. An hour later, the secretary buzzed him back. Linda Hunt would meet him that afternoon for a late lunch at Jackson's Steak House in one of Singleton's two affluent suburbs.

CHAPTER FIVE

"Oh, he's a devil. Smarter than anyone I've seen come through here in a long time." Ms. Hunt just shook her head. "Can't get to him. Can't make a dent. And we've been trying for months."

Jackson's was nearly full for lunch. As they took their seats at a corner of the restaurant, where no one could overhear their conversation, Linda Hunt leaned toward him and said in a low voice, "This is where the 'other side' comes for lunch."

"You mean the Republicans?" Jon asked.

Ms. Hunt took his arm and squeezed it gently. "Now, this is all off the record, right? Just between you and me? Jimmy said I could trust you."

Jon put his notebook off to one side. He wasn't quite sure where the "trust" part had come from—that was not something he and Jenkins had discussed—but he had no problem with talking "off the record" for a while. He just needed basic information, not direct quotes for a story, at least not yet. "Sure, no problem," he said breezily. "Now—the 'other side'?"

"Yes. What I meant was, you know—people who've made it, who know what they're doing, who raise their kids right—to be civilized, not animals. People who work for a living, who don't just live off welfare checks."

Jon immediately felt sick. This woman, whom he'd never met until now, had managed to make him feel completely ill at ease before their conversation had even begun. She was obviously what Jon thought of as a black-and-white thinker. He didn't see the world in black and white, in "us" against "them," the "haves" and the "have nots"—especially when he tried to apply his Christianity to the world around him.

36

There was a funny little story someone had told him once, which he'd never forgotten. Imagine, the story went, that you and everyone else were standing on the coast of California, looking out over the Pacific ocean. God is in Hawaii. He tells you and everyone else to jump in the ocean—on faith—and swim to him. Some do; many don't. But no one—no matter how gifted or talented or strong or sleek of mind and body—will come anywhere close to swimming all the way to where God is. Not in a million years, with countless tries. You can only get there with his help.

The world was a lot like that, Jon believed. When he heard people say they were better than someone else, he remembered that story. And he remembered that, by the only measuring stick that counts, everyone falls very, very short.

"Yeah, really?" Jon mumbled.

"Really," Ms. Hunt said, nodding. "That's why what Adams is doing is so awful. He's trying to hoodwink them."

"Hoodwink? Who?" Jon asked. He didn't pick up the menu. He wasn't sure he was all that hungry.

"You know," Linda Hunt said conspiratorially. "Good people, like you and me."

Jon shook his head. He didn't understand. "No, I'm not sure I do know."

A troubled look crossed her face. "Jimmy . . . he said that you were . . . you know, a Christian?"

"Yes," Jon frowned. "But what's that got to do with anything here?"

Linda Hunt leaned forward in her seat, relieved that her information had not been in error. "It means everything, of course. Adams is trying to convince people in churches—you know, good people—that he's like them, that he believes in the same things they do, and yet he's also pandering to the others at the same time."

"The others?"

Linda Hunt hesitated. "We're still off-the-record?"

Jon nodded curtly. "Yes, of course."

"Well," she responded, with just a slight pause. "You know—blacks and Mexicans and union workers and people who feed off welfare. The usual, you know, crowd of leeches they always get to vote for them."

Jon did his level best to hold his tongue. He needed Linda Hunt's perspective on Samuel Adams; he needed her knowledge of his schedule and his campaign. But it took every ounce of control he possessed just to continue sitting here with her. "But, Ma'am, aren't blacks and Hispanics and people who belong to unions ... aren't they ... can't they be Christians, too?"

Linda Hunt snorted. "Oh, yeah, sure, I guess. But you know what I'm talking about. Adams is trying to have it both ways. He's talking trash to trash, and then turning right around and talking about prayers in schools in neighborhoods around here. You can't do both."

"You can't? Why not?"

"Because they're totally different, totally separate."

"But if they're all in his congressional district—in *your* congressional district—isn't he supposed to represent *all* the people?"

Linda Hunt gave Jon the strangest look. "You learn in school about how democracy's supposed to work?"

"I took a couple of political science courses at Princeton."

Linda Hunt shook her head. "Well, kid, this ain't Princeton. Not by a mile. This is the real world. And here there's one side, and then there's the other. You can't go talking to both sides and get away with it."

Jon didn't say anything. From where he stood, Sam Adams seemed to be doing precisely that—if only because he seemed open to the possibility that you could actually talk to different levels of society—a sort of "all things to all men and women" mentality. Jon wasn't so sure he disliked that philosophy.

"Well, anyway," Jon said, grabbing his menu so he could fumble with his hands for a moment as he thought, "I need some help. I can't even find out what Adams is doing. And I thought maybe your organization could help me a little."

"Help you keep track of Adams?" she asked incredulously.

"No, no," Jon said quickly. "Keep me posted when you think he's doing something he shouldn't be—crossing the line, things like that. I'll take it from there."

Linda Hunt nodded. "I get it. Yeah, okay, sure, be happy to. I'll give you an earful." She suddenly leaned back in her chair, her eyebrows arched, a crooked smile starting to spread across her face. "In fact, I got something for you now. Tonight."

"Where?" Jon leaned forward in his seat.

"At St. Anne's tonight, about 7:30."

"St. Anne's?"

"It's one of the Catholic parishes out this way. They have a huge supper tonight, and Adams is dropping by, we've heard. You can watch him then."

"And you're not going?"

"Can't. I have a fund-raiser I have to go to."

"What's he going to talk about?"

Linda Hunt smiled. "You go see for yourself. You'll see right off what I mean. It's as plain as the nose on my face what he's trying to do."

"Is he invited to speak?"

"Go. You'll see," she said. "He doesn't have to be invited. He gets himself invited, once he's there. You'll see for yourself. Don't worry."

CHAPTER SIX

The little parish hall was jammed. Kids were everywhere, running in all directions, shouting, screaming. Mothers—and a few fathers— were trying to corral them, to keep some sort of order, but they weren't having much luck.

As usual when he found himself near children, Jon felt uncomfortable. Kids were foreign to him. He'd never spent much time around them. An only child, Jon hadn't had many friends while he was growing up. He'd been too introspective, too absorbed in his studying and projects in school.

In fact, as a child, Jon had always been content just to sit at home and read books or draw or maybe fool around with some project he'd started. His mother would try to get him to go outside and find a friend or two. Never one for confrontation, Jon had always said, sure, he'd go do something. Then he would just go off to another corner of the house and do something else.

As an adult, his habits weren't much different.

It wasn't that Jon was afraid of people. He just liked being alone. Then he didn't have to talk to anyone, and he could think whatever he wanted to think. It was that simple.

Two small boys, about three or four years old, zipped past him just as he walked into the room. One of them, carrying a stick, was bearing down on the other. The first boy tripped over his shoe and went sprawling to the floor, both hands splayed out in front of him to break his fall. Oddly, or so it seemed to Jon, the boy with the stick paused briefly to give the other a chance to get up, which he did, bouncing up immediately as if the fall had never happened and barreling on again. The second boy then began the chase again.

Jon shook his head. Man. All these families and kids. Why were they here, at this parish? What were they doing?

He glanced around. Round tables and fold-up chairs were crammed into every conceivable corner of what had to be the parish's gym. And almost all the tables were full by now. Up at the front of the room, dozens of covered dishes were spread out on several long tables joined together. People just wandered up and helped themselves. No signs, no directions, nothing told Jon what he was supposed to do.

But everyone here seemed to know what was going on and what was expected of him or her, even if Jon did not. Everyone talked to everyone else, quite loudly. There was plenty of laughter, plenty of serious nods as people tried to carry on conversations.

Jon stood just inside the doorway for almost five minutes, watching. This whole scene blew his mind. He couldn't fathom it, all of this family togetherness, all of this goodwill. This kind of thing had certainly never been part of the Abelson family experience. It amazed him.

Jon saw Adams, finally. Despite the crowd and motion and noise, Adams was easy to spot if you knew what to look for. Jon recognized him from the rally, of course, but he was also the only person in the hall who was moving from table to table. He didn't hurry. But neither did he tarry long at any table.

The man had an instinct, a way of moving that made him stand out. People naturally gathered around him to hear him speak as he moved easily, effortlessly from one table to the next.

Jon watched him for a few minutes before drifting over to listen in casually on one of his conversations. He'd introduce himself later. Right now, he just wanted to peek in.

Adams was informally dressed in black Levi jeans, a dark red, light-weight cotton shirt, and walking shoes. He wore no tie. He blended in well. It was, Jon noticed, quite a different outfit from what he'd been wearing at the rally. His sandy brown hair was cut close enough that it didn't obscure any portion of his clean-shaven face. It was a professional cut, made to look natural and easygoing. It had the desired effect.

Jon noticed immediately that every woman Adams walked up to changed her bearing and posture immediately. One woman handed her baby to a friend so she could talk directly to him. Several women actually took a step closer to Adams when he joined their table conversation. Several inclined their heads to listen closely to him.

41

The men had an almost opposite reaction to his presence. They shook his hand very firmly. Adams always returned the handshakes firmly as well, Jon noted. Many of the men then actually seemed to take one giant step backward. Several folded their arms in front of them. One man even drew a chair in front of him and leaned on it casually, the chair serving as a barrier of sorts.

Adams seemed—or pretended—not to notice any of this. Whether the person he was talking to was close at hand or keeping a distance, he carried on each conversation as if it were the most important conversation of the evening. He seemed to listen intently to each and every word, offering answers only when necessary and making sure he cut no one off.

Everyone seemed to know why Adams was there. They all knew him or quickly grasped who he was and why he was there. Jon finally moved in close enough—he positioned himself just a few feet from the table, near enough to another crowd of people so as not to stand out—to hear one conversation. Adams was talking to two women in their early thirties, neither with children, and both sitting alone at a table.

"It isn't right," the first woman said.

The second woman nodded. "It's like we're second-class citizens, Mr. Adams."

Adams pursed his lips thoughtfully. He held a finger up to his lips for a moment, a gesture Jon had seen him do more than once already that evening. It made him look thoughtful. "Liz, tell me. In your mind, what should be done about it?"

The first woman, who must have been Liz, seemed to brighten at the recognition and the question. "Well, give us something, some recognition. Women can preach in some of the Protestant denominations. Why not in the Catholic church?"

"So you'd like to see women priests?" Adams asked gently.

"No, no," said the second woman. "But we'd like some recognition that a woman is not just some sort of a prop for a priest in the church."

"And is that the way most women see it, that you're props?" Adams asked.

"Our friends do, yes," the first woman, Liz, said emphatically. "And we don't like it."

"Do your friends have something in mind, something concrete they'd like to do or say?" Adams said, his voice very quiet.

"Well, no, not really. Not anything specific. We just think it's wrong—the woman's role in the Catholic church," Liz answered.

"I see," Adams said. "You'd like a greater role, more voice, more recognition?"

Jon noticed how the two women reacted to Adams's questions. They nodded vigorously, convinced for some reason that they'd found a sympathizer to their laments. But Adams had never actually made a statement one way or the other; he'd simply followed up on their statements, using words and phrases the women were comfortable with. And it clearly made them feel as if he were truly hearing their concerns.

"Yes, exactly," the second woman said. "That's all we want."

"That's not too much to ask, is it? It's not like we want to storm the Vatican or anything," Liz said.

"No, of course not," Adams said soothingly, already starting to edge away from the table and the conversation and on to the next one. He did it gracefully; the women couldn't tell what he was doing. But Jon could. It was as if Adams had some kind of an internal clock. He had a certain, limited amount of time to spend with each person in the room, and he entered and left conversations according to that clock. Jon had no doubt that Adams would get to everyone of voting age in the room before he left.

A little girl about kindergarten age, screaming at the top of her lungs, whisked toward Adams, crashing into his legs. She ricocheted a little, wobbled, and then fell to the floor. With a quick good-bye to the two women, Adams knelt on one knee and offered the little girl a hand. She hesitated, then took it.

"You all right?" Adams asked her.

"I'm okay," the girl answered, blushing.

"Sure?"

"Yeah, sure."

Adams smiled. "Sorry my leg got in the way."

The little girl returned the smile, then an instant later was on her way again, racing to the next disaster. Adams stood up just in time to greet the little girl's mother, who had hurried over.

"Oh, Mr. Adams, I'm so sorry," she said. "I hope Melissa didn't—"

Adams waved it off. "No harm, no foul. Don't worry. I think we both came away unscathed."

The mother sighed. "It's so hard to raise kids. In today's society, they learn so much. Everything moves so quickly. Melissa wants to act and be like all the boys, you know."

They both glanced over at little Melissa. She was racing around with a pack of three other boys about her age. "I can only imagine," Adams said.

"You don't have children, do you?" the mother asked.

"No, not yet. Someday."

The mother took a step closer to Adams. Jon edged a little closer as well, to make sure he could still overhear the conversation. "You know, I try so hard to teach Melissa how to behave like a proper little girl. Not to just run around and try to be like all the boys."

"So you feel that it's hard to raise girls in today's society, that they get bombarded with all these conflicting messages?" Adams asked with that gentle, prodding voice.

"Yes, exactly!" the mother said, beaming. "They get so many conflicting messages. Be tough, be sensitive, be strong, be nice. Compete with boys, be your own person. It's hard. You know?"

"Yes, I know," Adams said, nodding. "And you're trying to teach her properly, is that it?"

"Yes, properly. Girls become women, and they have a proper place in society. My job is to raise my kids. It's the best job in the world."

"It's an honor to be a mother, isn't it?" Adams asked.

"It's the highest honor, the greatest duty. I can't imagine anything more fulfilling."

They both looked over at Melissa, who was now dangerously close to careening into a new crowd of adults as she whipped around the room with the boys. "She's a beautiful little girl," Adams said. "You must be very proud."

"I am," the mother said. "And my boys are real good kids, too. They're growing up right."

"Respect for their elders, I'll bet?" Adams said.

"Yes, they sure do have that. You need to learn respect. You have to; otherwise things get out of hand."

Adams shook the woman's hand and started to edge away, his internal clock clearly telling him it was time to move on. A moment later, Adams had managed to insert himself squarely into the center of a conversation with a group of six men.

Jon casually strolled over so that he was within earshot.

"The dumbest move I've seen in the past ten years," one of the men said.

"Moronic," a second said.

"What an idiotic deal," a third chipped.

"There *was* no deal with Kosar!" a fourth erupted. "They just let him go! Modell's an idiot and a rat fink. I hope he rots in Baltimore."

Adams raised a finger to make a point. "So you all think Modell's to be blamed for the Kosar move a few years ago?"

"Yeah, man, course he is," one of the men said, waving his arms like a human windmill. "First, he pays all that money to get Kosar. The guy

44

has two good years, gets us into the play-offs, then demands a lot more money—"

"Which he has a right to do," someone else offered.

"Yeah, sure, course he does. He succeeds, he's got a right to ask for the big money—"

"And then Modell gets nervous as he starts to write out the check—"

"All that money! Makes him sweat."

"Big time."

"So he deals the guy," said the windmill. "Just like that. One minute the Browns are a contender, get a shot, and the next, they're back to square one. Now, Modell's split, and we're stuck with an expansion team."

"Hey!" one of the men said. "I heard the new team owner's gonna offer the Dolphins a ton o' money for Marino."

"Yeah, right! In your dreams. Like the *new* Browns will have that kind of money."

"But what if they *did* go after Marino?"

"GO BROWNS!" the windmill cheered, holding both hands up high. The men on either side gave him high fives.

Jon watched Adams. He didn't say much. Apparently, he didn't have to with this group. Just listening to the men bemoan the Cleveland Browns' latest troubles seemed to be enough to "bond" with these guys. Just offering up a pertinent question every so often was enough.

"So you guys don't think much of the quarterback they have now?" Adams asked when the windmill had lowered his arms.

"A bum!"

"Hasn't got an arm. It's a rainbow every time he puts it up for any distance."

One of the men laughed. "And sometimes it's a rainbow when it's just over the middle to the tight end."

Everyone laughed uproariously. Jon didn't get the joke. He'd never seen this quarterback play, and he wasn't much of a pro football fan to begin with. But one thing was clear. These fellows didn't think the new guy was the quarterback of the future for the Browns.

"But didn't he take the Bears to the play-offs when he was there?" Adams asked. "Didn't he win a whole bunch of games for them?"

"Dumb luck."

"Had a great defense. They never scored on the Bears. So the guy didn't have to put many points on the board to win."

"And the Browns sure don't have that kind of defense."

"No way. They're a sieve in the secondary."

Adams nodded thoughtfully, taking all the comments in. Jon almost laughed out loud, wondering how any of this was even remotely part of a congressman's job. Maybe critiquing football teams was something you did in subcommittee markups.

The lambasting of the poor Cleveland Browns continued unabated for another few minutes, but Adams somehow managed to get in firm handshakes all around and then excuse himself. That internal clock kept ticking.

Half an hour later, Adams had either talked to or touched at least half the adults in the room. Jon found it increasingly difficult just to trail behind him, so he drifted over to the table finally and began to help himself to some of the food on it.

He'd just taken a bite of a ham-and-cheese sandwich when he felt someone slip up beside him and gently take his arm and ease it away from the table. Jon glanced up and jumped involuntarily. It was Adams.

"Over here," Adams said, gesturing toward a remote corner of the room, maybe the only place in the hall that wasn't jammed with adults or kids. Jon followed him meekly. He had a hard time swallowing the bite in his mouth.

Adams positioned himself squarely in front of Jon but with his back to the rest of the room. His eyes were curious, seeking, not especially brooding or angry. But Adams was clearly serious about what he was doing. He looked at Jon intently, and Jon had the strangest sensation of almost falling into those eyes. "All right, kid," Adams said in an almost playful tone of voice despite his gravity. "What's the deal? You were at my rally. Now you're here. You with Hunt? Is that it?"

Jon tried to catch his breath. Adams's eyes bored into his. Jon couldn't remember ever meeting anyone so intense. "Linda Hunt?"

The barest hint of a smile played across Adams's face. "Yes, my opponent, Linda Hunt. You here for her?"

"Why do you think—"

Adams leaned closer. Their faces were just inches apart. In the back of his mind, Jon knew that this was simply a technique Adams was quite consciously using to intimidate him. "Look," Adams said in a stage whisper. "Maybe you think you were being cute. But you've been shadowing every conversation I've had in this place since I walked in. Right?"

Jon didn't answer immediately. This guy *was* intimidating him. And that bothered Jon. Nothing had ever really intimidated him in his life. There had never been a challenge too great for him, a puzzle too complicated, a path too twisted to follow. He wasn't about to let this guy, this political wannabe, be the first to back him down.

"Yes," Jon said a little too loudly, finally finding his voice. "I was shadowing you. I listened to your conversations, or as many of them as I could."

Adams didn't flinch. But Jon could see a very slight change in his eyes. Hardly noticeable. But it was almost as if Adams was slightly amused by this turn of events. And a little curious. "And you're with Hunt?"

"No," Jon said firmly, able at last to return the intense stare. "I'm a new reporter for the *Gazette*. Jon Abelson. And I'm covering your race."

Adams raised his eyebrows slightly. But it didn't take him long to shift gears, maybe a couple of seconds. "A reporter? For the *Gazette?*"

"Yeah, and you have one of the rudest campaign staffs I can imagine," Jon said. "They wouldn't give me the time of day or even tell me what your public schedule is."

"Good for them," Adams laughed. "I told them to cut the *Gazette* off. I'm delighted to hear that they follow orders so well."

"You told them that?" Jon said, clearly surprised that Adams would admit it to him.

"Sure, why not?" shrugged Adams. "Your newspaper's never done me any favors. Why should I give them the time of day?"

"Because it's a newspaper," Jon said. "First Amendment rights and all that."

Adams chuckled. "Look, kid, the First Amendment's a wonderful piece of work. But it doesn't compel me to give you information. It just gives you the right to say what you want about me. Which the *Gazette* does abundantly, any old time it wants to."

To be honest, Jon had never thought much about the First Amendment, one way or another. But he wasn't about to back down from such a direct challenge.

"Mr. Adams," Jon said, his voice deadly earnest. "I'm going to cover your race. That's a given. You can cooperate or not. I don't care either way. But I'm covering your race. And I'm going to call it as I see it."

"You are, huh?"

"Yes, I am. Whether you like it or not."

Adams smiled broadly. It was a disarming smile, especially under the circumstances. "Well, kid, I'm glad to hear it. You can start your education tomorrow morning, then. Fifth and Main. The old S & L building, eight o'clock in the morning."

"I'm supposed to meet you there? You're doing something there?" Jon asked.

"See ya, kid. Or not. I don't care either way." Adams turned away. A minute later, he was thoroughly engrossed in a conversation with a knot of people gathered around the buffet table. As if nothing had happened.

CHAPTER SEVEN

When the alarm went off at seven o'clock the next morning, Jon panicked for a moment. He couldn't remember where he was, why he was there, what he was supposed to be doing. Then it came back. He was meeting Adams for some mysterious rendezvous.

Jon groaned and sank back into the pillow. He let the alarm go for nearly a full minute before reaching over and shutting it off, and then he could still hear the jangling alarm echoing in his mind.

At Princeton, Jon had carefully selected all his classes so that he had nothing before ten o'clock. And even ten-o'clock classes had been infrequent.

This getting-to-work-on-time stuff would be hard. It would take some getting used to. Fortunately, this flophouse the newspaper had put him up in was just five blocks from Fifth and Main, where he was to meet Adams; he could walk there in less than ten minutes.

He climbed out of bed, hurried into the bathroom, and turned on the shower. While the water heated up, he brushed his teeth, brewing a cup of instant coffee at the same time, which he carried into the shower with him.

He finished the coffee while he got dressed, hurried out into the morning air, and realized immediately that he would freeze on the walk to Fifth and Main. It was mid-May, and the summer heat had not yet arrived. It wouldn't warm up until mid-morning. Jon wrapped his arms around himself and hurried.

He found the old S & L building without any trouble and arrived a good five minutes before eight. The building still looked like a bank if you ignored the broken windows and the graffiti; even an old, boarded-up drive-through teller window was on the side of the building, facing the parking lot.

Jon peered through the front doors. No one in the lobby. The door swung open when he pushed, so Jon walked inside. It was dark, but he could hear voices farther in. His footsteps echoed as he walked across the lobby toward a set of glass double doors that led farther into the building. He paused at those and looked in.

Beyond the doors was a much larger room, one that must once have served as the central part of the S & L, where the tellers had waited on people and vice presidents had talked to people about car loans. Now, though, all the teller windows had been torn down, and the room was one big open space with a few desks jammed up against the walls.

In the center of the room were maybe a dozen gym mats shoved together. And on those mats, sitting in a semicircle, were about twenty young, black men, all gazing up at Sam Adams.

Only one other white person was in the room, a youngish man—perhaps in his late twenties—with black bushy eyebrows, a hooked nose that made him look like a hawk, closely cropped hair, a gold earring in his left ear, rounded spectacles, and a gold cross on a chain around his neck. He stood off to the side, neither part of the group nor next to Sam Adams.

Adams looked so out of place that it startled Jon. What *had* he been expecting? Jon wasn't sure, but he knew it wasn't this.

Jon eased through the doors. Every head in the place turned immediately and looked at him, making him profoundly uncomfortable for some reason. It was as if he were an intruder, an unwanted visitor from another planet.

Jon waved at Adams, who returned the wave and then beckoned for Jon to come over and join them.

"Guys, this is the reporter from the *Gazette* I mentioned," Adams said. Many of the faces on the black youths relaxed. But, Jon noticed, a few did not. "Jon," Adams continued, "come on over. Have a seat. You can listen in."

Jon settled in on one of the mats. He kept his distance from the others, who made no effort to include him in the group. But that was all right. None of these kids were his friends, nor would they ever be, most likely. He was here to observe Adams, nothing more.

Gradually, everyone turned his attention back to Adams. Only then did he continue.

"All right, as I was saying, today is Cherry Hill," Adams said. Jon noticed how easygoing Adams's tone of voice was in this setting. He made no effort to impress these guys, and clearly he didn't need to. They hung on every word.

"How many of you guys are familiar with Cherry Hill?" About ten hands went up. "And how many of you live there?" No hands went up, and Adams nodded. "Okay, good, that's what I thought. So we'll need a pretty thorough canvass. You guys all bring something to write with?" Most of the kids around Jon nodded or mumbled.

"We can do buddies?" one of the kids asked Adams.

Adams nodded. "Of course, Leroy. You know the drill. Like before. If you're more comfortable traveling with a buddy—for whatever reason—then go ahead. No problem."

"Where we meetin'?" a second kid asked.

Adams pointed to the floor. "Here, in four hours. I'll have lunch. Cherry Hill's not too far from here, so you can get there and back without too much trouble. Everyone can give their recon reports, and then I'll bundle 'em up and take 'em over."

Jon really wanted to raise his hand and ask Adams just what this was all about. But he'd find out soon enough if he stuck close to Adams and watched.

The kids started to get up and stretch their legs. Most of them wore their hair closely shaved. Not like the military, but awfully close to it. Many of them wore heavy boots. A few had leather jackets. Nearly all of them were dressed in just a T-shirt and either jeans or work pants of some sort, giving Jon the impression that these kids were following their own, private dress and conduct code.

As most of the kids started to file out of the room, two of them approached Jon and simply stood in front of him. They didn't say anything. It was as if they were waiting for him to say something to them instead.

"So you guys come here often to listen to Adams?" Jon finally asked them just to break the ice.

"Mister Adams," one of them said, "and, yeah, we come here a lot. The man's got somethin' to say, and we here to listen."

The other kid took one slightly menacing step forward in Jon's direction. "You from the *Gazette*, that right?"

"Yes, that's right," Jon said, trying not to let his eyes drift away from the young man's gaze. He didn't want to give the impression that he was afraid of him—even though he was, a little.

"So, man, why you be beatin' up on Mister Adams all the time?" the kid asked him. "Why is it? You got somethin' against him?"

51

"No, I don't have anything against him," Jon said. "I just got here. Why would I—"

"You said you was the *Gazette*, right?" the first kid said.

"Yeah," Jon answered.

"Well, then, answer my question. The *Gazette's* all over Mister Adams's case. All the time. Why's that?"

Jon didn't know how to answer. They were right, of course. The *Gazette* was all over Adams. But he wasn't about to admit that, here.

Jon glanced at Adams, who was now talking privately with the white guy Jon had seen when he first entered. Adams was, Jon guessed, fully aware of what these two kids were saying, how they were making Jon squirm. And Adams wasn't about to rescue him anytime soon.

"Look, you guys, I'm just a new reporter with the *Gazette,*" Jon offered lamely. "I came here today because Adams—Mister Adams—invited me. That's all. I don't have anything against him. Honest."

The second kid sneered back at Jon. "Yeah, right. You're like all the rest of 'em."

Jon gave him a quizzical look. "Why do you say that?"

"Man, I can just tell. I can tell." Both of them laughed and then moved off. They'd made their point. Now it was time to get started on with their mission, whatever it might be.

Jon breathed a silent sigh of relief as he watched the two walk away. Jon wasn't a racist. At least, he didn't think he was. But this whole setup made him nervous. These black kids clearly liked Adams. No question about that. But their dislike of Jon, for whatever reason, was palpable. Was that why Jon felt so profoundly uncomfortable here? Or maybe because he was a stranger here—to the town and to these kids? No, it was more than that. And whatever was causing it, the feeling was strong.

Adams finally drifted his way. Waiting until the kids were out of earshot, Adams softly said, "So, you made it."

"Yeah, I made it," Jon grinned weakly. "Barely."

"I saw a couple of my kids were beatin' you up a little."

"Ah, it wasn't much. They were just asking questions."

Adams didn't say anything right away. "They look out for me."

"I can see that."

"They don't mean anything by it, really. They just look up to me. And they think your newspaper's unfair to me. Which it is, of course."

"I can't speak for the *Gazette,*" Jon shrugged. "I can only speak for myself. And I don't have any hard ideas, one way or another. Except maybe that you have a couple of jerks on your campaign staff."

Adams laughed. "Yeah, maybe so. Politics attracts hard chargers. I think I have a couple of those working on my campaign."

Jon decided to change the subject. "You said they were your kids. What did you mean by that? They work for you?"

Adams glanced as the last of the kids left the building. He turned to the man at his side. "Jon, these kids were brought here to me by this man," Adams said admiringly. "Meet Sean Burns, a minister of the United Methodist church here in the downtown area. He introduced all of these kids to me, and keeps me in line. He keeps all these kids in line as well."

Sean Burns extended a hand. Jon took it. "Nice to meet you," Burns said.

Jon stared hard at Burns. He had beady eyes, almost like two black lumps of coal. They weren't exactly unfriendly. They were just unfathomable. "An interesting group of kids."

"They just need direction, that's all," Burns said. "We're giving them something to aim for."

"Burnsie's my right hand in this project," Adams said. "It was his idea. He finds the kids. They listen to him, and then to me."

"I see," Jon said.

"But they don't work for me. They don't work for anyone, for that matter," Adams said. "You need to understand that. It's important. They do their own thing."

"They have jobs?"

"Some of them. Not many. Hard for young, black men to find work, you know. Black teenage boys have the toughest time. That's why I started this. It gives them something to do, and I got a little funding for it from the city welfare agency, so I can give them pocket change."

Jon gave Adams a strange look. "So what is it exactly that they do? For pocket change."

"You know much about the city yet? Like what Cherry Hill is?"

"Nope."

"You know about subsidized housing projects?"

"Ghettos?"

Adams shook his head. "Not ghettos the way you're thinking of them. Cherry Hill's a housing project. Takes up an entire city block. It has a big courtyard inside."

"And you're sending these kids there? For what?"

"Mostly to look around, ask a few questions," Burns chipped in. "Some of the brave ones will go door to door and ask the neighbors a few questions."

"About what?"

"Almost anything," Adams said. "Are toilets getting fixed, do the police come through at all to break up the drug deals, are there lights on in the courtyard at night, have they seen many handguns around, any hookers. That sort of thing."

"And then what? They come back here and give these recon reports you mentioned?"

"Yes, exactly," Adams said. "They give me the information, and I disseminate it as I see fit. Sometimes to the local HUD office, sometimes to the police. Depends on the information. We try to give the right people the right information, so at least a few things can get done right."

"So you've had some successes?"

"Just two weeks ago I gave the police enough information to shut down a drug deal and put people in jail." Adams grinned. "That even made your newspaper."

"And today, what do you figure they'll find?"

Adams looked off toward the street. "What they find every time they go out. Despair, hopelessness, abject poverty, misery, and a great deal of anger."

Jon looked at Adams with just a little more respect than he'd had coming into this thing. "And you think you're making a difference with this program? You really do?"

Adams turned back quickly and looked directly at Jon. "You have any better ideas how to get these kids engaged? You see anybody else stepping up to help these kids or trying to get even the smallest thing done for a project like Cherry Hill? Do you?"

"No," Jon said softly, "I can't say that I do."

"Then don't be so quick to criticize," Adams said, his voice edged with a hint of anger. "You don't change a place like Cherry Hill overnight. Maybe you never change it. But at least some of these kids will learn something by trying."

"Okay. I'll keep an open mind," Jon said.

Adams nodded, apparently satisfied. "All I can ask. Okay, then, let's go take a look at Cherry Hill ourselves. Up close and personal. We'll get back before the guys do so we can fix lunch."

CHAPTER EIGHT

The walk over to Cherry Hill was depressing enough. As they got closer, even the litter in streets was different from that in other parts of the city—nasty, vile things. People stared at him as if he were from another planet.

But Cherry Hill itself was even more depressing. No hope seemed to be there, nothing redeeming or uplifting. Just misery, bitterness, and despair—exactly as Adams had said.

Jon couldn't imagine living in such a place. He couldn't imagine *any* human being living in such a place.

Every wall was covered with graffiti. Ugly, harsh words, the kind that offend almost everyone, words that spoke of unbridled anger from people who did not know where they would go or what they would do with their lives.

The "courtyard" of Cherry Hill, large and open, must have promised something even slightly grand when it was first built. Now, though, it was a dump, a place of filth and shadows, except for the barren center of the place.

There was trash in nearly every corner, every nook or cranny. No one ever picked it up, apparently. Beer cans, used syringes, and other used paraphernalia littered the landscape. It seemed completely out of place in a public square. It was hideous. Jon cringed.

Kids wailed incessantly. Every so often, a voice—usually a very loud, angry male one—would roar at the offending child to tell him or her to be quiet. Only they never used the words *be quiet*. Their words were more blunt, with emphasis on the profanity in the sentence.

Almost from the moment Jon entered the courtyard at Cherry Hill, he began to hear a curious *bang!* every few seconds, occasionally followed by a roar of anger or exhilaration. The sound vaguely reminded Jon of something, from years past, but he couldn't remember what.

He drifted across the courtyard toward the sounds, ignoring the stares that followed him.

In a far corner, Jon found an open door barely clinging to its hinges, with a darkened hallway beyond. The lights were broken. Jon ducked into the hallway and followed the sounds around a corner, trying to ignore the stench of human sweat that pervaded the space.

Jon stopped in his tracks. There, smack in the middle of the laundry room, was a whole pack of kids of all ages, gathered around a table of some sort, studying it intently. The whole scene, which Jon recognized immediately, seemed oddly out of place here.

It was a foosball table—chipped on all corners, cracked in a couple of places, the wood worn through in a whole bunch of places, but still a foosball table.

Jon had played the game in his fraternity at Princeton. One of his wealthier frat brothers had brought his own table to school with him and plunked it right down in the common area on the first level of the house. Like everyone else in the house, Jon had played it a lot, often until well after midnight. It was something to pass the time.

In fact, Jon had played it enough that he'd gotten pretty good at the game. Not a pro, by any means. But good enough to know what to do with the hard, white ball that skittered around the table between the wooden or hard plastic soccer players that swiveled around the sticks that were laid across the table.

Jon wandered closer. A few of the kids turned to glare at him but quickly returned to the game. All eyes were glued on the four players at the table. They were pretty good, Jon acknowledged. They passed the ball a little between back and front lines, and they could slam the ball hard when they had a shot. That was the strange *bang* Jon could hear echoing when he first entered Cherry Hill.

But Jon could also tell that they played the game wild. Not in control. The white ball hardly ever stopped moving on the table. It just banged forward and backward at lightning speed until someone managed to slam it into one of the goals. All four players basically tried to whack it hard when it came past. They didn't have a plan, a way to control where the ball went.

Jon smiled to himself. He could take these kids. It had been years since he'd played, but he knew he could. This game had an art to it, if you knew what you were doing. It involved passing until you could trap the ball with your forward line, then getting the ball to the middle player of that line. Slide it across the table, flick the wrist, and—*wham!*—the ball popped up into the corner of the goal before the other player could react.

Jon watched silently for a bit. Two bigger kids were on one side of the table, and it was clear that they were the champions here. Everyone else challenged them for supremacy, but no one could beat them. When one set of players was defeated, another took their place.

Finally, one of the younger kids looked up at Jon. "Hey, man, you play?" the kid asked, obviously sizing him up.

Jon shrugged. "Yeah, a little."

"Can I play witch ya?"

"You sure?"

The little kid, who had to be no more than seven or eight years old, gave him a gap-toothed smile. "Yeah, man. I be sure. Ain't nobody else done nothin' against 'em," the kid said, jerking his thumb over his shoulder at the champions.

Jon nodded. "What's your name, anyway?"

"Jimmy."

"Mine's Jon."

"Can I play front?" Jimmy asked.

"Why don't you let me start there and see how it goes?" Jon said.

"You know how?"

Jon smiled. "Yeah, I know how."

Jimmy thought about it for a couple of seconds, then nodded. He'd let the big white guy play front and see how he did.

Jimmy elbowed his way to the side of the table as the game began to wind down. As the champions slammed in the last, winning goal, Jimmy seized the handles at one end of the table. He held on firmly, despite the jostling from a couple of other kids who wanted a crack at the table. Jimmy turned and looked over his shoulder. "C'mon, man. I got it. We're up."

The crowd of black kids moved to either side, silently, to let him pass. The room got really quiet in a hurry. The two champions glowered at Jon. One of them was taller than Jon, and bigger to boot, even though he was only a teenager. Jon was, he admitted, feeling a little intimidated.

No words passed between challengers and champions, though. The big guy plucked the white ball from the end of the table and tossed it over to Jon. He caught it deftly and fitted the ball into the slot. It was coming back—the feel, the touch of the ball, and the handles. He could do this. He could remember.

Jon spun the ball hard with his thumb as he pushed it out the slot and onto the table. The ball hit the table and spun in the direction of Jon's front line. He rotated the stick slightly, elevating the flat "toes" of the nearest player, and grabbed the ball. Jon pulled the stick toward him, spinning the ball back toward him, and grabbed the ball with the player closest to him. Before his opponent could react, Jon lightly tapped the ball off the side of the player's toe, making the ball ricochet forward off the wall, around the player in front of him.

Jon caught the ball with his front line, popped it over to the center player, and jostled the ball a little until it was resting on the table, just on the inside of his center player's toe. Jon took his hand off the handle—his opponents couldn't get at the ball, so it didn't matter anyway—dried the sweat off his palm and then regrasped the handle. He glanced up briefly at his opponent, who was waggling his players back and forth in front of the goal.

The boy clearly had no idea what Jon intended. Jon moved his hand very quickly, pulling the ball all the way across the goal mouth. He spun the handle hard, with a quick flick of his wrist at the end. There was a very loud *bang!* as the ball slammed, hard, into the upper corner of the goal.

"Yeah!" Jimmy said at his side. No one else said a word. His opponent grabbed the ball from the goal and jammed it back onto the table to put it into play immediately.

The ball skidded onto the table. The opposing player spun his handle hard when the ball was in front of one of his men. Jon moved his own man in front of the ball. The ball smacked into Jon's man. Jon grabbed the deflected ball with his own front line, popped it quickly through the opposing line, and caught it with his own forward. He didn't wait this time. He positioned the ball quickly and pulled the shot across the goal and in before the opposing team could react.

"Yeah, man, two-nothin'!" Jimmy crowed.

Jon could hear the mumbles start. Their opponents said nothing, though, and jammed the ball back onto the field of play. Jon blocked the ball again and passed it to his forward line. This time, the goalie on the other side of the table was prepared. He positioned his own three players so Jon couldn't pull it all the way across the table to the far corner. So Jon just flicked his wrist, nicking the ball with the corner of his man's toe, and banked the ball into the corner of the goal diagonally.

The murmurs and mumbles got louder. It was clear to Jon that nothing like this had ever happened at this table. They'd never seen control of the ball, a game plan, defense, that sort of thing. They'd never seen someone take charge of the game and think shots through. At the Cherry Hill foosball table, everything was reaction, not action. Now they were seeing something new. And they weren't sure they liked what they saw, Jon could tell.

For his fourth goal, Jon scored with his back line. He shot the ball from midfield. The ball sped through three lines of defense and cracked the back of the goal. For the fifth and final goal to win the game, Jon switched places with Jimmy, caught and controlled the ball with his goalie, lined up the shot carefully, and cleared the ball through six separate lines of players.

A muffled roar went through the crowd as Jon and Jimmy defeated the reining champions, who reluctantly gave up their positions at the foosball table. Jimmy was beaming so much, his face looked as though it was about to burst.

Jon stepped back from the table. "Hey, look, I can't stay. I just had time for the one game." As the surprised and disappointed onlookers parted to make way for him, Jon skirted the table and headed for the door, with Jimmy trailing behind him. The two boys he'd defeated stood near the door, still glaring at him angrily. Jon extended a hand. One of them took it limply. "Thanks for the game," offered Jon. "You guys are great."

"Yeah, right," the kid said, glaring.

"No, I mean it. I'd been watching for a while. You guys both have real talent. I just play the game differently, that's all. Where I played, you learned how to control the ball, take it away from the other side."

The kid guffawed. "You did that, awright. We never touched it."

Jon leaned forward. "You can learn that, too. You can. Just learn how to pass it and catch it. Control it. Don't just swing at the ball when it comes past. Stop it. Pass it. Think about the shots. That's all I did."

"Yeah, uh huh," the kid grunted.

"Anyway, I gotta go," Jon said awkwardly. He knew he was crossing some sort of line, and it felt a little strange. "Just try it. You'll see. You can control a game just like I did. It isn't that hard."

The kid nodded but didn't acknowledge the encouragement. He just turned away and stared back at the table, where four new players had picked up the game. Neither of Jon's opponents looked at him again. For that matter, none of the kids in the laundry room looked at him.

Jon watched the game a minute or two longer. He felt strangely as if he'd entered some other dimension—if only for a few moments—where his world, his past, his way of seeing things had collided violently with another. He wondered what it meant. If anything.

But it was just a game, he reasoned. Just a stupid game. It meant nothing, not to him and certainly not to these kids. So why did he feel as if he'd just left a war zone?

"Hey, c'mon," Jimmy said at his side, breaking Jon's reverie. "Wanna see somethin'?"

"Yeah, sure. What?" Jon answered absentmindedly.

"You'll see."

Jimmy left the room quickly, bouncing with every step. Jon followed. Jimmy clearly knew every back way, every hallway, every door in the place. He took Jon through a series of hallways and through banged-up doors until they came to one door that, although it was the same size and color and made out of the same substance as all the others, was also entirely different.

A pretty wreath of dried flowers rested on the door. The number of the apartment was hand painted. There was a welcome mat on the floor. Jon glanced up and down the hallway. There wasn't another door like it in the place.

"Whose apartment?" Jon asked.

"Grammy's."

"Grammy? Your grandmother?"

"Yep," Jimmy said proudly. "And she's in charge of here."

CHAPTER NINE

Mrs. Jimmy Robinson, Jon discovered, had raised seven grand-children at Cherry Hill. By herself. All seven of them had made it at least through high school. Jimmy, named after her long-departed husband, was actually her great-grandson, the last of her brood. Jimmy's mom lived at Cherry Hill but worked all day.

Mrs. Robinson's home was bare but immaculate. A couple of crosses hung on the walls, and Bibles sat on the tables in two different rooms, leaving little question where the strength of her convictions came from.

"So how'd you manage it? How'd you make sure all of your grand-kids got through school?" Jon asked her as he sipped the ice water she'd offered. He'd decided to skip lunch with Adams. Mrs. Robinson was more interesting.

She smiled. Several teeth were either missing or crooked. That didn't seem to matter. Her face clearly reflected a richness within that more than compensated for the external flaws.

"I jes' stood in the gate," she said, her voice deep and husky from years of controlling rambunctious kids.

"The gate?"

"Man, she's there alla time, after school," Jimmy piped up from the couch, beaming.

"You mean the gate at the entrance to Cherry Hill?"

"Thatsa place," Mrs. Robinson said. "I stand there when the bus come. 'Fo' anythin' else, they gotta study."

"Yeah, I gotta do math and readin'. Then I getta go outside," Jimmy said.

61

Jon nodded. So. Standing in the gate, she had seen the kids get off the bus, then snagged them before they wandered off to something else, like trouble. They studied first; then they played. Apparently, it had worked.

"I'll bet you're proud of those kids, for getting through school."

"Ain't nothin' mo' impo'tent than that," she answered.

"Why?"

"'Cause it be a chance," she said flatly. "They on'y chance."

"Their only chance?"

Mrs. Robinson nodded. "I be stuck here fo' the rest o' my life. But they move on. They all got good jobs. Got money."

Jon looked around. "None of them live here now?"

Mrs. Robinson smiled. It was a huge, glowing, proud smile. "They all be gone, 'cept Celia, Jimmy's momma. Jes' come by to visit their grammy."

CHAPTER TEN

By the time Jon left Mrs. Robinson's apartment, he felt as if he'd been deprived of something all his life. Jon had never had someone like Mrs. Jimmy Robinson, who watched over his every step to make sure he didn't stray too far from the straight and narrow.

But, of course, there had been no need of that with him, at least not when he was Jimmy's age. Until his period of searching and rebellion at Princeton, Jon had always been a pretty good kid. A loner, introspective, not too daring. He hadn't been surrounded by the awful, soul-searing pitfalls that lurked at every turn in a place like Cherry Hill.

Before Jon left Cherry Hill that first day, Jimmy showed him around. Jon quickly discovered that very few Mrs. Jimmy Robinsons lived there. In fact, despair and defeat were so thoroughly a part of the place that they permeated nearly every thought and utterance Jon came across.

What really made Jon hurt in a way he hadn't hurt before were the older kids, the ones who could think and act for themselves. They were aimless, rootless, without any knowledge of what they were supposed to do next with their life—or any hope that it could be something good.

In affluent neighborhoods, kids had to go out of their way to find trouble. They had to unlock their parents' liquor cabinets or buy fake IDs to get booze or drive to another district to buy drugs or create other ways to harm themselves. As Jon had.

At Cherry Hill, trouble was always there, in front of them, behind them, all around them. An inescapable part of their life. It walked with them. They had to work to get away from it.

If they were lucky, the kids of Cherry Hill had someone like Mrs. Jimmy Robinson, who talked to them incessantly about staying straight and avoiding the gangs and the fights and the guns and knives and the drug deals.

If a kid were *very* lucky at Cherry Hill, he "graduated" from his childhood with a high-school diploma—as all of Mrs. Robinson's had done—and a chance to go somewhere. They left to find someplace that wouldn't lock them into the eternal cycle of poverty that trapped so many in places like Cherry Hill.

Most kids in America simply *expect* opportunities to come up and move on with their lives—and they get them. They move into self-reliant adulthood as if it were a given right. They don't do anything to earn it. They just move on.

At Cherry Hill, kids had to fight for that right to move into the world of self-reliance, responsibility, and opportunity. They had to fight with every ounce of courage and resourcefulness they had. And if they made it, they did so because they had fought and won—not because it was a right granted them.

Jon hated the thought of being a kid at Cherry Hill, of playing in the dirt piles as a three-year-old, of stumbling across a used condom and asking your grandma what it was.

He hated the thought of a nine-year-old who really ought to be spending his time playing second base in Little League being forced instead to spend his time thinking about how to keep out of knife fights.

It made Jon sick to look at the eleven-year-old girls who had to start making adult decisions years before that should be required of them, and then being forced to live with the consequences of those decisions. It sickened him. It wasn't right.

But did Jon have the power to do anything about it? He was a white guy, after all—the people of Cherry Hill were black. What could he do; what could he offer that would help them? Nothing. He was the enemy; he was their stumbling block.

Even so, Jon went back to Cherry Hill the next day. And the next. He had no agenda; he had made no decisions. The episode with Jimmy and the foosball table provided a small opening for him, and Jon used that opening to ask questions. Then he asked some more. Eventually, he wrote some of the answers down. And when people asked him what he was doing, he told them he was a reporter for the *Gazette* and that he was working on a story. And it wasn't until after he had said it that Jon realized it was true.

Jon had no idea what he would write about when he finished asking questions. But the funny thing was that he never really ran out of questions.

The supply seemed endless, and the replies he got were interesting and varied. When he came to the end of his first week in Singleton, he had a notebook full of quotes from many, many people at Cherry Hill. And lots more questions he would like to ask—questions to which no one, neither Jon nor the Cherry Hill residents he'd been speaking to, had any answers.

So he just sat down on Saturday morning and started to write. He wrote about what he'd seen, about what people thought of themselves and their little community at Cherry Hill.

What Jon wrote had no beginning, middle, or end; there *was* no end that he could see, just a kind of drift into the next day and the next fight to survive. But after several hours of pulling things from his notebook, a pattern began to emerge in Jon's mind. He gradually began to see what Adams was doing in Cherry Hill. Jon had no idea whether it would actually work or whether it would ever benefit Adams politically. Even so, Jon understood.

Adams, who was white, was developing a group of followers who could speak for him in these communities that made up part of what might become his congressional district. Adams himself, in person, would not likely be listened to and followed in Cherry Hill any more than Jon would—but the young men who'd been canvassing the places like Cherry Hill for Adams *would* be listened to.

And the word about Adams had clearly spread through those young men. Most of the people Jon had interviewed at Cherry Hill knew who Adams was. They knew he was running for an office of some sort, and they knew when they were supposed to go vote.

Virtually none of them knew which office Adams was seeking or what his responsibilities would be. But they knew his name, and when someone pointed them toward a voting booth some day, they would recognize that name and cast the right vote.

And Adams was also serving as an advocate for Cherry Hill—and getting results. Thanks to his discussions with HUD officials, city welfare officials, and the police, every so often something would happen. During Jon's week in Cherry Hill, a maintenance crew showed up and fixed a few toilets and water faucets, adjusted thermostats, and repaired broken windows.

And, once, while Jon was out in the courtyard, he watched as several police officers came charging into the place and scattered a drug deal before it could be consummated. No one was arrested, but that police presence said something. Two days would pass before the dealers showed their faces again.

It wasn't nearly enough to make a dent in the illness of Cherry Hill, Jon knew, although he wasn't sure what *would* make a dent. But at least Adams was trying, even if his motives were, in all likelihood, purely political.

That was just conjecture, of course, because Jon never asked Adams why he was doing all this. It seemed obvious enough. Adams needed a certain percentage of the black vote, and he was going after that vote the only way he knew how.

When Jon finished his sprawling first draft and read back over what he'd written, he grinned and shook his head. This wasn't what the editor of the *Gazette* wanted. Or, at least, it wasn't what *someone* at the *Gazette* wanted. They wanted him to take Adams out. They wanted scandal, corruption, something that would do harm to Adams's candidacy.

Well, tough. Regardless of what Adams's ultimate goals were, he was doing some small measure of good for the people at Cherry Hill and other communities like it. That's what mattered. And Jon made it clear in his article that it mattered.

Jon wouldn't tell Sam Adams that his first story—his first stories, actually—would be about Cherry Hill and the politics of poverty. He didn't much care whether Adams knew or not, or what anyone thought.

By Sunday morning—the first Sunday after he'd arrived in Singleton—Jon had, he thought, a coherent series of articles. He spent all Sunday afternoon organizing and reorganizing his notes and polishing his copy. When he was finished, he was satisfied. He had a snapshot of life at Cherry Hill and one politician's efforts to make a difference in the lives of the people who lived there.

First thing on Monday morning, he would take his stories to Lawrence Sanders. He hadn't talked to Sanders since that first day, although he'd been in the newsroom several times. Mostly, he'd been out at Cherry Hill, doing his "reporting."

Jon had no idea what to expect from Sanders. But, in a funny way, he didn't care. What would happen would happen.

CHAPTER ELEVEN

Lawrence Sanders didn't look up for a couple of minutes. When he did, Jon's heart sank. He'd failed.

"Son, we can't print this," Sanders wheezed. He took a long drag on his cigarette stub, exhaled slowly, and stared through the haze at Jon.

"I know it's different. But it's all true. Every last word," Jon answered. He'd already decided that he wasn't going to back down.

"I don't doubt that," Sanders said. "But it's not journalism."

"Why not?"

Sanders held up the copy and pointed a cigarette-stained forefinger at the first paragraph. "Where's the lead of this thing? This it? This thing about misery, abject poverty, hopelessness, despair? That's your lead?"

"Well, yes, it is," Jon said, clearing his throat. "That's what I found. It's the truth."

"It may be the truth, but it isn't a lead for a newspaper story. Leads have things like who, what, where, when and why. And maybe how, if you get around to it."

"But that's all in there," Jon protested. "You know 'who' and 'what' and 'where.' 'When' is now, and forever, if we don't do something. And 'why,' well, 'why' I can't answer."

Sanders smiled. He glanced back at the copy. "You're sure all that's in here, in the lead?"

"Well, kind of. Mostly it's in there, pretty close to the top."

"Mostly doesn't cut it, kid. It's all got to be there. You can't be a little of Hemingway, a little of Tolkien, and then a little of the Pulitzers, all rolled into one. You gotta say it all, right at the top. People's attention wavers after that."

"I know," Jon said, leaning forward in his chair. "But a place like Cherry Hill doesn't all fit into one paragraph at the start of a story. And what Sam Adams is trying to do there takes a little bit of explaining."

Sanders took another long drag of his cigarette. "Adams. That's the other thing about this, whatever you call this thing."

"It's a series," Jon offered.

"Yeah. A series. I guess we can call it that, for lack of anything else to describe it. Well, this series looks like a paid campaign ad for Adams."

"No, it isn't," Jon said, his voice starting to crack with the first twitches of anger he was feeling. "It's the truth. The *Gazette* has been trying to nail him for months. I don't have a clue why. I guess I don't care. All I know is that I went out with Adams. I saw what I saw. And I wrote what I heard."

"You got snookered, kid," Sanders said gently.

"I did not!" Jon said loudly. "I know what Adams is. He's a politician. He's trying to get votes. But that's all in there. Even if those people at Cherry Hill don't see it, I did. And it's in the stories. Tell me it's not."

Sanders sighed. "Yeah, it's in there, way down in the stories, where you talk about how he's setting up a political base for himself with these young followers of his."

"See?"

"Yeah, I see. But who exactly *are* these followers, anyway? Are they renegade gangs? A new kind of Boy Scout program? A cult, with Adams as their messiah?"

"I don't know. A club, I guess," Jon shrugged. "But what I do know is that these kids would do almost anything for him."

" 'Cause they're getting money from him."

"No, not just because of that."

"But they're getting paid?"

"Yeah, they're getting paid. But it isn't all that much. And they'd work for Adams for free. Most of 'em, anyway."

"For free," Sanders snorted. "I doubt it."

"They would. Trust me. They would."

Sanders looked down at the copy again. He shook his head. "There's just no way we can get these pieces into the paper, Abelman. No way. They'll never fly."

"It's Abelson, sir. And why not?"

"Cause they won't. I'll fight for them. But I'm warning you, right now, that they won't make it. And if they don't, you don't either."

"So I'll be fired before I even get a story in the paper?"

68

"No, not fired," Sanders grinned. "Remember. We never hired you to begin with. You were trying out. It's like spring training in the big leagues. You get your shot to make the club. If you don't, you were never on the roster."

"Those stories deserve to be printed, Mr. Sanders," Jon tried one more time. But he knew it was a lost cause. His Cherry Hill stories would never see the light of day.

"Maybe so," Sanders answered. "But sometimes life doesn't work that way. You don't always get what you deserve. All those people you wrote about at Cherry Hill—do they deserve what's happening to them there in that project?"

"No. Definitely not."

"True. And you may not get what you deserve out of all this either. Your stories may not make it. You may not get hired here. That's just the way it is."

Jon decided to take a risk. "Mr. Sanders, you and I both know that if those stories don't get printed, it will be because someone at the *Gazette* doesn't want them to be printed. And, if that's so, word will get out that your newspaper killed those stories."

Sanders rocked forward in his chair ever so slightly. The corner of one side of his mouth twitched. Jon couldn't tell if Sanders was trying to keep from smiling or simply gritting his teeth. "Boy, are you threatening me?"

"No, sir, I am not," Jon said evenly. "I am simply trying to tell the truth, to the best of my ability. The way a real journalist would."

"Hmmm," Sanders grunted. "So that's not a threat, this theory of yours that somehow these stories will get out whether we print them or not."

"It is not a threat. It's the truth," Jon said softly. "Adams has been trying to tell your readers what he's doing for months. Your newspaper won't print it. And if you don't print these stories, people will know. People will hear about it."

Sanders chuckled. "Well, I guess we'll see, won't we? I think you're dead wrong. Maybe not about the stories and about whether this newspaper will run them. But I know you're wrong about Adams."

"Are you going to print the stories or not?" Jon persisted.

"I'll let you know. But you listen to what I'm saying about Sam Adams, son," Sanders said, a rare look of deadly earnest on his face. "For what it's worth, you got taken for a ride. He isn't what you think. Trust me. He is not at all what you think you saw."

"I think I know what I saw."

"You do, huh?"

"Yeah. He's a politician. He needs votes, and he's getting them. But he's also helping people."

"You believe that? That he's helping them?"

"Sure I do. I saw some of those windows and toilets get fixed while I was at Cherry Hill."

"And that means he's helping them? Because a few things got fixed?"

"Do you see anyone else doing anything?" Jon asked. "Because I don't."

"Did Adams say that to you?" Sanders blew a huge cloud of smoke. "Did he ask you that same question? Is anyone else doing anything?"

"I don't know. I don't remember," Jon said angrily.

Sanders leaned back in his chair. "Look, kid, sit tight. I'll go to bat for you. But don't forget what I said. Look out for Adams. He isn't what you think. Just keep your eyes open, okay?"

Jon nodded. "Okay, I will."

Sanders nodded, then looked back down at his desk. Jon slipped out of the office without another word, not sure whether it was his last trip to this office or just the second of many such conferences with his new editor.

CHAPTER TWELVE

Jon didn't wait in the newsroom for his answer. Instead, he went back to his ratty hotel room, read a few pages of a new novel he'd picked up, watched a little television, caught a movie that evening, and walked around the city when he was really bored.

On Tuesday morning, unable to stand it any longer, Jon called Sanders from his bedside phone. Sanders didn't take the call, but his secretary promised him that Sanders would call him back later that morning.

Jon waited by the phone for two hours, drifting back and forth between despair and euphoria. He didn't know what to expect or even what to hope for.

He still wasn't sure he even wanted the job. The investigating and asking questions had been fun. The writing had been okay. But he still wasn't sure he was cut out for this journalistic stuff. He needed a job—but he also needed something he could become passionate about, something that would give his life a sense of destiny and purpose. That was one of the reasons he'd turned away from the academic life—and there didn't seem to be any more emotion attached to journalism, at least for Jon, than there had been to academia.

When the phone rang, Jon almost fell out of the bed. The phone nearly slipped from his hand when he picked it up because his hands were slick and cold.

"Look, Appleman, I don't have a whole lot of time," Sanders growled at the other end of the line, "but I have your answer. You gotta make a choice."

"A choice?"

"Yeah, a choice. I got your series approved."

Jon's heart leaped. "By who?"

"By *whom*," Sanders said gruffly. "And it doesn't matter by whom. By me. That's who approves stories."

"But you said—"

"Son, I said your series is going into the newspaper. You should be happy about that."

"Well, I am. But you also said I had a choice. What's the choice?"

"The choice is whether you want it to go into print, knowing what might happen." Sanders waited for his response.

"And what might happen?" Jon asked finally.

"For one, most likely you won't be hired on full-time at the newspaper if the stories go into print."

Jon was confused. "But why should that be, if the *Gazette* likes the stories enough to print?"

"Because," Sanders said, clearing his throat, "they'll go in as a one-time deal, with you listed as a special contributor."

"Not as a *Gazette* reporter?"

"That's right. Not as a reporter. We'll pay you $250 for the stories, and we'll each go our merry way."

Jon's blood ran cold. "I want to make sure I understand this. My choice, I mean. If the stories get printed about Cherry Hill and all, then I get paid $250. That's all. And I don't get hired on as a reporter."

"That's about the size of it."

"And if I choose not to let the stories run?"

Sanders didn't say anything for several seconds. "We're prepared to offer you a job as a reporter. That's your choice."

"Full-time? Salary and benefits and all of that?"

"All of that. There's a vacancy on our night-cops beat. You'd take that position."

Jon blinked furiously several times. "I won't be covering politics or Adams or any of that stuff we talked about?"

"The only open reporter's job at the *Gazette* is night cops," Sanders said stiffly. "You'd be covering all the local police and emergency stuff. You get a lot of bylines with the beat."

"But no politics?"

"Yep," Sanders wheezed. "Look, kid, I gotta go. It's your call. Take it or leave it. But let me know soon. We got other people stacked up in line waiting to fill that job."

A long silence filled both ends of the phone call. Jon understood the choice. Someone at the newspaper had heard—and understood—Jon's threat about the stories getting out anyway if the newspaper wouldn't print them. That isn't good for business, a scandal about censorship in a small town—especially when race is involved.

So they were trying to buy him off. He could get a job as a reporter at the paper—though not covering politics—if he kept his mouth shut. Or the stories could run, which would keep him from following through on his implied threat of going public. But, of course, if he chose the let the stories run, he had no job. Justice maybe, but no job.

"So that's the deal?" Jon asked bitterly.

"That's the deal," Sanders said. "Better'n most. And the only one we're offering. You're a good writer, kid. You've got the touch. I hope you don't waste it on some fool politician who's takin' you for a ride."

Jon ignored the dig. "How long do I have to decide?"

"Go have a cup of coffee. Then call me back."

"Wait. You mean—"

"See ya around, kid." There was a click on the other end of the line.

CHAPTER THIRTEEN

The first story in the series ran on the following Saturday, the worst day of the week for newspapers. No one reads Saturday newspapers; no one has time. They are doing more important things.

The story was on the bottom corner of the "Metro" section and jumped to the inside. "Cherry Hill Residents Fight Despair and Poverty," read the headline. "Politician tries to make a difference," read the smaller headline underneath. The story was by "special contributor" Jon Abelson.

Jon tossed the newspaper aside and stared at the $250 check sitting on top of the nightstand. He'd already decided to check out of the hotel on Tuesday, when the last story in the series would run. He had no plans. Maybe he'd go visit his parents for a while.

In the end, the decision hadn't been a hard one. Maybe if he'd truly wanted to be a journalist and to get his big break in Singleton, Ohio, it would have been a close call. But, of course, Jon had no burning desire to be a reporter. Or anything else, for that matter. So, presented with the first moral dilemma of his working life, Jon had found it easy to choose the high road.

He'd been staring at that $250 check on and off for almost a day. He knew that, to do proper justice to his lofty decision, he should just rip up the check. He'd chosen the right path, he felt, but the money was still sitting there.

But he also knew he couldn't just throw $250 away. That wouldn't be right, either. The newspaper *ought* to pay for his stories. But what to do with the money? Go buy a new suit, maybe, so that he'd have something nice to interview in wherever he journeyed to next? Hardly.

74

The thought came to him late that evening, as he watched a rerun of *Gilligan's Island* on one of the local channels.

First thing in the morning he'd go by Cherry Hill and give it to Mrs. Jimmy Robinson, who had figured prominently in his series. Yep. That's what he would do. And that night, for the first time since leaving Princeton, he actually got a decent night's rest.

CHAPTER FOURTEEN

The day started out cold, and Jon had left the window open during the night.

He showered and dressed in a hurry, then went to buy a Sunday *Gazette* at the newsstand in the hotel lobby. He settled into one of the smelly sofas off to the side of the lobby to read the second article in his series.

They hadn't even bothered to put this one on the front of the Metro section, he discovered. A little box on the Metro front page directed readers to page B12 for the second article in the Cherry Hill housing project series.

"Great," Jon muttered. "Be a long time before I'm famous at this rate."

But at least they hadn't butchered the story. It was mostly intact, with only a few minor edits here and there. He now had two successful "clips" under his belt. No job. Just two bylines.

He walked to Cherry Hill. It was about the only thing he could think of to kill time and to ease the growing knot of anger in the pit of his stomach over the events of the past week.

He would be glad to sign the $250 over to Mrs. Robinson and then move on to something else. He was ready to be done with this whole sorry affair.

By the time he got to Cherry Hill, he'd calmed down. He would find Jimmy's great-grandmother, give her the check, tell her good-bye, and wish her luck with the rest of her life. Then, he had decided, he would just pack his bags that afternoon and get out of town. He could order copies of the Monday and Tuesday editions of the newspaper by phone and have them mailed to wherever he was going. He didn't need to hang around Singleton just to buy the papers from a newsstand.

Entering Cherry Hill, Jon expected some kind of reception. After all, he'd made the residents there famous. Or, at least, less obscure than they'd been previously. He walked through the chipped and crumbling archway that led into the Cherry Hill courtyard. No one approached him. The usual kids were in the middle, playing with dirt or running around. He spied a drug deal in the making across the courtyard and several other groups of people talking, hanging out. No one looked his way, other than to glance his direction to see who the white boy was entering the place.

Odd. In a way, he felt as though he were coming home. He'd spent so much time here in the past week that the place didn't seem sinister to him anymore. It was familiar. He knew what lay behind these walls.

Jon took his time crossing the courtyard to the doorway that led to Mrs. Robinson's apartment. A boy, who appeared to be in his late teens, emerged from one of the apartments on the ground floor, slammed the door behind him, and marched directly toward Jon.

"You!" the kid said to him with undisguised hostility. "Whatcha doin' here, anyway?"

Jon was surprised. There was no mistaking it. This kid was mad at him. "I, um, I came by to give something to Mrs. Robinson," he said awkwardly.

"No, you won't," the kid said. "She's gone. She don't want to see you."

"What do you mean, she doesn't want to see me?"

"I mean, get lost. Don't show your face around here no more," the kid said, coming within a couple of feet of Jon before he stopped, breathing hard as if he were about to get into a fight or something.

"I know you," Jon said. "You were at that meeting, with Sam Adams."

The kid stuck his jaw out an inch farther. "Yeah, so? What's it to you?"

"And you don't live here, you said."

"I got friends everywhere."

"So you're visiting one here now?"

The kid laughed harshly. "Nope. I was waitin' for you to show up. I knew you would sooner or later. I would've looked you up, only the newspaper wouldn't tell me where you lived."

"I was staying at the Clarion Hotel," Jon said, feeling very depressed and isolated suddenly. "You could have asked around."

"I waited for you here."

"But why?" Jon asked.

"Because of what you wrote, all those lies. Cherry Hill ain't nothin' like what you said. Nothin' like it. Black folks aren't what you said. You got it backwards."

"But—"

The kid stepped forward, right in Jon's face. "You said we all a bunch o' thieves and dope fiends and crack heads. That we all some dead-end, nasty losers. And we ain't like that at all."

"I didn't write that," Jon protested lamely, knowing that the kid was at least half right. He *had* painted a gloomy picture, if only because the place had seemed that way to him.

"Yeah, you did!" the kid shouted. "You did. And it ain't like that 'round here or anywhere. We all family, even the junkies. They my brothers. I know 'em. They my kin. They ain't nothin' like what you wrote. Not no way."

The kid turned on his heels and stomped off, one fist raised high. Jon had no idea what it meant. Perhaps it meant that he was telling his family here, his brothers and sisters, that he had just told the white boy off, but good. Who knew?

Jon looked around and suddenly realized that there had to be a couple dozen pairs of eyes all staring at him. And he couldn't tell who else might be gazing out from behind curtains or through peepholes.

Jon felt as lost as he'd ever felt in his life. He had thought he'd done the right thing by telling Cherry Hill's story. But clearly he'd done something wrong. He'd gotten something very, very mixed up. This kid's anger was a testament to that.

Turning slowly as he surveyed the eyes looking at him, Jon began to see what the Adams kid had been so mad about. It had been right there in front of him the whole time.

He had written off Cherry Hill as just some awful housing project. But to its residents, it was a community of people who all knew each other, who had grown up together. They didn't see Cherry Hill as Jon did. They didn't see the filth and squalor as much as they saw faces and people they knew. Brothers and sisters. They were family, even those who went very, very far out of bounds.

Jon had painted a bleak picture of the place—*his* picture, not theirs. He'd used their words to describe it, but it had been his picture.

And he'd missed the only point that mattered in a place like Cherry Hill.

Sure, everyone wanted out, to move to a better place. But almost none of them would succeed in making that leap. So they lived as well as they could with what they had, knowing that it was probably all they would ever have. And Jon had spent a week with them, had asked all the questions he wanted, and had still missed it.

"Sorry," he said quietly and turned to leave—then quickly turned and headed back across the courtyard for one last stop.

As he drew near the laundry room, he could hear an occasional *bang* from within. But, curiously, they were not as frequent as they'd been the day Jon had arrived—maybe every minute or so.

When he came to the doorway in the dimly lit hallway, Jon didn't enter the room. He simply poked his head around the corner to see if Jimmy was inside.

He wasn't, but the usual crowd of kids, big and small, were gathered around the battered table. The two bigger kids he and Jimmy had beaten the first day he'd arrived at Cherry Hill were at the table, as usual.

Only, as Jon watched in some surprise, it *wasn't* as usual. The ball wasn't flying back and forth across the table, out of control, slamming from one end to the other.

The two kids Jon had whipped thoroughly were playing a different game now. They were playing Jon's game. The front player had already learned how to pass from one line to the next. He was still shooting fast, but he was attempting to line up his shots. He had a plan. He was thinking about his shots, playing defense, and learning from the game.

And it was clearly working. Their opponents were totally outmatched. These two kids had already been good, with quick reactions. They'd beaten the others before just by their quick, aggressive play. Now, though, they were thinking about what needed to happen next. They were quietly, surely controlling the game.

It was a little thing, not very important. But Jon could see something he had never before seen. And he felt very humbled, very small. He had totally underestimated the ability of the people in Cherry Hill, such as these boys, to learn and grow and to see how things were and how they ought to be.

He turned and left without saying a word to any of the kids in that room. He walked back through the courtyard of Cherry Hill, gazing at his feet. No one said anything to him as he left through the gate where Mrs. Jimmy Robinson had dutifully waited for her kids after school each day to make sure they got their studying done.

And once he was outside the gate, he realized that he still had the $250 check in his pocket. He hadn't given it to Jimmy's great-grandmother. So what was he supposed to do with it now?

And then it occurred to Jon that he knew exactly what he would do with it. Only one thing left made any sense to him.

CHAPTER FIFTEEN

Jon noticed that the "Adams for Congress" sign hanging over the campaign headquarters was crooked, tilted at a definite angle. *Has anyone who works here even noticed?* he wondered. *Do they care?*

When he walked in, he was surprised to see how sparsely furnished it was. Several card tables and folding chairs were spread out around the three rooms that made up the headquarters. Everyone was talking into his or her respective telephones feverishly, even though it was Sunday morning.

Jon waited in vain for someone to approach him and at least ask him why he was there. They all seemed extraordinarily busy—which seemed odd on a Sunday morning just before lunch.

Finally, he managed to get a young woman's attention. He pulled the $250 check from his pocket and waved it in the air. The young woman sighed and walked toward him.

Jon couldn't help but look her over as she approached. She was startlingly beautiful in the midst of this chaos and turmoil. Strands of her short, reddish-blonde hair hung over her eyes, and her jeans fit her exactly right. Her face had a sharp, chiseled look.

Jon watched her walk, watched the way she moved her body, and then immediately felt embarrassed. He averted his eyes for a moment and then looked back, certain his face was flushed.

"You need something?" she asked him, scowling angrily.

"Yeah, I'm a potential voter," Jon said. "Tell me why I should support Sam Adams."

"Go jump in the lake. And stop staring at me," the young woman said, and turned away.

"Hey!" he called after her. "Do you always treat people who come into your campaign office like that?"

"We do when we're this busy right before a primary," she answered over her shoulder. "If you have any business here, tell me now."

"The primary?" Jon asked. "I thought that wasn't until the end of the summer. And I thought Adams didn't even have an opponent in it."

"Yeah, well, things change," the young woman said bitterly.

"How'd they change? And why?"

She turned back toward Jon and eyed him closely. "And why're you so curious, anyway? Who are you?"

"My name's Jon Abelson. And I'm just curious. Plus, I have this $250 check I want to sign over to the Adams campaign."

She came back toward him a step or two. "The guy who's doing that series on Cherry Hill? That Jon Abelson?"

Jon smiled. It felt good. "Yeah, that's me. One and the same."

The young woman tilted her head. "And you want to do what?"

"Give Sam Adams $250—if you tell me your name, too," Jon said, enjoying the young woman's confusion. "I can give money, can't I?"

"Well, yeah, sure, 'course you can. And my name's Susan Smalley," she answered. "Just make the check out to 'Adams for Congress' and I'll give it to the treasurer."

Jon pulled the check from his pocket. "Well, Susan Smalley, I have to sign it over."

Susan looked at the check and raised an eyebrow. "This is a check to you from the *Gazette*. You're just giving it to us?"

"Yep," Jon said, feeling extraordinarily calm and self-assured. He kind of liked giving money away, he decided.

"But I don't get it. Why would you want to do that?" Susan asked.

"I'll tell you and then sign the check over if you'll tell me why you all are so frantic around here," Jon said, looking around the frantic head-quarters again.

Susan sighed. "Okay, quickly, but then I gotta get back to the phones. Basically, the central committee just jammed us, deliberately, and we have ten days to respond."

"The central committee?"

"Of the Democratic Party," she said, shaking her head at how anyone could be so stupid.

"And they jammed you? What's that mean?"

"It means they held an executive session yesterday and voted to get rid of the primary at the end of the summer."

"They can do that?"

"Sure," Susan said, laughing. "They can do anything they want, except change the date of the general election. They're the party. They do what they want."

"So why'd they do it?"

"Simple. They moved the selection to a delegate caucus in the district in two weeks. And then they picked someone to run against Sam at the caucus."

Jon was shocked. He'd had no idea that political parties could do something like that. He thought politics was kind of disorderly, maybe a little chaotic, full of big egos and lots of money. But this sounded— well—as though it ought to be illegal or something.

"What's this caucus?" he asked her.

Susan frowned. "You really don't know?"

"No, or I wouldn't have asked," he said, annoyed.

"It's the summer delegate meeting for the party. They have a bunch of 'em in each of the districts this time of year. Usually they roast hot dogs and complain about the weather. But this year, the central committee decided they didn't like the way the candidate slate was shaping up. So they changed the rules and handpicked a few folks in some of the races. One of them's going up against Sam now."

Jon was almost afraid to ask. "And who is it?"

"Man, you must have just gotten off the bus," Susan said, shaking her head. "Nobody can be this dumb. I mean, it's your own newspaper!"

"My newspaper?"

"The *Gazette*, you moron," she almost sneered. "Sam's caucus opponent is the publisher's son."

CHAPTER SIXTEEN

Jon stood staring blankly at Susan. Never in his life had he felt so stupid, so completely ignorant about how the world worked. No wonder the newspaper had been afraid of killing the Cherry Hill series. They couldn't afford even the *hint* of scandal, not with the publisher's son about to enter the race against Adams, hero of Cherry Hill.

How could he have been so abysmally dumb? He'd known *something* was going on, of course, some reason for the *Gazette's* obvious malevolence toward Adams. But he'd never guessed this.

Despite the shock, Jon came to a very quick decision. "Sign me up," he said to Susan.

"What?" she asked

"Sign me up. As a volunteer. I want to work for Adams's campaign."

Now it was Susan's turn to stare blankly. But Jon didn't care. Nor did he care, at the moment, how he'd manage to pay his bills for the next couple of weeks without a job. He may have been a dupe once, but it would be the last time. And the best way to repay those who'd duped him was to work to get Adams elected.

Now, of course, looking back, it was easy to put the pieces together. In fact, he was surprised how many of the pieces of the puzzle he'd actually had after that pig roast the first night. Susan supplied the rest by answering his questions during his first day of volunteering.

The publisher's son—James Jenkins II—was a young, eager, telegenic assistant vice president with the largest bank in Singleton, First Merchant. His dad, the senior James Jenkins, had gotten him the job at the bank, but young Jenkins had made the most of his opportunity.

He'd quickly become the point man for several very high-profile community "investments" for the bank. Jenkins was in every picture of a ribbon-cutting ceremony, the guy who made the deal happen. He was the bank's wonder boy, the kid who brought the groups together at the table so the loan papers could get signed.

Jenkins senior, meanwhile, had given one hundred thousand dollars to the central committee of the state Democratic Party for each of the past five years. And young Jenkins served on not one but three party conference committees—two in the economic development area and one for environmental regulation.

And now his dad had pushed him into the congressional arena, against Sam Adams. On paper, it seemed to be a mismatch. Unlike Jenkins, Adams was not a wealthy patron of the party, nor had he toiled for it as an activist. He was not part of the "club." The party would back Jenkins, not Adams. Jon had seen that—and heard it—at the pig roast.

All Adams had going for him was his background. He'd grown up in a lower- to middle-class family with no money, gone to college on an ROTC scholarship, and served as an aide to the Army intelligence chief and later right in the heart of the Pentagon for the chairman of the Joint Chiefs of Staff.

After serving his time in the military—where, by all accounts, he'd been a rising star, certain to become a four-star general had he remained in the service—Adams left to start a food cooperative business back in Ohio.

The food cooperative had been successful. Adams turned out to be very good at finding regular markets for food grown by smaller farmers in Ohio. He became their middleman. The farmers made money and didn't have to shop for markets.

Sam Adams became wealthy enough to forget his roots. But, instead, he turned his prowess at finding markets and building cooperatives into a network to help funnel some of the cooperative's surplus food into inner-city food drives around Ohio's big cities. He helped launch something called "Food for the Poor" in a half-dozen large Ohio cities. The program, like the cooperatives, was successful.

For the next several years, Adams had continued that pattern of successful entrepreneurship followed by a little philanthropy and Christian charity. His efforts to organize the restless and jobless black youths in some of the projects had begun as just such a venture.

When Adams had entered the political arena, he had approached it much as he had the other parts of his life—with a wing and a prayer and not much else. Susan said that Adams had once told her he didn't worry about what would happen next in his life because God always made everything work out for him. "He says he leads a 'destined' life," Susan said.

Politically, Adams was a neophyte. He hadn't begun to raise any serious money for a primary challenge because he hadn't figured he needed to. Now, he was clearly in trouble. His name ID wasn't nearly as high as Jenkins's, even in Singleton. Even worse, nearly all of the party delegates going to the caucus had heard of the Jenkins family. Anyone who gave one hundred thousand dollars to the party every year was very well-known to the party regulars.

In short, winning the nomination seemed impossible for Adams now that they'd changed the rules and thrown such a formidable opponent up against him. But Jon would do what he could to help. He felt almost as though it were his patriotic duty.

By the end of his first day of volunteering, Jon had decided that Susan Smalley was not only the most beautiful woman he'd seen in a long time but also the most energetic, spirited, and aggressive worker he'd ever met. She was everywhere at once, constantly on the phone and issuing orders to other workers.

Jon found himself watching her at odd times during the day. He liked everything he saw about her. She was tireless, completely dedicated to Adams, and attentive to detail. If Adams won this thing, he would have Susan to thank for it. She was ten campaign workers rolled into one.

He tried, at one point late in the afternoon when they both stopped at the overworked coffee machine to refill their cups, to ask her out. Sort of. He just mentioned in passing that he had no idea where anything in Singleton was. Like where a good place to eat might be.

"Lame. Very lame," Susan said, placing both of her hands around the coffee cup to sip the liquid.

"What?" Jon asked, feeling his heart flutter. For someone who wasn't used to being intimidated, he'd certainly found his share of it lately.

"If you want to ask someone out, do you always circle around it like that?" she asked, gazing directly at him.

Jon hesitated. "I wasn't asking you out," he said finally.

"You weren't?"

"Well, no, not really."

"So you were just curious about good places to eat?"

"Yeah. Like I said, I'm new here."

"And you planned on attending solo?"

"By myself?"

"Yes, that's what solo means. Without partner or companion. By yourself."

Jon smiled wanly. This conversation was not proceeding even remotely as he had hoped, but some vestige of pride prevented him from admitting to this self-assured young woman that he wanted to go out with her. "Well, yes, I guess by myself. Solo."

"So you have no desire to go out to dinner with me, is that it?"

"I didn't say that," Jon said defensively.

"So you will go out and get something with me? If I find someplace interesting?"

"I would go anywhere you tell me to," Jon said, feeling immensely stupid from the moment the words left his mouth.

"I'll bet you would," Susan sighed. Jon wondered how often guys hit on her. Probably all the time. "Look. I'll make a deal with you. We get something to eat together, then you come back here with me for the evening."

"With you?" Jon's head was spinning.

"To make calls," Susan laughed. "We have to get some of these registered folks in the evening. Can't get them at work."

"Oh, I see."

"You had something else in mind?" Susan asked mischievously.

"No, of course not," Jon said quickly, certain his face was now changing colors rapidly.

"Good," she nodded. "Didn't think so. Now, back to work. We have two weeks to turn this around. And I need your help."

"Yes, ma'am," Jon answered smartly.

CHAPTER SEVENTEEN

By the end of the evening, Jon never wanted to see a phone again for the rest of his life. He figured he'd made at least a hundred calls by 10:30 that evening. Susan matched him call for call. In between, they traded stories about how well the calls were going.

Their "dinner" had consisted of eight tacos, two bags of chips, and two Pepsis. To go. They ate at their desks.

The desk Susan had given him, which was now next to hers, consisted of a folding table, a rickety folding chair that had a habit of collapsing whenever he got up to go somewhere, and a telephone that smelled of cigarettes and coffee. The list of people she'd given him to call seemed to go on and on and on.

Several hundred delegates would attend the delegate caucus in less than two weeks. But Jon and Susan weren't calling the actual delegates. Adams would call each of the delegates personally before the caucus.

No, what Jon and Susan were doing—and what the other volunteers would do for the next two weeks as well—was locating registered Democrats who'd been active in the party in and around Singleton. And once they had them on the phone, they would ask those Democrats three questions: Did they know anything about Sam Adams? And did they know their delegate to the party caucus? And, lastly, if they liked Sam Adams, would they talk to their caucus delegate about him?

It seemed a roundabout way of drumming up support for Adams, but Susan explained that there was really no other way. They had to make Adams known to the delegates.

"It's the only way you can get some of these delegates to pay attention to Sam," Susan told him early that evening. "We can't just tell the delegates

88

to vote for him—we're his campaign workers; that's what they would expect us to say. Other people that the delegates respect have to call the delegates, and we have to find those people."

Actually, once Jon got the hang of it, he kind of liked it. And, on a half-dozen calls, he actually found people who knew of Adams, liked him, and also knew the delegate from their area. They promised to contact the delegate.

Whether they actually would, of course, was another matter. Still, Jon had the feeling that he might have accomplished something.

When they'd finally finished for the evening—because it was bordering on impoliteness to call people after 10:00—Jon could barely speak. Susan, though, still seemed full of energy. It was boundless. Jon wondered how he would manage to keep up with her.

"You'll learn," she promised. "You'll get caught up in it, I promise. It's a rush. It keeps you going."

Yeah, sure, Jon thought. *If I don't drop in my tracks from exhaustion first.*

CHAPTER EIGHTEEN

Adams showed up at the campaign office toward the end of the day on Tuesday, the last day of the Cherry Hill series in the *Gazette* and two days after Jon had signed onto the campaign. Jon already felt as though he and Susan had known each other forever. Other than the six hours of sleep he'd gotten Sunday and Monday nights, he had been at Susan's side constantly from the moment he'd walked through the campaign doors.

Adams looked bone tired. One of the volunteers whispered that he'd been out on the road, nonstop, since Sunday, personally visiting as many of the delegates as he could. Those he couldn't visit personally he would call the last week before the caucus.

Adams glanced briefly at Jon as he entered but didn't really acknowledge him. But a few minutes later, he leaned out of his little office and waved Jon in.

Adams was waiting for him at the door and closed it after Jon entered. He waited for Jon to take a seat, then pulled a chair from behind the desk and straddled it a few feet from him.

"Never thought I'd see the likes of you around here," Adams said with a wan smile.

"Never thought I'd be here," Jon answered.

"Liked your series, by the way."

Jon hadn't even bothered to read the fourth and final installment in the series that morning. He'd been too busy and too tired.

"Yeah, well, it's over now. Time to move on."

Adams sighed. Jon could see how tired he was. "I won't ask you why you're here," he said. "But I think I can guess. They probably didn't much like the direction the series took, did they?"

"No, they didn't."

Adams nodded. "Figures. They've known for awhile that they were going to run Jenkins. I guess I just didn't think they had the stomach to go through with it."

Jon leaned forward in his chair. "Why are they running Jenkins against you, anyway? I can't figure it."

Adams looked out the window. "Oh, it's a long story. I'll tell you about it sometime, when this is over."

"Is there a short version?"

Adams looked back. "The short version is that I was once the chairman of the local party around here. I went up against the central committee over something—over the way they were paying out soft money in races—and they hung me out to dry. I resigned my party position, and now I'm back running from the outside in."

"So you don't have the support of the party?"

"Support?" Adams laughed. "They'd like nothing better than to see me either leave the state or switch parties. It grates them to no end that I'm back, running a credible campaign."

"But now, with Jenkins and the money behind him?"

"Conventional wisdom has it that I'm dead in the water," Adams answered. But something about the way he said it made Jon look up. Adams didn't sound like a man who was whipped.

"But I take it you don't believe in conventional wisdom?"

"Not especially," Adams said. He leaned back in his chair. "It's been known to go in the other direction when circumstances warrant."

Jon eyed Adams closely. "And do circumstances warrant a change in direction?"

Adams didn't answer right away. He put the forefinger of his right hand to his lips, and began to rub it back and forth gently, methodically. It was his "thinking" mode. Jon had seen him do this at the Catholic parish the other night.

"Jon, can I ask you a question?"

"Sure. Shoot."

"You gonna stick around to see this thing through?"

"You mean the caucus?"

"No, I mean if I win the caucus and then run in the general election. Will you stay through the fall?"

Jon shrugged. "Hadn't really thought about it, to be honest. I was mad, so I signed up."

"And are you still mad?"

91

"Yeah, I guess. I don't like what happened."

"Are you mad enough to stick around and maybe get even?"

Jon could sense some sort of pitch coming, but he couldn't imagine what it might be. "I don't know. Maybe. What'd you have in mind?"

"I have to know. Will you stick it out and stay through the fall if we pull this out?" Adams was looking at Jon very intently now.

"Yeah, I probably will. I'd need some money to live on, but I can stay. *If* we win the primary."

"I can help with money," Adams said. "Not for the next two weeks, but for the general we can figure something out."

"So what do you need me for?"

Adams looked down at his shoes, still thinking. When he looked up, he'd made up his mind. "I have some information. But it needs some checking by someone with at least half a brain. And then, if it checks out, it needs to get into someone's hands. Someone with the means to make it public."

"And I have at least half a brain?" Jon asked, smiling crookedly.

"I'm betting my career on it," Adams said, deadly serious.

"You think I can get it into the right hands?"

"If it checks out, it shouldn't be too hard to maybe get one of the television stations that competes with the *Gazette* to go with the story. I think you can probably manage that. You seem to have pretty good news judgment."

Now it was Jon's turn to lean forward in his seat. "So what's the story?"

Adams cleared his throat. Jon couldn't tell if it was because he was nervous or because he wanted Jon to think he was. "You know what Jenkins's job is at the bank, First Merchant?"

"Yeah, a little. Economic development stuff. He puts deals together, and then cuts the ribbons at the ceremonies."

"That's right," nodded Adams. "But it isn't all he does, apparently."

"What else?"

"You weren't in Ohio for the last elections, two years ago. Did you hear anything about them?"

"No, I was at Princeton. I don't know a thing about Ohio."

"Well, three congressional seats were up for grabs, along with the governor's post," Adams said. "A whole lot of money came in the last week of the election. It went to those three congressional races and to the governor's race. Democrats won all four seats. The Republicans raised a stink—or tried to—at the time, but it all seemed to check out. The central committee had records and receipts to show that they'd received dozens of high-dollar checks, for one thousand dollars and two thousand dollars the last two weeks before the election. They showed a couple of them to people, and the uproar died down."

"Okay," Jon said, "so what's the problem? Sounds like somebody did a whale of a good job of fund-raising."

Adams looked directly at Jon. "Yeah, well, somebody did, but it wasn't what you think. The money didn't come from individuals."

That made Jon pause. "So where'd it come from?"

"It came from First Merchant, from James Jenkins," Adams said slowly. "A one-million-dollar loan went out to a small business, signed by Jenkins. Then the money was split up four ways for the races. The party has paid it back to the bank in installments over the past two years, through the business."

Jon narrowed his eyes. "And how do you know all this?"

"I just know it; let's leave it at that," Adams said, with a dismissive gesture.

"So what do you need me for?"

"I need to make sure it checks out, that there's some kind of paper trail, and then I need to get it into play."

"And how am I supposed to do that?" asked Jon.

"Well," Adams said slowly, "for starters, you could go by the business that got the loan and ask a few questions. Then you could go ask the Republicans for some of the names on the checks they heard about two years ago and go interview them. All it will take is for one or two of those people to admit they didn't give two thousand dollars the last two weeks before the election. Then, you can go back to the bank, over Jenkins's head, and confront them with the allegations. And, after that, you can get one of the TV stations to go talk to the same bank official and ask the same questions. The whole thing'll blow wide open then."

Jon took a deep breath. "And how am I supposed to do all this? As an Adams volunteer?"

"No," Adams said softly, "as a journalist. Just go ask a few questions. No one really knows you're working for me yet. And you're not, anyway. You're volunteering."

"But I'm not a journalist anymore."

"Yes you are. You have bylines. You can get another reporter's job any old time you want. That makes you a journalist."

"But I can't claim to be a journalist now. That would be misrepresentation. That isn't . . ."

"No," Adams said, cutting him off. "Don't even think it. I'm not asking you to do or say anything dishonest. All you'd have to do is say you've written some stories for the *Gazette*, you're working on a new story, and you just have a few questions. None of that is false."

"But I wouldn't be working on a new story," Jon protested.

"Yes, you would be. Just not necessarily under your own byline. The rest is certainly true—that you've written stories for the *Gazette* and that you have a few questions."

"Yeah, I guess," Jon said uneasily, not quite sure what to think.

"Look, Jon, think about it," Adams said with a calm, reassuring voice. He stood up. His physical presence was commanding, inspiring even. "This is just about the only thing that can save me. I need something like this to break my way, or Jenkins will walk all over me. You have to admit that wouldn't be fair, right?"

"Well, yeah, you're right, that wouldn't be fair," Jon said.

"And if this pans out, if it's true, then the public has a right to know. Isn't that also true?"

"I guess."

"So you'd be doing the right thing in bringing it to light. Correct?" Adams walked over to the door. "At any rate, just think about it. We'll talk first thing in the morning."

CHAPTER NINETEEN

Sometime in the middle of the night, after lying awake for hours, Jon decided that it would be all right. It was for a good cause. Adams was a good guy, and this Jenkins seemed like the worst kind of politician—someone who was getting by on his daddy's money and influence and had bent the rules something fierce to get ahead.

As long as he didn't actually tell anyone that he was still working for the *Gazette*, Jon reasoned, it wouldn't be lying. That was what it boiled down to. Jon would simply tell people that he'd written stories for the *Gazette*, which was true, and that he was working on a new story, which was also somewhat true.

And if someone asked him what he was going to do with the information he was gathering, well, he'd just hedge. No law compelled him to reveal why he was asking questions. As long as he didn't misrepresent who he was, he was okay.

It wasn't as if he were doing something unethical, like posing as someone else to go undercover or sneaking a tape recorder or a concealed camera into a closed meeting or secretly tape-recording telephone conversations—things some journalists had done in the name of getting the big story over the years.

Jon was doing none of that. Yes, he was blurring the line somewhat between the Fourth Estate and whatever estate Adams represented. But Jon hadn't actually received a paycheck from Adams yet, so he hadn't officially crossed the line. Not yet, at least.

He called Adams at home about 7:30 in the morning. A woman answered the phone. Jon had forgotten that Adams was married. No one

95

at the campaign ever said much about it, and his wife never came to the headquarters.

Abby Adams, Susan had told Jon, was one of those quiet but aggressive political wives who networked as much as possible, who was always out and around as much as her husband was, filling in for talks when she had to, and going to functions her husband wouldn't or couldn't attend. She and Adams had met in college ages ago. They had no children, for whatever reason.

Susan had confided that Abby had loved the years she and Adams had spent in Washington. She hated Ohio, really, and wanted desperately to get back to Washington's social circles. She'd do or say just about anything to get there.

Susan also warned Jon to be careful with Abby, that Abby didn't trust or care for staff much. Jon took her words to heart. He would mind his manners with Abby.

"Sam isn't here right now," she said.

"Oh. I'm sorry," Jon stammered. "I didn't mean to call so early, Mrs. Adams."

"Oh, this isn't early. What did you say your name was?"

"I didn't, but it's Jon Abelson, Mrs. Adams."

"Well, Jon Abelson, please call me Abby, if you plan to be working for my husband long," she said evenly. "And don't worry about calling early. Everyone does. Early. Late. Sam works at all hours, and everyone calls whenever they like. In fact, he's been up since five this morning, and you're about the tenth call."

"Oh, I see," Jon said, surprised.

"So please call back in, oh, about twenty minutes. He should be back from his morning run by then. All right?"

Jon nodded, forgetting that Abby Adams couldn't see him. It seemed strange to him that she didn't offer to take a message or a number where Adams could call him back. "Yes, Ma'am, I will."

"Very good."

Abby Adams hung up the phone. There was no good-bye. Jon placed the phone in the cradle gently. How strange. He hoped he hadn't offended her. Susan had been right. Abby Adams seemed difficult to read. Jon felt a little like a servant who'd been deftly and impersonally reprimanded.

Jon showered, dressed, had a cup of instant coffee, and then tried Adams again. This time, Adams answered the phone.

"Oh, good, it's you," Jon said.

"You get Abby when you called before?"

Jon could almost see Adams grinning at the other end of the line. "Yes, I did."

Adams laughed. "And you survived, apparently. Abby didn't mention that you called, which means she didn't take an immediate dislike to you. You're luckier than most. So. Have you thought it through? Do you have a plan?"

"Yeah. I thought it through. And, yes, I do have a plan."

"Great," Adams said enthusiastically. "I knew you would. You get things done. I can see that."

"But, Mr. Adams—"

"Please. Sam."

"Okay, Sam, there is one thing."

"Shoot."

"I will not misrepresent who I am. I will not lie. I am simply going to tell people I've written some stories for the *Gazette* and that I'm working on a new story."

"Which is true, of course."

"And if someone asks me if the story will go in the *Gazette*, I'm going to tell them the truth."

"Which is that you don't know, yet, where the story will appear. Right?"

"Yeah, something like that," Jon murmured.

"Good. Fine. Nothing wrong with that," Adams said enthusiastically. "So you ready for the name of the business?"

Jon sighed. "Yep. I'm ready."

"Okay, take this down. The name of the company is Evergreen Communications. It has a post-office box number for an address, so you're gonna have to do some legwork to get a street address. The only officer listed is Saul Shepard. Got it?"

"Got it."

"Okay, kid, you're on your own. Report back if you get stuck or if you make progress."

"Yes, sir, I will."

"And Jon, one other thing. It's important. You realize, of course, that you're doing this thing on your own, on your own time. Right? You understand that? You know what that means?"

A chill passed through Jon but then quickly went away. "Yes, of course. I know that. If it blows up, I'll just take off. It won't come near you."

"Good, then. We've got a deal. Go get 'em, Jon."

CHAPTER TWENTY

Evergreen Communications, it turned out, was incorporated not in Ohio but in Connecticut. Most of its board of directors were not from Ohio, either. It wasn't listed as a sub-chapter S corporation, either, but as a full-blown corporation.

Jon had gotten lucky. Instead of finding the usual sludge bureaucrat, he'd run across a middle-aged woman at the county tax assessor's office who was more than happy to help him find virtually any record he was seeking. The woman even walked him from office to office within the huge new government center on the outskirts of Singleton so that he could track down different records.

The woman had found everything from the actual articles of incorporation to the tax records over the past several years for Evergreen.

From what he could see, Evergreen was a profitable start-up corporation. It had generated, in fact, gross revenues of several million dollars in its first year, and that revenue stream had remained stable for the first couple of years. It had dipped dramatically in the past couple of years, however.

The corporation filings said Evergreen was a management consulting company, specializing in providing environmental counseling services to companies.

In fact, a couple of newspaper articles about Evergreen were in one of the files. They had done some work for companies around the state, advising them about how to comply with new Environmental Protection Agency or state environmental rules. So the company did a valid business. On paper, at least.

Jon decided just to call the company and ask for an address. He didn't lie, exactly. He just told them that he had to deliver a package. Which was true, kind of. He just didn't intend to deliver it any time soon.

The receptionist wouldn't give him the address at first. But Jon insisted that it was important, and the woman finally gave it out somewhat reluctantly.

Evergreen was in a new office building just off the interstate that circled Singleton to the north. The building had plenty of glass and covered most of an acre, although it was a lot higher than it was wide.

Jon parked in the middle of the lot and walked through the double doors of the building as if he owned the place. But no security guard was around to question him.

On the building directory, Jon could see that the place was filled with professionals—doctors, dentists, lawyers, and small businesses of one sort or another. Evergreen was on the eighth floor, along with at least a dozen other firms.

Jon took the elevator to the eighth and just sauntered down the hall. He didn't really have a plan. He just wanted to see the place for himself.

Evergreen's offices were at the end of one of four corridors on the floor. Nearly all of the offices had nameplates on the doors, which had no windows. All the doors were closed.

Evergreen's office door was like all the others. Deciding to take a small chance, Jon knocked on the door of the office directly across the hall from Evergreen then entered quickly and closed the door behind him.

The room he'd entered was a small reception area, with three small offices directly behind. An elderly woman glanced up at him from the receptionist's desk as he entered.

"Hello, may I help you?" she asked pleasantly.

"Yes, you can," Jon said quickly, keeping his voice low. "I'm looking for office space, and I'm thinking of moving into one of these offices, perhaps on this floor. I was wondering—Could you tell me what the working environment is like here?"

The woman looked a little surprised. "Oh, I guess it's fine, as offices go. It's quiet."

"Are all the offices like this one, with a small reception area and three others behind it?"

The woman looked behind her. "Yes, pretty much, I think. I've been in a couple of the others. And they look like this one."

Jon nodded. He felt a little uneasy telling white lies like this, but there was no actual harm in it, he reasoned. "And the offices on this floor.

Is there much traffic? Like the one right across the hall from you, Evergreen Communications. Do you see a lot of folks come in and out, usually?"

The woman frowned. "I never really thought about it. The doctor's office gets a lot, I guess, at the other end of the hall. But the one across the hall, no, I can't say that I've seen much traffic. In fact, that particular office is usually closed and locked. Someone comes by, oh, about every week or two, for a little bit. But that's about it."

"So you don't see your neighbors at Evergreen much?"

The woman shook her head. "Haven't a clue who they are. I've never spoken to them. They're never in. The person who checks in every so often isn't there long enough even to have a conversation with. In and out, mostly."

Jon tried hard not to show his excitement. "So I guess there isn't a whole lot of traffic in and out on this hall where you are, not with Evergreen closed most of the time?"

"No, can't say there's much here. It's not like we're neighbors. We pass each other in the hall, and that's about it."

Jon desperately wanted to ask for a description of the person who came in and opened the Evergreen office, but he felt as though that would be pushing it. So he tried something else instead. "You wouldn't, by chance, happen to have the name of the management company, would you? I wanted to talk to them about leasing a space."

The woman thought for a moment. She opened a side drawer to her desk, and rummaged around inside. "Well, yes, I seem to remember seeing something like that. Ah, yes, here it is," she said, smiling. "Smithson and Associates." She gave Jon a phone number.

"And would you have a first name, perhaps, of Mr. Smithson?"

The woman glanced back at her piece of paper. "Here it is. Yes, it's Ray. Ray Smithson."

Jon thanked her. He let the door to her office close, stepped lightly across the hall, and tried the door to the Evergreen office. It was locked. Jon smiled. He was onto something. He could feel it in his bones.

CHAPTER TWENTY-ONE

"So who is Ray Smithson?" Jon asked the next morning from a pay phone at McDonald's, where he was having breakfast. He'd called Adams's house three times before getting him.

Adams laughed. "Ray Smithson's involved?"

"It's his management firm that runs the office building Evergreen operates out of."

"Well, I'll be," Adams mused. "But it makes sense."

"Why?"

"Smithson's the secretary of the central committee. He doesn't say much publicly, but he's always right around the corner when something's happening."

"That connection alone's worth something."

"Not enough," Adams said firmly. "It has to be nailed down. Cold. No wiggle room."

"Okay, I'll get back to you."

Jon hung up the phone gently. Actually, he was glad that Adams hadn't wanted to just run with the news of Smithson's connection to Evergreen. Jon felt a little like a hunter who knew that his prey was close. He wanted to close in for the kill.

Which surprised him. He wasn't, as he had expected to be, turned off by this little investigation for Adams. Far from it. It was perhaps the most exciting thing he'd ever done. And it was for a good cause. Adams was a good guy. His opponent, Jenkins, was down in the slime, and he deserved to go down. Laws had been broken to get that money for the campaign, and Jenkins had been right in the middle of it. Jon felt as if he were doing battle with the forces of darkness.

Other thoughts pushed in on Jon, but he pushed those aside. He'd worry about them later. He wasn't breaking any laws. He was doing the right thing. He was convinced of it.

He wished, though, that he had someone with whom to bounce ideas off, someone who could tell him whether he was straying too far. Susan might be that person, but he'd never had that kind of discussion with her. Maybe someday. But, for now, he was left to fend for himself, with the occasional silent prayer of hope that he was doing the right thing.

Those frequent, informal prayers had become a habit with Jon since becoming a Christian after his first year at Princeton. He offered up his thoughts to God silently and in a constant stream as he went through the day. He didn't tell anyone what he was doing; he just did it. Trying to describe it to someone would have sounded foolish anyway. He felt as if God answered him when the situation warranted it—not in words, of course. It was more like a presence of thought that worked with his own thoughts, the way the wind will blow through your hair, moving it but not making it any less your own.

And Jon had sensed that wind moving through his prayers recently, telling him to be careful in all this. He was mindful of it. But he also felt a sense of urgency to get this job done. Adams needed answers quickly if he was going to prevail in this fight.

Jon's next stop was Linda Hunt, Adams's Republican opponent in the congressional race should he manage to survive the primary. Jon didn't tell her why he was calling. He knew it was a little dangerous, asking her for information. So when he told her that it was for a new story he was working on, he hinted that she'd be pleased with the story when it came out. She assumed, with the vanity of a politician, that he meant to do a favorable profile of her. Jon didn't correct her. She gave him the name of someone with the Republican Party's executive committee who lived near Singleton, a lawyer named David Grey.

Jon called Grey, gave him the same spiel, and asked for an appointment. Grey agreed, telling Jon that he liked the *Gazette* and that any friend of the *Gazette* was a friend of his. Jon didn't bother to explain to Grey that he didn't actually work for the *Gazette* anymore.

They met at a small diner for lunch. Jon wasn't especially hungry, so he just nibbled on a sandwich as they talked. Jon explained what he was working on, and Grey's eyes narrowed with guarded interest.

"You have something new on that?" Grey asked.

"Yes, I think I do," Jon explained. "But I need names."

"What kind?"

"I've been told that there were names on a couple of checks the party—your party—obtained a couple of years ago. I need those names."

Grey was dressed conservatively in a dark blue, pinstriped suit, black, tasseled loafers, and a tastefully designed silk tie that was pulled up tightly at the throat. His clothes contrasted starkly with Jon's casual attire. Grey leaned forward, careful not to let his tie droop into his meal. "And what happens if I get you those names?"

Jon almost smiled. He was growing accustomed to the rules of this weird game. "I help your party, I think. I expose something that should have come out some time ago."

"You know something?"

"Enough, I think, to make some folks uncomfortable. But I need those names."

Grey leaned back in his chair. He looked hard at Jon for several moments, studying him. He was looking for some chink in Jon's armor, some reason to question his motives. But Jon returned his steady gaze.

Grey smiled. "Be right back," he said, and excused himself. Jon watched him walk through the small diner to a pay phone. He spoke to someone for several minutes, wrote something down, and then returned.

He handed Jon a small slip of paper as he sat down. Four names were on it. No addresses or phone numbers. "You're sure of these?" he asked Grey.

"Yes, I'm sure," he said, nodding. "These were the names given to us, people who had written some of the checks. We tried getting to them, but none of them would talk to us at the time. I doubt they'll talk now. But it's all we have."

"Great," Jon said, pocketing the names. "This is exactly what I needed."

"One thing, though," Grey said, leaning forward again. "You have to keep me posted on your progress. I want to know if you get somewhere."

"I will," Jon promised with a straight face.

What he didn't tell Grey was *when* he'd get back to him. He'd keep him posted, all right, but not until he'd gotten everything moving.

It wasn't exactly lying. It was just pushing the truth off toward the horizon a little, for a later day when he could safely tell Grey what he'd found.

CHAPTER TWENTY-TWO

Sol's All-Night Dinner and Waffle House wasn't romantic, or pretty, or even sanitary. But it was the only restaurant open at 11:00 in the evening, and it was close enough to the campaign office that Susan and Jon could walk to it.

After his conversation earlier in the day with David Grey, Jon was dying to let Susan know about what he'd stumbled into. He felt badly that he wasn't helping Susan and the volunteers work through that long list of telephone calls. But what he was doing—if he pulled it off—would be worth much, much more to Adams's campaign than anything Susan and the others were doing. Susan knew it, too.

The restaurant was crowded, even at this hour. They took a booth off in the corner, away from most of the other night owls. John ordered a cup of coffee and a donut, Susan just coffee.

"So you're onto something, you think?" she asked him after the waitress had left.

"Yeah, actually," Jon said, nodding. "I don't know how much Sam has told you . . ."

"Sam tells me everything," Susan said, her eyes never leaving Jon's. "There is not a single, solitary thing that happens in this campaign that I do not know about. Not one thing." She drilled the thought into him with her eyes.

Jon took a deep breath. There were times, like this one, when Jon wondered who Susan really was. She was tough as nails. Driven. She didn't seem to need anyone. And yet Jon was drawn to her in a way he'd never been drawn to anyone before. Maybe it was that intimidating self-sufficiency of hers that attracted him.

"Okay, got it," Jon said, trying to smile. "Now, as I was saying." Jon told her about his encounter at Evergreen, about his certainty that Evergreen was a front, about his conversations with Linda Hunt and David Grey. He explained how he would go about tracking the names Grey had given him, how he would nail the whole thing down, tight as a drum.

"Do it quickly," Susan said, her voice tired. "We're running out of time. We need this, Jon. I don't think we can win without it. We're all counting on you."

Jon looked down at the table. He could hear the slight desperation in Susan's voice. No matter how many hours she put in, no matter how many calls she and the others placed to registered Democrats and delegates, it wouldn't matter. Jon had to take Jenkins out.

But . . .

Jon looked up. Susan was staring at him intently. "You know, I've been thinking about what I'm doing. Whether it's . . ." Jon's voice drifted off.

"Whether it's the right thing to do?"

"Yeah, that. What do you think?"

Susan didn't hesitate. "What I think doesn't matter. It's what you think that counts. It's your life. I can't pick your morality for you. Whether I think it's right or wrong isn't important."

"But it is," Jon insisted. "I'd like to know what you think."

"And if I told you that I think what you're doing is really deplorable, nasty, underhanded, and vile, would that change your mind?"

"Is that what you think?"

Susan laughed lightly. Jon liked the way the corners of her mouth turned up when she laughed. "Of course not. I was teasing. I think Jenkins is an abomination in politics, and I'd like nothing better than to obliterate him from the face of the earth. You're doing the Lord's work, so to speak, if you take the guy out. So by all means I think you're doing the right thing. No question."

"But am I, in fact, doing the Lord's work?" Jon asked softly.

"I don't know about that," Susan answered. "That's your call, I think. I'm not one of your typical do-gooder types. I let people figure things out for themselves. I'm not going to tell you whether I think there's some Lord who's calling the shots on a deal like this."

"But you believe in God?" Jon asked, knowing he was now charting a potentially treacherous course with Susan.

"Do I believe in God?" Susan asked rhetorically. "Well, I believe in something. A Great Spirit, as the native Americans might say. An

105

over-Spirit, as John Steinbeck might call it. The spirit of Nature and the Earth, as Wordsworth wrote about."

Jon looked at Susan in some surprise. "You've read about all of that?'

"Sure. I read almost anything I can get my hands on. I like to learn."

"And you believe in all that stuff, about the Great Spirit or whatever."

"Yes, whatever," Susan said simply. "I don't have a name for it."

"So it's not like you believe in God and Jesus Christ, as his Son?"

"Probably not in the same way you do, no," Susan said. "I believe in myself, and my own ability. I believe in those I trust. And I believe there is more to the world than just atoms and particles and molecules."

"Something spiritual?"

"Yes, something spiritual."

"But not Christian?"

Susan frowned. "Not Christian, not the way you think about it. If I met this man, this Jesus Christ, and he had something interesting to say to me, I'd listen. Just as I'd listen to any man or woman who had something worthwhile to say."

"So you don't dismiss the Christian faith out of hand?"

"Jon, I don't dismiss anything out of hand," she said forcefully. "Only fools do that. You listen, and then you weigh everything in the balance. If it's good to me—for me—then I accept it. If not, I ignore it, dismiss it, fight it if it's working against me. That's how I see things."

"So if I talk to you about my own Christian beliefs, you won't think I'm crazy or goofy or hold it against me?" Jon asked slowly. "Or if I make a decision that something's wrong or right because of my own beliefs?"

"Everyone makes their own choices," Susan said. "I'll always listen to what you have to say, Jon. But, in the end, *you* decide what's right for you. Or wrong. Not me. That's just the way it is."

CHAPTER TWENTY-THREE

First thing the next morning, Jon asked Adams to run a data search on the four names. He didn't ask Adams how he would do it. Adams didn't tell him. By the middle of the afternoon, though, Adams called back.

"I want you to meet me downtown," Adams said. "I have something for you."

"Where?"

"Outside the city administration building. Know where that is?"

"I can find it. What's going on?"

Adams laughed into the phone. "Oh, a little party for the mayor. My boys have a few questions."

Jon could only imagine what Adams had up his sleeve. If his "boys" were involved, then it was likely to be a demonstration of some kind, aimed at making news. "Is 5:30 okay?"

"Make it 4:30. You'll want to see this."

By 4:30, Adams's little "demonstration" was in full swing. It was garish. There were more than a hundred people outside the administration building, most of them wearing black, hooded masks. Many of them carried signs accusing the mayor and the city administration of refusing to clean up projects like Cherry Hill.

Adams was already addressing the crowd. Jon stood off to the side, listening. He'd only seen Adams in action a couple of times.

". . . and times are hard, right?" Adams called through the tinny, battery-powered microphone.

"Yeah!" the crowd answered in unison.

"Everything costs too much?"

"That's right!"

"Not enough police!"

"No!"

"Drug deals out in the open. Not enough food to eat. People talkin' about takin' it to the streets?"

"You got that right!"

"So what do we want? Justice! More money to clean up the streets! And we want it now. Not promises about tomorrow. We want it now!"

The crowd roared its approval. Adams handed the microphone to another speaker, who launched immediately into the same themes: Poverty. Crime. Not enough money to buy the necessities of life. Despair. The cameras took it all in.

Adams worked his way through the crowd and pulled Jon off to the side. He handed Jon a report in a loose-leaf folder. Jon opened it and scanned the contents.

Inside, there was a small dossier on each of the four people Grey had listed on the small slip of paper. Jon was a little surprised at how quickly and thoroughly the research had been done. The dossiers were so complete, so professional.

"How'd you—" Jon started to ask.

"Never mind," Adams said. "This is what you wanted, right?"

"Yeah, it sure is. I should be able to get to all of these guys, right now. Thanks."

"No, thank you," Adams said, grasping Jon affectionately on the arm. "This will really help, Jon, if you can unravel this thing. Give it your best shot."

"I will, Sam. I promise."

Adams nodded once, gave Jon another reassuring squeeze, and then turned to work his way back through the crowd. Jon watched the demonstration for a little while longer. The young men in the black hoods were working the crowd well. They had the place rocking.

The sight unnerved Jon, to be honest. Adams's "boys" were pressing the crowd's hot buttons so feverishly, it was more than a little scary. But Adams and Susan had both said it was time to go for broke. If they didn't turn this thing around, it would be all over.

Jon left a few minutes later. He'd looked at the report more closely as he'd watched the demonstration, and he'd decided on a course of action. Three of the names in the report were almost certainly dead ends. They were still in the state of Ohio, and all three had become very successful in the past several years. Their careers had taken off. Two of them now ran profitable businesses of their own. A third was an executive vice president at a large corporation in Akron.

Jon knew there would be no getting to those three. They had almost certainly been paid off—not through a direct cash payment, but through the ethereal "network" that seemed to pervade the political system. Friends of friends had helped at opportune times, making those three successful in their endeavors. They weren't about to jeopardize that success now.

In fact, Jon figured, even making inquiries about those three might jeopardize the mission. Word would get around that he was asking questions about an old problem, and everyone would start covering their tracks.

But the fourth name held distinct possibilities. The man, Jay Dooley, had moved out of state. He was a professor of sociology at the University of Michigan in Ann Arbor. He was tenured. He was faintly controversial and unconventional in academic circles. A couple of articles had been written about him, and they were in the dossier.

But there was something else in the dossier that startled Jon. He had no idea why it was in there, but it was. Just a sentence about two-thirds of the way through the report speculating that Dooley had crashed and burned in politics. He had once been a real up-and-comer in the party. He'd worked directly for Jenkins senior in a couple of big deals. But then he'd lost all of his money in a binge of gambling, and it had washed him out of politics.

Jon shook his head, chuckling wryly as he read through this section. This was so weird. It was like being in the middle of a war, with espionage and confidential intelligence reports and strategies for taking the "other side" out.

So Jay Dooley was a gambler and, therefore, something of a security risk to those in power who had trusted him. All of that interested Jon for only one reason: If that had eventually resulted in Dooley's expulsion from the "network," then he just might be willing now to talk about why his name was on a check written without his knowledge several years ago.

It took Jon less than half an hour to pack an overnight bag and begin the drive to Ann Arbor. He'd decided not to call Dooley first. He didn't want to spook the guy. Instead, he would just find out when the guy taught and show up at his class.

There wasn't much time left, and the trip alone would eat up two days of his time. But it would be well worth it if Dooley would talk. Well worth it.

He arrived in Ann Arbor just before midnight, checked into a Red Roof Inn off the interstate, and set a wake-up call for six the next morning. He went to sleep wondering whether he was off on a wild-goose chase—or was, in fact, about to alter the political landscape in Ohio.

CHAPTER TWENTY-FOUR

Jon was at the registrar's office by 7:30 in the morning. He had to wait for someone to show up; it was summer, and no one worked normal hours at the university during the summer. But Jon couldn't believe his luck. The only class Dooley was teaching that summer met at nine that morning, less than five minutes away in the central part of the campus at the Department of Sociology.

Jon found the classroom, then walked over to the Student Union for a cup of coffee to kill some time. He arrived back at the classroom just before nine, as the students were filing in.

It was a fairly large class, maybe fifty kids or so. Jon took a seat about two-thirds of the way back. Dooley arrived just at nine o'clock and started right into his lecture without much preamble. It was pretty good. Dooley was a good professor, better than most. He clearly cared about his subject, and he spoke with some flair and emotion. The students mostly paid attention.

Twice during the lecture, Dooley looked at Jon, apparently trying to figure out who he was. That was good; Jon wanted him to be a little curious.

After class, Jon waited in his chair. He kept his eyes riveted on Dooley, who stuck around to chat casually with several of the students, all of them young men who seemed to know and admire him.

Dooley glanced at Jon a third time, even as he was chatting with his students. Jon nodded once at him.

After the last student had drifted away, Dooley strolled casually toward the back of the room, eased his way through the rows of chairs, and took a seat beside Jon.

"You're new to this class."

111

"Yes, in a way," Jon answered.

"In a way," Dooley mused. "That's a funny answer. Not the kind I'd expect from a student."

Jon cleared his throat. "I was a graduate student at Princeton until a short while ago."

"And you're thinking about coming here?"

Jon decided to take the plunge. "No, I'm working, in Ohio. I've written some stories for a newspaper in Singleton. And right now—well, right now, I'm looking into something. I was kind of hoping you'd know a little about it."

"You write for the *Gazette?*" Dooley asked him nervously.

"I just finished a series on efforts to clean up a housing project there," Jon said evasively. "Now I'm working on something that happened several years ago. Something political."

Dooley looked straight at him. "I don't do politics. I'm a tenured professor here at Michigan. That's what I do."

"But you *were* involved with politics, with the central committee of the Democratic Party in Ohio several years ago, weren't you?" Jon asked, lowering his voice even though they were the only two people in the classroom.

"No, not really."

"Not really? You didn't—"

"I was a volunteer," Dooley said quickly. "Like thousands of other people. But that was awhile ago."

"But you did work for the central committee, didn't you?"

Dooley took a deep breath. "Look. What did you say your name was?"

"Jon Abelson. Pleased to meet you." Jon held his hand out. Dooley shook it. Jon noticed that his palms were cold and slick with sweat.

"Well, Jon, did you travel here just to see me?"

"Yes, I did."

"You're wasting your time. I don't know anything."

"Did you work for the central committee?"

"It was a long time ago," Dooley said. "And I didn't do much. I don't know anything. I was just some sludge volunteer."

Jon almost laughed. He knew a little about being a sludge volunteer. But he also figured that Jay Dooley had been just a little more than that.

"You did work for Jim Jenkins, didn't you?" he asked Dooley directly. "Jenkins senior. For the party. Right?"

Dooley didn't answer right away. "Jenkins doesn't know what you're up to, does he? No one at the *Gazette* does, do they?"

"No, they don't," Jon said truthfully.

"How'd you get my name?"

Jon decided to press. "Your name was on one of the checks, wasn't it? You were part of it?"

"Part of what?" Dooley asked. "What are you working on?"

"A story about how a million dollars was given to Democratic Party candidates illegally right before a critical election. How it was given through Jenkins's son, and then repaid later."

Dooley looked stunned. "There's no way—Jenkins would never let you loose on such a wild-goose chase."

"I don't think it's a wild-goose chase. I'm halfway there already."

"I don't know anything about it. It was a long time ago, and I just did volunteer work."

Jon could see he was going to have to do something, take a risk. Otherwise, Dooley would never talk.

"Mr. Dooley, I think you did more than that," Jon said, leaning forward in his chair. "I think you worked pretty closely with Jim Jenkins and his son. I think you were part of a couple of big deals. I think you let your name go onto one of those checks, and maybe even lined up a whole bunch of 'safe' names for other checks. I think you know a lot more than you're saying. And I think you left Ohio because it all made you uncomfortable."

"I really don't know anything," Dooley said, his voice a whisper.

"I think you do," Jon said firmly. "And I think something happened. I think you took a whole lot of the money that you made working with Jenkins, and you lost it all gambling. That's what I think. And now you're here."

Dooley blinked, several times. He looked like a little kid caught sneaking into the kitchen for a chocolate cookie after his mom had told him not to. "You're going to print that?" he finally managed.

"Is it true?"

Dooley looked away. Jon could see him close his eyes for a moment, almost as if he were praying silently. When Dooley looked back, Jon could see it, clearly. Dooley had made his decision.

"Look, my life has changed. I'm a new person. I'm not the same as I was then. I've committed my life to Jesus Christ."

Jon smiled. "Me, too."

Dooley relaxed. "Really? You're a Christian?"

"Yes, so I understand what you're saying. I don't want to print or say anything about your gambling. If you've asked God to forgive you for that, then that's good enough for me. I just want to know the truth."

"And that's all? You don't want to bring all this stuff out about me? Because if it came out, they could use it to justify revoking my tenure here."

"I give you my word," Jon said solemnly. "I don't want to expose you. I just want the truth."

Dooley nodded. "Okay, then. I'd like to make a deal."

"Let's hear it."

"I don't want to be in the newspapers over this. I want to talk to you anonymously. How do they put it—on background?"

"Yes, on background."

"So is it a deal? Can we talk that way?"

"Yes," Jon said, his heart leaping. "We can talk that way."

Dooley nodded. "Okay. Here's what happened."

CHAPTER TWENTY-FIVE

For the next half hour, Dooley talked and Jon took notes. It was an extraordinary story.

Dooley had been working for Jenkins junior, at the bank. But he'd begun to do work for the central committee as a volunteer and had gotten to know Jenkins's father as well.

Eventually, Jenkins senior helped him set himself up as a small businessman, in a consulting company very much like Evergreen Communications. Jenkins's bank had loaned him enough money to get it started, and with his ties to the party, the business had flourished.

Just before the election, Jenkins senior had asked Dooley to provide a list of names—people who could be trusted without question. Jenkins didn't tell him why he needed the names, but Dooley could guess.

He worked the network he'd built up over the years and compiled a list of about twenty-five people he was absolutely, rock-solid certain were loyal to the party.

Those twenty-five people, in effect, became one hundred thousand dollars. Each could be said to have given the maximum allowed—two thousand dollars each for both the primary and the general election. Their signatures were not actually on any checks; those fictitious checks would be made up only if it proved necessary, after the fact. But the willing names were needed up front, to be ready to speak in case something happened.

When the story of the cash infusion just before the election started to leak out, Jenkins and others in the committee decided to put a few canceled checks into "circulation" to quell the speculation and to preempt any official inquiry. So a few checks, properly signed by contributors—including Dooley—were circulated.

Newspaper reporters tracked Dooley down, as Jenkins had told him they would. And Dooley told the reporters that, yes, he had signed the checks, and that besides contributing to the party, he had helped organize fundraisers.

The strategy worked. The story faded in the face of corroboration from Dooley and other "contributors." There was no inquiry. Everyone assumed that the money had come in legitimately, through normal fundraising channels.

And, in fact, the money was eventually raised in just that way. The central committee of the party retired the debt shortly after the general election, through several fundraising dinners, a couple of direct mail pieces, and a phone-bank effort.

But the problem right before the election had been that they needed the money immediately, and there hadn't been enough time to raise it the old-fashioned way. So they had bent the rules a little and worked it all out later.

Some time after that election, as Dooley's business had begun to prosper and he had started to make a great deal of money, he also began to spend money like there was no tomorrow. He bought cars, went on trips, ate out at the finest restaurants, flew first-class to the Super Bowl and the World Series with big donors to the central committee. Dooley had it all, and there seemed no end in sight.

Until he'd started to place "little" wagers on sporting events. A thousand dollars on a Cincinnati Reds game here, two thousand on the Chicago Cubs there. Then ten thousand on the Cleveland Cavaliers. A hundred thousand on the Browns.

And, finally, $1 million on the Super Bowl. He bet that the winner of the game would win by more points than the odds makers' "spread." He almost made it. The spread was sixteen points. His team was ahead by three touchdowns—twenty-one points—with two minutes left in the game.

But they brought in a new quarterback, a rookie, to finish out the game. He'd driven his team down the field for a meaningless final touchdown. His team lost by fourteen points instead of twenty-one points.

Jay Dooley lost a million dollars, and nearly his life.

He'd tried to recover from the loss with a wild gambling binge, culminating in a trip to Las Vegas where he'd cleaned out his bank account in a desperate effort to just get back to "even." He came home from Vegas virtually penniless.

It was at that point—at the absolute rock-bottom, lowest point in his life—that he'd turned to Christ. Eventually, he was able to get out from under the last of his debts and begin to slowly rebuild his life. He taught at a junior college for a year, and then came to Michigan as an associate professor. He'd gotten a tenured position a year later.

He was not wealthy now. Far from it. But he was happy, he told Jon. He had put his gambling and his troubles far behind him, and he was glad to be out of all of it.

In the end, Dooley agreed to give Jon some of the other names he'd rounded up. Most likely, at least one or two of them would agree to say, on background, that they had not signed the checks.

It was quite a story. Jon only hoped that the TV station he gave it to would do it justice.

And, also, that they would protect Jay Dooley.

CHAPTER TWENTY-SIX

The images on the television set flickered, casting a shadow against the wall in Jon's darkened hotel room. The curtains were drawn. The sound was just loud enough for Jon to hear but not so loud as to disturb anyone in other rooms.

Jon sat on the edge of the bed and stared at the TV screen. He glanced at the clock on the nightstand, watching as it rolled over to 6:00. An instant later, the logo for one of the three local affiliates in Singleton, Ohio, flashed on the screen

Jon didn't know what to feel at that moment. He was on the edge of success. He had done his part, delivering the story to the premier political reporter at the local station, complete with Dooley's story, the Evergreen Communications background, and the names Dooley had supplied him—more than enough for any decent reporter.

But in the two days since then, things had gone slightly off course—not enough to jeopardize the story but enough to make Jon feel distinctly uneasy.

The *Gazette's* publisher, Jenkins senior, had gotten wind almost immediately of what was happening. He'd gone straight to the owner of the TV station and tried to block the story. He'd almost succeeded.

But Adams had also spoken to a couple of people. Jon didn't know who, but the story didn't die. Instead, Adams was told the station would need to have someone involved in the story, someone who'd been on the inside, who would be willing to go public. The station needed to make sure it was protected if it were to go ahead with this.

Earlier today, Adams had called Jon and told him that they'd tracked Jay Dooley down in Michigan. Jon had almost thrown the telephone against the wall. He'd given Dooley his word that he would protect him.

"There was no choice, really," Adams had told him when Jon had calmed down. "The station needed something concrete to protect themselves. Dooley gave them that. In the end, he was willing to confirm on camera just what he told you. Would he have done that if he didn't believe that confession, that honesty, was the best thing for him? Remember, Jon, you told me he's a Christian now. He's cleansed his soul, and the station can put the story on the air. Jenkins'll be out of business in politics, Jon— and you did it. You did it."

Jon held his breath as he watched the broadcast. The anchor read the lead-in to the exclusive. The reporter opened with the guts of the story, and then cut directly to an interview with Dooley just outside his home in Michigan. As Adams had said, Dooley confirmed it all.

The story had it all—pictures of the Evergreen office; graphics of the trail of money, where it went, and for what purposes; how the money was repaid; a picture of the check Jay Dooley signed, provided courtesy of the Republican party; and the obligatory prepared response from the Democratic Party that it was all a bunch of hogwash.

When the story closed, they went to a live, two-way conversation between the news anchor and the reporter. " . . . and we've learned that the U. S. attorney's office plans to reopen an investigation," the reporter told the anchor. "We've also been told that Jay Dooley—whom you just saw—may not be the most reliable of witnesses."

"And why is that?" the news anchor asked.

"Well, sources told us that he lost millions of dollars in a gambling binge several years ago," the reporter said solemnly. "His financial problems, as well as his associations during that time, may compromise his testimony."

"So there will be more on this?" the anchor asked.

"Yes, we've only seen the opening chapter in this story," the reporter said.

CHAPTER TWENTY-SEVEN

Every lobbyist, every journalist, every foreign dignitary, everyone of prominence in Washington, D.C., knows that two types of offices exist for members of the House of Representatives, the "people's house." Those who have power have offices in the spacious, marble-lined Rayburn Building. And the unfortunate others across the way set up camp in either the Longworth or Cannon buildings.

New members of the House get the worst offices, usually some cramped, infested cubbyhole up on the fifth or sixth floor of Longworth or Cannon. It is an immutable law. If you are a junior member, you get a crummy office. Period. No questions asked. Once you achieve seniority, you get to move over to Rayburn.

For those unfortunate souls—the legions of aides to the newer members of the House of Representatives—forced to work in the over-heated, undercooled offices in Longworth or Cannon, it is an exercise in endurance and professional horror.

If you sit close to the wall and don't scrape your chair across the uncarpeted floor, you can hear mice scurrying back and forth in the hollow walls. There are lots of mice. Exterminators come through all the time, but it doesn't seem to help much; the mice are back in force within weeks.

In the winter, the heat doesn't work quite right. On very cold mornings, it's ten degrees too hot in the place. On unusually mild mornings, the heat fails to kick in every so often and everyone pulls on a sweater.

In the summer, it's even worse, especially in July and August when it's so hot and muggy that all the mosquitoes die just to avoid the weather. Longworth and Cannon are supposed to be centrally air-conditioned. But that's just a lofty promise. Most people just bring in their own fans.

Legends say that the elevators in the place don't actually run on electricity. Instead, three fat trolls sit in the basement and pull the elevators up and down with large ropes and pulleys. They pull—or don't—when they see fit.

Veterans also know the rules about cafeteria food—never take a dessert near the front of the row because, more often than not, fingerprints can be found from people poking the cakes and pies to see if they're stale. Always check the expiration date of the milk. Don't ever pick an entree that has the word *stew* as part of its name, like "lamb stew." That's a clear signal that the kitchen ran out of something and just dumped leftovers into a big pot and stirred it up.

When walking the halls, get out of the way of men in suits or women in high heels running frantically down the corridor. Getting in their way can be hazardous to your health.

The phrase "working lunch" was almost certainly invented here. What most "working lunches" consist of is a Coke or Pepsi at your desk, a candy bar or chips, and—if you are very lucky and get there early—a can of prepackaged macaroni and beef from the ancient vending machines. As you work, you try to take bites between telephone calls.

Entire forests have been cut to supply the paper that keeps the offices well-stocked. Every desk has reams of paper piled haphazardly on it. Printers whir and click constantly under plastic covers in every corner of every office, spitting out words of wisdom that go to millions of people.

Those staffers who've been here awhile always advise their bosses to pick in the office lottery an office suite somewhere on the northwest corner of the buildings. Those offices are shielded from the blistering early morning sun. But more important, each suite on that corner of the building has at least a couple of spaces with a spectacular view of the magnificent buildings just across the street to the north.

Views are something that people war over in this claustrophobic community. Everyone wants to be able to sit at his or her desk and stare out a window, preferably at some noble or stately structure. Few people actually achieve such status. Those who do, guard their position jealously and fight off all challengers.

It is, in a word, a sorry place. The working quarters are cramped, the hours are hideously long, the tolerance for mistakes is almost nil, egos rage out of control, no parking is nearby, tempers flare, and vacations are few and far between.

But it is also the center of the political universe. People fought hard to win one of these lousy offices and to keep it.

"Congressman!" someone yelled

Jon looked up from his desk in a fifth-floor office at the southeast corner of the Longworth Building. Sam Adams ran into the office, threw his coat on a chair near his secretary's desk, and bolted into his own office.

Their office suite was farther from the Capitol building than almost any other congressional office. To make votes, Adams usually took the stairs and then ran across the street. Someday, he had vowed, he'd discover a system to track votes more easily and keep from running so much.

In fact, a whole group of younger congressmen, most of them from the business world, had devised just such a system. They spent their time in either the House gym or the policy offices in the Capitol building itself; they conducted all their business by phone or pager. They only came back to their offices in Longworth or Cannon when they had meetings they couldn't escape. You could find this group moving through the Capitol like a herd of cattle, roaming from one event to the next, cellular phones in hand. They were never more than a stone's throw from the floor when the House was in session.

Sam Adams wasn't that kind of congressman. He did everything by the numbers. He met with legions of constituents, who trooped through his office in a constant stream. He met with each and every interest group that called him and asked for an audience. He listened to all their concerns and requests with an attentive ear.

Adams churned out the maximum amount of "franked" mail allowed under the fairly generous House of Representatives' budget. Jon had proposed, early on, that they slap a big picture of Adams on the outside cover of the franked envelopes. No one ever actually reads the junk, he'd argued, so at least make sure people see Adams's face just before they drop the piece in the trash.

That and other things seemed to be working. Adams did constant polling in his congressional district—to test his name ID and to gauge where his constituency stood on tough votes like whether to keep Medicare from rising ten percent a year until it bankrupted the federal government or whether to ban the sale of Uzis in discount department stores.

More than two-thirds of the people in the district now knew Adams's name without prompting from the poll callers. That was very good for a freshman congressman in the second year of his first term in office. Adams was, in fact, in great shape going into his reelection year, considering that he had won the congressional race last year with a name ID well below the halfway mark. He had won that race easily, once Jenkins had been removed from the picture. The central committee of the party had urged Jenkins to go quietly into the night, and he had obliged.

Jon was never sure whether the Democratic Party leaders had known that he and Adams were behind the story. They must have at least suspected, Jon assumed. But it didn't seem to matter. Politics, it appeared to Jon, was more about delivering results than it was about loyalty. Yes, you needed a network of power behind you if possible. But if you chose to go your own way and you won, then the system made room for you—as long as you kept winning.

The proof of that to Jon was what was happening to Adams now as he geared up for reelection. He was now the incumbent congressman, and the Democratic Party in the state was helping him raise money for his campaign. They'd sponsored a half-dozen dinners, and they'd committed a pile of "soft money" to support him as well.

It boggled Jon's mind. Adams had deliberately attacked the system—their system—and yet they were now supporting him. It was a funny business.

Adams poked his head out the door. "Jon!" he bellowed. "Get in here!"

"What's up?" Jon asked as he entered Adams office.

"Close the door," Adams ordered, his back turned.

Jon reached behind him and swung the door shut. He took one of the two seats that faced Adams's desk and waited.

After the election, Adams had asked Jon almost offhandedly whether he wanted to come to Washington with him as his communications director. Jon had accepted immediately. He had no other plans anyway. He could always go back to journalism if this didn't work out, he figured.

In the chain of command, three others in the office had bigger salaries, more staff, and a longer list of responsibilities than did Jon. The administrative assistant, the director of the district office, and the legislative director all were much older than Jon and more senior.

But Jon and Susan, Adams's executive assistant and "Girl Friday," were, in fact, the real powers in the office, and everyone knew it. Jon and Susan were Adams's "get it done" people. Both knew how to feed Adams's immense appetite for news, information, rumors, or gossip—anything that might help him get the job done. Both knew that they would be with Adams long after the others had gone on to some other job on Capitol Hill.

Since coming to Washington, Jon and Susan were the ones most often at Adams's side. The AA was an experienced hand in Washington, plucked from another congressional staff. The district office director spent his time schmoozing with business types, mostly to raise more money. And the legislative director was another congressional staff retread who spent more time with other subcommittee staff and legislative policy types than he did with Adams.

Among the senior policy and communications staff, only Jon was truly "loyal" to Adams. Susan, despite her intense loyalty, was not yet a senior staffer. She was ambitious, driven, and smart. But she was young. She wouldn't move up for a year or two yet.

It was Jon's job to protect Adams, steer him clear of trouble, put the best face on difficult votes, and promote him to the public at large. He was the only member of the senior staff who had a personal relationship with Adams. In fact, the other people on Adams's Washington staff often turned to Jon for insight into how Adams would react to some new development in the office.

And yet, it seemed to Jon, *no one* really knew Sam Adams. What drove him? He didn't seem to have any real friends, not like the fraternity friends Jon had from college or those friends he'd made at church or in high school. Adams had no social or personal life to speak of. Virtually every night of the week, Adams was out after dinner at parties, shaking hands and raising money from the business community lobbyists who swarmed to those functions like bees to honey. Each weekend, Adams was back home in the district, speaking to at least a half-dozen groups, constantly on the move.

Adams walked to a small closet, whisked his shirt off, and grabbed a white, frilly one. It was late in the day. Jon knew this routine by heart. Adams kept a tuxedo in the closet for formal functions in the evening. He never went home to his apartment to change. He did that here. It saved time.

"I want you to come with me this evening," Adams said, as he slipped out of his pants and put the black tux pants on.

"To what?"

"A party in the president's honor."

"The president of the United States?" Jon asked. Instinctively, he glanced down at his suit and tie to see if he had any coffee or food stains on them.

Adams laughed. "Don't worry, kid. You won't get a chance to meet him. He'll spend the entire time in a receiving line."

"But he'll be there?"

"Yeah, he'll be there. But that's not why I'm going there or why I need you—and Susan, if she wants to come along."

"Why, then?"

"Because I want you to witness my pitch, firsthand."

127

"Your pitch?"

Adams turned sharply and looked directly at Jon. "Are you listening? Paying attention?"

When Adams did this to other staffers, they cowered. Even the AA got uncomfortable when Adams turned his withering stare in his direction. But Adams didn't terrify Jon the way he did the other staff. Jon knew that Adams needed him.

"I'm paying attention," Jon answered softly.

Adams nodded. "Good, because you'll have to act on what you see this evening. And I don't want you to make a mistake. We're about to enter a high-stakes poker game. I don't like to lose."

"Don't worry, boss. I can handle the mission," Jon grinned. He knew Adams hated it when he called him "boss."

"We'll see," Adams grunted.

"So what are you going after?"

Adams held a hand up. "Hold on. I want Susan to hear this as well." He reached down and flipped on the intercom to his personal secretary, Sharon Simpson, a sharply dressed, efficient, bright woman in her mid-forties. She had served three previous members of Congress with distinction and knew the ropes better than almost any senior aide on the Hill. "Sharon, can you send Susan in here? Thanks."

An instant later, Susan walked through the door to the "inner sanctum" and closed the door behind her. As always, Jon found it hard to control the slight flutter in the pit of his stomach when he saw her.

"You rang?" Susan asked cheerily.

"I want you to hear this," Adams said quickly with no preamble. "You can come along with Jon, if you like."

"I do," Susan said immediately, without knowing what she was signing up for.

"Okay, now . . ." Adams reached into his desk drawer and pulled out a bow tie. He wrapped it around his neck.

Susan, though, stepped around the desk and took the bow tie from Adams. "Here, let me," she said. "You talk."

"No, I can—"

"Talk," she commanded. "I can do this better than you can. We both know it."

Adams sighed in disgust, knowing that Susan was right. He shrugged at Jon and continued. "All right. Here's the deal. This administration needs a jump start to its second term. It wants change, big

128

change. The people want the government smaller, different. And I have a plan."

That hardly surprised Jon. "But you're just a freshman. Nobody pays any attention to freshmen. Not in this town. You'll have to wait your turn."

"Not necessarily. Not if I can bring the players to the table. Not if I can deliver the coalition to the White House."

"What coalition?"

"The one you're going to put together, of course," Adams said wryly, "after my pitch this evening."

Jon settled back in his chair. "Okay, I give up. What's the deal here?"

Adams scanned his desktop as Susan put the finishing touches on the bow tie and stepped away to make sure it was in place. Adams spied a sheaf of stapled papers, grabbed them, and tossed them to Jon. "Read that."

The document wasn't on any letterhead. It wasn't addressed to anyone nor did it have a signature. The first sheet was a "one-pager"— an executive summary of the contents of the paper itself, the kind of summary briefing clearly meant for very senior eyes.

There is an old rule of thumb in Washington. The higher up the food chain you go, the smaller the briefing materials required. Very important people have little time to review mounds of material. That is done by staff, who review the core material and condense it to its essence for the people who make the decisions.

By the time you get to the president, you'd better be able to state your case in about three paragraphs. If you can't, you've lost. Plain and simple.

The policy paper itself contained a radical, new proposal. There was a fever raging in Washington these days. Both parties were competing to see who could gut—or "reinvent"—the federal government the fastest, rearranging the deck chairs on the Titanic.

Some wanted to abolish agencies like the Food and Drug Administration or the Environmental Protection Agency. But that wasn't feasible. Others wanted to get rid of obsolete Cabinet departments like Commerce, Energy, or Housing and Urban Development. That was a little more palatable because they didn't have strong, supporting constituencies.

The proposal Jon was now staring at took a little from all the "reform" camps. Basically, what it proposed was a totally new approach to welfare. Every program that sustained the poor—from school lunches and food stamps to public housing and Medicaid—would be combined under one roof.

A new Cabinet department would be specifically designed to serve their interests and dole out the vast sums of money needed for that effort. It would be called the Department of Public Works.

It was a wonderfully simple, elegant proposal. All the money used to support the myriad of poverty programs would be pooled and then given out under one system. In some ways, this proposal was nothing new. Taxes that came in to the federal treasury, even under the existing system, were not differentiated as to how they were spent. No separate trust fund existed for Social Security. Money in the Treasury paid for everything anyway. Millions of Americans were wholly dependent on the Treasury for their health, housing, education, nutrition, and job security.

All this proposal did was consolidate everything, simplify it. In effect, the poor would be given a certain amount of money to spend, and they could spend it as they saw fit, within certain limits. Every program would have a ceiling. For instance, each family could spend up to $500 a month on health care, replacing the Medicaid system. They could not go above that ceiling. Each family could spend up to $150 a week on food—which they could purchase anywhere—or up to $800 a month for housing.

Whole departments and agencies would be abolished or subsumed into the new Public Works department. HUD would be abolished, for instance. Instead of building huge, new public-housing complexes, people and families would be given a stipend toward their monthly bills. They could live wherever their stipend would allow them to live.

Medicaid would be taken away from the states and the Department of Health and Human Services. Everyone who came under the system would have a monthly health-coverage allotment, enough to cover regular doctor visits and the occasional hospital emergency. If medical expenses for anyone under the system went beyond the limit, the hospitals and the doctors would have to come to the federal government for more money. They would not be allowed to turn patients away—not those, at any rate, who were covered by the proposed system.

Both Social Security and Medicare would likewise be swallowed up by the larger Public Works department. The Social Security Administration would be abolished, and Medicare would be pulled from HHS. Those two programs alone accounted for just about half of the new department's budget, and tightly controlling expenditures in both would guarantee that the budget would remain under control.

Of course, this proposal would make old people wholly dependent on one department of the federal government for their support and livelihood,

130

but that wasn't too different from the way things were now. In fact, it would make life easier: Everything would be paid for under one system.

In fact, if you were over sixty-five, you could qualify for a fairly large sum of money that would let you live at a Fortune 500 chain retirement home, eat out at a decent restaurant a couple of times a week, see a doctor regularly, catch a movie every so often, and even visit your grandchildren at Christmas.

Because everything would be consolidated and coordinated through just one department, Public Works, all payments could be centralized. It would relieve millions of small and medium-sized businesses of countless hours of paperwork and hassles.

People would get their allotted sum, its amount varying with demographics and socioeconomic status, and then they could "debit" against that account weekly. They would not be able to spend above that mark, though. The account set up in their name would not process any more than that.

A large super-computer company had already agreed to lease a system to the government to handle the processing of the claims, demographics, socioeconomic data, and centralized payments. It would be easy, actually. Nearly every large corporation had already given up on the networked personal computer revolution and gone back to large, central systems. Now the federal government was just joining the wave.

And last, the poor would not need to worry about how to pay for all the different services that supported them. They wouldn't need food stamps, their AFDC vouchers, their Medicaid card, their Social Security ID validation, their driver's license, their earned-income tax credits for their children, the school-lunch vouchers, the WIC credit vouchers, or their housing credit allowance.

Every major bank in America, Japan, Canada, Great Britain, France, and West Germany had competed fiercely to develop the "smart" card with a centralized debit system. That technology was already in place, and the federal government would simply need to flip on the switch to implement a similar government program.

"Smart" cards were fairly simple instruments. A microcomputer chip was embedded on the card. It stored "read-only" information, mostly financial. It allowed parents to give their kids debit cards for college without risking massive overdrafts. The card was credited with only so much money, and when the card ran out, it ran out.

But, over the years, the smart cards had become brilliant. Thanks to some revolutionary innovations by two of the leading computer-chip makers, the chips on the card now had the capacity to store life histories, send information to, and receive it from, scanners at every store in the country, and even give consumers who owned them detailed information and advice on their current economic status.

The cards helped them budget, for instance, by advising them if they were spending too much money too fast on food—based on a historic average stored in the chip—or if they were approaching their median spending on health care, again based on historic averages.

The FBI had worked with the big banks to teach them how to cross-match ID procedures with card ownership. If a smart card were lost, it couldn't be used by someone else. The card, through a new heat-sensitive pad on its reverse side, read both the fingerprints and the DNA of the person holding it. You had to press the card down to make it work, so there was no way to fool the system.

The system was foolproof. The only thing necessary to implement it nationally was the will of the people. Which was where the policy paper ended.

Jon looked up. "Where'd this thing come from?"

"It's a copy straight off the president's desk. Problem is, it's way too hot to handle. They don't actually want to make such a proposal. They'd get killed."

"So what are we going to do with it?"

"Good question," Adams said. "That's why you need to come with me this evening. I'll describe my plan more on the way to the Naval Observatory. It's a surprise birthday party for the president, for about a thousand of his closest and dearest friends."

"So we're your dates?"

"Not exactly," Adams chuckled. "Abby's going, too."

CHAPTER TWENTY-EIGHT

Abby met them on the street behind the Longworth House Office Building in the Volvo sedan she always drove. She was dressed in a conservative, tailored beige suit and small-heeled shoes. Her black hair flecked with gray was pulled back. She'd gotten some sun, because her cheeks had some color.

Jon wasn't surprised that she'd wanted the three of them to come down to the street, rather than coming up to the office to meet them. In fact, Jon couldn't remember Abby Adams ever setting foot in her husband's office suite since they'd all come to Washington after the election. Jon had seen Abby often enough over the past year or so but never in the office.

Abby was a strange woman. She was direct, to the point of being slightly obnoxious. She either liked someone or she didn't. And if she didn't like you, you knew it. There was no guessing with Abby.

Abby adored Susan. They were almost inseparable. Susan waited on Abby as a servant waited on her queen. But Susan was also tactful about it. She was not overly obsequious. She simply responded promptly to every whim of Abby's. Her wish was Susan's command—quietly, efficiently, and without complaint.

Abby also liked Jon. She'd liked him right from the start. Jon figured it was because he'd helped her husband get into office. On the other hand, maybe not—Abby seemed to go out of her way to show that she thought being the wife of a U.S. congressman wasn't such a big deal.

Abby wasn't the sharpest of dressers in Washington or the wittiest of congressional wives or the most ruthless social climber in Washington or the consummate networker. Instead, she was very good at *all* those things, to the point that Jon had noticed others often turned to her for advice.

Not staff, though. Staff were little slugs to be stepped on if they got in your way. Abby treated staff the way royalty used to treat their servants. But to those who held some sort of power or were married to it, Abby could be breathtakingly poised and articulate—as well as overpowering —if the occasion called for it.

Jon was sure that she'd be in rare form this evening. If she got her chance to get close to a Cabinet secretary or two or a couple of top lobbyists who could fill her husband's campaign coffers, then Jon knew she'd be at their side, armed with flattery and wit.

They had to park about five blocks up the street from the Observatory on Massachusetts Avenue. A sea of people extended in all directions. At least two-thirds of the members of Congress and assorted aides were there, plus a couple hundred top lobbyists who couldn't believe their luck at being invited to such an event.

As the four of them walked up the street, Abby and Sam held hands. It wasn't exactly an affectionate gesture, Jon knew; it was simply expected.

Jon was very much aware, as they walked, of Susan walking beside him. Their relationship had changed since they arrived in Washington. They'd been seeing each other when time permitted—and when both of them were in Washington at the same time on the weekends, which was rare considering how much time Adams spent back in the district—but they did not hold hands as they walked toward the Naval Observatory. That would have been unprofessional.

From the moment they entered the compound, Adams began working his way toward a particular spot on the grounds. As usual, he seemed to know what he was doing, so Abby, Susan, and Jon simply trailed behind.

As the sun descended below the tree line to the west, there was a stir in the crowd. Floodlights suddenly started sweeping the darkening sky above the Observatory. It was quite a light show, and the crowd murmured appreciatively.

Several moments later, Marine One came flying in low over the horizon, hovered over the grounds, and then settled near the spot where former Vice President Dan Quayle had once put in a putting green. The spot now served as a temporary helipad.

Adams had managed to find a spot just about fifty feet away from the rear porch entrance to the Naval Observatory's private quarters. He was quite close to Marine One as it landed, as he had no doubt intended to be.

Jon, Susan, and Abby were standing at his side as the mammoth military helicopter set down and the side door opened. They moved to the side as the Secret Service detail secured a path for the president.

President Will Simpson was just starting his second term in office. As the Democratic Party's nominee, he'd survived an extraordinary four-way presidential election, winning with just thirty-five percent of the vote. He'd been flanked by independent challengers on both the right and left, as well as the Republican nominee. But, in the end, he'd managed to rally all the old, traditional allies of the party to build a winning coalition that squeaked by.

Now, in his second term, the president was making a bold move to unite all the core constituencies of the party behind a central master plan that would make them wholly dependent on the state for their survival. If it worked, the party would control their destinies. If it failed, then the party would likely splinter and disintegrate.

As he walked past them, the president suddenly stopped, stepped toward Sam Adams, and held out a hand. Adams shook it briefly, then leaned toward the president and said something. Jon couldn't hear it over the roar of Marine One's rotors. But the president nodded back at Adams, and Jon could distinctly see him say "thank you" before moving on.

Within the next few minutes, the president shook at least two hundred hands on the way into his "surprise" birthday party and paused for the obligatory wave at the crowd—picked up live by CNN from a riser platform out on the lawn. As the president disappeared inside, Jon turned toward Adams.

"What'd you tell him?" Jon asked.

"I told him that I was going to take care of his problem," Adams said, deadly serious.

"He knew what you were talking about?"

"Of course he knew. I was handpicked for the job."

Jon was stunned. Adams, a freshman congressman, running point on an operation of this complexity and importance?

Adams had filled him in on a few of the details on the brief ride over. Basically, they were going to "float" the plan among the different coalitions and groups in Washington that might be reluctant to sign onto such a sweeping overhaul of the status quo. For instance, Adams himself would meet with the executive director of the American Association of Retired Persons (AARP) to sell them on the concept. Without proper stroking, AARP might foster a revolt among its vast membership.

Jon, though, would have the far more difficult task of trying to mobilize an army of support among the activist groups that backed causes for the "poor" and "disenfranchised" of society.

The guts of the Adams plan, though, was something that neither he nor Jon would ever put on paper. In a nutshell, both were going to promise to pay off certain groups for their active support of the concept. Jon would go to established groups that operated in the inner cities and ghettos and, in essence, promise funding for their leadership in return for their support of the plan. That would mean billions of dollars in support for inner city clinics or "education" programs in poor neighborhoods for drug abuse and mental health counseling.

Jon and Adams would pick the leaders in a new army. In return for their support, those leaders would get federal funding for a variety of new or slightly altered programs. It was simply a new twist on the old, time-honored patronage system.

There were precedents, of course. When the AIDS epidemic hit in the late 1970s, for instance, clinics sprang up across the country to counsel gay men who'd contracted HIV. The clinics got up to two hundred dollars from the federal Centers for Disease Control for every person they counseled right off the street. The AIDS clinics became a big business.

And hundreds of Medicaid and Medicare complexes across the United States had come into existence simply because there was money to be made off the federal government.

What the president—with Adams's help—was going to do was change the rules. New friends would be made. New alliances would be formed.

Jon leaned close to Adams. "How'd you do that?"

"Get picked?"

"Yeah. How'd you do that?"

Adams smiled. "Luck, kid. Like always. Now, you guys be good. I have to go inside and see a couple of people." An instant later, he was gone, working his way through the crowd.

As they watched him leave, Abby took Jon's arm. She'd been unusually quiet that evening. She pulled him close. Jon could smell her perfume. "If you believe that, my boy, then you're a fool. Sam worked his tail off to get this assignment."

"But how?" Jon whispered back.

Abby scanned the crowd that was beginning to push its way through the doors, following the president inside. When she found what she was looking for, she pulled Susan in close so she could hear as well.

"Two men are near the entrance, huddled together, talking," she said conspiratorially. "One's wearing a regular suit, not a tux. Quite fat. The other's trim. Looks like he just stepped out of the tailor's shop. See them?"

Jon peered past the sea of tuxedos and formal dresses. He spied the two men, one heavy and the other dressed sharply in an obviously expensive black tux. "The bald, fat guy and the James Bond look-alike?" he asked.

Abby smiled. "The fat guy is Nathaniel Watson. The guy he's talking to is Jonas Brownlee."

"Nathaniel Watson. I know that name."

Abby nodded. "White House counsel to two Democratic presidents. He's a partner in a law firm now, but he might as well be in the White House still. Everything like this goes through him, even now."

Jon gave Abby a strange look. "No way."

"Yes, way," Abby smiled. "At least a dozen of the Fortune 500 companies are his clients. Every president for the past two decades has called on him for private advice. Even the Republicans."

Jon shook his head. Washington was a weird town, he was discovering. You couldn't tell the players without a scorecard, and sometimes even party affiliation didn't help much.

Susan said, "That's Jonas Brownlee, one of the vice chairs of the Democratic National Committee?"

Abby nodded. "One and the same. Been around a long time. Came up through the ranks of the unions."

"So how'd they get involved in this?"

"I don't know," Abby answered. "I just know that Sam's been seeing both of them a lot. They were both over at the house twice, late, in the past month."

It angered Jon a little that Adams met with people like this without telling his staff. No law, of course, said he had to tell his own staff where he was going or whom he met with. But Jon sometimes wished Adams were just a little more forthcoming with information.

Susan, though, never seemed quite as surprised by this sort of thing as Jon was. She seemed to have ways to find things out before Jon did, so Jon sometimes confirmed rumors with her.

To Jon, it seemed at times as if Adams had whole networks that operated independently from his own professional staff—as if Adams worked in several different, distinct universes, and those in each never knew what the other was up to.

Jon often felt that the Sam Adams they saw in the office was only part of a very complex picture. He let them see only what he wanted them to see. The rest he kept hidden. Adams clearly had his own purposes, his own plan. Jon played his part blindly, never sure how much of it had been scripted by Adams or by other unseen, guiding hands.

Now two of those hands had names.

"Doesn't Sam tell you?" Jon asked Abby, half wondering whether he'd crossed the line.

Abby laughed. It was a bitter, ironic laugh. Jon had heard it more than once. "I wish. But Sam doesn't tell me anything. I'm as much in the dark about things as you are. I don't know where he is half the time. And even when he's around, I have a tough time figuring things out. So I gave up a long time ago."

Jon wanted to ask why she'd married him, then—but he *knew* that would be crossing the line. And he figured she had her reasons. Maybe she'd just decided to hitch her wagon to his star and then get out to push when the situation required it. As Jon had. "It's hard for me, too, sometimes," Jon said weakly.

"Yes, dear, but you're not married to him," Abby said, her eyes flashing. "Oh, well. Time to mingle. You two be good. Have fun." Abby whirled, and she was gone. Just like that. Off to the social butterfly races.

"So now what?" Jon asked, smiling.

"I'm famished," Susan said. "Let's eat."

CHAPTER TWENTY-NINE

The front entrance to the vice president's house was blocked by a huge line of lobbyists and other assorted well-wishers, all waiting to greet President Simpson and wish him a happy birthday, so Jon and Susan looked for another way into the house. They wandered through a massive pool and outdoor porch complex and, eventually, through a side entrance that led past a coatroom and a small parlor.

They tried to turn left and wound up in the kitchen. There were a half-dozen people scurrying around with trays of assorted foods. Jon and Susan turned to go back and nearly ran over one of the kitchen staff coming back through the doors.

"Can I help you?" asked the man, a middle-aged Hispanic with short-cropped hair and a fine mustache. He wore a tuxedo, but Jon could tell immediately that he was permanent career staff, one of the silent, unseen legions of people who served presidents and vice presidents from one administration to the next.

"We're lost," Jon said helplessly. "We were trying to find something to eat, and we wound up here."

The man smiled. "It is a common mistake. Please. May I be of service. Allow me to serve you here."

Susan glanced at Jon. This wasn't exactly their idea of a "power" dinner. But it probably beat waiting in line to try to get to the buffet table out in the main dining room. "Is that allowed?" Susan asked him.

"In my kitchen, I am lord of the manor," he replied, bowing slightly. "So, please. What can I get for you?"

Jon held out a hand. "My name's Jon Abelson. I work for Congressman Sam Adams." The man shook Jon's hand vigorously, bowing slightly as he did so. It was a curious gesture, one Jon had not seen in Washington before.

Susan also extended a hand, which the man grasped delicately. "Susan Smalley. I also work for Sam Adams."

"I am Juan Perez."

"And you're the chef?" Jon asked.

Juan shook his head. "No, Mr. Abelson. I run the household here at the vice president's residence. I have served three vice presidents."

"Oh, I see," Jon said. "I just thought, when you said that this was your kitchen . . ."

Juan smiled again. It was a disarming smile, designed to put people at ease. It had the desired effect. "I spend a great deal of time in here. It seems that vice presidents, their family members, and their guests often ask for something from the kitchen. Take your Mr. Adams, for instance. If I recall correctly, the last time he was here, he asked for a cappuccino and some mint cookies."

Jon's jaw nearly dropped. "The last time? When was that?"

"Congressman Adams has been here a number of times for meetings with President Simpson and several of his Cabinet secretaries," Juan said evenly. "Usually in the evenings."

Jon glanced over at Susan. "Did you know that?" he asked her.

Susan looked at Jon, unblinking. "No, I didn't. But you know Sam. He sees people all the time, and we don't always know about it."

"But the president of the United States?" Jon asked, trying not let his anger get the better of him. "Shouldn't we know about that?"

"Not really," Susan said, shrugging. "Sam always tells us things when the time is right. I'm not worried. And you shouldn't be either."

"I'm not worried!" Jon snapped. "It's just that—" He stopped and looked over at Juan Perez. But Juan's face was impassive, expressionless. A thought suddenly occurred to Jon. "At those meetings, the ones with Congressman Adams. There weren't two other gentlemen here as well, were there? Jonas Brownlee and Nathaniel Watson?"

Juan thought for a moment, unfazed and unblinking. "Yes, those gentlemen were here as well, I believe," he answered.

Susan took Jon's arm. "Hey! I'm hungry. Can we get something to eat now?"

Juan nodded and turned. Jon and Susan followed. Juan stepped deftly between several servers attempting to get food onto platters and out of the kitchen. Jon and Susan followed his lead, trying to keep out of the way. They chose an entree and several side dishes, and then Juan led them out the back of the kitchen onto a small, covered patio.

"You may eat out here, if you like," Juan said. "It is private. You will not be disturbed."

Jon looked around. "Is this . . . ?"

"It is where the kitchen help often come to eat or read," Juan said. "It is our place. But you are welcome here. Please. Enjoy your meal. I must get back to the other guests."

"Thank you, Mr. Perez," Jon said.

"It is my pleasure, sir. Enjoy the party." Juan almost faded back into the kitchen. He was gone in an instant.

Jon began to pick at his food in silence. The news that Adams had been here on several occasions was profoundly disturbing to him. Yes, he knew that Adams had his own networks and often kept his own counsel. But meetings with the president! What if some reporter should get wind of it and ask Jon about it? He'd sound so stupid denying it, only to find out later that it had actually happened. And he'd lose all credibility with the press.

"So it really doesn't bother you?" Jon finally asked Susan.

Susan was eating her own meal with gusto. She approached nearly everything in her life in the same way—with boundless energy and enthusiasm. It was one of the things about her that attracted Jon. Susan was always eager to move on to the next thing, the higher level, a new challenge. No mountain peak was high enough to sufficiently challenge her.

"Jon, relax," Susan said between bites. "You know how Sam is. He meets with all sorts of folks we never hear about. I don't know about you, but I don't want to hear about those meetings. If it isn't on the public calendar and Sam doesn't want to tell me about it, then that's fine with me."

"Well, it's not with me," Jon said sullenly. "What if some snooping reporter should ask about them?"

"Don't worry," Susan reassured him. "They won't. And you know it."

"But what if—"

"Eat, you!" Susan commanded. She reached a hand across the table, took Jon's hand, and placed it on a fork for him. It was a gentle, urging gesture. As he always did when Susan touched him, Jon felt a desire to touch her back, to keep touching her.

But he did as he was told. Neither of them mentioned Adams's meetings with the president for the rest of the meal. But Jon knew that he wouldn't forget what he'd learned.

They left their dishes in the kitchen and made their way back to the main part of the residence, where the other guests were. Neither of them knew anyone at the party, of course, so they spent the better part of the evening listening to the soft jazz quartet near the back of the room and watching Abby and Sam work the crowd. It was quite a show.

Sam was a perpetual motion machine. They spied him talking with four different Cabinet secretaries during the evening, including the HHS secretary.

Sometimes Abby was at his side. But, more often than not, she was working the crowd on her own, zeroing in on large groups of women.

In fact, both of them used the receiving line as an opportunity to meet and greet people. Both of them walked up and down the line, standing to chat with one person or another for a few moments before moving on.

Neither Jon nor Susan even considered getting into that line. It was easily taking people an hour or more to get through it. All for a handshake, a picture to hang on your wall, and the opportunity to tell your friends that you'd spoken to the president of the United States at his birthday party. It made Jon wish he were somewhere else.

Adams finally came up to the two of them as the evening was closing down. "All right, kids, I've made the rounds. You ready to get to work?"

Jon shrugged. "I was ready before we got here. Just tell us what to do."

"Okay," Adams said, placing a fatherly hand on Jon's arm. "First thing in the morning."

CHAPTER THIRTY

Jon almost turned around and walked back out of the Longworth office the next morning, thinking he'd walked into the wrong office by mistake.

A dozen or so young black men gathered in the cramped front office, several of them milling around Sharon Simpson's desk and the rest either sitting in the chairs in the small waiting area or simply standing in the center of the space.

Jon politely elbowed his way through the crowd and made his way to Sharon's chair. "What's going on?" he quietly asked Adams's personal secretary. "Who are these guys?"

Sharon frowned at him, clearly unhappy about the crowd gathered around her. "They aren't on the calendar, that's for sure."

"Did you hear from Sam?" Jon asked. To the public, Jon referred to his boss as "Congressman." Here in the office he used Adams's first name.

Sharon nodded. "Real quickly, from his car phone. He said some men would be coming by for a meeting and just to keep them happy until he arrived."

"Arranged by whom?"

"By the White House, with help from the DNC," he said.

Jon turned and studied the men. Now that he'd had a chance to gather his wits, he realized with some surprise that he recognized several of them. They'd been at that first meeting Jon had gone to with Adams back in Singleton. They were some of the young men from Adams's "club." And, since it was unlikely that they'd flown in from Ohio that morning, they must have flown in before Jon and Susan had even learned about Adams's plans.

"Who paid for their flight in? I hope we didn't," Jon said quietly.

"I don't know a thing about it," Sharon answered. "But my guess is they're not our responsibility."

"Good." Jon scanned the room again. None of the men looked back at him, or anyone else on the staff, for that matter. They kept to themselves, talked among themselves. They were here for a purpose, not to socialize. They reminded Jon of a picture he'd seen of paid mercenaries waiting for their orders.

The private line on Sharon's phone rang, the one that Adams always used. Sharon picked it up. "Yes?" She listened for a moment. "Okay, I'll tell him." She hung up the phone. "Mr. Adams is downstairs in the car. He wants you to meet him there."

"Right now?"

"Right now. He's waiting for you at the curb."

Jon shook his head. He took the stairs down, because it was faster. Adams's car was parked at the curb, the emergency blinkers going. Adams signaled for Jon to climb in.

As Jon slid into the passenger seat, Adams handed him a thick file. "Here," he said. "Read this while I drive around the block. I want you to be prepared before we start this meeting."

"With those guys up in the office?"

"Just read." Adams switched the emergency blinkers off and eased the car into traffic. Jon began to read.

On the top of the file were classified, internal field reports from FBI offices around the country. Jon scanned them quickly. At least a half dozen of them all said roughly the same thing.

Armed groups were beginning to position themselves for conflict in the large metropolitan areas of the country in cities like Washington, D.C., Chicago, Los Angeles, and Detroit. It appeared to be orchestrated on a national level of some sort, because nearly all of the FBI field reports indicated that weapons caches were the same, instructions obtained by informants were similar, and the goals—intimidation of local administration—were also similar.

In fact, each of the FBI reports predicted bluntly that there would be violence in these areas—some orchestrated, some me-too. There was no escaping the fact, the FBI reports said. Conflict was coming—and soon—to the inner cities of America.

There were also reports, based on eyewitness accounts from inside informants, of organizational meetings of what could only be described as quasi-terrorist cells from militant groups, both black and white. Their goals were murky, other than to incite violence. It was pretty scary stuff, obviously top secret, although Jon wondered how the FBI had managed to so thoroughly keep these developments out of the public eye.

The FBI was often called upon, Jon knew, to contain a certain amount of this kind of violence. But these reports made it clear that there had been a proliferation of these groups in recent years, to the point that now too many of these groups existed for the FBI to monitor and control.

The file also contained some clips from local newspapers in the areas, describing what seemed to be sporadic incidents of violence—street shootings, cars blown up, metro trains derailed, things like that. A few of those stories Jon had seen on national news, but there had been no suggestion that any of them had been linked. Now, based on what Jon had seen in these reports, the conclusion could be reached that some loose coordination was going on between these shadowy groups.

Last in the file was a confidential assessment of the potential for multi-city violence in the streets that summer in major metropolitan areas. The assessment had been prepared by the staff of the president's National Security Council, which included all of his top domestic and international intelligence and military advisors.

The NSC staff report predicted flatly that—unless fairly radical restructuring occurred in the way in which money, funds, and programs were delivered to the poor and disadvantaged in America's major cities—there would be a massive uprising in those communities. In short, the report concluded, people were fed up with the status quo. They wanted something different, and they would fight for that change.

Attached to the NSC document—and clearly prepared by the president's national security staff as well—was a brief description of one of the groups right in the thick of things, the World of Allah.

The World of Allah was a slightly less militant offshoot of two other black activist networks, one step removed from the Nation of Islam and the Black Panther organizations, according to the NSC staff document.

The Black Panther movement had been largely formed along military lines. The Nation of Islam, similarly, had been formed as a sort of elite paramilitary shock team. They'd made a name for themselves by going into housing projects to protect the residents there with a swash-buckling, in-your-face style.

Several young leaders from the Nation of Islam had left after a run-in with Louis Farrakhan, the charismatic, virulently anti-Semitic leader who'd made the Nation of Islam well-known nationally but who had a penchant for making outrageous statements that inflamed racial tensions.

Those leaders had subsequently formed the World of Allah, which had, not surprisingly, taken a different direction from the Nation of Islam. They had set up a vast network of more than two hundred clinics that served the indigent in the inner cities. They'd essentially formed buyers' clubs—almost like HMOs—and bought bulk medical supplies from brand-name and generic drug companies and then provided those to the clinics virtually at cost.

The World of Allah made money because they also demanded compensation from the drug firms—shipping and handling fees for moving the packages, essentially, in addition to the bulk drugs that they were practically given for free. Those terms were outrageous, of course, but the drug firms, fearing adverse publicity, complied. Providing the drugs for the clinics was a pittance in their overall budget, and the goodwill they received from the program was worth it.

Jon finished reading and closed the file. "Is all this true, the stuff about the violence?"

"Believe it," Adams said somberly.

"And why do you have this?"

"Because the president thinks we can help," Adams said. "That's what this meeting is about. We have to get folks into those communities to start talking. And we have to start proposing a huge change in the welfare system. We have to turn the whole thing upside down. We want the inner cities to start hearing about the plan we discussed last evening, and not from us."

"Those men up in your office. They're—what?"

"The first wave of ambassadors to the inner-city communities. Their tickets here were paid for by the DNC's task force on welfare reform."

"Ambassadors for what?"

"For change. Big change. Radical change. We have to plant the seeds now, in a hurry. We're going to turn the world upside down, Jon. These men are going to help us get the word out."

"The DNC has money for this kind of thing?"

"Sure they do," Adams answered, continuing to drift along in traffic. "The DNC always has money for grassroots projects and coalition-building activities. And if the president orders something, it's done. No questions asked. And he's ordered this."

"So who are these guys, exactly? I recognized some of them from back in Singleton."

Sam nodded. "That's right. Some are mine. The others are hand-picked by Jonas Brownlee from other groups. They'll be special

146

'ambassadors' for the DNC. Each will be assigned to meet with a different special African-American interest group. Once they've cut their teeth, they'll be on the road for the next month, meeting with groups targeted by the DNC."

"Then what?"

"Eventually, other 'ambassadors' will go to other groups as well—seniors who are active in the party, women, Hispanic-Americans, gay activists sympathetic to the plan, and union leaders."

Jon looked out the window. It was a big plan. But, if the FBI reports and the NSC assessment were right, it would take a plan of this scope to help. "You think it'll work?"

"It has to," Adams said. "This first wave is critical, and I want it done right. I want my own troops trained and moved into action. If poor blacks don't buy into the plan, then the other groups won't matter. The African-American community has to be mollified and made to understand that this is in their best interest. If we fail in that, then we've failed the president."

Jon looked over at Adams with renewed respect. He felt, at that moment, that he was at the control center of the universe. "What do you want me to do?"

Adams smiled. "I'm giving you the hardest assignment I can dream up. There's a clinic in the middle of a rampant drug district in southeast Washington. It serves the unofficial medical arm of the World of Allah. You read the description of the group in there."

"Yeah."

"Well, I want you to go there with a guy by the name of Jamal Wickes. He's up in my office with the others. The two of you are going to meet with Dr. Sira Sindar there."

"And what do we talk about?"

Adams laughed harshly. "What else? Money. Everything always comes back to that anyway. Even this."

CHAPTER THIRTY-ONE

Jamal Wickes was in his early twenties. His head was clean shaven. He wore black jeans, a tight black shirt, and a small gold ring in his left ear. He was also finishing up an M.B.A. at the Harvard School of Business.

Some day, Jon figured, as they rode down I Street toward the World of Allah clinic, Jamal Wickes would be someone to be reckoned with. But for now, he looked distinctly unhappy taking orders from Jon. He clearly did not like being paired with a white guy. But he kept quiet about it.

The clinic was in southeast Washington, deep in the heart of the drug district. One of the office interns was driving Jamal and Jon there. Jon stared dully out the window.

No white faces lined either side of the street. As they stopped at lights, black faces peered in at him as if he were some sort of invading alien. Jon felt uncomfortable and out of place. He did not belong here. Every probing pair of eyes told him that loudly and clearly.

The clinic was in a dilapidated brick building that had once been a tire and auto store. Now, the showroom was the waiting room, and the room where tires had been rotated once upon a time was reserved for private examinations.

On the second floor in a small office over the "showroom" of the place furnished with a seedy couch, a chipped, wooden table, and several folding chairs, they waited for Dr. Sira Sindar. The clinic's medical director, Dr. Sindar was the preeminent medical voice within the World of Allah network and one of the best-known faces of black activism in America, appearing on *Good Morning, America*, and the *Today* show regularly. Whenever a medical story with an ethnic dimension made the national news, they turned to Dr. Sindar for commentary.

He had a medical degree from one of the top black medical colleges, Meharry, and he'd developed a specialty in treating infectious diseases. So, when the AIDS epidemic had grown beyond the gay community and had begun to ravage the inner city, Dr. Sindar had been propelled forward as an activist spokesman.

He regularly debated leading government scientists from the CDC, NIH, or FDA, or top corporate officials over the pace and timing of medical advances to help the inner city. Dr. Sindar had become adept at accusing either the government or the private sector of blatant or inadvertent racism, without appearing to be strident about it.

Dr. Sindar delivered his messages with such a calm, reassuring, baritone voice that audiences simply took what he said at face value without questioning the underlying logic of what he was saying.

And what Dr. Sindar said, mostly, was that blacks were getting the short end of the stick. Much of their medical care was handled in either emergency room settings or indigent clinics such as this one in drug-infested southeast Washington. He demanded better care for his constituencies, and he would continue speaking out until he achieved at least some of his goals.

"Don't be mistaken," Adams had warned Jon that morning. "Just because Sindar's a doctor and smooth on television, don't misjudge him. He's on the governing board of the World of Allah, and that organization doesn't make a move that he isn't fully aware of. You get Sindar's support, and you have the World of Allah's support."

"Welcome!" a large black man said in a booming voice as he swept into the room, shaking their hands firmly. "I'm Dr. Sira Sindar."

"Jamal Wickes," Jon's partner said crisply.

"Jon Abelson. We spoke on the phone."

"So," Dr. Sindar said, sweeping a hand around the room. "Do you like my palatial office?"

Jon glanced around the place again. "Could use some work."

"Work, my boy?" Dr. Sindar laughed. "It needs more than that. Perhaps a good, clean fire and a new start."

"That can be arranged," Jamal said, grinning wickedly.

Dr. Sindar gestured toward the chairs. "Come. Let us sit and talk. I have only the most rudimentary understanding of the purpose of your mission this morning."

Jon took a seat. Jamal did not, choosing instead to lean against the wall beside the one window in the place.

"So you know a little of why we're here?" Jon asked him.

"Some, from my good friend, Jonas Brownlee, over at the DNC," Dr. Sindar said, instinctively lowering his voice a little as he invoked Brownlee's name.

Brownlee again. He was a legend in the party. He'd been a caucus vice chairman at the DNC for decades. He single-handedly controlled virtually every special-interest group with any clout within the party's ranks. If Brownlee said listen, you listened. If he said jump, you jumped and waited for him to tell you when to land again.

Once upon a time—in the early 1980s after former President Reagan had almost reduced the Democratic Party to rubble—a former chairman of the DNC had attempted to dismantle the special-interest caucuses—the black, gay, women, and union caucuses—within the party. He'd successfully dethroned the existing vice-chairs of each of those caucuses.

But he had failed to remove Brownlee. And, over the years, Brownlee had nurtured and then resurrected the caucuses. Now they were back in full battle armor and ready for a fight. Brownlee was their designated leader, and they didn't make a move without consulting him first and often.

Brownlee and Nathaniel Watson were probably a lot alike, Jon reasoned. Washington was, in many ways, a small town, run by a handful of men and women who simply kept changing jobs and titles. Worker bees flitted from hive to hive, but the queen bees remained, directing the work in progress at all times.

The public didn't know who Brownlee and Watson were and probably never would, unless some scandal brought their behind-the-scenes activities into an unfavorable light. No, the public heard about congressmen and women and senators and presidents and Cabinet secretaries who took credit—or blame—for actions. Yet the Brownlees and Watsons often dictated Washington's swirling policy discussions. The public recognized the faces of Washington. Brownlee and Watson knew and understood those faces and told them what to say.

"So you've talked this through with Brownlee?" Jon asked. Adams, of course, had not bothered to tell him how deeply Brownlee was involved in all of this. And Jon still wasn't sure which network Adams had tapped into.

"A little," Dr. Sindar said. "But not enough to have a sense of what is required. Or what benefit the World of Allah may accrue in such a glorious enterprise on behalf of the state."

"I think you'll appreciate what the World of Allah stands to gain by supporting this initiative," Jon said, choosing his words carefully.

He didn't want to overpromise. "But can you tell me a little about what you do?"

"The clinics, you mean?" Dr. Sindar sat back in his chair, which creaked heavily. "Happy to. This clinic is one of the first we started. We leased the space for a dollar and then asked every doctor we knew to give us just one day a month to come in here and see patients for free. Eventually, we found enough so that our clinic was staffed every day of the month.

"Then we went to the pharmaceutical and medical device companies. We asked them to contribute. After some discussion about how it might be in their best interest to help, we began to receive some free samples. But not enough, really, to adequately treat people. We would, for instance, get one free sample of an antibiotic, enough to serve one patient. But when the second patient came in the door, we had nothing to give.

"So we decided to go into the business of procuring and distributing medicines ourselves. The World of Allah hired a pharmacist. We opened other clinics in every major city in the nation. We negotiated prices with the drug firms. And we give people good drugs now for almost nothing."

"So it works?" Jon asked.

"Yes, it works. But not well enough," Dr. Sindar said, frowning. "We have very limited choices of antibiotics to give people, for instance. When amoxicillin doesn't work, we often don't have anything different. Plus, it takes our limited staff hours and hours to fill out all the paperwork to get Medicaid or Medicare money—or anything else from the government. So we could do much, much better with just a little more money and a better system."

Jon paused. "And if you had the money and a central purchasing system to make everything easier?"

Dr. Sindar smiled broadly. He had two gold teeth, which gleamed even in the dim, soft light of the office. "Why, we'd be in heaven, my boy."

"Then let us talk, sir," Jon said, scooting his chair closer to the desk. "Because I believe we are about to become allies in the good fight."

CHAPTER THIRTY-TWO

The phone rang. Jon opened one eye groggily. It was just after eleven o'clock. He picked up the phone. "Hello?"

"So what did you think of Sindar?"

"Sam?"

"Yes, it's me. Sorry it's so late. I just got back to the house. So what did you think of Sindar?"

Jon didn't even bother to ask him where he'd been. Adams was always so vague about that kind of thing. "Sindar's an interesting guy. Very into his World of Allah thing."

"Did you strike a deal?"

"Yeah. We have a deal."

"Good boy," Adams said. Jon could hear the excitement in his voice. "I knew you could handle it."

"You know, Sam, he's gonna want money. Maybe a lot of it."

"Don't worry. Money we can handle. There's always money for the right things."

"And *is* this the right thing, what we're doing?"

"Of course. We're helping people," Adams said confidently. "Never forget that. We're in it for the people, Jon. Always. We'd be nothing without them."

"If you say so."

"I do. Now get some sleep. You'll need it. Lots of work left."

Jon groaned and hung up.

CHAPTER THIRTY-THREE

"There he is. Right on time," the clerk said cheerily from behind the counter at the Bagel Bakery, a couple of blocks down Pennsylvania from the House office buildings. Jon glanced up at the clock on the wall—6:00. In the morning.

He and Susan had begun meeting there each morning before work began at the office. They had no choice, really. The plan Adams had put in motion was so huge, it threatened to overwhelm them. The only way they'd been able to manage was to meet every day for two hours to go over things before the new day actually started.

"Gimme something good," Jon growled. He was whipped. The long work days were taking their toll, but he wouldn't rest until the foundation had been laid, as Adams put it.

"The usual? A sourdough bagel with melted butter and a large coffee?" the bagel guy asked him.

"Yeah. Why not?" Jon leaned up against the counter. A faint tinkling sounded at the entrance to the shop as the door swung open. Jon didn't turn around. He knew it was Susan. No one else was crazy enough to be out at this hour.

Susan slipped an arm around his waist as she came up behind him. Jon squeezed her hand affectionately. He was convinced that they had one of the strangest "dating" arrangements in history. They never had a chance to actually go out anywhere. Instead, they spent their time at meetings over one thing or another, usually at odd hours.

"So did HHS finally come through with the money?" she asked, moving straight into business. As usual.

153

"At the end of the day yesterday," Jon said, frowning. "I was ready to kill somebody, it was taking so long."

"You? Kill somebody?" Susan said in mock horror.

The deal with the World of Allah had been easier to consummate than Jon could have imagined going in. But Adams had been right. It was the money. That had made all the difference.

Jamal Wickes was now the liaison between the DNC, Adams's office, the White House, and the Department of Health and Human Services. Jon had been surprised that Adams had chosen someone so young and so green for that important position, but now, weeks after he'd been put there by Adams, Jon had to admit that he was shrewd and effective. And, after weeks of pushing, HHS had come through with the cash for a variety of as-yet-unnamed projects testing ways to streamline health costs. Based on Jon's recommendation, Adams had told someone at the White House to start the paperwork in motion.

Jon then began pressing HHS to award five million of the money it had allocated to the World of Allah to start a series of pilot projects at clinics in a dozen major metropolitan city clinics. The money would be used to see how inner-city clinics would benefit from a central processing system. Last night, HHS had confirmed the award.

To be honest, Jon was slightly uneasy about all of this. He wasn't entirely sure what the World of Allah would do with the money given to them. He also wasn't convinced that the system was all that beneficial. It certainly benefited the World of Allah and the government. But did it help the poor?

In the end, Jon simply felt that he had to trust Sam Adams. If Sam said it was the right thing to do, then it had to be the right thing to do. Some of Sam's methods might be suspect, but Jon firmly believed that Sam's goals were in the best interests of America.

"How about the other groups?" Jon asked Susan.

"We signed the memorandum of understanding last night with the organizations willing to serve as guinea pigs in the grand experiment," she responded. "We have enough groups now in twelve cities to support a network to serve the poor."

"And Pony Express?"

"It's a go, Sam says. He spoke to the CEO yesterday afternoon."

Pony Express—a large, multinational corporation that had combined banking, telecommunications, and information-processing capabilities in a global network—was going to kick in nearly ten million to pay for

154

the smart cards and the computer-processing capabilities for the federal government's pilot.

"Great," Jon said. "Now that the HHS grant has finally come through, I'm going after the hospital chain today."

A for-profit hospital chain that operated in every major city in America had agreed—in principle—to provide medical services the World of Allah could not handle at a set cost under the pilot program. Jon simply had to make sure they signed the contract.

"What about the oil companies?" Susan asked as they got their food and walked back to "their table"—a booth at the corner of the restaurant that looked out on Pennsylvania Avenue.

"Three of them have agreed to let their gas stations accept the cards in the pilot cities, according to my DNC guy who's been doing that one," Jon said. "They'll sell the gas for about a buck a gallon, at first."

Several DNC staffers now worked nearly full-time in Adams's office in a little makeshift "war room" to handle the myriad of problems that were unearthed every day. When these hired guns came across a problem they couldn't resolve—such as how a family under the pilot program could pay for one item or another with "the card"—Adams or Jon got on the phone and called and called until they found someone at HHS, the White House, or even the private sector who could answer their question and solve the problem.

"My CD thing is almost ready to go," Susan said between bites.

"Yeah?"

Susan had leased a state-of-the-art computer that would be able not just to *read* the digital information stored on CDs, but would also be able to *write* to them. She planned to set it up in one corner of the office. Everything—all the loose ends of the project—would be stored on that computer and, thanks to a new, custom-designed program, tracked over time so that nothing would fall through the cracks.

"Yeah," she said with satisfaction. "I'm gonna call the program 'Genghis Khan.'"

"Good name."

"I thought so."

Jon looked at Susan, and then looked away. Even though they'd been seeing each other casually for a while now, Jon still felt at times as if he didn't really know her. It bothered him. He wanted to know Susan's heart, her soul, everything that made her what she was.

Susan was not a Christian, at least not yet. Jon was working on her. Susan had been raised in a household where they'd elevated atheism practically to a religion. Susan had read plenty on the subject of religion, and she and Jon, when they had time, had rousing discussions on the existence of God.

Susan argued that men and women had an innate sense of right and wrong and that they had to live by certain moral principles and standards established by society. Jon argued that moral principles were established by God through the Bible and that Jesus Christ taught humankind how to live by those principles.

No, Susan always argued—someone who lived two thousand years ago could not possibly help you live by moral standards in today's world.

Yes, Jon argued, he could, because Jesus Christ rose from the dead and works in your life today, through the gentle urging of the Holy Spirit, to teach you righteousness.

That was hogwash, Susan said. Where was the proof that God existed? Could you see him, touch him, talk to him?

He is everywhere, Jon would answer. C. S. Lewis had written that the supernatural is superimposed over the natural. God's transcendence is everywhere in the natural world.

They argued like that for hours—on those rare occasions when they had hours to argue. Susan lived by her own strict rules. She held herself to a certain standard, she said, and she didn't care what anyone else thought. She did what she thought was right.

But what would happen, Jon would press, when Susan's personal moral standards were put to the ultimate test—when she was confronted with a choice of doing good for a larger cause even though it violated her own standards? Would she violate those standards—and herself—for the greater good, or would she obey her own moral code? And what happens to you when you violate your own moral code? Do you repent? Is there any need to say that you are sorry?

Silly questions, Susan always responded. You do what you think is right, for yourself first and then for others if you can.

But to Jon they weren't silly questions, because they were part of the puzzle of who Susan was. Despite his intense desire to solve that puzzle and move closer to its subject, he knew that, for now, he would have to put his personal feelings for Susan aside—or at least not act on them. There was simply too much that needed to be done in a very short time.

One thing was certain, though. Despite a few fits and starts, Jon and Susan and the rest of Adams's team had become awfully proficient at their jobs. Jon kept the liaison personnel and the network leaders working together, Adams found the right buttons or decision makers to push, and Susan managed every detail, down to the last invoice and paper clip.

What they had established—without anyone really being aware of it but themselves—was a system in each of the pilot cities through which the poor could use one card to cover all of their basic needs. All of them. That was Adams's plan.

They would get their medical care at the World of Allah clinics, their food from community-based stores that obtained much of their food straight from the farms, their housing support through a new HUD pilot program, and their clothing from surplus warehouse chains that also accepted "the card."

And if some needs weren't covered, they could tell the community liaison who Jon and Adams had handpicked and sent in to ride herd. The problem would get fixed. The system worked. It was almost ruthlessly efficient.

Virtually no one in Congress knew the total picture. The staffs on each of the authorizing and appropriating committees knew of the pilot projects in their area of jurisdiction. But no single committee had jurisdiction over all of them.

HHS officials had a broader understanding, of course, because they covered some of the basic needs. A few at HUD also had an inkling of the scope of the project.

At the White House, Adams said, a small task force that reported directly to the president monitored the program. It was from that task force that Adams, presumably, got his authorization and marching orders. Jon was never quite sure. He just knew that when he took a question or problem to Adams, it was dealt with quickly.

By just the spring of his second year in office, Adams had become a "force." Old-timers in Congress said there was always one in every new Congress, a star who stepped forward as a freshman and pushed a new idea through the cluttered marketplace of ideas and actually achieved a significant public policy goal.

Just a week earlier, the White House had unveiled the varied components of the program at a lavish White House ceremony in the Indian Treaty Room of the Old Executive Office building. Nearly all of the Cabinet secretaries had attended to the details of how their departments would establish the pilot projects.

Families who would be served by the program were flown in so that they could tell their stories. Store owners came, too, to tell how much simpler the new system would be.

Dr. Sindar of the World of Allah almost immediately became the public face and champion of the program. Within days of the White

House announcement of the pilot program, every media outlet was clamoring for him to appear.

Overnight, it seemed, the public policy community of Washington had latched onto the program. In one bold stroke, Adams and the White House team had fused both welfare and health reform into an innovative program that might actually work. The fruits of their labors were there for the world to see.

Why had it happened so quickly? Because Washington, as well as the rest of the country, had tired of the endless debates over health care and welfare reform. Everyone was ready for some evidence that a new system would actually work. The pilot projects gave everyone that evidence.

Jon closed his eyes as he munched the last of his bagel. He was so tired. He just wanted to go off somewhere and sleep for three days. But, of course, that was impossible. He had a hundred calls to make that day, at least.

"So what happens today?" Jon asked.

"Calls, calls . . ."

"And more calls," Jon said wearily. "I know. I feel like the phone's part of my head now."

Susan reached across the table and patted his head affectionately. "Don't worry, poor baby. It's all for a good cause. Never forget that."

CHAPTER THIRTY-FOUR

Jon had seen the CNN report so many times during the afternoon and evening that he practically had the thing memorized. He had a tiny TV that sat perched on top of his computer terminal, and he always kept it tuned to CNN. Nearly every office in D.C. did the same thing. It was how you kept plugged in.

And keeping plugged in was especially critical for press aides to members of Congress. They had to know about breaking news in case their boss wanted to "surf" his way into the unfolding news event.

But today's big news wasn't a Washington story—not yet, at least. Three riots had erupted in three major American cities, almost simultaneously. And exactly as the FBI reports Adams had shown Jon had predicted.

Several buildings were burning in Chicago, after homemade bombs had blown out their windows. A handful of cars were burning in the streets of Los Angeles, and an oil-slick fire was burning on the Mississippi River near St. Louis.

What so absorbed Jon was that, for the first time, the blind and deaf national media had actually picked up on the possibility that, somehow, the acts of violence in these cities might somehow be connected through some subterranean network.

No notes were found claiming credit for the violence, of course. But there were subtle clues that, perhaps, the idea behind the outbursts had come from some common source.

CNN had interviewed people on the streets in all three cities, and their stories were full of despair.

"People just mad," said a middle-aged black woman, mother of three in a project in Chicago's south side. "They got no money to pay fo' things. It all be so expensive. Ain't no way none o' us can afford to live."

"They better do somethin' quick," said a young black man in his twenties. "Where there's no hope, there gonna be violence, like today."

In all three cities, the looters had come out in force almost immediately after the violence started. Storefronts were bashed in. Consumer items were stolen. The TV cameras captured fleeting images of people racing along the streets with their hands full of stolen items and fire in the background.

Somewhere in those three areas CNN kept profiling, Sam Adams had people trying to talk to the leaders of groups who worked in the inner cities. They were trying to get something started, bring some money into the system. Maybe it would help. Something had to work, or a dozen inner cities in America were going to blow sky high.

Maybe some day their efforts—his and Adams's and Susan's—to simplify everything and make it easier for the poor to survive in the inner city would stop all this madness. Jon didn't know. But he would trust Adams and his plan. He had to.

Jon glanced at the clock that hung, somewhat crookedly, over the entrance to the office. It was just after nine o'clock in the evening. He'd been at work for fifteen hours already that day. The building was quiet. Only a few mad staffers were still there, banging away.

Susan peeked her head around the corner of Adams's office. "You want any coffee?" she called.

Jon shook his head. "Nope. I've had about fourteen cups already today."

"Ever thought about just taking it intravenously?" Susan said, smiling.

"Only if it's covered by the card," quipped Jon.

"Well, you'll need something," Susan said. "Sam just called from his car phone, on the way back from that White House meeting. He said he has something important to talk to us about."

"Tonight?"

"Yes, tonight. Sam says we'll have to move fast to take advantage of an opportunity."

Jon groaned. He didn't want any more opportunities. He wanted a vacation.

Adams got there close to 9:30. Jon was nursing a cup of coffee when he arrived. They gathered in his office.

Adams sat behind his desk and rubbed his eyes. Jon could see that he was even more tired than he and Susan were. Adams never seemed to rest or sleep. He was always moving, always on the phone, always making some deal happen.

But when Adams looked up, Jon could see it immediately. A kind of hunger shone in his eyes, an insatiable appetite for something that was just within his grasp. It was an intangible thing, but Jon had seen it before.

"We have an opportunity," he said softly, looking directly at the two of them.

"What kind?" Jon asked.

"It'll require one whale of a lot of spadework to get it right," Adams answered.

"So what is it already?" Susan pressed.

Adams leaned back in his chair. "Either of you know anything about Senator Whitt Johnson? Know much about him? Where he came from, what he's done?"

"Nothing other than what I've read in the papers," Jon shrugged. "Seems like an okay guy. Keeps a low profile since the governor appointed him. Votes right, stays out of trouble."

"What about the reporters? What do they think of him?" Adams asked.

There was a small, tight group of Washington bureau reporters who covered the Ohio congressional delegation pretty closely. Almost too closely, in Jon's opinion. They reported on every little move that the delegation made.

Back in Ohio, for instance, the welfare and health reform program Adams had put together had been front-page news for weeks. Adams's face had been liberally plastered across several of those newspapers regularly. Adams was big news in Ohio, even if he was still fairly obscure on the national scene.

"They don't think he's messed up," Jon mused. "They seem to think he's done all right. Votes with the president, mostly."

Senator Johnson was a freshman Democratic senator who'd been appointed to fill Senator John Glenn's seat when Glenn had abruptly decided to retire midterm. Johnson had been CEO of a large manufacturing firm when he'd been tapped to fill Glenn's seat.

The appointment had been a natural. Johnson had been one of the state party's principal financial eagles for years and had served as finance chair for two gubernatorial and two senate races. Johnson was a bland political personality but a safe choice to fill Glenn's seat. He worked hard for the party—plus, he could raise money, which was just about the only thing that mattered in politics.

Senator Johnson would face the voters of the state for the first time in a general election later that year. He had no Democratic primary opposition, of course. But no fewer than three strong Republican candidates—

including the lieutenant governor and the state Senate Majority Leader—
were competing in a primary to take him out in the general election.

"So they don't think he's vulnerable?" Adams asked.

Jon shook his head. "Not really. His fund-raising is in pretty good
shape. The unions seem to like him. He hasn't said anything dumb. And
he looks good on TV."

"So the reporters like him?" Adams said.

"I wouldn't say they like him."

"Respect him?"

"No, not exactly," Jon said. "They think he's done an adequate job.
He's done all right for someone who was appointed."

Adams leaned forward in his chair. His face almost glowed with
intensity. "And if it came out that he had some problems? What would
they think then?"

Jon blinked. "They'd take him out," he answered, his voice almost
a whisper. "If they had proof."

Adams reached down and pulled a file from the black leather briefcase that never left his side. He slid it across the desk toward Jon. Susan
moved her chair close so she could look at the file over Jon's shoulder. Jon
couldn't help but notice that he really liked the perfume Susan was
wearing, but now wasn't the time for such thoughts.

It was a photocopy of an internal FBI surveillance document. It
almost looked like the original, which told Jon that Adams had been given
a clean copy straight out of the original file. In Washington, where documents were often used as smoking guns, you could always tell how "hot"
something was by how faded it had become through multiple copying
and faxing.

But this FBI document was on the first leg of what Jon was certain
would be many, many journeys. And he wondered, almost with a queasy
feeling, how many of those journeys he would be personally responsible for.

The document was the result of a joint investigation by the U.S.
Postal Service and the FBI. It was a report to the FBI director, detailing
the findings of a domestic surveillance of purchasing activities by a handful of American citizens in different parts of the country.

Jon skimmed over the first few paragraphs quickly. It centered on a
publication called the "International Boys & Men Club." Jon began to
feel quite ill as he read through the document.

A magazine published in Denmark contained pictures of little boys
in very explicit activities with men. The boys were of all different races,

and the magazine apparently promised to deliver discreet, confidential contacts with "chicken hawks" through a post-office box.

The FBI and postal inspectors had followed the publication to a handful of mailing addresses in the United States and had begun an investigation of the recipients of the magazine.

The laws against child pornography in the United States were strong, much stronger than those governing adult pornography. The powers granted federal authorities in regulating child pornography gave them wide discretion to tap phones, order surveillance of residences, open mail, and all sorts of things usually prohibited or discouraged in other policing activities. Men convicted of buying magazines like this were usually convicted and sentenced to prison for at least a few years. The FBI didn't usually try to actually catch the men in acts of pedophilia. That was difficult.

But that meant, of course, that the men usually served only a year or two in a low-level prison before being paroled, and then they were free to move to other parts of the country and pick up their activities under new identities. Often, the FBI found those same men receiving the same magazines under new names.

Toward the end of the document, he found it. The sentences almost jumped off the page. One of the mail drops was at a post-office box near Dulles International Airport, west of Washington.

Through a law passed when the airport was built, the post office at Dulles was part of the District of Columbia, even though it was not physically located there. Post office boxes there had a D.C. address. International mail that came in to Dulles went straight to the boxes there, without going through a central processing facility.

It was quite convenient for international travelers who did not have a Washington office or who wanted to pretend that they had one or who wanted to have confidential mail delivered to Washington without risking it being seen by others.

The FBI had tried for months, apparently, to discover who had opened the post-office box at Dulles. It had been purchased for a six-year period a little over a year ago in the name of J. Smith. The box had been paid for with $125 in cash.

There was no record of who J. Smith was, according to interviews with the post-office employees who worked in the office. The FBI had opened a number of the deliveries to the box, but nothing had been found in any of them to indicate who the recipient might actually be.

The FBI had eventually planted an agent at the post office for several weeks to discover who was receiving the mail. One day a courier showed up with a key, opened the box, and took the contents with him.

The FBI agent followed the courier back to Washington, where he delivered the mail to a huge law firm on K Street. The FBI agent, perhaps unwisely, asked the receptionist for the name of the recipient of the couriered package. The receptionist would not give out the name and called one of the partners to come talk to the agent.

From that point, the FBI's surveillance was clearly blown. The partner said the mail was privileged client-lawyer material and that the FBI had stepped over the line. There was no follow-up, other than to obtain a detailed printout of the list of clients of that law firm.

That list, naturally, was extensive. But one of the names listed, without any speculation, was U.S. Senator Whitt Johnson. He'd retained the law firm shortly after coming to Washington.

Several weeks later, the FBI document concluded, the subscription to the Dulles post-office box had been canceled. "J. Smith" had called the post office to cancel it. The money had not been refunded, at the caller's request.

Jon closed the file and handed it back to Adams. "And?" he asked. "Is that it?"

"No, it's not." Adams handed him a second file. This file contained several different documents from a number of different sources.

The first document was a State Department e-mail, coded "confidential." It was a summary report from the U.S. embassy in Norway, listing the itinerary for, and participants in, a U.S. delegation to a NATO summit meeting there. One of the participants was Senator Johnson. Unlike most of the other participants who were traveling with spouses, Senator Johnson traveled by himself.

The second document was another "confidential" summary of activities, this from the CIA station chief in Brussels, Belgium. It listed a series of NATO meetings and the participants in them. Nearly a dozen meetings had taken place in the past year. Senator Johnson had diligently attended each and every one of them, the only member of the American delegation to attend them all. He had, by default, become the principle U.S. point of contact for the discussions.

The CIA document went on to detail Senator Johnson's role in the delicate negotiations over the reshaping of NATO now that it had subsumed much of the former Warsaw Pact. The document lauded Senator Johnson for his willingness to travel so extensively in Europe on behalf of NATO, even though he was a first-term senator who had reelection responsibilities.

The third document was from the National Security Agency, and Jon wondered as he stared at it how it was that Adams had come to obtain it. It contained "codeword" clearance summaries of satellite surveillance data.

Jon looked up briefly. He had only a minimal clearance level, only what was required for a congressional staff member. He certainly did not have "codeword" clearance. "Can I look at these?" he asked uneasily.

Adams shrugged. "No harm in looking. Read on."

The NSA had the ability—in fact, it had perfected it a number of years ago—to zero in on actual locations on the earth for picture surveillance. This particular picture summary contained a blow-up of a section of a larger photo, showing the license plate of a car. According to the report, that car had been rented to an American citizen traveling in Copenhagen—Senator Johnson, the report said. The car was parked across the street from a building where young male prostitutes—some as young as ten years old—entertained foreign travelers.

That was the last document in the file. Jon closed this file, too, and slid it back across the table to Adams. Too shocked for words, he looked at Susan, expecting to see her similarly troubled. But Susan's face was flushed with excitement. He knew that look. Her mind was racing ahead to the opportunity these documents presented, if handled right.

"There's no proof that Johnson owned that box at Dulles," Jon sighed, trying to think it through.

"No, there isn't," Adams responded.

"And it's perfectly legitimate for Johnson to travel to Europe as much as he does," Jon said. "He's the ranking legislator on the NATO subcommittee, and the Ohio reporters have actually done stories on how he's carved out a niche for himself as the NATO expert in Congress."

"True," Adams said.

"I'm assuming that there's nothing else on his activities in Copenhagen, other than the NSA picture summary?"

"Not as far as I know," Adams said.

"There's no proof that Johnson went into that place in Copenhagen, then, is there?" Jon said, more to himself than to Adams.

"The car was in Johnson's name, though," Susan interjected.

"Yeah, but he could always say he just dropped someone off, or parked there and went somewhere else for a meeting," Jon said. "There were other establishments on that street, I'm sure."

"But it was right across the street from the place," Susan said heatedly.

165

"Not good enough," Jon said.

Susan started to object, but Adams held up a hand. "No, Jon's right. It's not good enough. There isn't any concrete, direct proof. Not enough for a court of law, anyway."

Jon laughed harshly. "But good enough for a reporter or two."

Adams nodded, pleased that Jon got it. "That's what we need to discuss."

A thought occurred to Jon. "So who knows about this? How wide is the circle?"

Adams pursed his lips thoughtfully. "Not many. Maybe fewer than a dozen people."

"Really? That's all?" Jon was surprised.

"Well, think about it. You had the NSA analyst, that person's superior, and then the NSA chief who sent this to his contact at the White House. You had the FBI agent who watched the Dulles box, his superior, and maybe one or two in the FBI director's office. The U.S. embassy in Norway is clueless about what it's reporting. It thinks Johnson is a hero to the NATO cause. The State Department is also in the dark. They just arrange Johnson's foreign travel to the NATO meetings. And, as far as I can tell, the CIA has made no attempt to monitor Johnson's activities outside the NATO meetings. That would be much, much too dangerous to the agency."

"So it really is a small circle, then?" Jon said.

"Looks that way." Adams answered.

"You know," Jon mused, "even if all this is true—and I'd bet the farm it is—it's a long stretch to show that he broke any laws. What he *may* have been doing in Copenhagen—*may* have—is legal there anyway. You can't be arrested for that. And if there's no direct link to the Dulles post-office box, he's also protected there."

Adams nodded. "True, but I don't think voters much care about the law in a case like this. If they have enough proof, they'll throw Johnson out on his ear, whether he actually broke a law or not."

"And do we have enough proof?" Jon asked, hoping that the answer would be no and that this whole ugly thing would just go away.

Adams leaned back in his chair. He put his hands behind his head and stared off into space. "Let me put it this way. First thing tomorrow morning I'm flying back to Ohio to meet with my treasurer and attorney about filing for the U.S. Senate race in Ohio. The White House thinks it might be a good idea. I'm coming right back to D.C., but the process will take about a week, and we don't have to let anyone know just yet."

"And what should we do?" Jon asked, knowing somehow that Adams already had that answer worked out.

Adams looked directly at Jon and smiled gently, almost apologetically. "The White House says there's a new NATO delegation flying to Europe in a day and a half. They're taking one of the Air Force planes. Several White House aides are going along. They'll visit four countries on the trip."

"Including Denmark?" Jon asked.

"Including Denmark. It's first on the trip."

"And Senator Johnson's part of the delegation?"

"That he is," Adams said. "Along with a couple of other special White House guests—you and Susan. And for your trip as tourists, my office is happy to provide a new Canon camera, complete with a lightweight tripod and a telephoto lens."

Jon closed his eyes. Somehow, he should have guessed. "Isn't that—well—kind of illegal?"

"Not at all," Adams said confidently. "You're part of the official delegation. And, as tourists, you can take pictures anywhere you like of any attraction that happens to strike your fancy."

"What if we don't come up with the pictures?" Jon said, his voice almost a whisper again.

Adams shrugged. "Not to worry. I think we have enough already. It would just be nice to nail this particular coffin real tight, don't you think?"

CHAPTER THIRTY-FIVE

Susan was excited about the whole thing—being part of an official White House delegation, traveling overseas, rubbing elbows with senators and their wives, and meeting a couple of top White House aides, including the president's national security advisor. She almost forgot why they were along for the ride.

Jon wondered vaguely if anyone else knew why they were on board. Because they were just congressional aides, they were mostly ignored. Which suited Jon fine. He just wanted to get there and back—with a clear, unambiguous shot of Johnson doing what he should not be doing.

Something about all of this kept nagging at Jon. He'd tried to talk to Susan about it, but she didn't seem to have any qualms about any of it. But that didn't surprise Jon. Susan saw life clearly in black and white—though only from her own perspective, not from God's.

"Look," she'd said. "Even by your standards—"

"Not mine. God's," Jon had interjected.

"Whatever. By your standards, what this guy is doing is flat-out wrong. Isn't that so?"

"Yeah. It's wrong," Jon had answered.

"And, the way I see it, he's doing actual harm to kids. What he's doing is wrong. And if we expose it, we're doing the right thing. There's no other way to look at it."

"Even if Sam profits by it?"

Susan had given Jon a funny look. "And what's wrong with that? He's a good guy and a good boss. We're all in it for the cause. You're his spokesman, for heaven's sake. You speak for him. Surely you must believe in what he's doing."

Still replaying that conversation in his mind, Jon looked across the airplane aisle at Susan. She was sandwiched between a senator's wife and a White House aide, chatting away happily. She didn't seem to worry that she was only a lowly aide. She just pushed her way into conversations, and no one seemed to object.

Throughout the trip to Copenhagen, Jon kept to himself. He wasn't in a mood to mix. Despite Susan's attempt to reassure him, Jon wasn't the least bit reassured.

Whenever he could, Jon watched Senator Johnson out of the corner of his eye. He tried not to look at him directly. He didn't want Johnson paying any attention to him whatsoever. Johnson mostly kept to himself. Twice on the trip over, he slid into a seat next to another senator and had an extended conversation. But, mostly, he kept to himself and read from files in his briefcase, did some paperwork, or read the news magazines he'd brought.

They were met in Copenhagen by a fleet of dark blue Town Cars and whisked off to their downtown hotel. The ride took a half hour or so. Jon spent most of that time trying to familiarize himself with the maps of Copenhagen he'd brought with him. The house he and Susan were looking for was in the seediest part of the city, where all the really nasty stuff happened.

Every major city in the world had its own version of a "red light" district. But Copenhagen was one of the rare cities where that district was protected from the reach of the law. Most of what happened in Copenhagen's "red light" district was protected activity.

Two others were in the car with them as they drove, so Susan didn't say much to Jon. Instead, she kept up a running conversation with the others. But when they arrived at the hotel—an older, brick building that was magnificently restored both inside and out—Susan invited him out for dinner. Jon wasn't hungry; it was actually close to lunch by his own internal clock.

"Why?" Jon asked her in the lobby.

"Because I overheard something," she said, her face a little flushed.

"What?"

"Johnson's going out to eat somewhere," she said. "I heard him mention something to that guy with the thing in his ear."

Jon smiled. "You mean the Secret Service agent-in-charge?" Even though no protected official was on board, because it was a White House delegation and several prominent American officials were aboard, meant that a small Secret Service detail was on board as well. They would generally keep tabs on everyone, although they were not charged with actual protection of any individual.

"Yeah, that guy. Johnson told him where he was going to eat."

"Because the agent has to keep track of him," Jon said, nodding. "And you got the name of the restaurant?"

"I did. So that's where we're going."

Jon shook his head. "You're good at this."

"I know," Susan laughed.

The restaurant was less than five minutes away. In fact, the hotel concierge told them, they easily could walk the distance. After they'd dropped their bags off in their rooms and changed quickly, they left for the restaurant.

As they walked, Susan took Jon's hand, interlocking her fingers with his. Susan loved to hold hands. In fact, she loved the sense of touch—caressing, holding, anything that crossed that mysterious bridge that separates two human beings.

Touch was a funny thing. Occasionally, when Jon was in a strange mood, he would imagine two distinct points in space, moving toward each other, the finite distance between them growing smaller and smaller—but never actually disappearing, only growing infinitely smaller. The sensation of touch belied that odd vision; it reassured you that the distance between two objects can disappear.

Susan squeezed Jon's hand hard. "It's nice being here with you."

Jon looked at her. They'd been dating on and off for more than a year now. In Jon's mind, that was fairly serious. He hadn't really dated others during that time. He knew that Susan had. She didn't say much about that, but it was understood that Jon couldn't just pick up the phone and find her free on a Friday or Saturday night.

"Yeah, it is," he answered. "But, remember, we have a mission. We can't go off sightseeing."

"Oh, I know. But we can enjoy the times we get, can't we?"

The restaurant was an American-style café, with both an outdoor and an indoor section, both very crowded. Susan opted to sit outside. They didn't see Senator Johnson anywhere. Jon went inside and casually searched there.

"Not inside either," Jon told her as he reclaimed his seat toward the edge of the terrace.

"You're sure?"

"I gave it a pretty thorough look."

"Then we'll keep a lookout here," Susan said.

They ordered a couple of coffees, then told the waiter to give them a while. They tried to talk, but Jon was preoccupied by his vigil—Susan, too.

Fortunately, they didn't have to wait long. A dark-blue Town Car parked at the curb just a few minutes after they got their coffee. Two men emerged.

One of them was Senator Johnson. But the driver was someone neither Susan nor Jon recognized. He looked to be in his early twenties. He had very short, light-brown hair. He was dressed casually in tight, creased blue jeans, cowboy boots, and a shirt that was unbuttoned at the chest. He wore a gold necklace that fit snugly around his neck. A small diamond earring glistened on his right ear. Johnson was dressed casually as well, in slacks and a cotton shirt.

"Who's that?" Jon asked quietly.

"Got me," Susan answered, keeping her voice low. "He wasn't on the plane, that's for sure."

"Where do you think he met him?" Jon whispered. "And who is he?"

Jon and Susan watched as the two took a table near the opposite edge of the terrace. They were far enough away, and enough tables were between, that it was unlikely Johnson would notice them. It was doubtful that Johnson would recognize them anyway; Jon and Susan had both gone out of their way to avoid even meeting him on the trip over.

When they sat down, Johnson's companion slid his chair around the table so that he was sitting at a ninety-degree angle from Johnson, rather than across the table. Johnson's companion seemed to be carrying most of the conversation.

Jon and Susan ordered their own meal, keeping one eye toward the opposite side of the restaurant at all times. During much of their meal, Johnson sat back in his chair. His companion, though, leaned forward, speaking intently. Occasionally, their hands would touch, a gesture that made Jon cringe.

Susan, though, was transfixed. She almost stopped eating. She couldn't take her eyes off the table across the way.

"This is gross," Jon said at one point in a low voice.

"I don't know," Susan answered. "Look at the way he looks at Johnson. They're lovers, don't you think?"

Jon closed his eyes. This whole thing was making him sick to his stomach. He didn't want to be here. He didn't want to see this, think about it, witness it. Everything about this made him profoundly uncomfortable.

Jon didn't care, really, what Senator Johnson or anyone else did with their personal lives. Sins were sins. And everyone—no matter how great or small—sinned. It wasn't a question of degree. Jon knew in his heart that what Senator Johnson was doing was wrong. He did not condemn him for it. It was just wrong, as other sins are wrong.

For decades, a debate had raged in American society over whether homosexuality is an "accepted," normal part of human behavior. To Jon, there was no ambiguity about it. It was wrong—no more and no less than other wrongs.

You are separated from God by your sins. It makes no difference what your particular transgressions are—deceitfulness or hubris or greed. Human beings make mistakes. They do things that are wrong.

Jon had asked God for forgiveness for both past and present sins. Through Jesus, he had been forgiven. And through the intercession and guidance of the Holy Spirit, he had learned how to walk with God humbly. That humility made it impossible for him to feel morally superior to Senator Johnson. But, Jon thought as he watched the senator's companion reach over yet again and cover the senator's hands in a warm gesture of affection, it didn't stop him from being repulsed by what he saw.

The senator and his companion got up to leave. Susan bolted back in her chair, as if she'd been shocked. "We have to get going," she said urgently.

"Why?" Jon asked.

"We'll be late to that house if we don't get moving," she said. "It just occurred to me. They might be going there."

They paid their tab a couple of minutes after Senator Johnson left and hurried back to their hotel, half running, half walking. Jon ran upstairs to his room to get the camera bag while Susan had the concierge get a cab for them. They were on their way within minutes.

The cab driver gave them a curious look as he drove into the heart of the seedy district. Even at this time of day, the prostitutes were already out, walking the streets.

Jon's heart sank as they approached the house. The dark-blue Town Car was parked out front. Susan had been right. And they had missed their chance for a photo; the sun was going down. They'd lose the light in about forty-five minutes.

They pulled up to the curb several houses down from the Town Car. The cab driver accepted the fare and tip without a word. He left without asking them whether they wanted him to wait.

"We missed them," Jon said glumly, staring alternately at the car and the house.

"Don't worry," Susan reassured him. "We can still get them coming out."

"But the light—"

"Don't worry," Susan said cheerily. "I just have a feeling. We'll get this."

They picked a vacant lot three houses down and set up the tripod behind some bushes, with a clear view of both the front door of the house and the Town Car. Jon felt like a voyeur, but Susan reminded him that they were doing it for "the cause."

They had to wait for more than an hour. The sun was fading badly. A few minutes more and they would lose the chance.

But their diligence paid off. Senator Johnson and the young man in cowboy boots emerged from the front door of the house, in full view. Jon snapped picture after picture.

Senator Johnson came out first, followed by his friend, who turned and said something to another person in the darkened doorway. Jon couldn't see whom he was talking to, but the senator's companion spoke intimately and with feeling to that person for perhaps thirty seconds, and then he hurried to catch up to Senator Johnson, who was now waiting on the passenger's side of the car.

Despite his misgivings, Jon couldn't contain his excitement. They'd done it! They'd gotten what they'd come for. They had pictures—of the house, the senator, his companion, leaving the house and getting into the car.

Just one, small problem kept nagging at the back of Jon's mind. He wasn't sure, even now, just what he had pictures of, and what he was to do with them. But that, as they said, was above his pay grade. Sam Adams would decide what to do with them.

CHAPTER THIRTY-SIX

As soon as they got to the hotel, Susan called Sam Adams to give him the news. Adams, Susan reported, was very, very pleased. They were moving exactly on schedule.

"Sam told me that, if we play our cards right," Susan reported to Jon after she'd hung up, "either the story will be out on the street within a month or there'll be enough rumors circulating to convince Johnson he'd better get out of politics quietly before his personal life gets splashed all over the front pages."

Jon desperately hoped so. But he'd never known politicians to go quietly into the night. Not anymore. They fought and clawed to stay on their exalted perches, right to the bitter end.

Susan tucked the undeveloped film safely in a secret corner of her vanity. They decided to wait and have the pictures developed back in the United States. And that would be soon because after talking it over, they decided just to catch a commercial plane back to Dulles first thing in the morning. There was no need now to go through the charade of staying with the White House delegation. There might, of course, be some risk that Johnson would later put two and two together, check to see whether anyone had left the delegation early, and figure out how the pictures had been taken. But that wasn't likely. There would be no definitive way to trace the pictures back to Jon and Susan. All Johnson would have is speculation that Adams was responsible, and by then it would be too late. The story would be out.

They arrived back in Washington while it was still morning because they'd been following the sun as it journeyed west.

Jon and Susan went to one of the one-hour photo places near the airport and waited while the film was developed.

"Please be careful," Jon pleaded with the teenage clerk as he took the film.

"Sure, boss," the kid said, as he popped a piece of bubble gum in Jon's face. "Guard it like it was my very own."

Susan placed a reassuring hand on Jon's shoulder. "Relax," she whispered in his ear. "This thing is nailed shut. Nothing's going to go wrong."

The pictures came out beautifully. There had been more than enough light. There was no mistaking who it was, and what kind of establishment he was leaving.

"That's it," Susan said, smiling broadly.

As they drove into D.C., Jon looked out the window at a state trooper sitting casually between the trees on the Dulles toll road that connected Dulles airport to downtown Washington. He wondered idly what those troopers did all day when they weren't pulling cars over for speeding.

"You know," Jon said slowly, "I'm not sure it's all over."

"Sure it is. Why wouldn't it be?"

"Well, for starters, how are we going to get these pictures into someone's hands?"

Susan frowned. "You know reporters, right?"

"Yeah, but I'm not sure any of them would take this story as is."

"Oh, come on. There's always a couple, right?"

Jon thought about it. He'd been so preoccupied with getting the pictures that he hadn't thought through what to do with them. But Susan was right. He knew a couple of reporters who'd do just about anything and take any risk to advance their careers.

One Washington correspondent for the *Cleveland Plain Dealer*, in particular, would sell his grandmother for a good, juicy story about an Ohio politician. He didn't care where the story came from or even whether it was completely accurate. As long as the story was somewhere in the ballpark on the truth scale, that was good enough.

And that was why Jon hated the thought of taking this story to him. But he also knew that he probably had no choice. A front-page story in the *Plain Dealer* guaranteed maximum statewide exposure. Even the threat of such a story in that newspaper would probably do the trick.

When they got to the Longworth building, Sam and Abby were waiting for them in the office. Most of the staff was out for lunch.

"Let's see 'em," Adams said. Susan pulled the photos from the folder and spread them out on Adams desk. All four of them crowded around.

175

"Oh, my," Abby exclaimed first. "So it's really true."

"It's true," Susan said.

Jon looked up to see Susan smiling radiantly at Adams. Adams was almost glowing. He knew. It was as if he could see the future. These pictures were his ticket to the national stage. They would, somehow, catapult him into the U.S. Senate, where every member harbored ambitions of running for president. And where every member actually had a decent chance of making that leap to the pinnacle of the American political system.

Jon also noticed something else, something he'd probably been subconsciously aware of for some time but found easy to ignore in the mundane day-to-day happenings of the office. But here it was, right out in the open: Susan clearly adored Adams—perhaps even worshipped him, if such a thing were possible. Was there anything, Jon wondered, that she would not do for him?

"This is it, then," Abby declared. "We file the papers for the Senate tomorrow."

"Not just yet," Adams said.

"Why not?" Abby asked him, a slight edge to her voice. Abby, Jon realized for the first time, took a very active role in shaping her husband's political ambitions.

"Because we absolutely cannot appear to be forcing this thing to happen," Adams said reasonably.

"But what if Johnson goes down, and others step forward to run before you get your chance?" Abby said tartly.

Adams held up a hand. "Abby, don't worry. I've taken care of that. If there's a sudden opening, the White House will have the national party publicly pick a candidate they'd like to see step into the race. Me."

"They'd override the state party?" Jon said, surprised.

"Yes, they would," Adams said. "They owe me that for what we've done with the state welfare projects."

"Won't that hurt you with the state party?" Jon asked.

Adams gave Jon the look he usually reserved for junior staff aides who'd done something colossally stupid like misspelling the name of a large Ohio city in a letter to a constituent. "Come on, Jon. Think," he said sharply.

"Oh," Jon responded, chagrined. "We're not exactly in good stead with the central committee anyway."

"There you go," Adams said, nodding. "Our direct mail is separate. Our fund-raising chairs are different. We never cross match the networks. We might as well *be* the state party."

"I still want to know why we can't file now, just to make sure," Abby insisted. "Just to be safe. In case the state party puts someone up first before the White House can act."

"Because," Adams said, turning his withering stare on his wife, "to be safe might just be unbelievably stupid. If this rolls out even slightly off center, it could ricochet. We don't want to get hit when the bullet comes back."

"I don't understand," Abby said testily.

"Let me try, Mrs. Adams," Jon offered. He could see now what Adams was saying. "We want to be in position to step forward immediately, the moment this thing breaks. When the national party raises Sam's name publicly, we want to have everything in order to file right away. But not before. That would leave a trail showing we knew this was going down."

"But that trail's already there," Abby objected. "You were with Johnson."

"It's a risk we had to take, to make sure," Adams said. "But now, we can minimize the risks. And that means we wait and see how this thing rolls out."

Jon watched as Abby glared at her husband. Jon was fairly certain Abby would not let this thing rest, that they would have further, more private conversations. But Jon was also certain that Adams would not budge. He could see the future—just as Jon could now—and he would hold firm .

"By the way," Jon said, trying to sound casual, "there may be something else here as well, something we should think about."

"And what's that?" Adams asked, clearly relieved to force the conversation in another direction.

Jon took a deep breath. He hated raising this, but he felt he had no choice. "You know, those pictures may not be what they look like."

Both Susan and Adams looked at him sharply. "How's that?" Adams asked.

"Jon, we saw the whole thing with our own two eyes," Susan added.

Jon stuck his hands in his pockets and stepped back to lean against the wall. "Okay, that's true. But what exactly did we see?"

"We saw the senator leave a house where young boys are prostituted," Susan said sharply. "That's what we saw. And we have pictures to prove it."

"Did we?" Jon asked softly. "Is that what we saw? Or did we see the senator pick up a young man, take him to dinner, and then accompany him to a house where young boys are prostituted?"

"So what's the difference?" Susan asked, agitated. Adams and Abby hung back, silent.

"The difference," Jon said deliberately, "is that we don't really know what went on in that house. That young man may live there, may work there, may have friends there. It may be a place where that young man and the senator simply meet. We don't know for an absolute fact *why* the senator was there."

Susan's eyes were flashing now. "Yes, we *do* know what went on in that house. Remember. Johnson had that subscription to that filthy magazine, the one with all those little boys in it."

Jon sighed. "I know. It looks that way. Everything points in that direction. But we don't know absolutely, not for certain. It could be, you know, that Johnson looks at those magazines, yes, but that he's just ... just ..."

"Just your regular, old, run-of-the-mill gay guy, who likes to look at awful pictures of little boys on the side?" Susan demanded. Jon had never seen her so angry.

"Well, yes," Jon said uneasily. He was beginning to wish he'd never brought the subject up.

"And that's not enough for you? Even that?"

Jon looked out the window. He didn't feel like explaining his views—his Christian views—about the immorality of homosexuality to this group right now. It would do no good. But neither did he feel like backing down from his uneasiness about convicting another human being in the court of human opinion without conclusive proof.

"All I'm saying is that we don't know for certain," Jon offered sullenly. "That's all."

"Look, folks," Adams interjected, "we're not a court of law. We don't have to prove anything. Let the voters decide. They're smart enough to see this thing for what it is."

Jon looked back at the group, clearly the only one of the four who harbored doubts about any of this. "But what if we're wrong? What if it isn't what it seems?"

"But it is," Adams said soothingly. "Look, Jon, it's almost a lock that Johnson was the target of that kiddie porn investigation. Right?"

"Yeah, I guess," Jon admitted. "It looks that way."

"And that alone is bad enough. Right?" Adams asked him. "I mean, the laws about child pornography are pretty tough in this country. Never mind what else you do."

"That's true," Jon said.

"So when you add that to what you saw in Copenhagen, well, doesn't it add up in your mind? Isn't that enough?" Adams looked directly at Jon. "Isn't it?"

Jon sighed. "Okay, I guess it adds up. I'm just saying you don't ruin a man's life without proof. That's all. I don't want to make a big deal out of it."

Adams nodded. "Jon, I hear what you're saying, and I respect you for it. But I think the proof's there, by and large. Besides the intelligence files, now we have pictures of him outside that house in Copenhagen. We don't need any more than that. I absolutely guarantee Johnson'll get out. Don't worry. He'll bolt before any of this goes public."

"And if he doesn't?" Jon pleaded.

"He will," Adams said. "Don't worry. It'll all work out in the end. You'll see. You have my word on it."

CHAPTER THIRTY-SEVEN

The Hawk and Dove was crowded at this time of day. People were already standing behind the filled bar stools at the popular dive about three blocks east of the Capitol on Pennsylvania Avenue.

For all the glamor and prestige Washington exuded to the rest of the country, the city itself wasn't much of a place to work. Not like New York, where there were a million places to go and a thousand things to do.

There were no nice parks near the Capitol to walk through. You could walk the Mall, if you wanted to join the thousands of tourists who were constantly roaming that very same Mall in search of the Smithsonian or the Lincoln Monument.

Washington was a great place to visit for a few days. But if you lived and worked in the city, there wasn't much to do beyond work. It was a tourist city.

If you went southeast from the Capitol, you landed smack in the middle of some pretty awful neighborhoods. The neighborhoods to the northeast were a little better, but not much. And there wasn't much to see there either.

Northwest of the Capitol was the White House and the so-called K Street corridor. Nearly all of the large law, public relations, or lobbying firms tried to locate within a few blocks of K Street, which ran east-to-west just a few blocks north of the White House. Southwest of the Capitol, you found many of the large buildings that housed the bureaucracy of the federal government. Not much to choose from.

So, for the congressional aides who labored fifteen hours a day for their ego-driven bosses, not much relief was in sight. You could play softball during the summer at some crummy field where the ball bounced funny, or you could go to a place like the Hawk and Dove and drink expensive beer.

Jon pushed his way through the crowded front room. He wasn't exactly sure who he was even looking for. The arrangements had been made for him by Susan, at Adams's request. Jon was meeting someone Adams said they could trust, someone who would delicately give their news to the reporter at the *Cleveland Plain Dealer* whom Jon had chosen to carry the story to Senator Johnson.

Someone waved at Jon. It was a man Jon had never seen before. Jon waved back and approached the table.

The man was well-dressed in a tailored, pin-striped, charcoal-gray suit, a pressed white shirt, an expensive silk tie, and tasseled Bostonian shoes. Jon had developed a funny habit of assessing the dollar value of people's outfits since he'd come to Washington. It was a fairly accurate way of assessing where people stood in the food chain. The more expensive the wardrobe, the higher up they were likely to be. Jon assumed other people figured things the same way.

He figured this guy to be worth at least seven hundred dollars—maybe more, if the suit was done for him by a personal tailor, which was all the rage among those who'd cashed in on government careers and now made several hundred thousand dollars a year in the shadow firms that fed off the decisions made at the seat of the national government.

"Jon Abelson?" the man asked, pushing back his chair and standing to meet him.

Jon nodded and extended a hand. He had to admire the way the man worked. He'd gotten to the bar early, locked up a table in the corner of the place. He'd taken a seat with his back to the wall, where he could keep an eye on the place. No other tables were within earshot.

"You're Ken Pierson? Right?" Jon asked.

Pierson nodded once and then offered a chair to Jon. Jon slid into the seat. He placed the envelope he'd brought with him on the table within Pierson's reach. Jon noticed how Pierson appraised the envelope, almost as a vulture would appraise fresh roadkill.

"Is that it?" Pierson asked.

Jon patted the envelope. "Yep. But I want to talk about this first."

"Of course," Pierson said, leaning back in his chair. He'd made an effort to appear relaxed by loosening his tie somewhat. But he'd kept the top button in place. That was another nasty part of the unofficial dress code for men in this town. You had to practically strangle yourself with your tie.

"So how'd you learn about all of this? Susan says you know Adams?" Jon didn't know much about Pierson, other than that he'd done some work occasionally for the DNC and, sometimes of late, for Adams and the state welfare-reform projects.

Pierson nodded. "Yes, I know Sam Adams a little. A fine man. Going places."

"You're with the DNC?"

"Not exactly. I have a couple of contracts with them to do project work for people they need work done for."

"Including congressmen?"

"Yes, a couple of members or their staffs."

Jon thought about that for a second. "Isn't that lobbying?"

"No," Pierson said confidently, "because I'm not working issues for a particular client who wants to influence Congress. I'm doing work Congress itself wants done. There's a difference."

Jon wasn't sure he grasped that difference, but he decided not to press it. "And you're an attorney with a firm?"

Pierson hesitated. "Yes, I am an attorney, and I work for a firm. A small one. Modest. We do different things. Adams's executive assistant . . . what's her name?"

"Susan Smalley."

"She didn't tell you this background?"

"Yes, she told me. She mentioned something about Nathaniel Watson, the former White House counsel?"

"He's a reference," Pierson said tightly. "But you don't need to worry about that, do you? That's not your job. Your job is to deliver. My job is to carry."

"Look," Jon said, holding up a hand. "I just wanted to check. Make sure I had it right and that I understood it. The stakes are high on this."

"I know," Pierson said. "But you don't have to worry. We can take care of this. I have someone lined up who knows your reporter friend at the *Cleveland Plain Dealer*—"

"I don't have any reporters who are friends, especially not this particular reporter," Jon said quickly. "That can be dangerous."

"Making friends with reporters?" Pierson said, grinning.

"Yes, especially with reporters."

"If you say so." Pierson looked at the envelope. "So, can I see them? The pictures and the files Susan described to me over the phone?"

Jon slid the envelope across the table, glancing around as he did so. But no one was paying even the slightest bit of attention. Everyone else was wrapped up in his or her own political minidramas.

Jon watched as Pierson expertly handled the pictures. He was careful to hold them along the edges. He didn't place his forefinger and thumb across the picture itself, which could produce a smudge—or a fingerprint. He glanced through the files quickly.

"These are copies?" he asked.

"Yes, they're copies."

"And I can take them with me?"

"Of course."

The way Washington worked, these files and pictures would be in circulation within two weeks if Johnson didn't bolt first. Once a document was "in play," it didn't take long for fax machines to disseminate it.

Pierson slid the envelope into his black leather briefcase beside his chair. "I'll report on progress."

"Great, but do me a favor. Let Johnson think about it first, okay? Don't send that stuff around until we know which way he's going."

Pierson smiled for the first and only time in their conversation. "Like I said, Jon. Don't worry. I know what I'm doing."

CHAPTER THIRTY-EIGHT

Abby lost her fight with her husband. Adams did not file his candidacy papers right away. They waited.

Two days after Jon's meeting with Ken Pierson, the rumblings started. The reporter from the *Cleveland Plain Dealer* called first the State Department and then the Postal Service. Adams heard about the calls within hours. Jon didn't ask him how or where he'd heard. He was just grateful that it wasn't being traced back to their office.

The reporter wasn't sending the documents around. He just asked the Postal Service to verbally confirm the investigation, which it would not do. The State Department generally acknowledged the contents of the cable from the CIA station chief in Brussels, because there wasn't much in it to begin with and nothing damaging.

Next, the reporter called the FBI to check on the child pornography laws and the specific investigation involving the P.O. box at Dulles, Adams told Susan after hearing from someone at the White House who'd gotten a courtesy call from someone at the Justice Department.

By the third day, the calls started to come in from the field. Word had gotten around Ohio that something was up. They had heard that Johnson had cut his European trip short and was flying back to Washington commercial.

The wild stories started flying on the fourth day—rumors that a disgruntled lover was going to hold a press conference or that Johnson had AIDS, or that he'd contracted syphilis from a liaison overseas. None of them were true, but that didn't stop the gossip, which was beginning to fly furiously among the staff of the Ohio congressional delegation.

The one-sentence release was sent out at the end of the fourth day. Johnson was holding a press conference in the Senate gallery the next day at 10:00 A.M. The release didn't say what the press conference was for, but everyone assumed that it was to announce he would not seek re-election. The rumors were still thick, but none of them really came close to the mark, Jon noticed.

Someone from the White House confirmed it for Adams late in the afternoon. As a courtesy, Johnson had let the DNC chairman and the political director at the White House know of his decision to retire and spend more time outside of the Washington rat race.

The unofficial word that went out from Johnson's office was that the senator had done his time, fulfilled his duty to the governor by taking the appointment to the vacant Senate seat, but that he'd decided politics in Washington wasn't for him. Johnson wanted to return to Ohio, where the grass was greener, people were nicer, and where you didn't have to work until ten at night all the time. Johnson was tired, and he wanted out.

Everyone who heard it knew that it was a story concocted to cover the truth, whatever that was. But no one dared challenge it. You didn't do that in Washington. It wasn't proper. The senator had retired for personal reasons, and that was all there was to it.

The next day, the *Washington Post* reported that Senator Johnson was announcing his retirement. The small, three-paragraph, boxed story on the front page was attributed to sources within the national Democratic Party.

The last paragraph in the *Post* story said that a likely contender for the Senate seat within the Democratic Party had already emerged— freshman congressman Sam Adams, a rising star in the party who had worked closely with the White House to create a plan for viable welfare reform. The article even hinted that Adams would get the primary nod without opposition. The article quoted two senior Democratic Party officials anonymously, both of them pumping Adams. Jon assumed that the nameless officials were Jonas Brownlee and Nathaniel Watson.

Adams waited until after the press conference to file his candidacy papers back in Ohio. By that afternoon, Jon was on the phone with every reporter in the Ohio press delegation, telling them of Adams's decision to seek the Senate seat being vacated by Johnson.

No story on the P.O. box at Dulles and the events in Copenhagen ever appeared in the *Cleveland Plain Dealer*. Would the paper have run the story if Johnson hadn't stepped down? Jon wondered. Probably. There was enough there to go with. So why didn't it run? It would've sold papers for sure. Politically, of course, no longer was there any need for the story to run; Johnson was stepping out of the footlights and off the stage. It would do no good to assassinate his character. At least not publicly.

But it still would have sold papers. Who had enough control over what a newspaper prints to kill a story that would sell papers?

By the end of the day, Jon had just about lost his voice explaining to the very last reporter what Adams's role had been in establishing the wildly successful welfare reform projects and why he was excited about the prospects of running for the Senate.

But it was all for the cause. It was all worth it. Adams was on his way. He'd made the quantum leap. And Jon had been instrumental in that leap. He would be duly rewarded, he hoped, if it all worked out in the end.

Jon hadn't yet thought about what that end might be. For now, it was enough that they had emerged from this thing unscathed. And Jon knew that the next few months would be brutal. A Senate campaign in a state as large as Ohio was a nightmare. But if anyone could manage it—Sam Adams could. Nothing seemed impossible with Sam.

Good or bad, right or wrong, Adams was on his way. And Jon was right there with him.

THE
SENATOR

CHAPTER THIRTY-NINE

Footsteps echoed down the hall, sounding ghostly, eerie. Usually the hall was crowded with lobbyists, staff aides, and visitors. But, now, at eleven o'clock at night, nearly everyone had gone home—everyone except one hundred senators, their principal aides on the legislation that was being filibustered on the floor of the Senate, and the handful of journalists stuck monitoring the debate.

At one end of the hall, Jon leaned over and whispered something to the cameraman spread-eagled on the floor, his camera flat on the marble tiles, pointed back down the long corridor. The cameraman pushed a button, and his camera whirred a little as the zoom lens adjusted. Jon stole a glance at the viewfinder. Perfect.

An instant later, two men turned the corner at the far end of the hall and began to walk toward the camera together, chatting amiably. One was a correspondent for the most popular network news magazine in the United States. The other was a freshman senator who had orchestrated the current filibuster on the Senate floor and who was personally holding troops in line to keep it going. The TV show was profiling the senator and his efforts.

Both men were miked. Jon could monitor their conversation as they walked, though very little of it would ever be aired. But it looked good. It looked very, very good. That was what mattered most in something like this.

Jon had "agreed" to let the producers and correspondent go well behind the scenes for this piece in the days leading up to the filibuster. He had agreed to give the network exclusive access to their strategy sessions as they prepared. The news crew had been allowed everywhere—even going along on the senator's workouts in the Senate gym.

189

The senator, the crew had discovered, did an enormous amount of business outside the walls of the Capitol. He was inclined to take very brisk walks—"power" walks—from the Capitol to the Washington Monument and back each morning, and he always invited some interesting or prominent or influential person to join him. Many did, and their conversations were always both private and fruitful. Staff aides were not allowed, but they always followed up diligently on the decisions or suggestions offered during those walks.

For the week before the filibuster, the crew had followed the senator as he met with White House officials, congressional leaders, interest groups, and constituents on the issue that was now front and center in the national consciousness.

It was a rare opportunity, and Jon, like everyone else on Adams's staff, was energized by it. With the Republican Party controlling Congress and the Democrats barely hanging on to the White House at the end of a Simpson administration that had run out of both steam and ideas in the past several months, even a freshman Democratic senator could have a huge impact if he chose the right issue to be an obstructionist on— especially if he were standing firm on something that had been at the core of his own party's values since the second World War.

Times had changed in Washington. Once, new senators had to be quiet, mind their manners, and obey the Senate leadership. But with the Republicans in charge of the Senate—and the Democrats badly split on whether they wanted to be liberals and defend the poor or protect the middle class where the votes were—those with the voice, the ideas, and the courage of their convictions were given the opportunity to take center stage.

In the Senate, the rules favored the rights of the minority. One senator could filibuster even the largest piece of legislation. And if he made the issue stick and attracted supporters, it took sixty senators out of a hundred to break the filibuster.

The key to success, of course, was to pick an issue so visible, so emotional, and so troublesome to vote on that the rest of the Senate would think long and hard before they voted to break the filibuster. That was how obstructionist, guerrilla tactics were used to drive ideology to the center of the debates on the Senate floor. It was the only tactic in Washington's arena of power politics that allowed one person to hold such enormous sway.

Jon listened in as the two men approached. This was the crucial night, the crucial vote. The marathon filibuster had begun three days earlier. Tonight Adams's opponents would try one last time to reach cloture, which would limit the time allotted to debate. If they failed, the supporters of the filibuster would win and the bill they were blocking would be sent back to the drawing board.

The Senate Majority Leader had kept the Senate in session around the clock for three days, trying to break the Democratic filibuster led by Adams. The strategy had backfired. Not only had the Republicans failed to break the filibuster, but also liberal Democratic senators who had, at first, been reluctant to join the effort of their more centrist colleagues were now beginning to join the effort in droves as the fight became divisive and partisan.

The two men stopped in the center of the long hall. The correspondent turned and addressed the senator. The camera whirred and zoomed in for a tight two-shot. Jon knew instinctively that this conversation would be at the center of the piece when it eventually aired.

"Senator Adams, why are you doing this? Why are you leading this fight on this issue?" the famous correspondent asked in his very best professional TV voice. "You are directly challenging your own party's leadership who do not want this issue raised. You are taking on the White House—your own White House—the liberal, special-interest groups, and the Republican Congress. Why?"

Sam Adams looked directly at the correspondent, not down the hall at the camera that had zoomed in for a close-up of his clean-shaven face. Jon had made sure Adams had shaved and worn a fresh blue shirt, even though it was nearing midnight. No shadows would show on Adams's face for this moment.

"Because it's the right thing to do," Adams said softly, his voice barely audible in the empty corridor. But his voice would carry in the broadcast. It would be heard by forty million people, and that was what mattered.

Sam Adams was playing to the people—not to the Washington establishment that constantly schemed and maneuvered to protect and maintain the status quo. In this filibuster, Adams had directly challenged the two central constituencies of both the Republican and Democratic parties. He had, in essence, proposed to abolish the two monsters—the welfare state and the military-industrial complex—that swallowed up so much of the taxes people paid and to which both parties respectively paid homage.

It had been almost two years since Adams had been elected to the U.S. Senate in Ohio by a lopsided 65–35 margin over a stumbling Republican opponent who'd never gotten his candidacy off the ground.

Adams had literally been propelled into office on the heels of his successful welfare-reform projects. The overall program had been such a resounding success that any politicians who'd had the slightest part in consolidating the sprawling mass of welfare bureaucracies into the initial state-level pilot programs were capitalizing on the public image, based on the program's success.

The card that was at the center of Adams's plan enabled the poor who enrolled in the program to get medical care when they wanted without having to wait in emergency rooms for routine care. It allowed them to shop for the food they wanted, live in better places, and even buy consumer items such as magazines, books, or candy. Several national amusement chains now allowed the card to be used to pay for things like movies and arcades.

And Sam Adams had become the hero and the champion of those who held the card. He had made it all happen. Public recognition of his role in the formation of the welfare-reform projects had developed slowly but steadily, thanks to Jon's diligent, dogged efforts.

Jon never rested. He was always on the phone, touting the successes of the program. And Dr. Sindar had become so good at shilling for Senator Adams that it was now second nature to him to credit Adams when the sun came up each morning.

The DNC liaisons—the youthful black activists—who'd been handpicked by Adams to run the projects at the state level across the country had all moved up into positions of prominence or influence in their communities and states. Several of them were now state health or welfare commissioners.

Within the past year, the pilot welfare-reform projects had been given permanent status in the states where they'd begun. Pony Express had created a national system for the cards to be used in all fifty states. But not all of the states had yet accepted the system because Congress and the White House had not ordered it. At least, not yet.

But the situation was changing. The issue had moved front and center in Washington as the federal deficit crisis threatened to shut down both the economy and the administration—and as mounting inflation, violence in the streets, and general discord among the poor created incendiary conditions America's major cities.

Both President Simpson and a Republican Congress had made an effort to tame the deficit monster by reducing expenditures for Medicare, Medicaid, and Social Security while holding military spending to current levels. But the effort had collapsed when the elderly complained bitterly over efforts to reduce Medicare. Washington was buried in a blizzard of letters and postcards from confused older citizens who were convinced that they were going to have their Medicare benefits reduced—even though the administration's proposal was really attempting only to reduce the annual increase in Medicare spending from ten percent down to five or six percent a year. Older citizens represented the single largest voting block in America, and no one wanted to risk their anger.

So Medicare spending was left unchecked, and military spending started to rise again. Efforts to balance the budget collapsed, and the national debt began to go through the roof again. Now interest on the national debt threatened to bankrupt the country, and no one had any solutions.

No one, that is, except Sam Adams. His theory was simple, elegant, and attacked the very foundations of both parties.

Adams had proposed a drastic plan to reduce the welfare state by one hundred billion a year for the next five years and to reduce military expenditures by an equal amount. At that rate, the national debt would disappear, he predicted, and the United States would be debt free.

To accomplish that, Adams proposed to nationalize his welfare-reform projects and finally create the centralized Department of Public Works he'd been aiming for all along. Everyone would get the card—at least those people who had some part of their lives subsidized by the federal government—and everyone would take part in a centralized payment system. The efficiencies alone would probably save the money they needed.

On the military side, Adams proposed to pull American troops home from every corner of the globe and deploy them on the streets of America, stationed wherever the violence predicted by the FBI had continued to sharply escalate, turning cities into ugly war zones.

He would also hire all unemployed former police officers in the country and put them back to work helping police America. But this would not be a police state, Adams was quick to point out. This was simply helping communities "take back" their streets and neighborhoods.

By ending America's costly military commitment to NATO and trouble spots like the Middle East and redeploying the military to civilian situations, the U.S. would save tens of billions of dollars. The plan worked on paper. All it required was the political will to deliver.

Adams had been proposing his plan for months, in caucus after caucus, forum after forum. People had listened politely but had largely said nothing. It was, after all, such a huge change in the status quo—and that frightened people. The system continued unchecked.

Until the day the Treasury Department had issued a statement that in three months, it would be unable to pay its obligations on the national debt unless Congress sharply raised the national debt ceiling and allowed much more money to be printed.

Simply stated, not enough money existed to pay the interest on the debt. Tax receipts were down and debts were escalating. The country would either need to print more money—risking the kind of inflation that had swamped Germany before World War II—or figure out a way to float until government expenditures could be reduced enough to allow taxes to pay the government's bills.

Adams had seen his opportunity and had moved immediately. He told reporters at a National Press Club speech that now was the time for the national government to solve the budget problem once and for all. Washington could not hide this time. He even invoked the ghosts of his ancestors, telling the media that his namesake was rolling over in his grave at the sight of Washington lacking the courage to save itself.

The media ate it up. Adams provided them with great copy for "thumb-sucking" stories about the giant Washington mess. Adams also made great copy as a national reformer, capitalizing on his heritage to push bold, new ideas.

Adams had vowed to personally filibuster the Senate vote on raising the national debt ceiling—which was required in order for the Treasury to pay its bills—until Congress and the White House agreed to consider his plan. Then he had begun to build public support. He'd taken the plan straight to the people, and the media had given him a platform. Story after story—many of them fed by Jon—had given Adams a chance to argue his case directly to the people.

Slowly, the tide had turned in Adams's favor as governors—who liked the idea of increased state budgets and control—and the activist network Adams and Jon had put in place began to deliver massive numbers of people who supported the welfare overhauls. And when people began to rally behind the call to bring America's troops home to help out, Adams knew he had a chance.

Now, on the eve of the critical vote to break his filibuster, Adams stood at center stage. He had pulled together an unlikely coalition: the liberals of the Democratic Party, who realized that he was perhaps their best hope of winning back the town they'd all but lost. The White House was theirs, but that would be lost in just a year if they didn't change the core of their party somehow. And, in fact, reducing welfare spending through a centralized system wasn't such a bad thing the liberals figured. Yes, overall welfare spending would go down, but Adams's system actually gave the federal government more control over people's lives. And controlling people's lives meant controlling how they voted. It was a time-honored political rule.

Also belonging to Adams's alliance were the dozens of police and fraternal groups with whom he'd been meeting. Their response to his plan to merge military and police work was overwhelmingly favorable for a simple reason: Tens of billions of dollars were going to be transferred from overseas military missions directly into the hands of those who would help organize the domestic police and military operations.

And also, surprisingly, standing with Adams on this issue: isolationists and immigrant-bashers in the Republican Party. The Adams plan brought America home and gave the states—not the feds!—the troops to patrol the streets and defend the borders from immigrant hordes.

Jon stared hard at Adams as the TV correspondent nodded at Adams's last response. One more piece of the puzzle was left. *Ask it*, Jon thought. *Ask the question.*

"So, in your heart, do you think you can win this fight, Senator Adams?" the correspondent asked.

Adams smiled—a picture-perfect smile, just enough teeth to show confidence. "Yes, sir, I do. We will win this fight. We have no choice. We've run out of time. If we do not act now, our country is in grave jeopardy, and this is the only way out. I think the people know it. Now, we just have to convince Washington."

The correspondent held his position for a couple of seconds, and then turned down the hall to face the camera. He made a slashing motion across his throat. The cameraman turned his camera off. Everyone relaxed.

"Thanks for all your help," the correspondent said to Jon as they all gathered at the end of the hall. "We've just about got this thing in the can. It'll be ready to roll this weekend."

"Great. Call if you need anything else," Jon said, with his best fawning smile. Jon had learned the fine and high art of playing the enormously helpful and grateful servant to the powerful media personality. He hated the role, but—as Adams always said—it was all for the cause.

"I think we've got everything covered," the correspondent answered. "We just need to set up in the gallery now to catch the last bit of floor debate and then the vote later this evening. That should do it." The correspondent turned back to Adams. He raised an eyebrow. "So you really think you can win?"

Adams laughed. "Didn't I just tell your viewers I thought so?"

"Yeah, but that was for the camera, for the public," the correspondent smirked. "What do you really think?"

Adams leaned in close and looked directly at him. "We'll win. I can feel it. People want a change like this—a big change, one they can see every time they walk out their door or go to the grocery store. It makes it all real to them. Tangible. The card is something they can hold on to, and police cruisers in their neighborhood are something they can see with their own two eyes."

"But here in Washington?" the correspondent said. "Washington doesn't ever do things like this."

Adams laughed harshly. "Yeah, well, forget about Washington. That's not where the game is anymore. It's with the people."

"But people are idiots," the correspondent said cynically. "They don't know anything."

"Maybe, but they're smart enough to know what they want," Adams said. "And they want just one thing. They want to be safe. If you give them that—if you guarantee that they won't go hungry, that they'll have a place to live, and if you guard their neighborhoods—they'll support you. And that's all we're doing here."

The correspondent shook his head. "But such a big change . . ."

"It has to be big," Adams said firmly. "That's the only way left. Everything else has failed."

CHAPTER FORTY

Susan could barely keep her eyes open at breakfast at the Bagel Bakery the next morning. She was, Jon knew, every bit as tired as he was. Keeping that filibuster going around the clock had been a marathon, and Susan had worked tirelessly, endlessly, arranging for other Senate offices to support the cause.

But they had won. The filibuster had prevailed, and both the White House and Congress had agreed to come to the negotiating table to take up the Adams plan before the national debt ceiling was raised.

For the past two years, Jon and Susan had continued to see each other only sporadically in fits and starts. They both lacked time for a real, lasting relationship, even if that was what both of them wanted. Maybe later they both joked, when they were out of politics.

Jon wasn't sure how Susan felt about him. When they were together, she was loving and caring. She listened to him with endless patience.

But, despite their years together, Susan didn't reveal much about herself. That wasn't in her nature. She seemed more comfortable listening to Jon, helping him with his problems.

In fact, Susan was like that with everyone. She seemed to have a knack for listening to everyone's problems—the office confessor. Everyone came to her with their problems, great and small.

Adams, of course, relied on her more than anyone did. When a sensitive job needed to be done, if Jon wasn't doing it, then Susan was. She was at Adams's side more than anyone else in the office now. More often than not, Jon would spend his time working the phones and making things happen, while Susan responded to Adams's more immediate needs.

Jon did not begrudge Susan that role. Actually, it was kind of nice. Jon was much more at ease by himself anyway, and he didn't exactly like the thought of waiting on a senator hand and foot.

"So. We did it," Susan said, smiling.

"Yeah. We did." Jon sighed. "So now what?"

Susan looked up, a mischievous twinkle in her eyes. "Oh, you know, with Sam you can never guess. He's always working on something."

"True," Jon laughed. "He probably wants to be emperor of the world some day."

Susan didn't laugh. "And why not? What would stop him?"

Jon gave Susan a curious look. "Oh, just the Constitution, the United Nations, NATO, Russia, China, and the European community leaders."

"Mere details," Susan said, smiling this time. She reached a hand across the table and took Jon's hand. "We need to find more time together, don't you think?"

"Yes, we do," Jon said, feeling a warm glow spread through his weary body. "There will be time, later."

"Later," Susan repeated. "First things first."

"That's right," Jon grinned. "First we make Sam Adams emperor of the world. Then we find time to be together."

CHAPTER FORTY-ONE

Jon watched as the heavy gate swung open. He glanced around. No other cars were on the street. Just theirs. Pennsylvania Avenue was closed, and only very prominent people were allowed through the northwest gate of the White House grounds by car anymore.

Reporters lined the roadway entering the White House grounds. Camera after camera peered in through the darkened windows of the black Town Car.

Jon and Sam Adams sat in the back seat together. Adams looked immensely serene. This was his moment. He seemed to be intently soaking up every last detail, every look, every glance, every turn of the lens as it attempted to find and then narrow its focus on his face.

"You ready?" Jon asked as the car began to slow in front of the permanent, three-tiered riser just outside the double doors that led into the lobby of the West Wing of the White House. The risers were there so that the media wouldn't surround White House visitors like wild beasts anymore during impromptu press conferences. Not that it stopped them.

Adams turned toward Jon. Susan had expertly taken out the wrinkles beneath his eyes and applied a little color to his cheeks—not enough to be conspicuous but enough to make sure he looked superb on television.

The cameras started rolling the moment Adams stepped out of the car. "Senator, Senator!" several shouted. "Will the president sign the bill?"

Adams paused just long enough to hold up a hand. "I am hopeful," he said, speaking directly to the cameras aimed in his direction. "For the sake of the country, for the sake of the party, I am hopeful that he'll sign this bill."

Congress, in the end, had buckled to the weight of public pressure. The whole country, it seemed, was anxious to close off its border and be sheltered by the federal government. They wanted the card. And they wanted their military might aimed at their own streets of violence, where it would make a difference they would see every day, rather than the bloody streets of Bosnia, Iraq, or Rwanda.

The Adams plan had been approved by Congress in numbers close to those necessary to override a presidential veto. Adams was here to try to persuade the president to avoid that confrontation by signing it.

But it was all just a big con game. President Simpson had no intention of vetoing the bill—not in a million years. A veto would doom the party, and the president knew it. But the game must be played, and one of the most important rules was that it was a president's prerogative to ask for something in return for his signature on a significant piece of legislation.

Adams would be the courier of that quid pro quo. Jon was fairly sure that his boss and the president had already discussed it and that this event at the White House was nothing more than a public relations stunt. But he wasn't certain. Nothing was ever that certain in politics.

The bill had been passed at a critical time. The country was desperate for a big change. Inflation had just hit double digits for the first time in years. The prime lending rate was already at fifteen percent and rising. Unemployment, which had remained steady in the six percent range for a decade, had ballooned to ten percent in the past year, while twice the normal number of banks had closed. And the number of people who'd sunk nearly to the poverty level had almost tripled.

More big riots had erupted in Chicago, Detroit, and Los Angeles that summer. More were predicted for the summer ahead. The FBI and other agencies had engaged in a constant running war with armed militias in rural America, a movement that had barely been slowed by the 1995 tragedy in Oklahoma.

"Senator!" several reporters yelled at once. But Adams waved and turned to enter the West Wing. A marine opened the door smartly to let him enter. Jon followed behind closely, choosing to ignore the shouts of the reporters echoing in his ears.

When they entered, Jon went to the receptionist just to the right at the end of the short hallway. The receptionist looked up from her desk. "Senator Adams?"

Jon nodded. "We're a little early."

"That's fine," the young girl said, smiling sweetly as she undoubtedly did with every visitor. "Someone will be here in a moment."

Jon took a seat. A huge bowl of peanut M&Ms sat on a large table in front of one of the couches. Jon took a handful to calm his nerves. Adams looked completely at ease, standing and gazing at one of the many original oil paintings that hung in the lobby.

An instant later, the entrance swung open again. The man Jon had seen just once at the surprise birthday party for the president at the Naval Observatory—Nathaniel Watson—walked toward them, looking enormous in the narrow hallway. Watson didn't so much as glance at the receptionist, choosing instead to walk straight to Senator Adams. "Sam," Watson said brightly. "A fine day for a presidential signature, eh?"

Adams turned. His smile was instantaneous and genuine, Jon guessed. The two men shook hands warmly. "Nate! Didn't expect you here," Adams said.

Watson glanced around the lobby. He looked straight at Jon, back at Adams, and then back at Jon. Jon felt distinctly uncomfortable under the portly man's gaze, but he did not look away.

"One of yours?" Watson said, turning back to face Adams.

"Since my first campaign," Adams nodded.

Watson took Adams by the arm and guided him over to the couch, where the two carried on a hurried and hushed conversation. Watson was quite animated. Adams looked subdued as he listened to whatever news Watson was bearing.

After several minutes of discussion, Adams got up and walked over to Jon. "I need you to do something," he said very quietly so only Jon could hear. "Discreetly. Don't draw attention to yourself."

"What is it?" Jon asked.

Adams glanced around again, but no one was in the lobby other than the three of them and the receptionist, who was paying no attention. The marine was stationed outside the double doors.

"I need you to meander over to the press room, wander around a little, and see if you can pick up anything."

"What am I looking for?"

Adams took a deep breath. "Nate says a plane's down over West Virginia. Dropped out of the sky."

"A plane?"

Adams's eyes bored into Jon's. Their intensity frightened Jon a little. "Jon, the vice president was on his way to a fund-raiser in Charleston, in Air Force Two. Just about now."

201

Jon felt a silent sonic boom whipsaw through his brain. Watson, Adams, the White House all swirled through his mind in an emotional hailstorm.

But everything righted itself quickly. The instincts honed through years of working with Sam Adams asserted themselves, and Jon began to weigh this news against the cause. Something needed to be investigated here, and the results of Jon's investigation might have a bearing on the political future of Sam Adams.

"How—?" Jon started to ask.

"Nate just got a call from someone," Adams said. "That's all I know. I need you to nose around. See if the press has caught wind of it yet. The second they do, come back here and wait for me. We'll decide what to do when I leave my meeting with the president."

Jon nodded crisply. He knew his mission, and he would carry it out faithfully. He knew what Adams was thinking. In fact, Jon had become so adept at anticipating what Adams wanted done—what he was likely to want done tomorrow, in fact—that the two of them didn't need extensive conversations anymore. It had been months since they'd had protracted discussions about anything. Adams wanted something done. Jon did it, almost instinctively.

It had been months, too, since Jon had seriously questioned his own motives or the direction of his career or his reasons for doing things for Adams. It had become very easy to let Adams chart the course. Adams was the navigator. Jon was simply the first mate, following orders, doing what had to be done to keep the ship afloat and moving in the right direction.

And Jon knew without Adams's telling him that this was an opportunity. If the vice president's plane had gone down and no survivors were found, the nation would mourn. But, for Adams, it was a chance to seize the proverbial brass ring.

Adams was the man of the moment in the nation's consciousness. His name would naturally come up as a possible successor to the vice president, especially if he—and Jon—played it right.

The vice president had been virtually assured of taking the torch from President Simpson when their term ended in less than a year. The vice president had paid his dues. The party's presidential nomination was his for the asking.

In fact, the succession was so certain that no other likely contenders had emerged. No senator or governor had stepped forward to try to wrest the prize from the vice president. With the primary season in full swing, the bloodbath had all been on the Republican side, not with the Democrats.

The vice president had raised millions of dollars, nearly all of which he'd been able to save for the general election in the fall. And the party leadership wanted it to stay that way.

And now? If the worst had happened, there would be an enormous, gaping hole at the center of the party. Someone would need to step forward to be anointed. That prize would go to the person smart enough and quick enough to move in and claim it. Opportunities like this, tragic though they might be, rarely happened in the world of national politics, and those who seized the moment were rewarded beyond their wildest hopes. Those who hesitated or faltered became political footnotes.

Adams clearly had no intention of being a footnote. He wanted the entire chapter of the history book. And Jon's job was to do everything in his power to make certain those pages were written.

CHAPTER FORTY-TWO

As Adams and Watson went in to see the president, Jon went back out the hallway, turned right at the driveway, and sauntered to the press room around the corner of the West Wing offices. He ducked through the doors and stopped. The room was mostly empty. A bank of TVs were mounted high to the left, at the back of the briefing room. There was no one to the right, near the stage and podium from which the White House press secretary held his daily press briefings.

Jon noticed three reporters lounging to his left, near the small cubicles where many of the reporters made their phone calls. Jon walked over casually to listen in on their conversation—which turned out to be about the latest Redskins trade. No hint of urgency, no indication that anything had happened.

Jon wandered across the room to the CNN and Associated Press booths. If something had happened, one or both of those news organizations would suddenly spring into feverish action.

The CNN booth was empty. Jon scanned the room; no one connected with CNN was there.

The AP booth had just one person in it, a young woman with a fierce, strained look on her face who was scribbling notes furiously, the phone cradled on her left shoulder.

Jon walked past the desk, slowing just enough so that he could glance over the woman's shoulder at her notes. Her scribbling was hard to read, but Jon could make out the words *Webster Springs WV* and *Air Force Two* on her pad.

Jon's heart started to pound. So it was true! He had no idea where Webster Springs was, but every instinct told him it was between Washington and Charleston.

Jon continued past the desk then turned into the next aisle and doubled back. Desks in the cramped White House press space were crammed back-to-back, with nothing more than partitions erected to separate the desks somewhat. He walked quickly to a desk that was shoved up against the AP desk and took a seat, fairly certain that the reporter had not seen him. He leaned toward her desk, only a foot or so away, concentrating on what he could catch of her end of the conversation.

"Okay," Jon heard her say. "VP's plane down in the mountains. East of Webster Springs. Andrews has lost contact. Don't know what happened. Air Force jets scrambled. Be there in a few minutes. Got it. When's it moving on the wire?" There was a pause as the woman listened to whoever was on the other end of the line.

"I understand," she said, her voice excited but under control. She was young, but she was a pro, and news was news. Even big news like this. "I'll phone whatever react I get from the press secretary in a few minutes."

Jon heard her chair scraping back. He rose and watched as she vanished into the bowels of the press office complex, presumably to find the press secretary.

Jon knew he had little time to act. He tried not to appear to hurry as he returned to the lobby—but when he arrived there, he realized that his appearance was of no consequence. The entire atmosphere of the place had changed. Four Secret Service agents now stood in the lobby. Aides ran through the doors at either end of the lobby, one of which led to the West Wing office complex and the other to the Roosevelt Room and the suite of offices that surrounded the Oval Office.

The receptionist spied Jon as he entered. She beckoned to him. "You're Jon Abelson, with Senator Adams?" she asked.

"That's me."

The receptionist turned to a young man sitting beside her and said, "You can take him in."

Jon felt a flood of panic. The young man who wore a White House ID badge around his neck stepped over to Jon. "Follow me," he said.

"Where am I going?" Jon asked, fear constricting his voice.

"The president's office," the young man said.

"The Oval Office?"

"That's the place."

Jon swallowed hard. His arms and legs felt as if they had lead weights attached to them. He found it suddenly hard to breathe. Everything seemed to be moving in slow motion.

They left the lobby through the doors to the left, turned right, and then left again. They walked past two offices. Everywhere Jon looked people were running, shouting into telephones, or pounding madly on keyboards. It looked as if the whole place had gone into meltdown.

They paused at a large, rounded foyer. Six agents were stationed outside the Oval Office. Something clicked in Jon's brain. It was, of course, a national emergency if the vice president had been killed—but there was something else going on here, something he didn't understand yet.

Jon leaned toward the young White House aide. "You're sure I can go in there?" Jon whispered.

"According to my instructions."

They waited at the rim of the foyer while an agent had took a hand-held scanner and ran it down both sides of Jon's body to check for concealed weapons. "Just a precaution," the agent said.

Jon thought that unusual—but, then, so many kamikaze attempts had been made on the president's life in recent years that no amount of security would surprise him.

Despite his efforts to remain calm and professional, Jon felt a terrible paralysis seize him the moment he stepped through the door to the Oval Office. He glanced to his right at the president's desk. Two agents were stationed at either end of the desk, flanking President Simpson. The president was on the telephone. The two agents glared at Jon.

To the left at the other end of the oval-shaped room, were couches and chairs and tables. Senator Adams was standing off to the side, talking in hushed tones to Watson and two other middle-aged men. No one else was in the room.

Jon caught Adams's eye as he entered. Adams raised a hand, and beckoned for Jon to come join them. Jon glanced back at the president, who was listening intently to someone at the other end of the telephone line, and then threaded his way among the furniture to get to the four men.

"Well?" Adams asked as Jon approached. "Have they caught wind of it yet?"

The paralysis that had seized Jon gripped him tightly. He felt completely unable to speak. He opened his mouth, but nothing came out.

"Does the press know yet, boy?" Watson said sharply.

Jon glowered at Watson. The tone of the man's voice snapped him out of his paralysis. He didn't like this guy. "Yeah, they know," Jon managed to say. "Or, at least, one of them knows."

"Who?" Adams asked.

"An AP reporter," Jon said. "I saw her notes. I heard her talking to someone, maybe an editor."

"And?" Adams asked. The other three men all looked intently at Jon.

"And AP's going to move something on the wire, probably in a few minutes. Something about the VP's plane going down near a place called Webster Springs. Andrews Air Force Base has lost contact with the plane. They're sending Air Force jets out to look. The reporter is looking for the press secretary right now for a comment."

The two men standing beside Watson and Adams reacted to the news by closing their eyes. Watson's expression was hard to read, but he looked energized, maybe excited. Adams looked serene, collected, even thoughtful.

"Won't be long now, then," Watson said harshly. "We'll have pictures on CNN within a half hour, I'll bet."

There was a sound, a soft "click," at the other end of the room. All five of them turned in unison and looked at the president. No one said a word. The room was deathly still. Jon held his breath.

"It's true. Air Force Two is down," the president said, his voice sounding tired. "About the only silver lining in all of this is that there weren't a whole lot of people traveling with the vice president. Most of his staff is back here, and he didn't have any guests aboard on the trip there."

"Art and Jonas weren't on board?" one of the men with Adams asked.

The president smiled wanly. "No, thank God. Art flew in for the event from California, and Jonas had a conflicting event and had to take a late commercial flight in from National. Neither were with him when . . ." His voice trailed off.

The next forty-eight hours would be painful for the president, everyone in the room knew. While the vice president had not been an intimate of President Simpson, the two men had nevertheless developed an uneasy alliance over the past six years.

Senator Adams took a step forward. "The press is going to move a story on this any minute now, Mr. President," Adams said, taking credit for Jon's reconnaissance work. "Is there any hope, sir, that it's not what it sounds like?"

The president shook his head. "Doesn't appear so. Not based on the other reports."

"Other reports, sir?" one of the two men asked.

The president looked hard at Jon, apparently trying to determine who he was and whether he could be trusted. Then he shrugged and turned to look out the window. When he swiveled back, he had a look of intense sadness about him.

"It looks like it was a surface-to-air missile," he said somberly. "From a mountain ridge. The plane probably exploded in midair. No survivors."

CHAPTER FORTY-THREE

The briefer sent over from the Pentagon was no lieutenant or some other lower officer; he was a four-star general. General Don Ashland reported directly to the chairman of the Joint Chiefs of Staff. As key White House staff gathered in the Roosevelt Room for the briefing, Jon was amazed that he was still being included as part of the "event."

"Thank you," General Ashland said to the small handful of aides gathered in the Roosevelt Room for the confidential, closed briefing. The president was in his own office with Senator Adams and several others. Jon would fill Adams in later. "I'll be brief. As you know, the major wire services such as the Associated Press have already filed stories. All four of the major television networks have told our public affairs staff that they've chartered helicopters. They're flying stringers to Webster Springs—which is a small town near the heart of the mountains of West Virginia—to file on-site reports.

"To get to Charleston from Washington, planes fly over the Appalachians. Webster Springs is on a direct line between the two cities, near two prominent ski resorts located on the tallest of the mountains in the area.

"Now," the general continued, glancing down at his own notes, "let me tell you first what the public is hearing. The AP story is sketchy. It's apparently based on at least two eyewitness accounts from somewhere near Webster Springs, as well as White House sources. According to the eyewitnesses, there was a loud, midair explosion as Air Force Two flew over the area. At least one of the witnesses said the plane broke up before coming down.

209

"The AP story also speculates erroneously, based on information from unknown sources wandering the halls of the White House here, that several prominent guests scheduled to attend the fund-raiser in Charleston might have died in the crash as well. I can tell you, categorically, that that portion of the AP story is not true.

"The story correctly identifies billionaire Arthur Demontley as the event's host. Mr. Demontley, as many of you know and as AP explains, is chairman of a huge defense firm, Nuclear Waste Control, Inc., that manages nuclear waste storage problems for the Pentagon. He has also been President Simpson's national finance chairman for his last two elections and is widely known as the president's closest outside advisor. Mr. Demontley is now also serving, at the president's request, as a fund-raiser for the vice president.

"In addition, the AP speculates that a top Democratic Party official, Jonas Brownlee, organized the fund-raising event and may also have been aboard Air Force Two. Now, as I said, while AP may be correct about the role of these two gentlemen in pulling together the Charleston fund-raiser, we do not believe that either Mr. Demontley or Mr. Brownlee was aboard the plane. We are attempting to locate them to verify their safety.

"That's what the public is hearing. We, however, have some additional information. We expect, for one thing, to have photos momentarily, sent via satellite from the Air Force jets that scrambled to the site. In addition, the AP report is silent on what might have caused the explosion. Our own surveillance efforts—which I will not identify here—picked up a short-range missile signature."

General Ashland paused to take a drink of water. The room was silent as listeners waited for him to continue. Now was not the time for questions. Those would come later.

"As all of you know, both the military and the intelligence community have been concerned for years that something such as this could happen. International arms merchants have been peddling former Russian surface-to-air missiles—the kind that are easy to transport and fire—to anyone with enough money. These missiles have been used by revolutionaries in civil wars for at least a decade. We have all believed for some time now that it would be only a matter of time before such missiles fell into the hands of those with the will to fire at unarmed domestic targets—such as Air Force Two.

"Air Force One, as many of you know, contains sophisticated radar and tracking technology. We also routinely fly decoy Air Force Ones. But the vice president's plane, Air Force Two, flies solo with only minimal support." The general paused momentarily to make his point. "It was, to put it bluntly, a sitting duck for a determined hunter.

"Because the plane was basically a retro-fitted commercial jet, it had no ability to evade the kind of surface-to-air missile routinely used to bring down helicopters or low-flying planes in wars. All that was required was the right timing, the right flight path, and a position near a mountain summit as Air Force Two flew over.

"That is, apparently, exactly what happened," the general concluded somberly. "I can tell you that, at this moment, we are deploying fully into the area, as is the FBI and every other part of the combined military and intelligence forces of this country. We will find those who fired that missile. We will leave no stone unturned."

CHAPTER FORTY-FOUR

After General Ashland's briefing, Jon and several others returned to the Oval Office. Adams didn't say much as Jon filled him in. He was distracted and unusually distant, as if he were calculating some move twelve steps away.

Jon was still finding it difficult to believe that he was in the middle of all of this. He felt awkward standing off to the side of the Oval Office as it began to fill with people again, but no one seemed to care that he was there. More people just kept filing in. President Simpson was known for his willingness to listen to a number of advisors when decisions needed to be made. At a time like this, it wasn't uncommon for him to seek the counsel of dozens of people. So Jon stayed in the room and listened to the buzz as the White House staff reacted to the horrible news.

General Ashland entered and handed a portfolio of pictures to the president, who looked at them briefly and then handed them back to the general. Jon wasn't standing close enough to see the pictures, but he had picked up some details already from the conversation around him: Bits and pieces of Air Force Two had been scattered over a quarter-mile of pastoral countryside. There were almost certainly no survivors.

"All right, everyone," the president said loudly after the general had taken the pictures back. Every head in the room turned to hear him. "We need to make some sort of statement to the public."

The president's press secretary, Mark Cromwell, took a step forward. "We have two hundred reporters demanding to know what caused the explosion, sir. Are you going to confirm—"

"I'll confirm what I want to confirm!" the president exploded. The room grew still. The pain was evident on the president's face—the same pain that was etched on the faces of the handful of vice-presidential aides who had not been aboard Air Force Two with their boss and who now stood huddled for comfort near the American flag.

Cromwell didn't back off, though. It was his job to keep the press at bay. "But we have to say something, sir. We can't just let speculation run wild."

The president glared at his press secretary. "Is their speculation any worse than the reality?" But it was a rhetorical question; he knew Cromwell was right. He turned to Senator Adams just a few feet away. "Senator," the president said to Adams, "are you willing to help me here?"

"Whatever you need," Adams said firmly. "Just tell me."

The president reached over and opened a folder on top of a pile on his desk. He glanced down at its contents. "This is your bill, creating the Public Works Department?"

"It is," Adams answered.

"And if I sign this, it authorizes the use of military force here in the United States in domestic situations?"

"Yes, sir, it does."

"Then bring the press in here!" the president barked. "They can watch me sign this. The nation's business must move forward. We cannot let an event like this send everyone into a panic. We simply cannot."

"But what will you tell them?" Cromwell asked. "I think it's a great idea, signing this bill. It'll show the country the White House is still working in the middle of this tragedy. But what will you tell them about the explosion?"

"The truth," the president said grimly. "As much as I'm able." The president turned to Adams. "And then, Senator, with your help, I'd like to turn the military loose in West Virginia to find those . . . those . . . people who did this."

"I give you my word I will help in any way I can," Senator Adams said solemnly. The president nodded at Adams and then turned back to his staff.

"Okay, folks," the president ordered, "let's take five minutes to prep, and then we'll let the press in for the bill-signing ceremony. We'll give 'em five questions—no more—and then they're out. We'll confirm the explosion, that Air Force Two went down, and that there are probably no survivors."

"And that's all you want to say?" Cromwell asked.

"For now," the president said wearily. "It's not like I can just tell them that someone—presumably our own citizens—shot the vice president's plane down. Not until we have proof."

CHAPTER FORTY-FIVE

Jon had never seen so many reporters pile into a room. There wasn't so much as standing room for one more person in that portion of the Oval Office facing the president's desk. The lights from their video cameras lit the room up brilliantly.

Sam Adams stood just off to the side of the desk. There hadn't been time to call any of the Cabinet secretaries or the congressional leadership to be there for the bill-signing, so it would be just Adams and President Simpson. The president's chief of staff and press secretary hovered nearby, off to the side and out of the shot.

"The president has a brief statement first, and then he'll take a few questions," Cromwell said loudly, trying to be heard above the din. One of the reporters started to shout a question, but Cromwell raised a hand sharply. "Please—the president, first."

President Simpson entered the room from a side entrance a moment later and walked immediately to the desk. Cameras started rolling. Jon, who was pinned against the wall about halfway between the reporters and the president's desk, could see some of the reporters jockeying to get as close to the front as possible.

All four networks were carrying the event live. Jon could just barely see a monitor off to the side of the bank of cameras. Adams would be in the picture—in the shot—when the event happened. Even in the midst of such a tragedy, Jon could not contain his excitement at being a witness to this piece of American history—and to this giant step forward in the career of his boss. Sam Adams was, indeed, fortunate—in the proverbial right place at the right time.

"In a moment," the president said slowly, speaking directly to the cameras, "I'll take your questions on the tragedy that has occurred a short while ago in West Virginia. But, first, it is important that the nation's business go forward, even in times of adversity and tragedy such as this.

"With that in mind, I am today signing into law legislation creating a new Department of Public Works and authorizing the redeployment and use of American military forces in the continental United States. It is a bold proposition, one which I endorse wholeheartedly."

The president turned to Adams. "Senator, the nation is grateful for your leadership on this crucial issue at this critical time." President Simpson turned back, pulled the folder in front of him and quickly penned his name to the documents inside the folder. Then he looked up.

Five reporters immediately tried to get the floor. "Mr. President!" they all shouted at once. The president pointed a finger at an elderly woman, a senior correspondent with AP.

"Mr. President, is it true—can you confirm that Air Force Two exploded over the mountains in West Virginia? And that the vice president was aboard?" the reporter asked.

The president nodded solemnly. "First, let me say that we are in the process of trying to determine what exactly happened in West Virginia. And let me add that our hearts go out to the families of those who were aboard—"

"So it's true? Air Force Two exploded and went down?" another reporter shouted.

The president glanced at Cromwell, who merely shrugged. There was little hope of controlling the White House press corps, not under these circumstances with this kind of news. "I am saddened to say this but, yes, we have confirmed that there was an explosion aboard Air Force Two and that the plane went down somewhere east of Charleston, West Virginia."

"Are there any survivors?" a reporter yelled, ignoring the usual protocol of waiting to be recognized.

The president hesitated. "It is too early to speculate on that."

"But our reports say the plane was scattered over the countryside," a reporter said. "Is that true?"

"It does appear that it was a powerful explosion, of a cause and origin as yet unknown," the president said.

A half-dozen reporters tried to jump in. "Survivors!"

"Are there survivors?"

"Have you heard from the plane?"

"Is anyone alive?"

The president held up a hand, silencing the questioners. "I will say this. My heart goes out to the families of those who were aboard. But it does appear, based on preliminary reports, that there are not likely to be any survivors of the crash. It was, apparently, a very powerful midair explosion."

There was an audible gasp in the room, even among the cynical and hard-bitten press corps. Jon could only imagine what the reaction must be among people watching this live in front of television sets across the country.

"Mr. President," a reporter near the back of the room yelled out, "is it true that the vice president's plane was shot down? We've talked to someone here in the White House who said it was possible that someone intentionally brought the plane down with some kind of explosive device and that other prominent people were aboard with the VP. Can you confirm that?"

The president gritted his teeth. As usual, the White House had been unable to hold a secret for longer than a half hour. "We have no confirmation of anything like that," he answered.

"But is it possible? Could someone shoot Air Force Two down, right here in the U.S.?"

"Something caused the vice president's plane to explode in midair," the president said firmly. "We do not, as yet, know what caused that. But—and I give you my word on this—we will not rest until we determine exactly what happened. And if some group is responsible for such a reprehensible act, those responsible will be brought to justice."

A senior reporter for the *New York Times* stepped forward. "Mr. President, is it true that your national finance chairman, Arthur Demontley, and a senior Democratic Party official, Jonas Brownlee, were aboard Air Force Two and were killed in the crash as well?"

The president cast a brief, angry glance at the reporter. The press could be so brutally cold-blooded. "It is true that Arthur was hosting the event for the vice president. But I am thankful to God for small miracles in such a tragedy," the president answered somberly. "Arthur, who, as you all know, is also a close friend of mine, was not aboard the aircraft. He was flying in from another part of the country for the event."

"And Brownlee?" the *Times* reporter followed up.

"Jonas was not aboard either," the president answered.

Every reporter in the place scribbled furiously. Every camera whirred. "And what will you do now, Mr. President?" someone asked. "What will you do now?"

The president glanced at Senator Adams. "We will immediately initiate bipartisan efforts to investigate this. Thanks to the legislation I just signed into law, we will be able to use the full authority of the military to help with the investigation."

"Last question!" Cromwell shouted.

"Mr. President!" someone in the front row yelled. "Whom will you select as your new vice president if, in fact, there are no survivors? Whom will you pick to succeed you to run in the primaries? Do you have someone in mind yet? A list of possible candidates?"

The president's face contorted with anger for a brief moment and then vanished as he composed himself. "That question," he said quite deliberately, "is simply not proper. Not at this time. We will rapidly determine what happened today, and then we will take appropriate action. That is all I can say at this time."

"So you don't—" the reporter began.

"That is all I will say at this time," the president said. He rose, beckoned for Senator Adams to follow him, and then left the room by a private door. The press corps bolted for their doors as well.

CHAPTER FORTY-SIX

Jon woke at 3:30 in the morning and couldn't get back to sleep, even though he was exhausted. He'd been up until after midnight, going over the events of the day with Susan in their customary haunt at the Bagel Bakery on Pennsylvania Avenue.

And it wasn't just the adrenaline and the excitement, either. Something was pulling at the corners of Jon's mind. He'd mentioned it to Susan, but she'd laughed at him. It was silly to read anything into any of this, she'd said. It was a truly unfortunate tragedy, she'd said, and that's all. Some crazy people must have gotten their hands on an old Russian missile and used it to shoot down the vice president's plane. It was a pure fluke that Adams had happened to be around as the thing happened. He *always* tries to be at the center of things, Susan had pointed out, just so that he can take advantage of opportunities like this.

By early evening the night before, CNN and the other networks had had pictures—from the air with telephoto lenses—of the wreckage of Air Force Two strewn across the wooded hillside. It was obvious even to an untrained observer that the plane had exploded violently in midair and that there would be no survivors.

Shortly after 9 P.M., the White House had issued a statement making it official. There were no survivors of the Air Force Two crash. The cause of the explosion was unknown, but the FBI and the military had been called in to investigate.

The White House statement contained one other detail—one that had caught Jon by surprise. The president had appointed a task force to spearhead the joint investigation. The task force was headed by Senator Sam Adams.

Adams had called Jon at the office shortly after the White House statement had been issued. He had apologized for not getting word to Jon beforehand, but there had been no time. He had not left the president's side during the entire ordeal, and he himself had learned of his role in the task force just before the White House announcement.

The call had been brief because Adams needed to return to the Oval Office. His instructions to Jon were simple—don't comment on the cause of the crash and simply confirm that he, Adams, would convene the task force immediately to gather information from the various arms of the investigation.

Jon stared at the ceiling. Trying to get any more sleep was hopeless. Not tonight. Maybe not for many nights to come.

"Oh, brother," he grumbled, and then rolled off the bed. He shuffled into the small kitchen of his rented townhouse just off Capitol Hill. He fumbled for the light, found the coffee, piled twice as much as he needed into the filter, filled the pot, and switched it on.

He went outside in the darkness and searched around the steps for the *Washington Post*. He was in luck. Because he lived in close, he'd already gotten his copy.

Still standing on the steps, Jon opened the paper. The night was clear, and the moon provided enough light to make out the banner headline screaming across the top of the paper: "Missile Shoots Down Air Force Two." "Vice President Feared Dead," read the subhead.

There was a huge, aerial picture of the wreckage of the plane. Jon grimaced. There could be no survivors from this crash.

Jon flipped the paper open to the jump page. A second picture dominated the inside—of President Simpson with Senator Adams at his side.

Jon had spoken briefly to a *Post* reporter, Laura Asher, at 10 P.M. about Adams's role as the head of the presidential task force investigating the incident. Accompanying the aticle was a separate sidebar, by Asher, about the task force and what it might hope to accomplish. Jon began reading it as he stepped inside.

Buried in Asher's story, attributed to anonymous White House and Democratic Party sources, was speculation that Adams was at the top of the list to be tapped as the next vice president, once the death had been confirmed.

Asher had asked Jon directly about it. Looking back on the conversation, Jon felt a little uneasy about his response. He'd immediately gone off-the-record. "Adams and I were in the Oval Office when the news came in. One of the first things the president did after he took the call was to turn to Adams and ask for help in handling it. They seem to have a strong relationship already, and the president relies on his help."

"But how *likely* is it that Simpson will pick him?" Asher had persisted. "We're still off-the-record?"

"Of course."

"Then I'd say it's certainly a possibility. Maybe even a good one. Stay in close touch with me on this, Laura. As the task force proceeds, I think I can be helpful to you. And vice versa."

Nothing more had been said. Both Jon and Laura were pros; she understood what he meant.

And there, in her story, was clear speculation that Adams was a likely candidate for the vice presidency, that he was in position to lead the party and to assume that mantle at the party's nominating convention at the close of the primaries in August.

That one story in the *Post* would be enough to put Adams's name at the center of every conversation that would take place over the next week or so about what to do in the wake of the tragedy.

The right place at the right time. That thought kept going through Jon's mind. Adams always seemed to be in the right place with the right information. He was, indeed, a truly fortunate person. Blessed, even.

And Jon, because he'd hitched himself to that star, was going right along with him. Jon looked up at the night sky. "Lord," he whispered in the still, night air, "what have I gotten into? Is all of this your will? Am I doing the right thing?"

Jon didn't listen for an answer, though. His mind was reeling with possibilities. Big ones.

The thought of the White House, of all that power and glory, sent shivers down his spine. There was a good chance that he would be there—in a very short time. Every instinct screamed to Jon that it was inevitable, that Adams would be chosen as vice president and that he, Jon Abelson, would go to the White House with him.

And with that selection, Adams would become the heir apparent to the leader of the Democratic Party, giving him a very, very good chance of winning the party's nomination in August and then becoming the next president of the United States.

Just like that. In one blink of an eye, Jon's life had changed. He didn't know what today held, what tomorrow would be like, or what the coming weeks would yield. All he knew was that he was at the center of a storm, one he could not control. Only Sam Adams seemed able and willing to control the forces that were buffeting a confused nation.

CHAPTER FORTY-SEVEN

Jon woke again at 6 A.M. after managing to catch another hour of sleep. No rest for the weary—the national media were demanding answers, and they wanted them immediately. The networks had, of course, all tried to dispatch their own crews the day of the shooting. But the military had already sealed off a wide perimeter by the time the news crews had got there, and no one was getting through. Today a "pool" of media would be allowed into the area to cover the developing story. The military was simply not going to allow a mob of reporters and cameramen anywhere near the site; access would be tightly controlled and limited.

Jon rode with the reporters to the site of the explosion near Webster Springs. The White House press corps had voted collectively on who would make up the "pool" crew: one network camera crew that would feed the pictures to the other electronic media, a wire-service reporter, a news magazine correspondent, and Laura Asher from the *Post*, who would feed her notes of the scene to the other print reporters back at the White House.

Also along for the ride was Cromwell, the White House press secretary, and several military attachés with public relations experience.

Jon knew that it would be difficult, if not impossible, for anyone to sort out who was actually in charge of the investigation, especially in these initial stages. It was true that Sam Adams headed the task force—that's why Jon was along—but the White House clearly perceived itself in charge, while the military similarly felt it commanded its own troops. And Air Force Two was, after all, a military plane.

The wise thing to do, Jon decided, would be to stick close to the reporters, avoid getting in the way of either Cromwell or the military attachés, and avoid conflict. He could serve Adams better by listening first and planting suggestions later.

Laura Asher didn't even bother to talk with the military aides on the helicopter flight across the mountains. Jon could guess why. They weren't likely to give up much information, even off-the-record, so what was the point? And Asher didn't need to work Cromwell over, either. Cromwell was a pro. He gave up information when it was useful and kept his mouth shut at all other times.

Which left Jon as the target of her solicitousness and gentle inquiries. Jon admired the way she worked. She was all sweetness and light, but every question had a point, every answer led to another probe or inquiry. Asher never rested. She wanted this story in the worst way.

And that desire, Jon had already seen, made her the ideal partner for a strategic alliance. The opportunity here was to position Adams as the prime mover in this crucial investigation over the next few days, to keep his profile so high that speculation about his succession to the vice presidency would be inevitable. So Jon would offer information in return for premium space for Adams's name in Asher's stories—and for continued speculation on Adams's future role in the administration. In fact, Jon had a valuable piece of information he planned to offer to Asher today, a small piece of the puzzle given to him by Adams for just that purpose this morning before they left.

Asher and Jon were huddled off to one side of the helicopter as they started their descent toward the crash site. They could just begin to see some of the wreckage not yet collected.

"So that's what's left?" Asher said, peering through the window. "That's Air Force Two?"

"Looks that way," Jon sighed.

"Not much left, is there?"

"Nope. They nailed it good."

Asher turned her head sideways to look at Jon. "They what?"

Jon shrugged. "Figure of speech. Whatever caused the explosion."

Laura Asher leaned in a little closer. "But you said 'they.'"

"Yeah, I guess I did," Jon said, drawing her in.

"So, do you know something? Does the task force have information?"

Jon hesitated. "You have anyone else on this story, other people working on different angles?"

Asher gave him a strange look. "You know we do. We must have about half our staff on the thing, I'd guess."

"So who's covering the political angle?"

"You mean the presidential primary stuff, the next vice president kind of thing?"

"Yeah, that." Jon waited for her answer.

Asher looked out the window briefly at the countryside where Air Force Two went down. "Kind of a sick thing to think of right now in the middle of all of this, isn't it?" she offered quietly.

"Life goes on. So do you know who's covering that angle?" Jon persisted. You could never let a reporter like Laura Asher push you around. She'd use every trick in the arsenal, including trying to claim the moral high ground to move things the direction she wanted them moving.

Asher looked back at Jon and smiled. It was a wicked, bemused, faintly cynical smile. She'd played this game many, many times. She was a pro. She could handle someone like Jon in her sleep.

"Me, I guess," she answered. "If I want. Something like that's always up to me."

Jon nodded. "Good. That's what I thought. Do you happen to have anything in your notebook yet about who the White House has on their list, what the party plans to do about the primaries?"

"Not as yet," she said softly. "But I can, in short order. Maybe not for tomorrow but for the next day, certainly. And for the weekend wrap-up, where we speculate about all sorts of things. Like what caused the explosion."

"And might the *Post*'s informed speculation focus on how Sam Adams—who's heading this task force investigation and who just pushed through a major domestic policy centerpiece—would be a logical, consensus choice?"

"It might," Asher chuckled. "Assuming we can find a few people to actually say just that, which shouldn't be hard."

"And will you—will the *Post*—make that effort?" Jon asked, laying the quid pro quo squarely on the table.

"Yes, I give you my word," she said without hesitation. "We will follow up along those lines. Now, what caused the explosion, Jon?"

CHAPTER FORTY-EIGHT

The front page of the *Post* the next day carried an exclusive story, quoting anonymous sources that Air Force Two had been shot out of the sky with an old Russian surface-to-air missile system purchased several months ago in Eastern Europe.

The missile system had changed hands several times before landing in the hands of an "extremist, right-wing Christian militia" based less than thirty miles from Webster Springs.

"The Bible-toting, fundamentalist Christian sect is believed to be the largest, best-funded militia of its kind on the eastern seaboard," the *Post* reported. "Members are outfitted with everything from radar-scope rifles to laser-guided bombs. Sources close to the White House investigation of the Air Force Two bombing have confirmed that this militia group is at the center of the inquiry."

The *Post* article also reported, again according to anonymous sources, that the FBI had warned several months earlier that it was only a matter of time before such a weapon fell into the wrong hands. The FBI had, in fact, specifically named this particular militia group—the Christian Armada—as a prime candidate for acquisition of such a weapon.

Webster Springs turned into a town under siege within hours of the *Post* story. Hundreds of reporters mobbed the town by late morning. Not since the Oklahoma bombing had there been a story like this, and no one in the media wanted to be left out.

By the end of the day, every resident in Webster Springs, it seemed, had been interviewed at some point by a member of the media about the reclusive, secretive militia that operated out of a converted farmhouse on the outskirts of town.

The Christian Armada had been formed about a decade earlier by a best-selling author who had used the profits from his book about the coming apocalypse to set up an elaborate fortress atop of one of the tallest mountain ranges in the area.

At one time, several hundred men had been attached to the Christian Armada, the people of Webster Springs said. These men did not bring their families—only men lived at the Christian Armada compound. They drilled regularly, and the town of Webster Springs often heard gunfire echoing in the hills near the Christian Armada camp.

These days, the Christian Armada's numbers had dwindled, but they were still a force to be reckoned with, said the townsfolk—who had no doubts at all that the militia was capable of this heinous act of terrorism.

By evening, the FBI and the military had surrounded the Christian Armada compound, holding a perimeter roughly a half-mile from the walls of the compound on all sides. No one got in or out. The *Post* story had, in effect, preempted the task force's investigation of the Armada, forcing them to confront the militia directly.

But the leaders of the Christian Armada weren't coming out willingly. They would not negotiate with the FBI—or with anyone else for that matter. Their phone lines were cut. No one knew how many people were inside the compound.

Adams told Jon just after dinner that the Pentagon was making plans to send an elite team in that night, just in case the paramilitary forces inside the compound decided to turn violent. They didn't want a repeat of Waco—no one wanted that—but they had to be prepared for any eventuality.

"But are you sure they did it?" Jon asked him.

"Sure enough," Adams answered. "Everything points that way. And they *act* guilty, don't they?"

They did act guilty. The members of the Christian Armada had retreated to their compound, weren't responding to direct inquiries, certainly had no shortage of weapons, and, according to faxed dossiers of several of the militia's leaders, had the necessary training to use the weapon that had launched the missile at Air Force Two.

In short, they had everything except a motive. Jon was struggling with that one. Why would a well-armed militia like this one do such a thing, when their whole world would so clearly come crashing down around them? The crime was too easy to trace back to them. It was suicide.

The answer, the media speculated among themselves, was that the Armada *wanted* to bring the apocalypse down on their own heads. They wanted the confrontation. They welcomed it. It was part of their religion.

Well, Jon thought, they were about to get it.

Still, something was not quite right about how this came together. He would need to sort through all of that later. Right now, he had a job to do and opportunities to take advantage of.

CHAPTER FORTY-NINE

The military high command set up an outpost for the media pool, essentially an over-sized RV with few amenities. They weren't right at the perimeter established by the FBI and the military, but they were close enough to hear anything if violence broke out.

The rest of the media were stuck back in Webster Springs, forced to interview anyone who dared to venture out of their homes. The few at the outpost fed the rest hourly reports via cellular telephones.

CNN tried early in the day to position a camera to take pictures of the compound under siege, but the military officers ordered them to take it down. They didn't want any pictures of any sort on television, on the off chance that someone on the outside would be able to somehow convey information about troop or weapon position to those still inside the compound.

Everyone was waiting for something to happen, for some communication or movement from the compound. But there was nothing. No evidence, even, that anyone was inside. Jon knew better; he'd seen the reports of what was likely to be there. They had enough firepower to start a small war.

The media were biding their time, waiting for the military and the FBI to overreact, as they had at Waco. But Jon figured there was little chance of that. The federal government had learned its lesson at Waco. There would be no overreacting, not this time, despite the overwhelming public sentiment in favor of "taking the place out," as one CNN report said. Refusing to pay taxes was one thing; shooting down the vice-president's plane—or bombing public office buildings full of people—was something else.

Shortly after dark, Jon wandered out of the RV to get some air. Laura Asher followed him. Even though only eight of them were in the RV, it was still cramped. Cromwell had gone back to Webster Springs for the evening. Jon was the only nonmember of the news media spending the night at the perimeter.

"So?" Laura asked him when they were outside.

"So, what?" Jon responded. He'd gotten used to Laura's almost constant, hovering presence. He knew she would attack any misstep, but he felt as though he knew what he could get away with with her—and what he couldn't.

"So what do you figure's going to happen?"

Jon shrugged. "I would guess, at some point, the Christian Armada will send someone out to negotiate. What choice do they have?"

"You think they'll give up that easily?"

"What are their options? Start a war? They'd get wiped out immediately. They must know that."

Laura peered into the settling darkness of the woods. There was movement and noise in both directions, but it was impossible to tell what was happening. Soldiers could conceivably be moving all around them, but there was no way for them to know it. "They didn't come out at Waco," she said softly.

"We never gave them a chance," Jon countered.

"I'm not sure they would have anyway. And I don't know that they will here either."

"So what's your guess?"

"That—"

But Laura never finished her sentence. A deafening explosion came from the direction of the compound. Jon and Laura, frightened beyond reason, lurched a step or two away from the sound, clutched each other's arms, and then turned to watch in horror as an immense fireball erupted skyward in the darkness, silhouetting the pines of the surrounding forest. Behind them, the rest of the reporters and cameramen crashed through the RV door and out into the night.

Within seconds, a series of new explosions followed, all of them coming from the direction of the compound. It was clear, even from the limited vantage point of the media command post, that the compound itself had been rocked by the explosions. What they did not know was what had caused them.

Within minutes, Jon and the rest could see and hear troops massing in huge numbers, all of them moving toward the complex. The media

229

pool tried to move with the troops, but several officers ordered them to stick close to the RV.

"But we've got to see what's happening!" one of the TV crew yelled at the officer.

"Not until I say so, you won't," the officer yelled back.

"Then send us someone who can tell us what's going on down there," Laura demanded.

"We'll try," the officer nodded, and then vanished into the night.

"I'm not sittin' here," one of the cameramen said. "I'm gonna get into position to shoot something." He shouldered his camera and began to move into the woods.

"You shouldn't—" Jon started to say.

"Don't try to stop me, man," the cameraman said. An instant later, he was gone.

It sounded to Jon and Laura as if whole armies were moving through the forest, descending on the Christian Armada compound. Crashing noises and crunching sounds came from all directions.

Through the trees, they could see an orange glow against the darkened sky. That could only mean one thing: The compound was burning. It might be completely destroyed, judging from the size of the glow and the explosion.

Several minutes later, the cameraman came back—escorted by two soldiers. But he was smiling. He didn't say anything until the soldiers had deposited him at the RV site and moved off into the woods again.

"Get anything?" Laura asked him. The others gathered around.

"Yeah, I was able to roll some film," the cameraman said, unable to contain the smile spreading across his face.

"And?" the AP reporter said impatiently.

"And the whole place is burning to the ground," the cameraman said. "The flames from the buildings are higher than the treetops. It's a big fire. It must have been a whale of an explosion."

"Could you tell how it might have started?" the AP reporter asked.

The cameraman shook his head. "No way of knowing. The whole place is burning. It's an inferno. Whatever started it, it was quick, and it cooked the place in a hurry."

The AP reporter pulled her Nokia cellular phone from her belt and quickly punched in some numbers. She got an editor on the line, and within seconds was dictating a story based on the cameraman's observations and on what they'd all heard and seen. The Christian Armada compound had been destroyed. No one knew yet exactly how.

CHAPTER FIFTY

Susan flew into Webster Springs that evening, hitching a ride with Senator Adams, several top Pentagon brass, the new National Security chief, the FBI director, and the president's chief of staff. They arrived just before midnight and took several vehicles to the compound. Jon met them at an entry point the military had established on the perimeter, and Senator Adams cleared him to accompany the group into the compound, which had been secured hours before by the military.

The reporters back at the pool site were all clamoring to get into the compound, upset that the reports they had filed so far had been based only on those details provided by military spokesmen. But the military wouldn't budge. They weren't letting anyone in.

Susan and Jon sat at the rear of the last vehicle, as they made their way in. They exchanged glances but no words. They'd try to talk later, after everything had calmed down.

Even from one hundred yards away, Jon could see that little of the compound was left standing . It was a smoldering ruin. Soldiers were spread out across the grounds, pulling charred and twisted pieces of metal or other debris from the rubble. As they drew closer, Jon noticed that there were zipped body bags off to the side, presumably containing the remains of some of the Christian Armada members caught in the blast.

The vehicles rolled to a stop and everyone stepped out. They were met by yet another four-star general.

"Any survivors?" Senator Adams asked immediately.

"None that we can determine," the general answered.

"Any indication yet what might have happened?" someone else asked the general as they all gathered around him.

The general grimaced. "As near as we can determine, it was self-generated. It certainly wasn't from any incoming on our side. There are signs of a blast that started inside the compound and blew the roof and the walls outward."

"Can we see?" Senator Adams asked.

"Certainly. Follow me," the general replied.

They all stepped carefully through the rubble. No survivors would be found from a blast like this. No chance. Heavy wooden beams, some of them ten or twelve inches across, had been smashed to splinters; the same force applied to a human body would not have left much for a doctor to repair.

The general stopped about fifty feet into what had formerly been the Christian Armada compound. He pointed to several twisted hulks of metal lying off to the side. "See these? Launchers. Capable of firing the kind of missile that hit Air Force Two."

"Any ID on missiles still at the site?" someone asked.

"No, but it won't be long before we have a positive ID on this equipment. No markings, of course, but it's almost certainly Russian. We'll know shortly."

Jon moved closer to Susan. "What's happening on the outside? I haven't heard a thing since I've been here," he whispered to her.

Susan reached out and squeezed his hand affectionately but only for a moment. "The whole country's gone completely crazy over this thing. And the polls are going off the chart. They wanted the place blown to smithereens. I think they're going to be disappointed when they hear that the Christian Armada blew themselves up."

Jon glanced at the growing rows of body bags. "The public *wanted* this kind of carnage, with all of these people dead?"

Susan followed Jon's gaze. She sighed. "I don't know that they wanted to see people killed—"

"*Americans* killed," Jon interrupted softly.

"Yes. Americans," Susan continued. "But they certainly wanted justice. They wanted to know who was responsible. And then they wanted something done about it."

"They got their wish," Jon said. He felt a longing at that moment for something he hadn't heard very often in the past couple of years—the still, small voice that had guided him since he'd become a Christian, that had helped him make sense of a chaotic world. Surrounded by so much carnage, by the cold-blooded brutality of the vice president's assassination, by the obvious and frightening desire for revenge by the American people, Jon was struggling to see any hope or meaning in any of this.

The men who had died here in this compound had professed to be Christians. And right now, across the country, millions of Americans—many of them also claiming to be Christians—would be happy to learn that these men had died in this hellish inferno. Where was the moral sense in any of that?

"At least we didn't do it," Susan said.

"Do what?"

"Blow this place up, like we did at Waco."

"Yeah, there's that, I suppose," Jon said glumly. "For whatever good it does."

The dignitaries left the compound a short time later. Susan left with Senator Adams and the others. Jon returned to the news media pool for a debriefing.

Tomorrow, the aftermath of the carnage would begin—the endless inquiries, second-guessing, the public drama of determining whether the Christian Armada was, in fact, responsible for the shooting of Air Force Two.

But one thing seemed certain, Jon knew. Senator Adams would emerge from all of this as a national leader, someone people could turn to. He had, once again, been in exactly the right place at the right time.

CHAPTER FIFTY-ONE

On Friday, two days after the Christian Armada compound had been destroyed, the *Washington Post* carried an exclusive story on the remains of the missile system discovered inside the compound. The story was quickly picked up by the rest of the media and was accepted as truth nationwide.

The system had, indeed, been Russian once. And it had been capable of firing exactly the kind of surface-to-air missile that had blown Air Force Two out of the sky over the mountains of West Virginia.

The story carried Laura Asher's byline, and it was based on "sources close to the investigation." The truth was, there had been just one source for the story, but that source had provided all Laura Asher had needed. She had merely confirmed a couple of details with others so that she was able to say with a straight face and a clear conscience that she had multiple sources for the unattributed story.

In addition, the *Post* also reported the Pentagon's preliminary findings that the Christian Armada had destroyed itself. There was evidence that explosives had been strategically placed throughout the compound, designed to go off simultaneously in the event of an attack on the compound. For whatever reason, those explosives had been set off deliberately, the *Post* quoted knowledgeable sources as confirming.

On the following Sunday, as promised, the *Post* carried a story "above the fold" on its front page about the search for a new vice president. Although the intense search was still underway, the newspaper reported, a leading candidate had emerged.

Senator Sam Adams seemed to be everyone's consensus pick, the newspaper reported. He was a relative newcomer to the political scene, but everyone recognized his leadership abilities. Not since John F. Kennedy, who'd become president at a very early age, had a star emerged so quickly within the Democratic Party, the *Post* said.

Adams had it all, according to observers of the Democratic Party. The *Post* provided a detailed recap of Adams's stellar military career, speculating that, if he'd chosen to remain career military, Adams would have been a four-star general by age fifty. Then the newspaper gave a history of the entrepreneurial years that had made him a millionaire—but from which he had turned in the unusual direction of setting up a regional alliance to serve the needs of the poor. And, the newspaper concluded, his efforts to set up youth clubs in the inner city—first begun in Ohio— had expanded nationwide at the same time his pilot welfare-reform projects were set up. Now nearly twenty such youth clubs were working in major cities in the United States. All of them owed their start to Adams.

Adams was the logical choice, the paper said, quoting multiple party and White House sources. No one else, really, had emerged. No one combined the talent, skill, luck, and timing that Adams so clearly possessed.

Sunday, on the early morning TV shows, several senior White House aides confirmed that Adams was on the short list to be considered as the next vice president.

By late Sunday morning as folks were leaving church, it had become conventional wisdom in Washington that Adams was the front-runner.

The Republican Party started to scramble for information on Adams. So did Democratic Party leaders, many of whom really knew very little about the man who might very well become their next standard-bearer.

Adams called Jon at home after NBC's *Meet the Press*. Jon hadn't been to church. In fact, he hadn't been to church in a very long time. He kept promising himself that he'd find a church in DC to attend regularly once things settled down. But somehow he never got around to it.

"I'm calling a hearing on Tuesday," Adams told him.

Jon had not seen much of Adams since that day in the Oval Office. They had barely talked when Adams had visited the Christian Armada compound, and they'd spoken by phone just twice since then. Adams had been swept up in the maelstrom.

"A hearing?" Jon asked. "How can you manage that so soon?"

"We have to," Adams said firmly. "The president insists. We have to close this thing out. We can't have a repeat of Waco. No long ordeals. We did the right thing by surrounding the place. We were not responsible for what happened there. We did everything by the book. We need to lay it out for the American public."

"You have enough to go with for a hearing?"

"I think so. We have plenty of pictures, along with reports from the intelligence files we can make public. I've already cleared it with the president."

"Reports?"

"On what some of the Christian Armada was up to."

"How? From where?"

"Phone taps, credit card records, travel records," Adams said nonchalantly. "Things like that."

"You have all that on the Christian Armada already? That was quick."

"We've had it for months, Jon," Adams said. "The FBI's counterterrorism center has been tracking them for some time."

After the Oklahoma City bombing that had leveled a federal building, Congress had approved some fairly radical antiterrorism legislation. More than one thousand new federal law enforcement personnel devoted solely to countering terrorism had been hired. A domestic anti-terrorism center, run by the FBI, was created.

The legislation had also made it much easier for law enforcement agencies to track telephone and credit card records and allowed them to tap phones—without going back for a new court order—when suspected terrorists moved their operations.

"They have?" Jon asked. "The Christian Armada? I hadn't even heard of them a week ago."

"Nobody had. At least, not the public at large," Adams said. "But, trust me, the FBI had them squarely in their sights. We've got more than enough information to close this thing down. It's airtight. They were responsible for the attack on Air Force Two, Jon. I'm certain of it. After Tuesday, the American people will be, too."

"I hope so," Jon said softly. "Because everyone's seen the pictures of that compound now. It was reduced to rubble."

"They did it to themselves, Jon. Don't ever forget that. We had the right place, the right people. Their own actions confirm that," Adams reassured him. "And we had to move in swiftly with as much military might as we could, if only to be prepared. Thank God we didn't have to use any of that force."

"I'm not sure God had much to do with any of this," Jon said quietly. "So—I suppose you want me to spin this out to the national print reporters following the *Post* story and the talk shows this morning?"

"Yes. On background, of course. No fingerprints."

"You know me."

"Yes, I do. If you need some background, you might go into the office real quickly. The file's sitting on my desk. Go ahead and look through it, but don't fax anything out from it. It's just for your own edification. To help when you talk to some of these reporters."

"I'll do that."

"And Jon?"

"Yeah?"

"That was a nice job with Laura Asher. A real nice job. It set the tone just right. Launched it perfectly."

Jon smiled. It *had* been a nice piece of work. "The *Post* only quoted anonymous sources," he said, laughing. "So what makes you think I had a hand in it?"

"Like I said, a great job," Adams responded. "Now, get to work on that hearing. We're not there yet. We're close, but we're not quite home."

"Senator?" Jon asked, before hanging up. "You're seeing a lot of the president right now, aren't you?"

"Yes, Jon, I am," Adams answered. "We're together often. He's intensely interested in the details of the investigation. I brief him regularly."

"That's what I thought," Jon said, nodding to himself. "And it's the president who picks the vice president, isn't it?"

"He's consulting others," Adams answered. "but it's his decision to make in the end."

"Kind of puts you in the right place at the right time, doesn't it?" Jon said evenly.

Adams didn't answer immediately. When he did, there was a funny edge to his voice. "You know, Jon, the Lord puts people in places of critical importance in times of great turmoil and trouble. This is certainly one of those times. And if God puts me in the White House, well, who am I to say no to that assignment?"

"You can't, of course," Jon agreed, wondering why he suddenly felt so cold. In the years Jon had known him, Adams had never invoked God's name. Not until just now.

"No, I can't. I must respond to God's call to service. You, more than anyone else, should know that. There's a time and a place for everyone. This is my time, I think. God has placed me here," Adams said. "But we're not all the way home just yet, Jon. Go take a look at that file on my desk. And make those calls to the press."

"Yes, sir, Senator," Jon said smartly.

"I'll be at the White House most of the day tomorrow. Susan's handling all the details for the hearing. The logistics, witnesses, statements, pictures, that sort of thing. You can work with her on it. You do get along with her, right?"

Jon chuckled. "Yeah. Susan and I get along fine."

"Okay, look, I gotta run. I'm having lunch with the president in an hour. You can reach me through the White House operator if there's an emergency, okay?"

"Okay," Jon said. "But there won't be. I'll take care of things."

"You always do, Jon."

CHAPTER FIFTY-TWO

The file was labeled "Confidential," and it was sitting off to the side of Adams's desk, just as he'd said. Jon picked it up and settled down in the senator's chair to read it.

The Russell building was deathly quiet. Other than the guard at the front desk, who'd let him into the building, Jon hadn't seen anyone else during his walk through the empty corridors. Most of the aides who did their work on the weekends came in on Saturday, then played on Sunday.

Jon flipped through the file first, just to see what was in it. He ran across several documents labeled "Codeword Armada." They were prepared by the Center for Research and Anti-Terrorism Activities—CRATA.

CRATA had sprung up after the Oklahoma City bombing. It was housed in a massive, modern, three-sided building south of Washington on the western shore of the Potomac River in Virginia. It now had more than a thousand employees, all dedicated to just one proposition—spying on Americans and American groups to see who might be "subverting" the state or thinking about it.

It occurred to Jon that he probably should not be reviewing these particular CRATA files. They were labeled "codeword," the highest security level. Jon was not cleared for "codeword" documents. But the senator had told him to look though the file, so he put his qualms aside and dug in.

CRATA had developed an interest in the Christian Armada several years earlier. A handful of descriptive narratives of their activities were prepared, Jon assumed, by someone within CRATA to reveal how the group worked.

Whoever had prepared the reports seemed to have had almost a bird's-eye view of the group's activities, as if the observer had been hovering overhead in a helicopter. Later, there were detailed notes on conversations of the group—transcripts, as if someone had been right there listening in.

The most damaging documents were the field reports from an agent who had infiltrated the group and the compound a year earlier. He described in intimate detail how the group operated. The agent, of course, remained unnamed, and probably only his controls knew his identity.

The Christian Armada convened on the weekends. Most of the men were not from the Webster Springs area but drove in from outlying areas in West Virginia and Virginia. They drilled and trained on Saturday, held a prayer and worship service for most of Sunday morning, and then played out a "war game" scenario on Sunday afternoon.

The files were explicit about the mission of the Christian Armada. They were in training for the day when their own government would turn against its citizens. They were preparing for a day they felt was inevitable—the day when the government would hunt them down as criminals.

Jon saw immediately that there was more than enough in the files to convict this group in a public forum. The agent had provided transcripts of conversations inside the compound in which group members talked about proactively doing something against the government.

In fact, there were three separate reports—all filed by the agent inside—detailing how the group had actively plotted to take out key members of the federal government in a crisis, including the president or vice president, to send the signal that the Christian Armada was willing to "stand and fight."

There it was—the smoking gun. Jon pulled those three reports from the file. He would ask Susan and Adams later just how much leeway he had to leak portions of them to Laura.

Jon also read through the detailed descriptions of the men's activities on the weekend. At another time, the whole thing might have struck Jon as almost comical: grown men leaving their families to go play war games at some secret location in the woods of West Virginia. Almost like little boys, with their cap guns and plastic rifles prowling neighborhoods in search of the "bad guys."

But it wasn't funny now. Many of the men described in this file were now dead. They would play no more games in the woods.

240

The reports went into great depth, especially the later documents, the ones from the past six months or so. They had, indeed, tapped the phone lines of many of the men who'd joined the Christian Armada. There were extensive credit card and financial histories of the leaders of the group. Several of them had apparently grown rich off the Christian Armada. The men who joined the group paid an annual fee to be part of it, and they also supported the creation of a supply depot full of weapons, food, and other basic goods. But what the members did not know—and what the CRATA documents revealed—was that a handful of the leaders of the group had formed their own company to handle the purchasing of goods and services for the group. This allowed those leaders to funnel all the members' contributions into their company.

At the apex of its popularity, more than one thousand men had been members of the Christian Armada. And each of those men had contributed at least one thousand dollars to the cause, some of them substantially more than that—which added up to a lot of money, possibly several million dollars a year.

Quite a little scam, Jon concluded. It would make extremely good material for a hearing. A name sprang into Jon's mind, something catchy and simple, something he could spin out to the press—the "thousand-thousand club." A thousand members, contributing a thousand dollars each, added up to a million dollars. It had a nice ring to it.

The public would react instinctively and angrily, Jon knew, to the news that the leaders of the group had deceived their own members and become rich off the group. The press loved to bash Christian groups for money scams. That, coupled with the three reports from the agent who'd infiltrated the group, would be more than enough to convict the group in the public's mind. Adams was right—they had enough to put this thing to rest.

As Jon closed the file folder, something caught his eye. He reopened it and looked more closely. The top of one of the pages was ragged. Like most of the remaining pages, it had been faxed from somewhere, and the name of the originating office was still there. Jon checked a few of the other pages. All seemed to have been shaved to remove the name of the originating office. This page, perhaps, had been out of position when the shaving was done.

Imprinted on the upper right-hand side of the page were the words "daystar.com." Jon recognized that as an on-line name—apparently the on-line name of the organization or company that had faxed the document.

Jon glanced through the document quickly. It was a surveillance report of some of the earlier activities of the Christian Armada—one of the oldest documents in the file dating back a couple of years.

Jon placed the document back in the file folder and closed the cover, making a mental note to check into it, just to satisfy his curiosity. Perhaps daystar.com was a computer program at CRATA dedicated to domestic surveillance. He'd find out.

But, for now, he had more than enough to convict the Christian Armada. He'd have the whole thing—the three documents from the agent inside and the reports of the financial scam—in the newspapers by Tuesday morning, before the hearing.

The timing would be perfect. The papers would report the financial shenanigans of the group and the conversations about taking out national political leaders in a crisis, and the TV folks would blow it sky high.

Of course, no one was left standing from the Christian Armada to answer the charges. No one had stepped forward to defend them, including any of the family members left behind.

Dozens of the wives had been interviewed, of course. But nearly all of them had professed ignorance of the activities of the Christian Armada. They had made no attempt to defend or even explain what the group had done. They'd simply been overwhelmed with grief over the deaths of their husbands in the national disaster.

But Jon had what he needed, and it was imperative to close this thing out. Once he did, the path would be cleared for Senator Sam Adams to go to the White House as the next vice president of the United States.

CHAPTER FIFTY-THREE

Jon loved the end of the day in Washington. He'd gotten into the habit of taking a walk at the western end of the Mall before heading home to his apartment, stopping only at the Lincoln Memorial.

Tonight, Monday, the night before the hearing, he was taking that walk even though he wouldn't be heading home for some time yet. And he'd talked Susan into going with him. They were holding hands, strolling along the north side of the reflecting pool. The sun had only just disappeared behind the Lincoln Memorial; there was still plenty of light.

Most of the tourists had gone back to their hotels, unwilling to take chances at night in unfamiliar territory. Only "native" Washingtonians braved the Mall at dusk. That's why Jon liked being out here at this time of day.

Jon always felt comfortable with Susan. Sometimes, they'd walk without talking. Other times, they'd discuss things that had happened in the office. It didn't seem to matter much whether they talked or not. Susan liked to listen, and she was easy to be around.

Lately, she'd been under increasing pressure as Adams had given her more responsibility. Preparing for tomorrow's hearing had been her biggest assignment yet, but Jon was confident that she'd handled everything down to the last detail. And anything not yet nailed down would be handled when they got back to the office; they would be there, Jon knew, at least until midnight.

"Did you get it in?" Susan asked as they neared the wide steps that led up into the Lincoln Memorial.

"I always do."

"I know. Just thought I'd ask. And will it come out the way you want?"

243

Jon smiled. "I think so. I gave the full set of documents to the *Post* on both the agent inside and the money scam."

"To Asher?"

"Yes."

"And she took it without question?"

"Without question."

"So the story will say . . ."

"That the Christian Armada was planning to kill a national political leader and that the leaders got rich off the members of the group."

"The headline?"

"Christian Armada Planned to Kill Vice President, CRATA Documents Show," Jon answered. "Something like that."

Susan nodded, satisfied. "Good. We've got the CRATA director coming to testify, and we have the agent inside on videotape in shadow, talking about the group—"

Jon stopped walking and turned to face Susan, releasing her hand. "You've got the agent inside?"

Susan's face lit up. "CRATA gave him to us immediately. We told them we had to have him to lend credibility to the charges against the Christian Armada. We said his accounts of what went on inside the group and what it was plotting to do were absolutely crucial to what we were presenting."

"And they bought it?"

"Sure. Like they had a choice. We told them the president demanded his testimony, even if it was in shadow so no one could determine his identity."

Jon paused. "And do you know who he is?"

Susan shook her head. "But CRATA says he's the man. That's good enough. And I've seen parts of his testimony. It's first-rate. Great stuff. There's no question what the group was up to."

Jon nodded. "So who else have you lined up?"

"We've also got the IRS commissioner coming by to talk about how they were planning to go after the leaders for tax evasion."

"Were they?"

"Close enough. They'd at least looked at the group's tax filings before the event."

Jon took Susan's hand and started walking up the Mall again. "Sam's ready," he said. "We went over his opening statement before dinner. He's going to wave the documents around for the cameras and talk about how criminals like this should never again be allowed to target national leaders. By the way, you didn't line up anyone to defend the Christian Armada, did you? Like a couple of the wives maybe?"

Susan slowed and gave Jon a funny look. "Now why would I do something stupid like that?"

"Oh, I don't know. Out of fairness, maybe."

"And who was being fair to the vice president and all his staff aboard that plane?" Susan said, her tone icy. "Did they have a chance to defend themselves against those ruthless, cold-blooded killers?"

"It was just a question," Jon said soothingly.

"Well, it was a stupid one. I'm surprised you even asked it."

"Did any of the wives ask to testify?"

"No, and we didn't go out of our way to give them the chance, either. You don't think we should have, do you?"

"No, I guess not."

They walked up the steps to the memorial in silence. They entered the cavernous front entrance. It was always a thrill for Jon to look up at the huge likeness of Lincoln in the memorial, no matter how many times he saw it.

Jon left Susan's side and wandered over to the base of the memorial. He caressed the metal sculpture, smooth from tens of thousands of hands doing the same thing, day in and day out.

"By the way, you ever heard of something called 'daystar'?" Jon asked casually.

Susan stared at him, her face blank. She didn't approach the memorial. "What's that? A new constellation?"

"I don't know. That's why I was asking you."

"Where'd you see it?"

"At the top of one of the documents in the Christian Armada file, on Sam's desk. It said 'daystar.com' at the top of a fax. I was just curious if you knew anything about it."

Susan shook her head. "Never heard of it before."

"There's no daystar office over at CRATA, is there?"

"Not that I know of, but I don't know all the offices over there. Could be. Why? Does it mean something?"

Jon shook his head. "Oh, I don't think so. It's just that, obviously, some of our material for this hearing came from daystar, and it was something I'd never heard of before. Just curious."

"Sorry," Susan said. "Can't help you."

"No problem," Jon answered.

In fact, Jon had made several discreet calls in the middle of the morning, after he'd made his calls to Laura Asher at the *Post* and several of the other national print reporters to give them the leaked documents.

There was nothing remotely like "daystar" at CRATA. He had pinned that down pretty well with just three phone calls. And there was no "daystar" of any sort affiliated with any of the committees or sub-committees in Congress, or with any federal agency, for that matter. He'd had someone who printed the federal directory look through his computer program closely, pulling rank to get the search done right now. It had turned up empty.

So Jon was fairly sure that, unless "daystar" was part of the so-called "black" budget—the budget for ultra-top-secret programs—at either CIA, NSA, or NRO, it wasn't affiliated with the government. And Jon doubted that there was a "daystar" component to any of those "black" budgets. He had a friend on the staff of the Senate Armed Services Committee with code-word clearance, and he'd said there was no "daystar" component to either agency.

Jon had felt a little guilty taking the time to track this down when there was so much to be done on Adams's behalf, but his curiosity had been piqued when he'd discovered that there was no "daystar.com" at CRATA. That had surprised him. If the material in Adams's file hadn't come from CRATA, where had it come from?

But he'd have to get to that later. Right now, he had a hearing to get through. And Senator Adams had said that there were developments at the White House that might be announced soon. He'd had a wicked smile on his face when he'd told Susan and Jon about it. Jon could only assume that it was the news they'd all been holding their breath about for days.

"This daystar thing—you think it's anything we should talk about?" Susan asked.

Jon hesitated, wanting to tell Susan about the calls he'd made. But—no need to complicate her life with extraneous matters right now. "No, not really," he said finally.

"You sure?"

"Yeah, I'm sure. It's nothing. Just something I was curious about."

Susan walked over to Jon then and wrapped her arms around him. She gave him a warm kiss. No one was around to see it, so Jon returned the kiss with as much passion as his tired body could muster.

"We won't keep anything from each other. Promise?" Susan whispered in his ear.

"I promise," Jon said.

"It's just you and me against the cruel, cruel world," she said, chuckling a little. "We have to stick together."

"Like glue," Jon answered, turning his head to kiss her again. They kissed for a long time. Jon had the strangest sensation that Susan's mind wasn't entirely concentrating on him, but when he opened his eyes briefly, hers were squeezed tight. The thought passed.

Susan pulled back. "We gotta go," she said, her voice hoarse. "I have a ton of work to do before the night's out. But you remember the promise you made to me here tonight. Okay?"

"Don't worry," Jon said, smiling. "I will."

CHAPTER FIFTY-FOUR

The headline on the front page of the *Washington Post* Tuesday morning was even larger than Jon had hoped for. It was stripped completely across the top of the paper. "Christian Armada Made Plans to Kill Vice President," it screamed.

There, Jon thought as he stared at the paper on the steps of his apartment. *It's done. The group will be tried and convicted in the public's mind by the time the hearing convenes this morning. The decision to send the military in to surround the place will be declared justified, once and for all.*

The hearing was held in the largest room in the Russell building, and it was completely full. Standing room only. There were at least two hundred members of the media. Jon had stacked risers at the back for the TV cameras—five-high, an all-time record. The cameras on the fifth level looked down on the senators seated at the front of the room almost as if it were a stage show or a sporting event shot from the back of the auditorium.

Jon stood off to the right in the committee staff entrance and watched almost with detachment as the proceedings began. There would be no glitches, no mistakes in this hearing. Susan had done a magnificent job.

Jon watched as Susan moved to Adams's look. She had virtually replaced the staff director and the senator's own chief of staff for this hearing. She was omnipresent. Adams whispered something into her ear; five seconds later she was whispering that same request to a staff aide.

They were becoming quite a team, Susan and Jon. Susan was the inside person, always carrying out Adams's wishes. Jon was the one facing outward; he was part of the inner circle, but he was the one who made things happen in the real world. They worked well together.

As scripted, Adams held up the critical documents during his opening speech. The cameras all zoomed in for the requisite close-up. Every red button was glowing as he read the relevant portions of the documents to the audience, the parts about targeting national leaders.

Jon knew that every bit of testimony from each witness would be flawless. Susan had gone over their prepared testimony in minute detail, omitting or deleting anything that might raise a question. There was no room for error. The stakes were too high.

Still, even Jon was stunned at the power of the testimony by the "inside" informant on videotape, as he spoke of the inner workings of the Christian Armada leading up to the moment when Air Force Two was blown up. The room was spellbound by the words of this man, who had been filmed with a screen between him and the camera that distorted his features completely. His voice had been altered as well.

But his words had not. Loudly and clearly, they painted the picture of a group obsessed with their perception of a federal government out of control, of a group that feared that same government would come after them, of a group that had clearly and distinctly talked of targeting national political leaders because they were in a "time of war" with the state.

Because his testimony was on videotape, there was no opportunity for anyone to ask him questions. But that didn't seem to matter to the media or anyone else in attendance. This was a first-person account of why the Christian Armada had plotted to assassinate the vice president of the United States. No additional testimony was needed.

By the time the CRATA director began to testify, in fact, some of the electronic media were getting anxious about moving out to file their story for that evening. They had the information they needed. They were ready to lay it out to the public.

Jon, in fact, decided to duck out for a cup of coffee himself during the CRATA director's testimony. He already knew what the guy was going to say. He could make it back in time for the question-and-answer session.

As Jon left the hearing area, he was surprised to see how heavy security was. Usually, just a couple of guards were posted next to an entrance to screen visitors as they entered. Today, they had no fewer than half-a-dozen armed military guards at the entrance and two more stationed in the hallways that led to the hearing room.

Jon was heading down the stairs to the cafeteria on the ground floor when he heard a woman's voice calling out plaintively, almost wailing: "But they killed my husband!"

"Ma'am, the hearing is closed now," one of the guards said sternly. "It's full. No one is allowed in."

Jon stopped and turned to watch. A middle-aged woman was trying to force her way past the guards at the entrance. As Jon stopped, one of the military guards from the other direction began to approach him.

"I have to get in," the woman pleaded. "Please let me through."

One of the guards reached a hand out to restrain her. "Ma'am, I'm sorry, but you cannot."

Jon turned to the guard approaching him and flashed his Senate ID in his direction. The guard nodded, albeit reluctantly, and returned to his post. Jon hesitated and then began to move in the woman's direction.

As the woman saw Jon approach, she looked directly at him for help, her eyes wide with both fear and anger. "Please, you must help me. I want to see the people who killed my husband. That's all I ask. Please help me."

Jon showed the military guards his Senate ID. They glanced at it quickly, then stepped aside. Jon walked around the heavy wooden metal detector that blocked the entrance to the building. He took the woman by the arm and guided her to one side.

"Were you married to one of the members of the Christian Armada?" Jon asked her softly. "Is that why you're here?"

The woman looked up at Jon, trembling. She was dressed simply in jeans, a cotton blouse, and tennis shoes—not like the typical visitor to a Senate hearing. "Please—can you help me?"

"Did you call ahead?" Jon asked her. "Did you try to get permission to attend this hearing?"

To Jon's surprise, the woman nodded. She wiped a tear from her cheek and sniffled once, loudly. "Yes, I did. I wanted to defend my husband. But they wouldn't let me in. They said I couldn't speak. But I came here anyway . . ." Her voice trailed off.

Susan had said that none of the wives had called. But here was one, and she very much wanted to testify. Jon didn't question Susan's judgment. It would have skewed the hearing to let a woman like this testify. In fact, she might very well have stolen the show had she been allowed to speak.

"Where'd you come from?" Jon asked, frowning.

"I drove here, from Petersburg."

"Is that in West Virginia?"

The woman nodded. "Yes, three hours west of here. Our home . . ." The woman looked down at her shoes and burst into tears again. Jon almost reached out to hold the woman, to comfort her. But the guards were staring at him as if he were committing some crime by even talking with her, so, instead, he gestured toward the exit. "Please, let's go outside and talk for a moment. I can explain about the hearing."

The woman looked back at the guards, then at Jon, and decided that it was hopeless trying to get in anyway. "Okay," she mumbled. She turned and left the building. Jon followed closely behind.

He pointed to a cement bench on the grassy divide between the street and the entrance to the building. They both took a seat. The woman sat at one end of the hard bench. Jon sat at the other, uncomfortable in her presence. In fact, every instinct he'd learned in Washington screamed at him to run far, far away from this woman—nothing but trouble could come from this.

But Jon didn't run. And the reason was that, just barely, Jon was hearing a voice that he hadn't heard for many months. A still, small voice, telling him to pay attention. Jon was torn. Should he—could he—block out the voice? Ignore it if it couldn't be blocked out?

He reached across the cement bench and held out a hand. The woman accepted it, her hands cold and trembling; she held onto Jon's hand for a moment longer than usual then released it.

"My name's Jon Abelson. I work for one of the senators in the hearing."

"Elizabeth Brown. You can call me Liz. Everyone does."

Jon almost smiled. "Well, Elizabeth Brown ... Liz ... I'm sorry you weren't able to get into the hearing. But the guards were right. The place is packed. No one's getting in right now."

She glanced at the ID that hung around Jon's neck. "You got in, I bet."

"Yes, I got in. I work on the Senate staff. I can get into hearings like this. It's my job."

The woman blinked once to fight new tears. "It's not fair. Not right. My husband didn't do anything wrong. He was a good man, a good husband, and a good father. We raised good kids."

"I understand."

"Do you?" she said, her voice rising. "Do you know what it's like to watch your husband get a phone call and leave in the dead of night, and then hear that he's killed himself two days later? No reason. Nothing. Do you know what that's like?"

Jon narrowed his eyes, ignoring her obvious pain for the moment. "A phone call? What kind of phone call did your husband get?"

The woman looked confused. "I don't know. Don't remember. It was like some of the others. About that group."

"The Christian Armada?"

"Yeah, the Armada. He went to that place every so often. The call was about that. I remember Sonny—that was my husband's name, Sonny—telling me that he had to get everybody together for a training session. There was also talk about a traitor or something."

"A traitor?"

The woman sniffled. "Yes, something about how big things were about to happen but that they had to deal with someone who wasn't one of their own first."

"Did they know who it was?"

"Sonny didn't say, but it didn't sound like they did. Only that they were sure someone had been doing something wrong."

"So why did your husband go back to the compound after that call, Liz?"

"It was all about getting everyone together. They all had to be there. Whoever called him said it was real important to get the whole thing lined up."

A car sped by just a few feet from where they sat. Jon barely heard it. "Lined up?"

"Yeah, my Sonny was one of the 'captains.' That's what they called him. Captain Brown."

Something clicked in Jon's mind, like the tumbler to a lock. "And, as captain, he had the duty to call other people in the Christian Armada to get them to join him at the compound? Do I have it right?"

"Yeah," the woman said, nodding. "That was what he did. He had his own troops. He made a whole bunch of calls to his men after that, and then he left ."

"Do you . . . do you remember who called him?" Jon asked, not sure where he was heading. Husbands lied to their wives all the time for all sorts of reasons. And maybe this woman had been lied to by her husband— except that the still, small voice was telling him to hear her out.

But the woman shook her head. "No, he never told me about any of that. Said I didn't need to know, that it might harm me when they came after our family one day."

Jon grimaced. Sonny Brown obviously had bought into the grand conspiracy stuff in a big way. "And you believed him—that people would come after your family?" he asked her gently.

"Well, it happened, didn't it?" she shot back. "Didn't it? My Sonny wouldn't kill himself. None of those men would. They just wouldn't." The woman started crying again. "He wouldn't do that. He loved our kids. He did."

Jon sat there silently. He didn't know what to do or say. He would never convince her that the Christian Armada—including her husband—had placed explosives throughout the compound and had then set them off in the face of the military presence surrounding it.

Jon thought about telling the woman that the Christian Armada had been wrong, that God did not call Christians to war—at least not physical warfare. But he would never convince her of that. Not right now, at least.

What to make of this woman's story? It could be important. But, far more likely, it was misguided, the imagination of a grieving widow.

"Mrs. Brown, do you remember when your husband got that phone call?" Jon asked finally.

" 'Course I do," she answered. "I'll never forget. It all happened so quick. First, he got the call, then he called his buddies. He left that night. The next day, that plane got shot down—"

"The vice president's plane, Air Force Two?"

"Yeah. It was all over the news. And then, the day after that, they—we heard they'd surrounded the camp. And then we all heard that they'd ... that they'd killed themselves." She was crying uncontrollably now.

Jon waited for the sobs to subside. It took a while. "Did you hear from him at the compound?" he asked gently.

The woman shook her head. "They didn't allow phones in the place. Said it wasn't proper. Didn't need them."

Jon thought. It was possible that Sonny had gotten the call to come to the compound because the Christian Armada leaders had already made the decision to take out Air Force Two, and they needed the "troop" reinforcements at the compound. That was the most likely scenario.

But not the only one. What if this woman were telling the truth and her husband hadn't been planning to do anything?

Sonny Brown had been one of the Christian Armada's leaders, a captain with men under his command. Was it possible that he would have been in the dark until the last minute about what the group was planning? That didn't seem likely. No, Sonny Brown had simply lied to his wife, Jon convinced himself, and didn't tell her what his group was planning.

"Mrs. Brown, did your husband tell you anything about the call, anything at all? What it was about? Why he had to leave in such a hurry?"

"No, just that they had an emergency training session. Mandatory for everyone who could get there."

"And just a training session?"

"That's what Sonny said."

"And would he have lied to you maybe to cover up what he was getting into? Maybe to protect you?"

The woman looked directly at Jon. Her eyes did not waiver. "Sonny didn't lie. Not to me. Not his whole life."

CHAPTER FIFTY-FIVE

It was the strangest thing. Jon heard the words—heard them quite distinctly—and yet they didn't seem to register. The words that would change Jon's entire world had no impact—as if it were all preordained, something that was simply going to happen as a matter of course.

"President Simpson has decided to select me as his vice president," Sam Adams told Susan and Jon in the privacy of his Senate office after the close of the hearing. "It will be announced tomorrow morning at a news conference."

"Who knows right now?" Susan asked him.

Adams looked out the window. He looked supremely happy, content, enjoying the moment. "Just Abby, and now you." He glanced back, giving Jon a half smile. "And God, of course. It all seems like his kind of idea, don't you think? A certain kind of justice?"

Jon ignored the comment. "The White House staff? Do they know, do you think?"

"I think the chief of staff has some idea," Adams said. "Others are guessing. More will probably get wind of it today." He swiveled back and forth a little in his chair. "I've told some of our network, of course. Jamal Wickes. Nathaniel Watson. Jonas Brownlee. Dr. Sindar. They all needed to know. I've put in a call to Arthur Demontley to ask for his support and help in the coming months."

"And they'll all keep quiet?"

Adams gave Jon a withering stare. "What do you think?"

Jon grimaced. "They'll do as you say, of course. I know, I know. They can be trusted."

"Without question," Adams said. "You should know that by now."

255

Jon decided to change the subject. "You know that, if White House staff knows about this, it'll absolutely be out by tomorrow. In the papers, I mean."

Adams waved off Jon's concern. "It's all right. The president expects that. We both do. The timing is perfect, actually. Thanks to your hard work, we got the story we needed for the hearing today. The networks will carry the story we need tonight. And if the vice presidential selection is in the newspapers tomorrow—beautiful! Time to move on. Time to heal the nation's wounds."

Inwardly, Jon winced. Yes, it all fit. And he, Jon Abelson, had coordinated much of that plan, for better or worse. He had helped make it happen.

"So when do we move over to the White House?" Susan asked, her face flushed with excitement.

"Immediately, I think," Adams answered. "They need us there right away, for the sake of the country."

A thought occurred to Jon, one that he'd almost put off during the events of recent days. "And the campaign? The presidential campaign?"

"We start that immediately, too," Adams answered somberly. "I will need your help, both of you. We can use the campaign staff in place already, but we need to add some of our own. Those loyal to me. That's why I've told Brownlee. He'll line up the political support. Jamal will let the network know. And Watson can help Demontley with the fund-raising side. You understand, of course, about the absolute necessity of having our own people in place?"

They both nodded. The campaign staff in place to help the previous vice president was competent and gifted at the fine art of national politics. But they were not loyal to Vice President-elect Sam Adams. And that counted for everything in the world of politics.

So Jon and Susan would need to build that loyal network and build it very rapidly. Fortunately, most of the people they would need were there for the choosing, a direct result of their years of hard work building the welfare and domestic reform projects in the states. Plenty of people owed their success to Sam Adams and would help at a moment's notice.

In fact, just a few phone calls would get the whole thing moving. The welfare and military reform project had basically given them team leaders—people like Jamal Wickes—who could mobilize a virtual army on Sam Adams's behalf in nearly every key state in the country. Almost as if a master plan had been crafted, waiting for just this moment, this opportunity.

"We'll get to work right away," Susan pledged. "Don't worry. We'll have it in place."

"I'm not worried," Adams smiled. "You always get the job done. Both of you. This will be no different. Just on a bigger stage."

As Jon and Susan left Adams's office, Jon noticed two men standing somewhat awkwardly near the office suite door. Both had coiled, plastic wires protruding from their ears. Jon ducked his head back into the senator's office. "Those men out here," he asked. "Secret Service?"

Adams nodded. "The president thought it was best to get a detail in place now, before the announcement. Just to be safe."

Jon closed the door and walked back to his desk. He nodded to the two Secret Service agents as he walked past. Both men nodded curtly but did not smile. They had a job to do, made even more critical by the events of recent weeks.

When he got back to his chair, Jon's first thought was to pick up the phone and call a few reporters discreetly with the news. But everything had changed now. He couldn't just do that kind of thing anymore. The stage, as Adams had said, was much bigger now. Other players were involved. It wasn't so simple.

So it happens just like that, Jon thought. *One day, you wake up, go to work, and lightning strikes. You go to work the next day in a building where the leader of the world also works. Nothing's the same after that.*

257

CHAPTER FIFTY-SIX

Jon parked his car on the narrow street that encircled the Ellipse south of the White House and started the long trek toward the Old Executive Office Building immediately west of the White House.

A curious thing. Jon was now a full assistant to the vice president of the United States. He was a senior White House aide, part of the inner circle to the second most powerful man in the United States. And yet he couldn't get a parking place even remotely near the seat of power. All of the VIP parking spots were already taken, the ones inside the White House grounds between the OEOB and the West Wing.

In fact, several of the former vice president's senior staff still held those parking spaces and refused to give them up. They were one of the most coveted prizes in Washington, those parking spots, and unless they were fired and thrown off the grounds of the White House, the former vice president's staffers were not going to relinquish their spaces.

Vice President Adams had decided—wisely, Jon believed—not to dismiss any of the former vice president's staff, at least not immediately and not without cause. He would assimilate his own Senate staff with the existing vice presidential staff. They would "work together," at least through the election in November. Adams needed them to carry on the vice presidential duties, after all. They knew what they were doing. And they all needed jobs. There was nowhere for them to go.

Which meant, unfortunately, that Jon had to do the work the office demanded, without the title or the perks of the office. He also had to take a slight cut in pay, at least for a few months until Congress granted a special supplemental request for additional staff expenses.

Jon was given a nondescript title—counselor to the vice president—because the former press secretary remained on staff. Susan became Adams's executive assistant, because the former vice president's chief of staff and executive secretary were both still in place.

But, despite the titles, people in the White House complex knew who was who in the Adams's inner circle. Titles could be handed out or conferred at will. Power could not.

Jon flashed his ID badge to the guards at the southern gate. They buzzed him in. It had taken him ten minutes to get from his car to the OEOB. But Jon smiled as he began to climb the long, wide steps on the eastern side of OEOB. He might not have a parking space, but he had the access. He had the ear of the vice president. In fact, there was a private meeting that morning—the kind of meeting that was most certainly not on the vice president's public calendar—that spoke volumes about who was in charge and who was not.

The vice president's chief of staff would not be in attendance, nor would his press secretary or his national security advisor. But Jon and Susan would be—the only representatives of Vice President Adams's staff. They would be joined by Nathaniel Watson, Dr. Sindar, Jamal Wickes, Jonas Brownlee, and Abby Adams.

Jon didn't even bother to check in at his own office. He headed straight for the vice president's ornate OEOB office, dominated by a huge table with nearly twenty chairs surrounding it. Brownlee, Dr. Sindar, Jamal Wickes, and Susan were already there, along with Abby and Sam Adams, who gestured for Jon to close the door behind him as he entered.

"Glad you could make it, Jon," Adams said cheerfully.

"Had to walk a ways," Jon muttered.

Jon scanned the room. It was huge, easily more than one hundred feet long. Everyone was seated on couches near the fireplace at one end of the room. Adams's desk was all the way at the opposite end, practically out of sight.

"We were just talking about the firebombing incidents in Detroit last night," Adams said. He pointed at Jamal Wickes.

"We've had people talking to groups there throughout the night," Wickes said, "trying to mediate. But I'm not sure how much luck we'll have."

"What happened?" Jon asked. "I saw the reports on CNN, briefly."

"Well, what you didn't see was a communiqué one of the groups sent to Washington, demanding more money. Or else," Wickes said. "We're pouring millions of dollars into some of these communities, and it still doesn't seem like it's enough."

"Too bad you can't just write a check and get some of these people off your backs," Brownlee said, laughing.

"Man, we're tryin' hard to do just that," Wickes grinned. "We're funneling so much program money into some of these places, you wouldn't believe it. But they were so far down to begin with, I'm not sure there's enough money in the world to make them feel like they're back up to ground level."

"So what can you do?" Jon asked.

"What we're doing. Just more of it. Keep talkin'," Wickes said grimly. "It's our only hope. We have to keep talkin' or else these places will blow higher than that Christian Armada compound."

"You're doing the best you can, Jamal," Adams said. "That's all you can do—that's all any of us can do. We have to try."

"But it just isn't good enough, Mr. Vice President," Wickes said.

Adams and Brownlee exchanged glances. Jon noticed Brownlee's slight, almost imperceptible nod of his head.

"Jamal, if you do your best and then you fail, no one can fault you," Adams said softly. "But, you know, sometimes even tragedy leads to something good, something grand. If we have anarchy in the streets, if we have poverty beyond the capacity of humanity to endure, if we have a moral sickness that is eating out the heart and soul of our society—well, then, maybe it's time for change. A new society. A new way of seeing the world. A new way of living. A new law of the land, one that recognizes the fundamental rights of every individual. Perhaps a new way of governing that *forces* people to share equally so that no group of elite individuals holds too much power, too much wealth, too much sway over their fellow men and women. Sometimes anarchy and violence leads to something better. That is my fervent hope in this very uncertain time. And that is what we will all strive for in the coming months."

Jon listened to Adams, not so much understanding his words as listening to their rhythm. Adams had never been prone to oratory. He was all action, all getting things done. But this transition to the vice presidency, moving into the center of power in the world, was beginning to change him. Listening to Adams, watching him, Jon could actually see the change. Sam Adams, previously always the man of the people, was taking on a regal bearing.

Jon had never heard Adams speak like this before. A new society, forged in the crucible of America's chaos, violence, and turmoil? It almost sounded to Jon as though Adams welcomed that chaos, that he embraced it because it forced the nation in a new direction. His direction.

"I will try to help, sir," Wickes said immediately.

"I will too, Mr. Vice President," Jonas Brownlee offered.

"I'm sure you all will," the vice president said warmly. "That's why all of you are here today, because we all share that common ground. So let us begin. We have a long road ahead of us between now and the election. We will need every ounce of strength and courage if we are to prevail. But the path we choose may change the course of history."

CHAPTER FIFTY-SEVEN

Over the course of the next two hours, Jon, Susan, and the others set out a strategy for the election. It was not a complicated strategy, but it would require all of their talents and contacts. Jonas Brownlee would make sure that the party apparatus swung in behind Adams. Nathaniel Watson, who joined the meeting halfway through, pledged that Arthur Demontley and the others who had been raising significant sums of money for Adams's predecessor would continue to help. Wickes and Dr. Sindar, who also joined them late, pledged that their network would turn out the votes on election day. Those who carried the "card" already saw Adams as their hero, Wickes said. It wouldn't take much to persuade them to carry that conviction into the voting booth.

Since the day of his swearing in, Vice President Adams had sky-rocketed into national awareness. He came with almost no baggage. He had no skeletons in his closet, so to speak, and the national media didn't seem inclined to search all that hard to find any.

Adams was ideal for the role of healer. He was young, energetic, a veteran, someone with ideas. He was a natural leader. It had been a long time since anyone in the Democratic Party had so invited comparison with John F. Kennedy.

Adams seemed prepared for the role. He was already beginning to "grow" into the job, as new as he was to it. The media were even beginning to write that kind of nonsensical drivel about how quickly Adams was gaining "gravitas" in the job. It was almost enough to make Jon sick.

Even so, Jon was busy adding fuel to all those fires—how quickly the new vice president is being assimilated into the power structure at the White House, how much the staff respects his insights, and so on. Adams would need every bit of good press Jon could muster to win this election. And Jon would do everything in his power to make sure the image of Adams in the media was the best it could be. That was his job, and he would not fail in it, no matter how cynical or manipulative it all seemed.

The meeting broke up by midmorning, and Jon went back to his cubbyhole office to return calls. Dozens of call slips were spread out on his desk. Since the transition, the press secretary and his staff had stopped trying to speak for Adams. Only Jon could get in to see the new vice president, so the others were simply dumping the many requests for Adams on Jon's desk.

Glumly, Jon sorted through them. MTV wanted Adams to host a special for kids. Both Jay Leno and David Letterman wanted him to appear as a guest. Oprah Winfrey and Phil Donahue wanted Adams to tell his life story to their millions of viewers. *Parade* magazine wanted a cover story, as did *People*, *Time*, and *Newsweek*.

And Jon could hear the phone ringing off the hook in the outer offices, most of them calls from other organizations wanting a piece of Sam Adams.

Jon was accustomed to dealing with the media. He just wasn't used to this kind of traffic or the urgency of the requests. Everyone wanted Adams, and they wanted him yesterday.

In the wake of the Air Force Two bombing, a pall had come over Washington. Time had seemed to come to a grinding halt. Now, with Adams in office, everything shifted suddenly into overdrive. The party had a candidate, a horse, to back. Workers had someone to fight for. Activists had a mission and a goal—get Adams elected to the White House.

Overnight, Adams had stopped being a real, flesh-and-blood person. He'd become a national figure, someone everyone talked about and very few actually knew. Adams no longer had friends. Now he had people who wanted access, people who wanted to serve or help—and others who wanted to block his ascent to the highest office in the land. Everywhere he went, an entourage followed.

On day two of the transition, for instance, Jon had staged a simple event. Adams had signed his name in the vice president's ornate OEOB desk, beside the names of Dan Quayle, George Bush, Walter Mondale, Gerald Ford, and LBJ. The cameras had rolled. Adams had cracked a few jokes about the spike marks Eisenhower had left on the floor of the vice president's office when he used to wander around in his golf cleats, and the media had gobbled it up. Adams was a star.

Jon had stood behind the cameras in the background, feeling as if he had stepped out of his own life into someone else's. It had all seemed so unreal, so hokey, so staged, so scripted. But everyone had known what was expected and had played their roles.

Sam Adams would be president soon. Everyone felt it, knew it, almost as if it were inevitable. And they all wanted to be there to be part of the mysterious event that transformed one man into the leader of the world. They wanted to be able to tell their friends and their children that they were there.

Everywhere Sam Adams went now, every person he met, every meeting he attended, every telephone call he took, every event he took part in—it was all part of the grand game. Adams had been anointed, almost—as he had intimated to Jon and Susan—by the mysterious finger of God.

Even the cynical, jaded White House staff saw it. In fact, they were perhaps the worst offenders. In White House meetings, many of them jockeyed for position next to Adams or deliberately entered conversations he took part in. They all wanted to "be there" as the succession occurred. No one wanted to be left out.

People seemed willing—eager even—to devote whole parts of their lives to serve Adams, as if they weren't whole until they were following someone who could lead them confidently into the future.

Adams was that person. He had the vision, the drive, the image, the look and feel of a natural leader of men and women. Most people had little trouble thinking of him as a leader—as their leader.

There had been a time when Adams could walk the streets anonymously. Now, when he walked among the people, everyone stopped and stared, approached him to say a few words, followed his entourage for a little while, or pointed and whispered.

And Adams had changed. His personal presence was different somehow, larger than life. It was the same kind of transformation seen in cardinals who become pope, or athletes who command center stage at world championships.

Adams's gift, the one that had carried him so far in politics, now seemed almost supernatural. Adams had always been a good listener—to the point that those talking with him felt as if they could reveal their cares and worries to him and that Adams took those things to heart.

Now that same quality meant that people confessed their innermost desires and wishes to Adams as if they were speaking to a deity. When

Adams said a few words in return, it was as if they'd been handed divine words by an oracle.

Strangely, it all made Jon feel small, rather than more important. Only Adams mattered. Everything else was simply apparatus and machinery to support his singular presence within the grandness of the White House. Jon felt as if he'd lost some part of himself. He was no longer Jon Abelson. He was an appendage of—and a conduit to—the man who was about to become the leader of the most powerful nation on earth.

It was an awful feeling. Yet Jon could not escape it. He was drawn to the power and the glory of it all, like a moth drawn inexorably to the light. The quest for power at the center of the vortex was an intoxicating, mind-numbing thing.

The notion that absolute power tended to corrupt absolutely was true. Yet part of Jon refused to believe it—or more accurately, wanted to test that principle firsthand to see if it was true.

Had the events of the past months changed Jon? Yes, he was sure that they had and that he was continuing to change. But that didn't matter. This was an opportunity much too big to miss, whatever the cost to himself or to others.

Jon had a front-row seat—one of the few in the world—for an unfolding drama of global importance. Very few witnessed the way in which the world was shaped and molded. Jon was being given that opportunity. He wanted to experience every moment of it.

Later, when the world had stopped spinning so madly, Jon would take time to figure it all out. For now, he would do what he had to, with each step along the path.

CHAPTER FIFTY-EIGHT

The plane lifted off the ground from National Airport. As many times as Jon had flown out of this airport, as many times as he'd seen this exact picture outside his window as his jet had pulled up from the ground and then banked hard to the left over the Fourteenth Street bridge, Jon was still fascinated with the view of the Mall grounds off to his right.

The place was majestic—to Jon and to nearly every tourist who ever came to visit the nation's capital. The Lincoln Memorial, the Washington Monument, the Capitol Building, and RFK Stadium, all in a row. It seemed to have such perfect symmetry.

"Pretty, isn't it?" Susan said from the seat beside his. She leaned over to gaze out the window with him. Her hair brushed against his face.

"Yeah, it is," Jon muttered.

Susan leaned back in her seat. "You really don't mind this? You're sure?"

"I'm sure, Susan. This is important."

Officially, they were going to Chicago for an important speech Vice President Adams was going to give at a project. It was a pivotal speech, one in which Adams planned to pledge a vast change in the way Washington treated the poor and downtrodden in every city in America.

But, unofficially, they were also going to meet Susan's parents, who lived in Park Ridge, a suburb of Chicago. And it was all making Jon very nervous. With their professional lives moving practically at warp speed for years now, they had no real time for a personal life outside the office. They had said nothing about marriage, engagement—nothing ever about making a commitment.

And yet, here they were, on their way to meet Susan's parents.

266

Despite his feelings for Susan, a gaping question hung at the center of their relationship, one that he seldom confronted but could never fully get past: Susan was not a Christian. She didn't share Jon's own religious beliefs. That had seldom caused friction between them because Jon had so rarely talked about his faith in the years they had known each other. But it was still there, the one, huge stumbling block that stood in the way of total commitment on Jon's part.

"You'll like my folks, Jon. I promise," Susan said as the plane began to level off.

"I know I will." Jon turned to look back out the window. "By the way, you worried at all about this speech Sam's giving?"

"No, why? Should I be?"

"Oh, I don't know. It's just that . . ."

"What?"

"That it's nice and all to talk about helping the poor and the down-trodden. But the poor and the downtrodden don't vote much. It's the people who are making fifty thousand a year and have to pay off a mortgage and put three kids through college who vote. And they don't want to hear about helping the poor."

Susan laughed. "You really are getting cynical in your old age, Mr. Abelson. Whatever happened to all those ideals?"

"Reality hit me."

"Well, try this on for reality," Susan said quietly, seriously. "Sam's having it both ways. People trust him as a patriot and as someone who's willing to help the average guy, the middle class. But people also think of him as someone who helps out the less fortunate."

"Yeah, well, maybe," Jon scoffed. "I know it looks like he's getting support on the one hand from the black community, thanks to Wickes and the others—and, on the other hand, that his promilitary stuff with the new domestic military activities and his strong stand on the Christian Armada thing has put him in good stead with the average white family. I just don't know how long that's gonna last. It's a tough balancing act. The two don't exactly go together real well."

"They only have to go together through the election," Susan reminded him. "After that, all bets are off."

When they landed in Chicago, they rented a car and drove to Park Ridge for a quick lunch with Susan's parents at Susan's childhood home. Susan had been right. Jon immediately liked both of them, and they seemed to like Jon. Susan's father was an accountant with Paine Webber, and her mother had been a full-time mother and housewife her entire life. They chitchatted about life at the White House and about Washington. No one said anything about marriage or children, to Jon's immense relief.

Shortly before supper, Jon and Susan returned to the city for the vice president's event. His speech that evening was to christen a new community center in a housing project. A huge crowd was expected. It was a big deal, one of the biggest the community had ever seen.

When they arrived, the vice president was waiting in a holding area backstage. Jon and Susan had to fight their way through the crowd, larger by thousands than had been estimated. None of them really cared what he was going to say. They just wanted to hear the man who might be their new leader.

Adams was sitting by himself in a corner of the holding area when Jon and Susan arrived. He was reviewing his notes for the evening. He didn't look up as Jon approached him.

"Sir, are you ready?" Jon asked him.

When Adams did look up, he had an intensity, a fierceness, about him. That was not unusual with Adams, especially before big speeches when it was critical that he be "up." But it still took Jon by surprise. Adams's charisma seemed to grow by leaps and bounds with every day of the presidential campaign.

"Yes, Jon, I'm ready," Adams replied. "How's the crowd?"

"Large. Very."

"The media?"

"Lots," Jon smiled. "All waiting for you to trip up. So don't."

They both laughed. Adams rarely made mistakes in his public speaking, not back in the Ohio days when he had urged people to "take back" their communities, and not now when he was urging the people of the nation to "take back" their own lives and their towns and cities.

The Secret Service detail walked up as they were talking and stood off to the side respectfully, waiting for Jon's conversation to end.

"Sir," the agent-in-charge said when Jon had finished, "I just wanted to remind you that we've had those reports—"

Adams held up a hand, cutting him off. "Yes, yes, I know. But, like I've said, I can't just stop campaigning because we've had reports from some of these groups. It was to be expected after the Christian Armada incident. But there will always be reports. I can't hide. I won't hide. I have to be here."

The agent nodded. "I understand, sir. I just wanted to remind you. We've done our best to secure the area, but there can never be total security at an outdoor event like this. Please be careful at the rope line. Go slowly so we can go in front and behind."

"Don't worry. I'll be a good boy," Adams said, smiling.

After the agent left, Jon looked at Adams. "What reports?"

"Oh, the usual bunch of nonsense," Adams scoffed. "The same old thing—some hate group might be planning something."

"But some of those reports prove to be true," Jon said. "Remember the guy who tried to fly his plane into the West Wing?"

"Not real bright, that guy, was he?" Adams laughed. He got up and placed his notes into his suit pocket. Jon stepped aside to let him pass.

"Be careful, sir," Jon said.

"Always am," Adams said, and then moved to the doorway.

Jon and Susan followed Adams onstage a moment later. As Jon looked down into the sea of thousands of faces, he glanced over at the vice president. Adams was walking slowly, surely, across the stage to the rope line, almost shining with charisma, clearly swept up in the emotion of the shouts and cheers gushing toward him in waves from the crowd. He made his way through the rope line—slowly, allowing the Secret Service agents to follow his steps—and then returned to the stage. He took his place behind the podium, the vice presidential seal on the front of the podium.

Just as he was beginning to speak, a sudden, sharp *crack!* was heard above the roar and rumbling of the crowd. A fraction of a second later, pieces of wood and plastic flew off in all directions as a bullet tore through the vice presidential seal and the podium.

Jon, transfixed, saw the whole thing happen as if in slow motion. He heard the report of the rifle, saw the pieces of debris fly off into the air, heard the bullet exit the podium and bury itself deep into the floor behind Adams, saw the Secret Service agents reflexively lunge toward Adams.

The bullet had missed Adams by maybe six inches.

Pandemonium immediately erupted. The crowd heaved to one side or the other, as people tried either to protect themselves or to see what was happening. Adams was surrounded immediately by Secret Service agents. Agents at the back of the crowd fell on the would-be assassin, pushing him to the ground.

Adams was hustled offstage, toward Jon and Susan. At least a dozen agents moved him toward the holding area.

"No!" Adams shouted. "I don't want to go back there!"

"But, sir!" the agent-in-charge shouted.

"I will not be intimidated by these groups!" Adams shouted. "I will not!"

The agents grabbed both of Adams's arms, physically restraining him. They began to march him toward the holding area. Jon stood to the side, helpless.

Adams continued to struggle, trying to pull both arms free. "Let me go!" he ordered. "Right now! I demand it!"

The agents hesitated. They had their orders. Their job was to protect the vice president, even if it meant sacrificing their own lives in the line of duty. But they had never confronted a situation like this where their charge was refusing to be protected.

Adams got one arm loose and then another. He turned to go back to the stage.

"You cannot, sir!" the agent-in-charge said.

"I can, and I will," Adams said. He pushed aside two agents who made an effort to restrain him and strode out onto the stage, where only moments before someone had tried to end his life. He walked to the podium and grabbed the microphone. Secret Service agents surrounded him on all sides but did not try to pull him off the stage. "Please, everyone. Remain calm. Do not panic. I am all right. I am all right," Adams said loudly into the microphone.

The crowd had been in motion, streaming in all directions. But at the sound of Adams's voice, everyone turned to look back at the stage. Cameras on risers at the back of the crowd continued rolling tape. Jon knew, as he watched the drama unfold, that what Adams was doing would elect him president of the United States. Without question.

"Please. Hear me out for a moment. I want you all to know something." The crowd hushed a little. "It is important. I want you to know that I give you my word, as we stand here tonight, that I will not be intimidated by the threat of violence in our society. I know that many of you every day, as you walk the streets of your neighborhood, are faced with the same fear that I felt tonight—the fear that someone you do not know will harm you in a place you thought was safe.

"Our homes should be safe, but they are not. Our streets should be safe, but they are not. Our neighborhoods and communities should be safe, but they are not. There should not be violence in our towns, in our cities, in our streets, and in our communities. But there is, and we have seen its terrible face tonight.

"But I give you my word, in the face of such awful evil, that if I become your president, I will change this. I give you my word that I will do everything in my power to make our homes and our streets safe again. This I pledge to you. Thank you."

Only then did Adams allow himself to be escorted off the stage to the relative safety of his holding area. And as Jon watched Adams leave the stage, he couldn't help but think that somehow, in all this madness, Adams had been the only one to remain calm, to see once again the opportunity in adversity. And he had acted when no one else would.

THE
PRESIDENT

CHAPTER FIFTY-NINE

"Mr. Abelson, the president is on line one."

Jon nodded at the aide who'd poked his head through the doorway to deliver the message. The aide closed the door quietly.

"Jon, I need you to look into something," Adams said on the other end of the line. "It's fairly urgent. Someone will bring the papers down shortly."

"Thank you, Mr. President," Jon answered somberly. "I'll take care of it right away."

"You always do, Jon," President Adams said with that calm, reassuring tone that engendered trust. "And Jon? Be discreet, okay? I don't want the circle wide on this one. Let me know when you have news to discuss."

"Yes, sir," Jon said and hung up the phone gently. He stared out across the spacious room. He had one of the best office suites in the West Wing. He'd chosen spaciousness over direct access to the Oval Office. Most White House aides fought and clawed to get an office as close to the president's as possible. Not Jon. He didn't need the proximity. He could see the president any time he wanted, so he chose an office suite on the second floor, down the hall from the Oval Office and up a flight of stairs.

As communications director to the president, Jon shaped the president's image and, in some areas, the new administration's policy. But Jon had a much broader portfolio even than that: He was the president's alter ego, and everyone in Washington knew it. Jon spoke for the president. He was the president's voice.

Almost from the very moment he'd returned to the stage after the assassination attempt, the country had rallied behind Adams in a way it

275

never had in its history. The nation saw courage in Adams's actions—personal courage—and it rewarded him with unprecedented adulation.

The man who'd fired the bullet at the vice president, it turned out, was from a right-wing extremist group, a man with a history of mental illness who babbled on about how Adams was to blame for the Christian Armada incident.

The election itself had been almost anticlimatic. Adams had been carried into the presidency in the fall on an unprecedented wave of bipartisan support. He got votes from Republicans and Democrats alike, winning with more than sixty percent of the vote. His Republican opponent had not carried a single state. It had been a landslide greater even than Nixon's or Reagan's reelections.

The campaign itself, of course, had nearly destroyed them all. Jon had learned to live on three hours of sleep at night. Presidential campaigning was now an art, honed by national political activists in the 1970s and 1980s. It was now a question of finding the right candidate, then filling the media with messages tested a hundred times with focus groups and selected polling.

Sam Adams had hit some very deep chords in the American electorate. By centralizing the welfare state and guaranteeing economic security to tens of millions of people—while simultaneously guaranteeing safer streets through the added police and military forces—Adams had changed the face of America overnight.

Once they saw it in action, people welcomed the security of a strong national government that met their basic needs—economic security and personal safety. Adams had almost single-handedly restored America's belief in the role of government. It's hard to argue against something that's working.

Jon, of course, had been at Adams's side virtually every waking moment during the campaign, continuously spinning in a hundred different ways, in a hundred different forums. But the central messages remained unchanged—*we will protect you at home and on the streets*. And people believed him.

The first one hundred days of the Adams administration had been extraordinary, beyond anyone's hopes, really. The Department of Public Works had become firmly entrenched, thanks to the tireless efforts of Secretary Sira Sindar and his chief of staff, Jamal Wickes. Almost half the adults in the country now had the card and relied on its many benefits.

Adams's first budget had been passed almost without change. Most of his domestic policy proposals were now working their way through the congressional appropriations system without much controversy, and the national debt problem was improving, slowly but steadily.

One serious problem remained—the very real threat that pockets of urban violence could spread soon during the summer months, despite Adams's improvements in the welfare system. Jamal Wickes and his "troops" in the large urban cities said that no amount of money could heal the unrest among the poor who had been disenfranchised for so long that their hopelessness had turned to bitter, uncontrollable rage.

President Adams had proclaimed, often and loudly, that he would use the combined might of the military and national police force to quell uprisings. But Jon wasn't sure that force would be any more effective than additional money in stopping the violence.

There was a knock on the door. One of Jon's four front-office aides brought the package in and set it down on his desk. "From the president," the aide said. Jon nodded his thanks and opened the package.

It was a proposed Executive Order, drafted by White House counsel Nathaniel Watson. There was a "white paper" attached to it supporting the policy, and Adams had penned a brief note on top for Jon's eyes only.

"We need this, Jon," Adams had written. "You can discuss with Captain Johnson over at CRATA. Run it by the community. Confirm with them the seriousness of the unrest. Then convince them that it's an absolute necessity to tighten the screws. We have no choice. We have to act now before it's too late."

Jon knew the "community" Adams meant was the network of activists who now served Public Works Secretary Sindar and who jumped to the commands of Jamal Wickes. Jon sighed as he thought of the nearly impossible task of trying to convince them that troops needed to come storming in soon.

Wickes had a huge pot of money to play with at the new Public Works Department. By combining several departments, the budget for their department was easily in excess of several hundred billion dollars.

"We've got more money than God," Sindar had once joked. But it was nearly true. Jon could not imagine that much money—or how it was all being spent.

In the past six months, Wickes had done a brilliant job setting up accounts for groups in nearly every urban city in America. He'd briefed the president recently on the progress, and it was astounding. There was a real network with real resources in these cities.

Jon scanned the proposed Executive Order that Nathaniel Watson had drafted. Watson had arbitrarily given it a "confidential" seal, which

277

meant that very few would actually see it once it had been signed and placed in the safe.

Executive Orders were weird documents. They authorized the president and the White House to do certain things, yet the public never heard about most of them. And those that were signed as part of the national security apparatus remained entirely secret.

This particular Executive Order would be one of those secret documents. Essentially, the document authorized the president to order increased domestic surveillance of groups and people who might be agitating to increase the unrest in major cities in the country. It expanded the counterterrorism activities of CRATA to include routine surveillance of a whole new set of organizations.

But the order went even further. In the event of major unrest in the country, the document authorized the president to order troops to quell the violence. In essence, the president could declare martial law and shut down all functions of the national government until peace had been returned to the cities.

Presidents could not arbitrarily declare martial law in the United States. American presidents were not dictators. Congress spent money and wrote laws, and the Supreme Court interpreted those laws. Presidents were mostly implementers of the laws created by others.

But this Executive Order, Jon knew, had the potential to shift that balance of power if there was major unrest and the troops were called in. Congress would try to challenge it, but in a climate of national fear and panic, the president would prevail with the public.

The white paper described how unstable the situation was in major cities like Los Angeles, Chicago, and New York. It predicted that flare-ups or something worse would happen this summer. It set out a plan for mediating and reconciling the conflicts in the cities, once the new domestic military forces had been put in place to keep the violence from spreading.

No author was listed at the end of the documet, nor was it on any agency's letterhead. But at the bottom of the last page, immediately under the last paragraph, was a single line that identified the creator of the document: Daystar Communications.

Jon blinked. It had been many, many months since he'd seen that name on top of the document outlining the activities of the Christian Armada, but he had not forgotten, even though he'd never tried again to trace it. What was Daystar Communications? And how did it figure into this?

Almost without thinking, Jon flipped the intercom switch. "Get me Captain Johnson. Over at CRATA," he barked to the unlucky soul who'd picked up the line.

"Captain Johnson?" the aide asked.

"Just ask CRATA's directory for his office. They'll find him."

"Yes, sir," the aide said and hung up.

Jon flipped the switch back down. He could hear a faint, nearly forgotten echo in the back of his mind, that still, small voice telling him to take a deeper look at this. But it had been a very, very long time since Jon had heeded that voice. In fact, it had been a very long time since Jon had even thought about that voice—or, for that matter, about what was right or wrong, much less acted on those thoughts.

He had become a creature of action. You did what you had to in order to get the job done. That was how you succeeded, especially in this place. Do the job. And don't ask too many questions about it. If the cause is just, make sure it prevails—any way you can.

In fact, Jon rationalized, you could argue that there really wasn't any clear black or white—right or wrong—in a place like Congress or the White House, only a million shades of gray. Everything was somewhere on that spectrum of gray. Things were good if they succeeded, bad if they failed.

By that standard, Jon was good. He nearly always succeeded. He got jobs done. That alone was the gold standard in Washington, the standard against which everything was measured.

The intercom buzzed. Jon flipped the switch back up. "Yes?"

"Captain Johnson on the line," the aide said briskly, exuding an air of accomplishment at having found the captain so quickly with a minimum of fuss.

Jon smiled. He enjoyed watching junior aides learn the ropes of Washington. "Thanks." He picked up the telephone, cutting off the intercom. "Captain Johnson?"

"Yes, sir, Mr. Abelson," the captain answered. "I was expecting your call."

"You were?"

"They told me the Executive Order was moving through the system and that you might have a couple of questions."

"I see," Jon said. "Well, they were right. I do have a couple of questions."

"Shoot."

Jon took a deep breath. He'd have to be careful here. "Will CRATA handle all of the surveillance activities?"

"We'll authorize and supervise them," Johnson answered immediately. "There will be constant monitoring and review."

"But CRATA won't actually do the work?"

"No, not the actual work. That would be . . ."

"Too dangerous?"

"Something like that. Plus, we can't buy that much equipment without congressional authorization."

"Not even with the black part of your budget?"

"Our black budget isn't that large. Can't accommodate it."

"Got it," Jon said. "So who's handling the contracting?"

"You mean, who's in charge?"

"No, I mean, who's actually doing the work?"

Captain Johnson paused, obviously wondering just how much he was authorized to tell Jon. "We plan to use Daystar," he answered finally.

"Daystar Communications? The outfit that prepared the white paper supporting the policy?"

Jon could almost hear the relief on the other end of the line. Jon already knew the name, clearly, so Johnson didn't have to worry that he'd leaked something he should not have. "Yes, sir, we use Daystar a lot. They have the capability for this project."

There were hundreds—maybe even thousands—of "beltway bandit" firms ringing Washington, D.C., who handled all manner of top-secret projects for federal security agencies. Nearly all of them were run by former government officials who, after leaving their agencies, simply continued the government's work from the outside. Obviously, Daystar was one of those.

"It's a big project," Jon mused.

"Daystar has the low-orbit satellites already in place. They've purchased long-distance phone access. They have pieces of the cellular and PCS systems as well. They can handle it."

Jon nodded. So whatever else it was, Daystar was something of a telecommunications firm in its own right. "And they can be trusted?"

Jon could hear the dead silence on the other end of the line. It must have sounded like a colossally stupid question. "You know the president is the chairman of its board? Right?"

"The president?"

"Former President Simpson. He's Daystar's chairman. He joined up several months ago after leaving office. But you knew that, of course."

"Yes, yes, of course," Jon mumbled. He was having a hard time understanding this. He couldn't connect the dots.

"So we have no problem whatsoever contracting with Daystar for this work," Captain Johnson said firmly.

"Oh, obviously. I understand."

"Good. Other questions?"

Jon thought quickly. He didn't want the conversation to end on this topic. "How soon do you go up?"

"Immediately. The sooner the better. We already have reports of unrest, groups preparing for marches in the streets. We have to be ready; we have to get there first—for the sake of the country."

"Certainly. For the sake of the country," Jon grimaced. He'd heard that often enough. "So you don't have a month or two to test this out?"

"No, sir, we don't even have a week or two. School's out soon, and we expect this summer to be brutal. No telling what might happen in July or August, with so many folks out on the streets."

Jon sighed. "Okay, I get the picture. I'm sure you'll have your Executive Order soon. Maybe in a day or two."

"Very good," Captain Johnson answered, clearly delighted at the news.

"Keep up the good work," Jon said. "I'll be in touch."

As Jon hung up the phone, he shook his head. Simpson chaired Daystar's board? Lots of former presidents and vice presidents agreed to chair or sit on boards of directors after leaving office. But something else was here—something he was missing.

Jon closed his eyes. The remnants of a conversation he'd had once, the memory of which still made him uncomfortable because he'd failed to follow up on it, drifted into his mind.

What was it Sonny Brown's wife had told him outside the Russell Office Building that day? That her husband had never lied to her?

Jon pulled out a pad of paper and wrote "CRATA" at the top. CRATA had been organized, in part, to monitor groups like the Christian Armada. Jon wrote "Christian Armada" just below CRATA, and drew a line between the two. But, according to that document he'd tripped across in Adams's file, someplace called "daystar.com" had carried out the initial surveillance work on the Christian Armada.

Jon wrote "Daystar" and connected it by line to "CRATA." Had Daystar been a CRATA contractor, monitoring the Christian Armada?

Jon stared at the page, at the lines connecting the three names. He suddenly felt very much alone. He was at the center of the universe, at the right hand of the most powerful man in the world. Virtually anything was his for the asking. And yet, Jon knew, he was alone. He had no real friends—only allies of convenience.

He could turn to no one, really, with these questions. Susan, perhaps. But she was now the president's chief of staff, and the demands of their jobs in the new administration had once again pushed them apart. So far, nothing had come of their trip to meet Susan's parents. It had, in fact, been weeks since they'd shared a quiet moment. They had been so consumed by the transfer of power to Adams following the election that they had not once discussed their future together.

He could ask no one about this. He had no friends on something like this, only enemies. Even asking questions was dangerous.

Jon pulled the piece of paper from the pad, crumpled it up, and tossed it into the waste can. He began to write new names down on the blank pad of paper in front of him.

There was work to be done for Adams. He'd need to place at least a dozen calls today to make sure that key members of the Sindar-Wickes network were okay with this new policy. Then he would bless the project and the Executive Order as the president had demanded.

But Jon would also ask a few questions. Carefully. Discreetly. Without raising suspicion. He had to, if only for his own sanity and peace of mind. A connection was there. He was certain of that now. And a long-ignored voice was urgently whispering that he had to find that connection.

CHAPTER SIXTY

"National Guard seals off streets in downtown Los Angeles. This is news at the top of the hour," said the tan, well-dressed anchor on CNN, which Jon always kept on near his desk. It was just after lunchtime in L.A., late afternoon in Washington.

"After shots were fired and police called for help, the mayor of Los Angeles today asked the National Guard to seal off several streets of downtown Los Angeles," the news anchor said after the commercial break.

"There were reports of at least two injuries in the shootings, but no deaths. Both the governor of California and President Adams authorized the use of the National Guard to quell the immediate threat of violence."

Jon watched the film of National Guard trucks on the move and some of the residents on the streets disappearing into their homes as the trucks rolled in. He grabbed the remote control, turned the volume down, and returned to his work.

He had an answer for the president on the Executive Order. Jamal Wickes's network wanted more money. A lot more money. They, too, wanted to put local people on the streets and in the projects to quell the unrest and the unease, hoping that locals would be effective enough to keep the military out of their neighborhoods. Jon, speaking for the president, had agreed to their demands.

Jon called for an aide and sent the draft of the Executive Order back to President Adams with his blessing. "Public Works will need to pump some more money into the projects, but it's worth the investment," Jon wrote in a note to Adams. "They'll plan a major push by the end of the month. You'll have people crawling all over the place, but they'll support strong-arm tactics if necessary."

He made only one other phone call during the afternoon. He placed it himself from a pay phone near a cafeteria below the street on Pennsylvania Avenue. Jon knew they kept extensive computer records of all incoming and outgoing calls at the White House, and he didn't feel like having this particular call on the books.

The call was to the regional Bell Atlantic office. After explaining that he worked for the president of the United States, he arranged for an appointment with the general manager at five o'clock. Jon didn't tell him why, and the general manager didn't ask.

Jon left the office a little early, telling his staff he had a few errands to run. No one questioned him. No one ever questioned him.

The Bell Atlantic office, which was less than fifteen minutes from the White House, served much of the mid-Atlantic region. It was one of the spin-offs from the break up of Ma Bell, but it was now a huge phone company in its own right.

The general manager was a kind, elderly man approaching retirement. Jon had assumed that the man would take the safe route, check with his superiors, perhaps make Jon file paperwork. But he didn't. He listened to Jon's story and agreed immediately to authorize a search of their extensive computerized phone records. He seemed eager to help the White House with a discreet investigation.

Jon was surprised how easy it was. He gave the general manager Sonny Brown's name and city, the approximate window of time—from three days before the Air Force Two bombing until the day after the incident. A half hour later, Jon had his printout.

Jon stood outside the Bell Atlantic office a few minutes later and stared at the printout. As he'd expected, dozens of calls were listed, both incoming and outgoing. But nearly all of them were "304" numbers, which meant they were local West Virginia calls. Jon felt fairly certain he could disregard those.

Elizabeth Brown had said the call came in the day before the bombing. Jon scanned the numbers on the printout. Most of the calls on the sheet were outgoing calls, placed from Sonny Brown's home, almost certainly to the members of the Christian Armada, summoning them to their post.

In fact, there were just eight incoming calls on the day before the bombing. Six of them were local "304" calls. The seventh was from a "703" exchange—which was Virginia—and the last was from a "301" exchange in Maryland.

As Jon stood there, cars rushed by in a steady, monotonous stream. This was rush hour in Washington, and everyone was pushing hard to get home.

That's what I should do, Jon thought. *Forget this. Go home. Bury the past. I don't want to know.*

Jon looked up at the sky, searching for an answer. It had been months—maybe years—since Jon had offered a sincere prayer to God. His old habit of constant, conversational prayer had died long ago. There had been no time. His life had been a constant rush of activity from one crisis to the next since he'd pulled into Singleton, Ohio, a century or two ago, looking for a job.

Jon tried to form the words for a prayer. But the words would not come to him. It had been too long.

But hadn't he learned that God hears your prayers even when you don't know the words to speak? That he listens to the cries of your heart? So did it matter that Jon didn't know what to ask for? God would hear. He always did. In his heart, Jon knew that. What Jon did not know— what he was afraid to even think about—was whether God would honor his request.

Jon felt as if bits and pieces of his soul had flaked off over the past weeks and months. He wasn't sure what was left or how much. Perhaps nothing more than a hard, cynical, embittered lump without much light or goodness to it. Perhaps nothing at all. Only God knew.

But even if Jon couldn't—or wouldn't—pray, he could at least dial a telephone. He looked down at the printout again. There were just two numbers to call, really. He walked back to the building and found a pay phone just inside.

Jon tried the "301" number first. The phone rang five times, and then a female voice answered. "Hello?"

Jon almost hung up, then found himself saying, "Hi! I'm calling from Washington, D.C. I got your number from Elizabeth Brown in Petersburg, West Virginia."

There was a brief pause on the other end of the line. "Liz? You got my number from Liz?"

"Well, yes," Jon lied, feeling uneasy about it. "We were talking a while ago."

"When?" the woman asked. "When did you see my sister?"

So this is Elizabeth Brown's sister, Jon thought. Strike her from the list. "Oh, a few weeks ago," he responded, deliberately trying to be vague. "I don't remember exactly."

"Why are you calling me? Is this about the trip Liz was planning to Washington? To talk about Sonny?" the woman asked.

"Trip?"

"You know, to talk about Sonny? To that woman who called her?"

"What woman?"

"Liz didn't say. Just some woman, who answered one of the letters she'd written to the president. You know, about what happened to my brother-in-law down at Webster Springs."

Jon took a deep breath. "You don't remember the woman's name?"

"No, sorry. I don't. But isn't that why you're calling?"

This was clearly a dead end. He was glad, though, that he hadn't identified himself. "Look, I'll follow up with your sister," he said quickly. "We just have to be thorough, you know. But I have to run now. I'll be in touch."

"But wait!" the woman said. "You didn't tell me who—"

Jon hung up. His hands were ice cold. He hated doing this kind of thing. He almost decided against making the call to the "703" exchange. But he'd gone this far; might as well close the loop. He punched in the number carefully.

"Hello," a female voice answered sweetly, professionally. "Daystar Communications. May I help you?"

Jon froze, his mind paralyzed for an instant. "I—I, uh, well, was wondering if you could possibly give me your address," he stammered finally. "I have a, uh—a package to deliver and the address is all garbled."

"Deliveries should be made to 6573 Dolly Madison Boulevard in Mclean," the woman answered smoothly.

"Oh, great," Jon said. 6573, 6573, 6573, he thought, trying to memorize the number. "That helps a lot. Say, what's Daystar do anyway?"

"Daystar is a telecommunications company," the woman answered, a trace of irritation in her voice. "Is there someone on our professional staff you'd care to speak to?"

"Oh, no, I guess not. I was just curious."

"Well, please call if you have any further problems in making the delivery."

"I will. Thanks," Jon said and hung up.

Jon pictured the crumpled piece of paper he'd tossed into the waste can back at his office in the White House, the one with the lines connecting CRATA to the Christian Armada and to Daystar Communications. There were two new lines to add to that page now.

So who called Sonny Brown? And why? That was the million-dollar question, the one he desperately did not want to find an answer for.

CHAPTER SIXTY-ONE

Jon leaned forward and looked at the faces. "Okay, we need something visual, something huge, something dramatic. We need that one magic visual, the one that tells everyone in the country that they absolutely, categorically have to deal with this. Right now."

Heads nodded around the table at the eastern end of the Oval Office, away from the president's desk. Nearly every one of Adams's senior advisors had gathered for the late-night session, after most of the White House staff had gone home for the day.

Jon glanced at Susan, who was running the meeting with her usual ruthless efficiency. She ignored him, completely focused on the task at hand. Susan had turned into quite a player. She had Adams's utmost confidence, and she used that relationship to keep control of the staff.

"What'd you have in mind?" Nathaniel Watson asked him, his heavy jowls quivering slightly as he asked the question.

"I don't know," Jon mused. "Maybe the president's giving a national address from the Situation Room. Something that's never been done before."

There were several audible coughs in the room, which was just the reaction Jon was looking for. Out of the corner of his eye, Jon could see that Adams was nodding slightly at the suggestion. Jon knew he had a winner.

"You can't do that! That's—that's a clear breach of national security!" sputtered one of the aides gathered at the table. "That room's for wars and coups. Things like that. You can't have—"

"President Adams is the commander in chief," Jon said forcefully. Everyone in the room was silent. "If he chooses to give an address from the Sit Room, he gives an address from the Sit Room. If he chooses to talk to the people from aboard Air Force One, he does it. If he wants to talk to the people from his bedroom, wearing his pajamas, he does it."

Jon watched with some amusement as several aides instinctively looked at Adams to see whether Jon had gone too far, talking about the president speaking to the nation in his pajamas. But Adams was now smiling broadly.

"I like it," Adams said. "The Situation Room is a great backdrop."

"With a huge map of America highlighting all the major trouble spots right behind you," Jon said quickly.

"And a chart beside it that lists the locations of major conflict in the past week," Susan added.

"How many have there been?" Adams asked.

Susan looked at her briefing book. "Four major conflicts through today and at least a dozen minor ones."

"And we're defining 'major' as what again?" the president asked, mostly for the benefit of everyone else in the room. Jon knew that Adams had memorized every inch of the briefing book Susan held.

"A major conflict is an armed confrontation between two groups," Susan said. "Fortunately, only one of the conflicts ended in actual violence, with two deaths."

"But the potential for many more is still there," Adams said.

"Very much so," Susan confirmed.

"And our intelligence says that we expect at least a dozen more in the next two to three weeks, right?" asked Adams.

"Correct," Susan said.

Jon held up a hand. "Don't forget. The media's going bonkers over the one that ended in two deaths. They're reporting it like the apocalypse is right around the corner. They're using the incident to predict that there will be massive urban violence throughout the summer."

"A prediction that feeds on itself," Adams said softly. "Unless we step in now with a firm hand and put a stop to any threat on the streets. Which, of course, is exactly what I promised to do if I became president, in case any of you here don't remember."

There was a deep stillness in the room. Everyone knew why they were there that evening—to reach a consensus recommendation for the president on a course of action.

In the past three days, there had been four armed confrontations between black militant groups and white extremist groups in different parts of the country. In one instance, during a black-pride parade that attempted to duplicate the so-called "Million-Man-March" on Washington of 1995, the two sides had opened fire. Two people—one of them a parade-watcher not affiliated with either group—had been killed.

The media had gone completely on overload covering the increasing tension and violence. The black militant groups had retreated into tight war councils and sent spokespersons out to brief the media. The white extremist groups involved did no talking to the media at all.

Adams had sent Dr. Sira Sindar out initially, both on TV and to several of the groups, in an effort to calm people down. Jamal Wickes had also tried to use the World of Allah leaders and councils as intermediaries, but it didn't seem to be working. Everyone was simply waiting for the next flare-up, the next round of deaths. Which could come at any moment.

The president, realistically speaking, had only two possible courses of action. The first option, preferred by nearly every member of his senior staff, was to give a nationally televised address and make an appeal for both sides to "stand down." Adams would set up a mediation board to hear grievances from all parties and use that forum to try to negotiate some sort of cease-fire in the growing hostilities.

The second option, which had only lukewarm backing from a few aides, was for Adams to take a much stronger course of action—to send troops into the cities, impose curfews, jail rabble-rousers quickly, and ban public events that might lead to confrontations.

With either option, the president would go on national television to address the nation. That's what Jon wanted the visual for, something to give absolute clarity to the president's central message, something that illustrated perfectly the true nature and extent of the hostilities and the president's duty to do something about it.

"So you want to impose a national curfew and send more troops in?" Jon asked Adams.

"I'm leaning that way," Adams said grimly.

Nathaniel Watson shifted his considerable bulk on the couch. "Jamal Wickes' report? Did it offer any hope?"

"Wickes and several World of Allah leaders met with three of the groups in Chicago two days ago," Susan responded. "They aren't backing down."

Adams stood up and paced the room. "I'm going on national television in forty-eight hours. I'm speaking from the Sit Room. I'm going to announce a national curfew and more troops. Any strong objections?"

The president was greeted by silence. "Good. I'll take that as support for the decision. Now, I'll need to follow up immediately. I want one big event scheduled every day for the next week after the announcement. Something that shows decisiveness and purpose."

"Like a face-to-face mediation session with a black militant group, arranged by the World of Allah one day? And an attempt to reach out to one of the militia groups on another day? Maybe a day on the streets directing some of the troops in a large city on another? Stuff like that?" Jon asked.

"Exactly like that," Adams said. "Something the media can shoot, something that shows action. We have to let everyone know we're in charge, that we have everything under control."

CHAPTER SIXTY-TWO

Jon turned up the volume on his car radio to hear the lead story on WTOP, Washington's all-news radio station. "Police were involved in gun battles in New York City and Chicago today," the news commentator read, over a background of gunfire from automatic weapons. "Efforts to halt the violence so far have failed. The mayors of both cities have asked the president for immediate assistance."

Jon flipped off the radio. He stared out his car window at the building just across the street. He didn't want to know what went on inside that building. It wasn't his business. He had no real reason to pursue this.

But if I don't, then who will? Jon thought miserably. *There's no one else.*

Jon had pushed this away for as long as he'd dared. He had done nothing beyond simply writing the four numbers down on a slip of paper in his Capitol Hill apartment—6573. On Dolly Madison in Mclean.

It had not left his mind, though. In fact, more often than not, it was all he could think of. But he had been paralyzed by the dread of what he might find out.

Finally, in the dead of a sleepless night, he had realized that unless he made the effort to find out, he would never have any peace. He had to try.

It had been hard enough just finding the time. Adams was consumed with every detail of the presidential address—and, by extension, so was Jon. The current outbreaks of violence in several large cities had made the address even more urgent.

It would be one of the most significant presidential addresses of the century. No president had ever done what Adams was contemplating nor had there ever been such need—except perhaps in the days leading up to the Civil War. Jon had simply had no chance to get away, until now.

The building, as it turned out, was set back from the major thoroughfare through Mclean, an affluent northern Virginia suburb that was home to some of the wealthiest residents of the Washington area. The building had its own private drive, complete with an armed guard station and a heavy security gate at the perimeter. Every other office building in Mclean was close to the road and open to the public. But not 6573. No name adorned the building.

Jon parked across the street and watched the traffic in and out of the private drive for awhile. Every few minutes, a commercial vehicle delivering something pulled up, spoke to the guard, and then entered the grounds.

After a few minutes, Jon decided to take the risk. He left the car's blinkers on, grabbed an innocuous package of old "white" papers that had been lying on the floor of his car for months—policy papers that had no identifiable markings—and walked across the street to the guard gate.

"Can I help you?" the uniformed guard asked him.

Jon held out the package. "Somebody sent me here with this package. Said to deliver to Daystar. You know which floor Daystar's on so I can deliver it?"

The guard gave him a curious look. "Gotta be more specific than that."

"Why's that?"

"Daystar's the whole place," the guard said, jerking a thumb over his left shoulder toward the building. "You need an office to deliver it to. Can't just drop it off. It'll never go anywhere."

Jon tried hard not to look surprised. "The whole building, huh?"

"That's right. So do you have a name?"

Jon decided to gamble. "Well, they said Simpson's office. I could deliver it there."

The guard shook his head. "*They* said that? Who did?"

"Captain Johnson's office, over at CRATA," Jon lied.

The guard relaxed at the mention of the CRATA captain's name. Clearly, that was a name he was familiar with. "Okay. I guess it's all right to run it in real quick. Just drop it off at the front desk inside. They'll take it on up to Simpson's office on the top floor."

"I'd be happy to take it up myself."

The guard shook his head again. "No one gets up there without security clearance. And you ain't got that."

Jon smiled. He didn't want to press his luck. "Okay, fine. I'll just run it in. Be right back out."

The guard pressed a button beneath the window. The gate swung open slowly. Jon walked briskly up the drive and entered the smoked-glass doors.

The lobby was mammoth. A lone desk sat in the center. Jon walked up to it slowly, trying to look around without appearing to. There was no directory listing who was on which floor, as nearly every building in Washington had. Clearly, the occupants of this building were known only to those who trafficked here.

As Jon got to the desk, he reached out and handed the package to the receptionist. "To Simpson's office," he said simply.

As she looked at it, Jon leaned over and stared hard at her desk. As he'd hoped, there was a brief directory in front of her. He frantically tried to read the names upside down.

One familiar name in the middle caught his eye, to his great surprise—"Brownlee, J." There were three numbers beside the name, which Jon took to be his extension. He read and memorized them.

"Is that all?" the receptionist asked him sharply. "Or is there something else I can help you with?"

Jon jerked his head up. "Um, no, that's all."

"Well, good day, then," the receptionist said curtly.

"Yeah, okay," Jon said, beginning to back away from the desk. "See ya."

She didn't respond. Jon turned and hurried from the building and back down the walk. He waved to the guard as the gate swung open. His mind was racing as he crossed the street.

Was it the same Brownlee? Did he have an office there as well? And why?

There were no laws barring DNC officials from sitting on boards or from serving as corporate officers. It had always been frowned on because of the possibility of conflict of interest. But it was not illegal, and many officials of both national parties had long mixed and matched politics with business.

Jon drove around the corner, found a pay phone, and parked the car. He dialed Daystar's main number.

"Hello, Daystar Communications. May I help you?" answered the receptionist, the same one Jon had spoken to on his first call. Jon gave her the three numbers he'd memorized. "One moment please," she replied professionally. "I'll connect you."

The phone rang twice. "Mr. Brownlee's office," a woman said.

"Jonas Brownlee's office?" Jon asked, holding his breath.

"Yes, this is Jonas Brownlee's office," she answered. "May I help you?"

"Oh, gee, I didn't realize Jonas had an office at Daystar," Jon said quickly. "Has he been there long?"

The secretary said nothing for several seconds. "Mr. Brownlee has been here five years," she said finally. "Are you a friend of Mr. Brownlee's?"

"Five years? Jonas has been there five years? I had no idea. I'd lost track," Jon said, barely keeping the surprise out of his voice.

"May I ask who's calling, please?" the secretary said sternly.

Jon knew that he was sounding like an idiot and that he'd better get off before it was too late. "Oh, just an acquaintance. In town for the day. But, hey, look, I have a plane to catch. Just thought I'd ring Jonas. I'll call next time I'm in town, when I have more time."

"I'm sorry, sir, but you didn't—"

Jon hung the phone up without saying goodbye. This was getting to be a habit, hanging up on people in the middle of a conversation.

He took a deep breath. Five years put Brownlee at Daystar well before the Air Force Two bombing, well before the time when Adams had become a United States senator. Right about the time Jon first came to Washington.

Maybe it was a coincidence. But Jon didn't believe in coincidences —not in this town, at this level, with people like Jonas Brownlee. Washington was a town of connections. It lived, breathed, danced, and sang with connections. There were no coincidences. Everything was infused with layers of meanings and levels of connections.

"So who talked to you, Sonny? Who put it in motion?" Jon asked out loud. But no one heard the question. And Jon wondered if he'd ever find anyone out there to answer it.

CHAPTER SIXTY-THREE

The clerk was very nice. Nicer than he had to be, which was unusual for any bureaucracy in Washington—especially considering that Jon hadn't shown the clerk his White House ID.

The public documents room of the Securities and Exchange Commission was swarming with people—mostly young, brash reporters sifting through 10K and 10Q corporate filings for that day.

The SEC was an extraordinary place for financial information junkies. Every corporation in America—those that were publicly held, at least—were required by law to notify the SEC of anything that might affect the price of their stock.

Which meant that the financial media was constantly sorting through the multitude of SEC filings in an effort to unearth tidbits and goodies about what corporate America was up to at that moment.

"So you just want the corporate board?" the clerk asked.

Jon nodded. "Yeah, but I'll take anything else, if you have it."

"Now, you know I need a FOIA to do the search, right?"

Jon spied a blank piece of paper on the cluttered counter. "Can I borrow a pen?"

The clerk smiled crookedly and handed him a pen from beneath the counter. "Knock yourself out."

Jon quickly scrawled a request. "Under the Freedom of Information Act, I hereby request documents on file at the SEC pertaining to a company called Daystar Communications." He signed it "Adam Smith" and handed it to the clerk.

The clerk read the note and started to laugh. "So what's your sequel to *The Wealth of Nations* going to be, Mr. Smith?"

Jon didn't waiver. "Oh, I've been exploring the poverty side of the equation for awhile. You know, just to balance things out a little."

"Makes sense," the clerk grunted. He did not ask Jon for an ID. "Well, let's see what ye old computer has for us today." The clerk sat down at the computer and typed in a few commands. He stared at the screen for awhile. "Hmmm," he said and sat back in his chair, shaking his head. "Never seen this before."

"What? What'd you find?"

The clerk typed in a few more commands. "Well, I'll be." He looked over at Jon. "You know Daystar's not publicly traded, right?"

"Yeah, I assumed that. I hoped you'd have some sort of filing anyway because they do government contract work."

"Nope," the clerk said, shaking his head. "I got nothing on 'em. It's not required. But there is something in the computer. Actually, two things."

"What?"

The clerk looked around, but there was no one close to them, and all others in the room were frantically doing other business. "There's a locked file on Daystar with a special security seal."

"A locked file? What's that mean?"

The clerk glanced back at the computer screen. "That's what I looked up. I'd never seen it before."

"And?"

"It's a protected file. It has special status. Only the chairman has access to it. Even our general counsel has to get permission from the chairman to look at it. And then only if he's got a federal court order."

Jon stood quite still. "You've got to be kidding. I've never heard of such a thing."

"Me neither," the clerk said quietly. "But this file I called up describes locked files as ones that have fairly unusual corporate boards, with nontraded shares of stock issued to raise capital for the company."

"What do you mean, fairly unusual?"

"Like the entire board is made up of CEOs from other publicly traded companies," the clerk said softly. "You know, Fortune 50 types, who have all sorts of vested interests in government policies and actions."

Jon nodded. He could see it now. "So while Daystar's not publicly traded because its board is made up of company heads who just might want to influence policy in Washington, there still has to be a filing with the SEC."

"Yep," the clerk said. "My guess is all these guys got together, chipped in a whole bunch of their own money, issued nontraded shares of stock to themselves, and formed a company."

"They can do that?"

"Sure. It's a free country."

For now, Jon thought. "What about the security seal?"

"Don't know about that," the clerk said. "It probably means they do secret stuff for the government."

"Which makes it impossible for anyone other than the SEC chairman to look at the file."

"That's about the size of it," the clerk said somberly.

Jon extended a hand. "Thanks," he said, shaking the clerk's hand. "You've been a big help."

"Yeah, right," he said. "But do me a favor?"

"Sure. What?"

"I don't wanna get in any trouble, so don't tell anyone you were here, okay? Or that we talked?" he said with pleading eyes. "This thing's kinda weird, you know?"

Tell me about it, Jon thought ruefully. "Don't worry," he said. "I was never here."

CHAPTER SIXTY-FOUR

As Jon stood gazing at the massive camera that would film the president's address from the Situation Room in the basement of the White House in less than forty-eight hours, the thought came to him out of the blue: the informant. The guy who testified in shadow at the congressional hearing. Who was he? Is that footage still around, the raw stuff that wasn't used for the hearing?

There was a decent chance that it was. The committee's staff had filmed the guy's testimony at the DNC's studio. With any luck, they still had the raw video around somewhere in the senate storage area, maybe up in the attic.

But Jon knew he wouldn't be able to try to find it till evening, if then. So much work still had to be done before Adams spoke to the nation and so little time. To make matters worse, he and Susan had a meeting with Adams in less than half an hour to go over the text of his speech.

No one, not even Jon, had seen what the president was going to say. He had insisted on writing the speech himself. He was getting dozens of suggestions from every key member of the senior staff. But the speech itself was being put together by Adams himself, by hand, at his desk in the Oval Office.

Jon and Susan would get a glimpse of parts of it this afternoon. He looked at the bank of TV monitors in the corner of the room. Pictures of more clashes with police and violence in several cities flashed across the screen on one of them from the latest news update on CNN. Jon watched the pictures for a moment and then turned away.

The latest word from Sira Sindar and Jamal Wickes was that the World of Allah network was not going to be able to contain the violence.

In fact, the infusions of cash through the network had actually encouraged the progressing confrontations. As the money flowed into some of these communities and they grew financially independent, they also grew more militant and more willing to agitate for change.

Now, without presidential action of some sort, there was no doubt that violence would increase in many of the ghettoes. People were tired of talking. It was time for action, even the self-destructive kind.

"I want to do a sound-and-sight check," Jon said to the aide who would operate the camera and who was here today so that Jon could check out the system. The aide took his position behind the camera as Jon moved behind the makeshift desk they'd set up in the Sit Room for the broadcast. A huge map of the U.S. served as the backdrop. Jon sat in the leather chair and stared at the unblinking eye of the camera then looked away to the monitors.

"Four score and seven years ago, we had world wars," Jon said. "Let's hope we don't have another one right now." He got up from the chair and moved closer to the TV monitors.

"Can you play it back?" he asked. An instant later, Jon saw his own face on the screen. *This will work*, he thought triumphantly as he watched the playback. The backdrop was exactly right, and the setting of the room was perfect. The room was drenched in national security atmospherics, and it would speak powerfully to the people.

As he had for years, Jon thought only of how it would all play, how it would all look and sound to people. Whether it was right or wrong—that was really Adams's responsibility. And Adams wouldn't be doing this if he didn't basically think it was right. And if Adams thought it was right—well, for a long time now, that had been good enough for Jon.

All for the cause.

"Looks good," Jon signaled to the tech aide. "We're ready to roll tomorrow evening."

Jon made his way up to the Oval Office to meet with Susan and Adams. He bumped into Nathaniel Watson on the stairs. Actually, because of Watson's considerable bulk, Jon had to squeeze up against the rail of the narrow stairwell to let Watson pass by.

"Ready for the fireworks?" Watson asked him.

"All set. Now we just need the speech."

"No problem," Watson said. "It's in place."

"You've seen it?" Jon asked, surprised. "I thought Sam was working on it himself."

"Oh, he is, he is," Watson said quickly. "I've just seen bits and pieces of it. Not all."

"Yeah, well, Susan and I are about to get a peek at it ourselves," Jon said, trying to ease his way past.

"Make it good, Jon. We need it."

"I'll do my best." Jon squeezed past and continued his way up the stairwell. Watson labored heavily to get to the bottom and disappeared around the corner. *How odd*, Jon thought. *He's seen the speech. I know he has.*

Jon had almost fifteen minutes to kill before he met with the president, so he ducked into Susan's front office to wait, just down the hall from the Oval Office.

"She's running late, Mr. Abelson," Susan's secretary said as he entered. "She's over in the East Wing, meeting with the First Lady."

"Oh, on what?" Jon asked.

The secretary shook her head. "I don't know. It's just the two of them."

"I see," Jon said, settling in on the couch. Susan and Abby often met, just the two of them. It was one of Susan's greatest strengths, her relationship to the president's wife. It was a relationship she had cultivated for years.

"Can I get you anything? Something to drink?" the secretary asked him.

Jon thought for a moment. There was something, actually. A file he'd been meaning to check that he was certain was somewhere in the chief of staff's file archives in the back room.

"You know, if you don't mind, I think I'll have a look at something in the files," Jon said.

The secretary looked over her shoulder at the door off to the side. There was a small closet inside with many of the old files. "In there?"

"Yep," Jon said, rising. "Something I've been meaning to check."

"You know, Ms. Smalley doesn't like—"

Jon held up a hand. "It's fine. Susan won't mind. Trust me."

The secretary smiled. She knew of their special relationship. "Well, because it's you, I guess you're right. She won't mind."

Jon moved past her desk, opened the door to the small closet, and switched on the light. The room was musty. It hadn't been used in awhile, he could tell.

There were two file cabinets in the closet, containing all of the old files from Sam's congressional races and his House and Senate terms. Somewhere in here, Jon was sure, was the old task force file on the Air Force Two bombing.

It took some work, but he eventually found it at the bottom of one of the two cabinets. It was in a special section all its own, separate from the congressional stuff.

Jon pulled the file loose and leaned up against the wall. It was thicker than the last time he'd looked at it. Susan had jammed all of the written testimony from the task force hearing into it, and it appeared as if there was some follow-up briefing material from CRATA toward the back as well.

Jon started near the front, leafing through the documents. He stopped when he came to the old surveillance document detailing the activities of the Christian Armada. The top of the page, the one on which he'd remembered seeing the "daystar.com" fax logo, was neatly cut. The "daystar.com" logo was gone.

Jon quickly leafed through every page of the early documents, just to make sure. But there was no mistake. Someone had removed all traces of Daystar's involvement with the monitoring of the Christian Armada.

Jon took a deep breath. If someone went out of his way to make sure Daystar wasn't even remotely connected to the Christian Armada incident, what did that mean? It meant either that some laws had been broken or that there was some serious money at stake. Or both.

Jon flipped to the back of the file to the CRATA briefing material he hadn't seen before. It was a listing of all the charred remains and the twisted hulks of military equipment in the Christian Armada compound.

Jon read through the document. As everyone knew, they'd confirmed that, in fact, Russian-made surface-to-air missile equipment had been on the grounds. The equipment had been essentially destroyed in the explosions at the compound, but there was no doubt that it was the same type of missile used in the attack on Air Force Two. No doubt at all.

All of that had come out at the task force hearing, the one that had put all the speculation to rest. The Christian Armada was responsible for the attack. They'd plotted to kill a national leader, they'd acquired the means to do so, and they had been given the opportunity when Air Force Two flew over Webster Springs to the Charleston fund-raising event. It was cut-and-dried.

There was just one brief, puzzling statement about two-thirds of the way through the CRATA document, from a logistics and equipment review. The missiles found in the rubble at the Christian Armada compound, it seemed, had not been loaded or armed. In fact, none of the military hardware and equipment discovered at the compound appeared to be battle-ready. Most likely, the report said, it had been in storage.

But the logistics report speculated that this was excess equipment, that the actual missile used to bring down Air Force Two had been the only one loaded and battle-ready. The others were extra, the report speculated.

But what if that wasn't the case? Jon thought. And what about the launch platform used to fire the missile? Where was it? Why wasn't it listed in the report? Maybe because it was never there.

Jon felt a tight knot in the pit of his stomach, one that had been forming for some time. He replaced the file carefully, left the small closet, and closed the door behind him. He had one telephone call he wanted to make before he went into his meeting with Susan and the president. "I'll be back," he told Susan's secretary.

He took the stairs up to the second level of the West Wing three at a time. He waved at his staff and then whisked into his office, closing the door behind him. He flipped though his rolodex quickly and found the DNC political office number. He dialed it and held his breath.

"Political," someone answered.

"Hi, this is Jon Abelson over at the White House."

"Yes, sir!" the aide said on the other end of the line. Everyone there knew Jon. He called frequently.

"Can someone there do me a real quick favor?"

"Sure, what?"

"You guys keep a log of events on the computer there, right? Fund-raisers, who attended, how much they gave, that kind of thing, right?"

"Yeah, we have that."

"Okay, can you look something up for me?"

"Now?"

"Yeah, right now. Just call it up. It was a fund-raiser in Charleston, West Virginia, last year—"

"The one where Air Force Two was shot down?"

"That's the one."

"Sure, hang on. Let me pull it up on the screen." Jon could hear him typing away at computer keys for a few moments. "Okay, got it. What'd you need?"

"Who actually organized the fund-raiser?" Jon asked. "Who put the thing on and made it happen?"

Jon waited patiently. "Looks like . . . yeah, looks like it was just a two-way deal. Not much staff involved," the aide said. "I have confirmation letters going back and forth between Jonas Brownlee and Arthur Demontley. Jonas proposed and Demontley accepted."

"Any staff notes around for the thing? Follow-ups? Proposed lists, that sort of thing?"

"No. None. It was a personal deal between Brownlee and Demontley."

"Isn't that unusual? Cutting out staff like that?"

"Yeah, a little," the aide said. "But Brownlee does deals like that all the time. He's got more connections than the Mafia."

"And Demontley? He's done this sort of thing, too?"

"For Jonas? Yeah, sure, all the time," the aide laughed. "You know how tight they are. Demontley has raised a bazillion dollars for Jonas over the years."

"I know," Jon said softly.

"So's that it?" the aide asked. "Is there anything else?"

"No, that's great. Thanks. It's what I needed."

"You looking to do another fund-raiser soon?" the aide said. "Call me if you need our help."

"Will do," Jon said. "Don't worry. You guys are great."

"Always here to help."

Jon put his head in his hands after hanging up. Arthur Demontley had been former President Simpson's national finance chairman for both his election and then his reelection effort. No one was closer to Simpson than Demontley, though only those in Washington's political circles knew that because Demontley stayed out of the news so well.

Demontley and Brownlee had invited the vice president to Charleston, West Virginia. They had orchestrated the fund-raiser, presumably with the president's blessings. It was all so straightforward. Who would have guessed that such an event would end in such unmitigated tragedy?

Jon thought back to the day of the tragedy, the unfolding news in the Oval Office, and the questions about Brownlee and Demontley at the press conference. It hadn't occurred to Jon at the time just how fortunate it was that neither of them had been aboard Air Force Two when it went down. The usual protocol, in fact, was that honored guests for such functions flew aboard Air Force Two with the vice president. That's the way it worked.

But Demontley had not, and neither had Brownlee. Yes, how fortunate, Jon thought bitterly. How very, very fortunate, both for Mr. Brownlee and Mr. Demontley. Funny how fortune smiled on people, how some survived while others did not. It was a curious thing.

The intercom buzzed, startling Jon. He shook the cobwebs from his brain and flipped the intercom switch. "The president is asking for you," his office aide said.

"Tell them I'll be right down."

"You were supposed to be there already, you know."

"I'll be right there!" he snapped. "Just tell them that!"

"Yes, sir," the aide said meekly. "I'll inform them."

CHAPTER SIXTY-FIVE

On the way to the Oval Office, Jon passed three offices, and all three of them had TVs tuned to CNN. The news that hour was grim.

Sira Sindar, Jamal Wickes, and several leaders from the World of Allah—all of them acting on the president's behalf—had gone to meet with several leaders of armed militia groups and representatives of a handful of black militant groups in Chicago. They'd met at a neutral site.

Negotiations had broken down almost immediately, however, with both sides storming angrily from the site. There seemed no hope of reconciliation in the immediate future, the commentators speculated.

It reminded Jon of a factional war, the kind most Americans only heard about in far-off places like Burundi, Zaire, Guatemala, or Peru. Not in the heartland of America.

But the tensions had been building for years. All it had taken, in the end, was a match or two thrown on the kindling, and the whole place had gone up.

Susan and the president were waiting for him when he arrived. The guard stepped aside as Jon entered the Oval Office. Susan was fuming. She hated waiting for anyone, even Jon. "We've been here for awhile, you know."

"Sorry," Jon said quickly. "Had a few things to take care of."

"More important than this, I can only imagine," Susan said sarcastically.

"Okay, you two," the president said soothingly. "We have more important things."

Jon took one of the two leather chairs that faced the president's desk, next to Susan. Jon was surprised at how good Adams looked. He had no bags under his eyes, and he looked well rested. He'd been preparing for this moment, it seemed.

Jon faced the president. "The speech? Is it ready, I hope?"

"It is," Adams said. "Susan already has her copy."

Jon glanced over at Susan. "And? How is it?"

Susan smiled. Despite the setting, Jon couldn't help notice how starkly beautiful she was; every feature seemed chiseled out of some luminescent material. "It's brilliant. But judge for yourself."

Adams handed a copy of the speech across the desk. Jon began to read it silently.

The opening was straightforward. It described, in short detail, the state of affairs in America—how, for the first time since the Civil War, armed groups of Americans had begun to face off against each other in widely spread locations across the country. Negotiations had failed. Increasing the numbers of National Guardsmen and police on the streets had failed. Citizens were afraid. People cowered in their homes in many neighborhoods, from coast to coast.

Jon turned the page and began to read what Adams had written with his own hand.

> Every option has failed. We are at a crossroads. That is why it is time for something that will stop the violence now. Drastic times call for drastic measures.
>
> It is for this reason that I am imposing martial law in the United States this evening. Until peace has been restored, I am invoking the full power, might, and authority of the military.
>
> For a time, the military will effectively run the governments in every major city of the country. Once peace and tranquillity have been restored, power will be returned to the municipalities.
>
> But, for now, this must be done. There must be an end to the violence and the terror. This is the only possible course of action. I trust history will judge us fairly for our actions.

Jon looked up from the text, unable to believe what he had just read. No president in history—not even Abraham Lincoln at the most despairing moment in the Civil War—had ever taken such a drastic step. The Founding Fathers had carefully crafted the Constitution to forbid this very thing.

"No president has supreme authority. He shares power," Jon said quietly. "You can't do this."

"Yes, I can," Adams said forcefully. "And I fully intend to."

"But the Supreme Court and Congress won't let you."

Adams shook his head. "You forget. The Court *interprets* laws. They don't act."

"But Congress does. And they will here. They'll have no choice," Jon said, playing the devil's advocate.

"Not here, they won't," Adams said. "They control the money. Not the military. And the military has more than enough money to operate for weeks—independent of Congress, if it has to. The military will do as I say, not as Congress says."

"The Joint Chiefs support this?"

"Yes. They've already sent the orders."

"And Watson said you can do this?"

"He has. There's no precedent, obviously. But by the time Congress gets around to doing anything, we will have done what we needed to do."

"Which is sending in troops to take over the cities," Jon said tightly.

"Yes," Adams answered. "But only until we have things under control. Not a moment longer."

"And if you don't get things under control?" Jon asked. "What then?"

"First things first, Jon," Adams said, trying to sound reassuring. "We'll worry about that later. Right now, we have to try. This is our only hope."

Jon glanced at the TV set in the corner of the Oval Office. The sound was turned down, but there was no mistaking the pictures that flickered on the screen: The violence had progressed from automatic weapons to heavy mortar fire and shelling—not in some remote foreign capital, but in an American city.

"I guess you have no choice," Jon sighed. "And I suppose you want a little cover, some hint of this in a newspaper before the speech?"

"That would be nice, Jon," Adams said, smiling broadly. "Just enough so that people aren't totally shocked by this course of action. But not enough detail to get Congress up in arms before the speech."

"In other words, you want me to work my usual black magic," Jon said, his heart heavy.

"That's right," the president said. "You are my voice and my vision, Jon. Help prepare the way."

CHAPTER SIXTY-SIX

For the first time since signing on with Adams in Ohio years before, Jon felt reluctant about—even repulsed by—what he was trying to accomplish. An American president's seizing control of the country, as if he were a dictator? It went against every principle Jon had ever learned about democracy.

Even worse, Jon was a full partner in it. He had helped create the network that now was feeding the violence. He had helped craft the policies and had sold them both to Congress and to the public, via the willing media.

Never a history buff, Jon had at least read enough about World War II to know that one of Adolph Hitler's greatest allies and trusted aides had been Paul Joseph Goebbels. And what had Goebbels been good at? Propaganda. Or, in the language of today's world, public relations.

Everyone always joked about "PR," as if it were some stupid, trivial thing. Which it usually was. At the level of presidential politics, though, public relations took on a new meaning. And Jon practiced that black art at its highest levels.

He dialed Laura Asher at the *Washington Post* first. He went off the record immediately, laid out the possible options and what the president might—or might not—speak to in his national address the following evening, during prime-time television.

Asher was an old hand at reading the hidden text. "So is he considering martial law? Is that an option?" she asked him.

"Let's just say that one of the options under consideration is a more direct role for the military and the president in the efforts to reduce and eliminate violence at the local level," Jon said evasively.

Asher whistled. "So he's considering martial law. Congress won't be happy about it, will they?"

"We will fully consult and cooperate with Congress," Jon pledged, knowing it was a hollow promise. Maybe even a lie.

"Yeah, sure," Asher said cynically. "Like Johnson consulted Congress during the Vietnam War."

"These are all options, Laura. Understand? Just options. Nothing's set in stone yet."

"I understand," she responded. She'd played this game for a long time. She knew her role. "I'll play it straight."

"Thanks," Jon said—then, just before hanging up, added on impulse, "Hey, by the way, can I ask you something?"

"About this?"

"No, something old. The Air Force Two bombing."

"What about it?"

"During your investigation, did you ever come across anything that maybe made you think it wasn't what it seemed like?"

Asher grunted. "Yeah, we heard from a whole bunch of the wives. Plus, a couple of former members of the group who said it was just a club, really. Not some kooky group bent on annihilating themselves."

"The wives all said the Christian Armada didn't do it, right?"

"Yeah, but, I mean, what'd you expect? They were all clueless about what their husbands were doing. So we didn't put much stock in it. Why'd you ask? Something up?"

"No," Jon said quickly. "Just curious. It's nothing."

"You know all these groups are gonna go ballistic when you go the martial law route. When Adams makes it public. You know that, right?"

"*If* he does, Laura," Jon said, smiling at the reporter's effort to wheedle more out of him than he was willing to give.

"Hey, by the way, is this one all mine? I have any competitors?"

"It's all yours," Jon said. "So appreciate it. And do it up right."

"Deal. Good luck. You'll need it."

CHAPTER SIXTY-SEVEN

Jon called ahead and found someone who actually knew where the stuff from the old Air Force Two bombing task force had been stored up in the attic of the Senate Russell Office Building. Jon knew he'd be at the White House for most of that night, so he decided to go home, grab something to eat, take a shower, and then come back to work for the evening. But on his way home, he stopped by the Russell building.

The task force boxes were jammed into a far corner of the attic at the back of a locked cage along with at least fifty boxes from three Senate Labor and Human Resources Committee hearings. None of the boxes were labeled, so Jon just dug in.

He hit pay dirt in about the fifteenth box. At the bottom, he found five VHS tapes. One of them was labeled "witness #1" on the side.

Jon took all of them and returned the cage key to the committee staff. If this wasn't the right tape, he'd be out of luck. He didn't have time to search the entire attic.

Back at his apartment, he put some frozen cheese enchiladas in the microwave, opened a can of Pepsi, and sat down in front of the TV. The first of the five videotapes was a series of interviews with different people in and around Webster Springs, talking about the radical nature of the Christian Armada.

Jon found the shrouded task-force witness on the third tape. It really was a raw tape. The camera moved in and around, up and down. Tech people walked back and forth in front of the camera. Sometimes the sound worked; sometimes it didn't.

Five minutes into the tape with the camera rolling, the witness entered the room and walked behind the partition. Jon rewound the tape to the point at which he'd entered the room.

Jon put the video on "pause" and advanced the film frame by frame. Seven frames later—thanks to the wizardry of digital technology—he had a clear image of the witness just before he walked behind the partition.

Jon stared at the image on the screen for a long time. Here he was, the informant whose testimony had pounded the last nail in the coffin of the Christian Armada.

The man was white, perhaps in his early thirties. He wore a gold earring in his left ear. His hair was extremely close-cropped. He wore small, rounded spectacles. His nose was curved, like a hawk's beak. He had big, black, bushy eyebrows.

It had been nearly five years. The memory of their first meeting—in that old, decrepit S & L building back in Singleton, Ohio, with Sam Adams so long ago—came hurtling forward in Jon's brain at the speed of light.

It was the minister of the United Methodist church in downtown Singleton, the same man who had first introduced all of the young, black men of the city's ghetto community to then-candidate Sam Adams and who had later been the driving force behind the continued organization of those young black men.

Jon remembered that morning vividly. Adams had described "Burnsie" as his right-hand man in the ghetto project. And Jon knew that the man had continued to do occasional work back in Ohio for Adams over the years, though Jon had never been involved because he worked in Washington. But Jon had a good, long memory.

Jon closed his eyes. He did something he should have done long before this, regardless of how unworthy or how uneasy he felt about it. He only hoped it was not too late, either for him or for the country.

Dear Lord, he prayed silently. *I have been so blind. How could I have let this happen? How could I have been a part of this? How could you have let me?*

But, in his heart, Jon knew the answer to those questions. Like countless men and women through the ages, Jon had been blinded by the allure and seduction of power. He had chosen not to look, not to see. And now it was, perhaps, too late.

Only one more piece of the puzzle had not yet been uncovered. Tomorrow morning, first thing, he would attempt to find it.

And what he would do then, Jon did not know.

CHAPTER SIXTY-EIGHT

The drive to Richmond, Virginia, took less than two hours against the rush-hour traffic. Many people commuted north on I–95 toward Washington early in the morning. Very few commuted south on the highway toward Richmond, so Jon had a relatively easy drive.

He'd been at the White House until two o'clock in the morning feeding the speech into the TelePrompTer, making sure all the props were in place, then checking and rechecking everything. There was no room for mistakes. The speech was too important.

Jon had, of course, been distracted while he was working; he had much on his mind. But he was a professional, and he did what needed to be done. It was his job, and he was good at it.

So when he left his apartment before dawn, he'd managed to get just a couple hours of sleep. The two cups of coffee from McDonald's helped a little, but it would still be a very long day.

The Virginia Secretary of the State's office was in downtown Richmond, near the heart of the city. Jon parked at a garage and made his way to the office on foot.

He knew from past experience that every corporation in the state of Virginia—even those that were private and wished to remain out of the public eye—had to file a listing of their officers with the state in the secretary's office. It was the law; no one could avoid it.

You couldn't request a copy of that filing over the phone or through the mail. But if you showed up in person, the office had to give you a copy of the filing. Everything else about the corporation could be kept confidential, except that filing.

Jon arrived at the secretary's office just after it opened for business. No one else was there. Jon filled out the paperwork necessary to obtain a copy of the filing and then settled in with his copy of the *Washington Post*.

Laura Asher had, as usual, done a masterful job. Her story led the paper. "President Considers Martial Law," read the headline. The story went on to describe the options being considered by the president, including imposing martial law. The trial balloon had lifted off the ground without a hitch; now it was time to see who fired at it.

Several minutes later, the clerk in the secretary's office returned with the copy of Jon's request. She handed a plain manila folder to Jon.

"No problems getting it?" Jon asked the clerk.

"No, it was in the archives under the name you requested," the clerk said with a disinterested yawn. "It was filed with the office, oh, I'd guess, about five or six years ago. Hasn't been touched since. This is the only thing in the file."

Jon went back to his seat and opened the manila folder gingerly. There was a copy of a single piece of paper inside. It was a listing of the initial officers of the Daystar Communications company.

Only four names were listed. Jon's hands trembled as he stared at them. All of them were names he recognized. Three of them did not surprise him. Only the fourth did.

The president of the new company was Ken Pierson, the lawyer Jon had met in a Capitol Hill bar when they'd "pushed" a U.S. senator from office, the lawyer who had said he did occasional work for Jonas Brownlee. He had obviously set up the company, done the necessary legal work, and filed the papers. Nathaniel Watson was listed as vice president. The treasurer was Arthur Demontley.

But as Jon stared at the fourth and final name, the one that held the most direct link to the administration, he felt as if some outside hand, a hostile one, had taken control of his life. The world seemed to come to a slow, grinding halt.

The secretary of Daystar when it was first formed was someone new to Washington at the time, someone just learning the ropes. But this person had apparently learned quickly—or had been given her marching orders quite well—for she now held one of the most powerful posts in the world.

At Daystar's founding, its secretary had been Susan Smalley, now chief of staff to the president of the United States. The last piece of the puzzle clicked effortlessly into place, but the echo in Jon's mind sounded more than anything else like the *clang* of a dungeon door shutting.

CHAPTER SIXTY-NINE

There were seventeen urgent messages on his pager and at least twice that many on his voice mail. But he didn't care—about that or about anything else. Everything seemed gray and colorless.

On the drive back to Washington, Jon could not escape the inevitable conclusion his mind was drawing as, over and over and over, the details all stacked up neatly like building blocks. He would tear them down and try to stack them some other way, but each time they went together in the same way, all pointing in one direction to just one monstrous but inescapable conclusion.

It was simply not possible. It simply could not be. And yet, Jon knew it was true.

There were two courses in life, two choices, two ways of viewing the world and humankind's role in it. Jon had always known that. He had just forgotten it for a while.

In the first view—the one in which God does not exist—there is no inherent meaning to life. You are born, live for a time, and then die. Whatever you achieve in life is done by your own hand—or with the collusion of others who submit to your will. What makes this view attractive is that there are few limits to what you might achieve. You are bound only by the laws of society (and then only if you can't find ways to circumvent them) and by your own ability to achieve power, wealth, fame, glory, or whatever goal you have set for yourself.

Few people in history have taken this view to its utter, most logical extreme. But it could be done. In fact, it had been done by those such as Adolph Hitler. For those who did not believe in a God who deals in eternal justice, the only laws that circumscribed their actions were those made by humankind, and then only if men and women existed who had the will and the power to enforce those laws.

Susan subscribed to that worldview. She lived by it absolutely. Over the years, Jon had tried to convince her of the second point of view. He had never succeeded. Susan did not believe in God. She believed in herself, in Sam Adams, perhaps in Jon. She would do anything within reason to achieve her goals. Anything at all, it seemed.

According to the opposite view, the one Jon had always believed he followed, God existed. By virtue of his existence and his nature, God also dominated the meaning of life. Jon believed that every person's existence was meant as a chance to draw near to God—not to achieve personal glory, power, fame, or wealth. God breathes life into every person. They owe their very existence to him.

Two thousand years ago, Jesus Christ came to earth with a promise to any and all who followed him and who believed in him. For those who did so, Jesus promised eternal life—and the opportunity to draw near to God.

You get two choices in life. If God doesn't exist and life has no inherent meaning, then you may choose to do everything within your power to experience as much and to accomplish as much as you possibly can before you die. Do everything, try everything, make as much money as possible, accumulate as much as possible. There are no rules. You do what you want—to whomever you want, whenever you like—and hope you don't get caught. Human beings are nothing more than obstacles in the way of your path to whatever you desire.

Jesus is the other choice, the other path. In that choice, life has meaning. You exist for a reason—to learn who God is and how you personally fit into God's universe. With that choice, actions have moral consequences. Everything you do, everything you say or choose, has an impact on others around you. There are clear, defined rules. They are not the world's rules. They are God's rules.

Jon had once seen the truth of this clearly without shades of gray. The first time he had recognized it, he had been "born again." He had become a new person, in many different ways. He had learned to see the world and everything in it with different eyes—through God's eyes, not necessarily his own.

Now, so many, many years later, Jon wondered just how far he had strayed from one path toward the other. He didn't know. Only God could judge a man's heart, and he would judge Jon's some day. No other could sit in that judgment seat, not even Jon himself.

CHAPTER SEVENTY

Jon pulled up to the southwest entrance to the White House complex. He didn't bother to flash his White House ID; the guards recognized him. The heavy metal gate swung open slowly, majestically, allowing the car to enter.

Jon parked his car in his reserved space between the Old Executive Office Building and the West Wing. Susan's car was there, of course, along with every other car belonging to a White House VIP.

Before entering the compound, Jon looked around. The sun was shining brilliantly. The grounds were stunning, magnificent at this time of year. Everything seemed impossibly green. Flowers bloomed everywhere.

Dozens of White House correspondents were already on the front lawn, doing live stand-ups as a prelude to the historic speech this evening. Several senior White House aides and Cabinet secretaries were being interviewed as well.

The place was buzzing. And deep inside at the very heart of the compound, Sam Adams was preparing for perhaps the most important address any president had made in recent history.

One of the correspondents spied Jon and frantically tried to get his attention. Jon simply waved and quickly ducked inside the building. He had no desire to speak to the press right now. He wasn't sure what he'd say.

He hurried up the two flights of stairs to his office, stopping only briefly to say hello to two White House aides on their way down. One of them mentioned in passing that the president and the chief of staff were both frantically trying to find him. Jon mumbled his thanks and kept moving.

317

He was mobbed by his staff as he entered his front office. One of his secretaries thrust an entire sheaf of telephone slips in his face, demanding to know why he'd failed to return any of her frantic pages.

"The president's about to send the military out to find you!" she hissed. "Where have you been?"

Jon placed an affectionate hand on her shoulder. "Look. I'm sorry. I had something important to do. It couldn't wait."

"More important than the president of the United States?" his secretary practically shouted.

Jon almost smiled, wondering if perhaps his sense of humor were returning at last. "Yes, actually. A higher power was knocking on the door," he said mischievously.

"There is no higher power!" his secretary snapped. "You serve the president. He's your boss, or have you forgotten?"

I wish, Jon thought. *Oh, how I wish I could just forget all of this, forget that it ever happened, and go somewhere else. Anywhere.*

"I know," Jon said, sighing. "So. Give it to me. How many messages do I have to return immediately, and which ones can wait?"

His secretary handed him just two slips of paper. "Actually, you can ignore all of them if you'll just deal with the president and the chief of staff. I'll hold everyone else off."

Jon gave her a quick, affectionate hug, distinctly out of the ordinary for him. It startled her. "You're the greatest," Jon said, knowing that this might be one of their last conversations. "Tell the president I'm on my way down."

"Move," she said gruffly, returning to her desk. Jon saluted smartly and left the office the way he'd come, working his way through the complex to the Oval Office.

Susan intercepted him just outside the Oval Office doors, out of earshot of the military guards. She stormed out of her own office and grabbed him by the arm. Their eyes locked. Jon could see something—an intensity, almost bordering on hatred, really—that he had not seen before. Susan had let her guard slip, he realized, in the passion of the moment.

"Where have you been?" she said through clenched teeth.

"I had something to do," Jon said evenly.

"You should have been here!"

"I was, until two in the morning," he said, his voice surprisingly calm. "Everything is set. It'll go off like clockwork tonight."

"You saw the *Post* this morning?"

"Yeah, sure," Jon shrugged. "It was what we wanted."

"You don't think it went too far?" Susan said viciously.

Jon shook his head. He actually didn't care at this point whether it went too far. "No, not really. It floated the option, which was what we all wanted."

"Yeah, well, we have just about every member of Congress breathing down our neck this morning."

Jon laughed bitterly. "Don't worry, Susan. It's too late. Your little master plan is too far along. Nothing can stop it now. It's all worked quite well. Everything will be in place by tomorrow morning."

Susan let go of Jon's arm. Her body tensed even more than it had been, and her head cocked a little to one side, appraising him carefully. "What's that supposed to mean?"

And at that moment, at long last, Jon could feel a welcome friend with him, one he had pushed away for a very long time. "I think you know exactly what it means," Jon said, every part of him now attuned to that still, small voice—the guidance of God's Holy Spirit—whose crucial help he had ignored for so many years now.

"No, I don't," Susan protested cautiously.

"Yes, I think you do, Susan," Jon answered in a clear voice. "I've seen the corporate records of Daystar. Just this morning, in fact. I saw your name. I know what happened. I know what Daystar's done. I know. Trust me."

Jon watched as his words were heard. He watched as Susan's face distorted into an ugly, enraged mask. "Don't point any fingers, Jon," she hissed. "You're a part of this, too. Just like me. Like all of us. It's what you wanted. What we all wanted. You can't deny that you want this. You can't. You've worked every bit as hard for it as I have."

Jon almost felt sorry for her. "You know, I have one question, though," he said softly. "It's the one question I can't really answer. I know you set up the Christian Armada as a decoy. I can't prove it. But I know it was you. Or Daystar—"

"You don't know a thing," Susan said coldly. Her words pierced Jon as nothing else could have.

"You made that call to Sonny Brown, didn't you, Susan?" Jon said. "You were the Washington insider, the one Sean Burns introduced to the Christian Armada leaders. You called Sonny Brown the day before Air Force Two went down, didn't you? It was you who made that call and set things in motion. Either that, or you ordered someone to make the call."

Susan's face contorted even more. Her jaw was clenched so tightly that every muscle in it bulged out. But she did not respond to the question.

Which meant that Jon had his answer. He would never be able to prove it in court, of course. But he knew. "I thought so," Jon continued. He moved toward the Oval Office doors.

"You can't go in there," Susan ordered, shaking free of her momentary paralysis and moving to cut him off.

"Yes, I can," he answered. "And I will."

"You work for me. You can't go in there."

Jon stepped deftly to one side and moved down the hall, to a point just outside the doors to the president's office. Susan did not follow him. "I don't work for you now, Susan," he said as he put a hand on the doors. "And I am going in to see the president, whether you like it or not."

CHAPTER SEVENTY-ONE

The president was standing behind his desk, staring out at the rose garden, when Jon entered. No one else was in the grand room. But Jon knew they were not alone. You were never alone when you were in the White House. Someone was always listening.

"Mr. President," Jon said after a moment.

Adams turned to face Jon. He was wearing a stiff, white shirt, a tie loosely knotted around his neck. His dark-blue suit pants were neatly pressed. Every hair was in place; his face was without a single line or wrinkle.

"We've been wondering where you've been, Jon," the president said, his voice barely bridging the gulf between the two of them. "You disappeared mysteriously without a trace."

"We need to talk, Mr. President," Jon said, slightly amazed at how calm he felt. It was extraordinary, in light of the circumstances.

"Certainly, Jon," Adams said easily, moving toward him.

"Not here. I'd like to talk outside on the grounds. Perhaps we can take a walk. Just the two of us."

Adams held his finger up to his lips, thinking. "You know there are press and all sorts of people everywhere on the grounds today. Are you sure?"

"Yes, sir, I'm sure," Jon said. "If you don't mind. I would appreciate it if the agents could give us some room as well."

The president hesitated for only a moment. Then he pulled his suit jacket from the back of his chair, leaned over his desk, and pressed the intercom button. "Tell the agent-in-charge I'm going for a walk on the grounds. I don't want to be disturbed. They can watch from a distance."

"But, sir—" his secretary protested.

"I need some fresh air," the president said. "Jon's going with me." He released the button then stepped to the side door, beckoning for Jon, who led the way to the garden and then out the back and down toward the Ellipse. There was enough room to walk there undisturbed.

Jon and the president had walked perhaps a hundred feet or so onto the immaculate White House lawn south of the complex before word reached the White House press corps. In less than thirty seconds, more than one hundred TV cameras hastily assembled on the paved drive at the southern end of the White House residence. The Secret Service kept them all in place, forcing them to shoot with long lenses. Their boom mikes would not be able to pick up conversation from that distance.

Secret Service agents moved around the perimeter of the grounds. Beyond them, people crowded against the metal fence to stare at the president taking a walk with a trusted aide.

This was, ironically, one of the few places in the world where Jon could truly be alone with the president of the United States, here at the center of the huge south lawn in the open air, watched by hundred of pairs of eyes. No one could tape-record a conversation here. There were no Secret Service agents close at hand, no aides waiting in the wings to curry favor or jump at the president's call.

They stopped almost directly in the center of the grounds. Adams turned and faced Jon directly. The TV cameras were rolling, Jon knew. He wouldn't be surprised if at least some of them had cut in live, just for the pictures alone.

"What's on your mind, Jon?" Adams asked him finally. He had deliberately chosen to stand with his back partially to the cameras. No lens, no matter how long, could pick up his words. Jon, likewise, stood at an angle to the president, although it made little difference to him whether lip-readers could pick up his conversation from the film.

"I went down to Richmond this morning, Mr. President," Jon said. "I see."

"I had a look at the filing for the officers of Daystar Communications. I saw the names, all of them."

"Daystar's a private company," Adams said evenly.

"Yes, sir, with a former president as its chairman and your chief of staff as its secretary. And, of course, two officers who were directly involved in making sure Air Force Two flew over Webster Springs on its way into Charleston."

The president deliberately placed his left hand in his pocket and placed one foot over another, striking a casual pose for the benefit of the

322

cameras. "Daystar was not involved in that unfortunate incident," he said. "There's nothing that shows that."

"Perhaps not. But Arthur Demontley and Jonas Brownlee were. I know why they weren't on Air Force Two that day. And Daystar had been monitoring the Christian Armada. They had that group squarely in their sights, the perfect target. And when Susan called Sonny Brown, it was all set. All it took was one clear shot and the deed was done. History was made. The vice president was dead. Long live the new vice president."

Adams thought before he spoke, his face an impassive mask. "It's all conjecture, Jon," he answered finally. "Pure fantasy."

"No," Jon said, feeling the heavy burden lifting from his heart as he uttered the words. "It isn't. I recognized the man who infiltrated the Christian Armada, who set them up, and who testified behind the shroud at the task force hearing. I met him with you that day in Ohio. Why did Sean Burns do it? Maybe he has an intense hatred of groups like the Christian Armada—maybe he believes they're part of the forces of darkness. I don't know. But I *do* know that Burns is your man. He belongs to you. You own him."

The president stiffened slightly but not enough for any of the media to notice. He waited and then chose his words carefully. "It doesn't matter. It's meaningless."

"Mr. President, I know what happened," Jon said, his voice strong and clear. "I can't prove it. No one would believe me anyway. But I know what happened. I know what Daystar did. I know you picked the Christian Armada as the best possible decoy, infiltrated the group, and arranged the vice president's trip. The explosives were already in place at the compound, probably put there by Burns. It wouldn't take much to set them off once the group was inside. Push one remote control switch, and the place is incinerated."

"The entire world knows what happened there, Jon," Adams said. "It was as plain as day to everyone. They killed the vice president and then killed themselves. Every shred of evidence points in that direction."

Jon shook his head. "That's what everyone saw. It's what you wanted them to see. It made such perfect sense, no one even bothered to question it. Everyone knows those groups are crazy. Everything said in their defense could be easily discredited. They were the perfect decoy."

"Jon, please, this is ridiculous," Adams said, his words barely audible. "You know me. Why would I do something so—so patently evil?'

"Because you've done it all your life. I've just never seen it. Until now," Jon said softly. "In a world where God does not exist—in your

323

world—there is only one law. Do whatever it takes to succeed. Whatever. There is no other law. That's what you've done since I've known you. People—like Jay Dooley or Senator Johnson's lover—are simply props, later discarded. You will do whatever it takes to seize power. It makes absolute, perfect sense."

The two of them gazed intently at each other. The world looked on, wondering what they must be discussing on such a historic day with the leader of the world poised to seize total, absolute control in his own country.

"You're out of your mind," Adams said finally from across the abyss that had appeared between the two of them. "You'll sound like a fool if you try this in public. You know that, don't you? You'll look ridiculous in the light of day."

Jon looked up at the brilliant blue sky and smiled. "You know, you're probably right. People will believe a lie when it's told well. The bigger the lie, the better. The truth looks very strange beside it."

"And you have nothing," Adams said softly. "Only your imagination and your absurd conspiracy theory. And that won't last long under public scrutiny."

"I know," Jon said with more than a trace of sadness. "That's why I won't be able to do anything. But neither will you. You can't risk this going public, either."

"You would be destroyed in that process, Jon—not me," the president said. "You, of all people, know that."

"Yes, I do," Jon answered. "That's what bothers me most. That your lie sounds so much more convincing and real than my truth. Justice is warped by what people perceive."

"There is no truth, and justice is determined by those who hold the power," Adams answered with a harsh, guttural laugh. He could see now that Jon was harmless, nothing more than a minor obstacle. Jon, despite his experience and resourcefulness, was not a threat. "That is so obvious that any fool ought be able to see it. But they can't because they're blind. Spare me any more talk about truth, Jon. What matters is who succeeds. Who is victorious? Who has the force to take what he wants? *That* is truth. There is nothing else. The only justice is what those in power will to happen."

Jon turned away from the president to begin the long walk back to the White House. "There will be justice someday, Mr. President," he vowed. "Maybe not today. Maybe not in our lives. But there will be justice. Not the justice of this world but eternal justice. God promises that."

"There is no God," Adams called to him as Jon walked away.

"But there is, Mr. President, and some day, you will discover that," Jon answered, more to himself than to Adams as he exited the stage of the most powerful drama on earth. "Trust me. You will find it someday."